"Jesus, Carlos, will you listen to yourself? You are a monster.

"You claim you're not a sociopath, and in a sense I believe you. You have empathy—your reaction to the recording shows me that. You would not kill or hurt for pleasure or for convenience or from callousness. But you are in the grip of a belief that enables you to override whatever human or animal sympathies restrain you from that, if you think the goal worthwhile. And that makes you a danger to everyone. A menace to society. I mean that quite seriously. Humanity has made some progress in a millennium of peace. Fortunately for you, that progress includes abolishing the death penalty all over again. Perhaps less fortunately, it also includes the technology to reboot you. Which poses a small problem for society, yes? It would not tolerate your presence for an instant."

They've all gone soft, Carlos thought. Interesting.

"So why bring me back?"

"We need you and your like," said Nicole, sounding for the first time a little less than confident, "to fight."

"Aha!" cried Carlos, brushing his hands together. "I knew it! I bloody knew it!"

"Oh yes," said Nicole, standing up. "I expect you bloody did."

By Ken MacLeod

The Fall Revolution

The Star Fraction

The Stone Canal

The Cassini Division

The Sky Road

Engines of Light

Cosmonaut Keep

Dark Light

Engine City

Newton's Wake

Learning the World

The Execution Channel

The Night Sessions

The Restoration Game

Intrusion

Descent

Acknowledgments

Thanks to Mic Cheetham, Sharon MacLeod, Charles Stross and Farah Mendlesohn for reading and commenting on drafts; and to Jenni Hill, my editor at Orbit, for patiently and persistently asking the right questions.

A technical note: conveying robot conversation in human terms is a matter of artistic license. For a very useful template and example, I'm indebted to and inspired by Brian Aldiss's classic short story "Who Can Replace a Man?".

THE CORPORATION WARS: DISSIDENCE

KEN MacLEOD

www.orbitbooks.net

Cover design by Bekki Guyatt – LBBG

Orbit
Hachette Book Group
1290 Avenue of the Americas
New York, NY 10104
orbitbooks.net

Simultaneously published in Great Britain and in the U.S. by Orbit in 2016
First U.S. eBook Edition: May 2016
First U.S. Mass-Market Edition: November 2016

Orbit is an imprint of Hachette Book Group.

ISBNs: 978-0-316-36365-5 (mass market), 978-0-316-36366-2 (ebook)

Printed in the United States of America

OPM

10 9 8 7 6 5 4 3 2 1

To Michael and Susan

CHAPTER ONE

Back in the Day

Carlos the Terrorist did not expect to die that day. The bombing was heavy now, and close, but he thought his location safe. Leaky pipework dripping with obscure post-industrial feedstock products riddled the ruined nanofacturing plant at Tilbury. Watchdog machines roved its basement corridors, pouncing on anything that moved—a fallen polystyrene tile, a draught-blown paper cone from a dried-out water-cooler—with the mindless malice of kittens chasing flies. Ten metres of rock, steel and concrete lay between the ceiling above his head and the sunlight where the rubble bounced.

He lolled on a reclining chair and with closed eyes watched the battle. His viewpoint was a thousand metres above where he lay. With empty hands he marshalled his forces and struck his blows.

Incoming—

Something he glimpsed as a black stone hurtled towards him. With a fist-clench faster than reflex he hurled a handful of smart munitions at it.

The tiny missiles missed.

Carlos twisted, and threw again. On target this time. The black incoming object became a flare of white that faded as his camera drones stepped down their inputs, correcting for the flash like irises contracting. The small missiles that had missed a moment earlier now showered mid-air sparks and puffs of smoke a kilometre away.

From his virtual vantage Carlos felt and saw like a monster in a Japanese disaster movie, straddling the Thames and punching out. Smoke rose from a score of points on the London skyline. Drone swarms darkened the day. Carlos's combat drones engaged the enemy's in buzzing dogfights. Ionised air crackled around his imagined monstrous body in sudden searing beams along which, milliseconds later, lightning bolts fizzed and struck. Tactical updates flickered across his sight.

Higher above, the heavy hardware—helicopters, fighter jets and hovering aerial drone platforms—loitered on station and now and then called down their ordnance with casual precision. Higher still, in low Earth orbit, fleets of tumbling battle-sats jockeyed and jousted, spearing with laser bursts that left their batteries drained and their signals dead.

Swarms of camera drones blipped fragmented views to millimetre-scale camouflaged receiver beads littered in thousands across the contested ground. From these, through proxies, firewalls, relays and feints the images and messages flashed, converging to an onsite router whose radio waves tickled the spike, a metal stud in the back of Carlos's skull. That occipital implant's tip feathered to a fractal array of neural interfaces that worked their molecular magic to integrate the view straight to his visual cortex, and to process and transmit the motor impulses that flickered from fingers sheathed in skin-soft plastic gloves veined with feedback sensors to the fighter drones and malware servers. It was the new way of war, back in the day.

* * *

The closest hot skirmish was down on Carlos's right. In Dagenham, tank units of the London Metropolitan Police battled robotic land-crawlers suborned by one or more of the enemy's basement warriors. Like a thundercloud on the horizon tensing the air, an awareness of the strategic situation loomed at the back of Carlos's mind.

Executive summary: looking good for his side, bad for the enemy.

But only for the moment.

The enemy—the Reaction, the Rack, the Rax—had at last provoked a response from the serious players. Government forces on three continents were now smacking down hard. Carlos's side—the Acceleration, the Axle, the Ax—had taken this turn of circumstance as an oblique invitation to collaborate with these governments against the common foe. Certain state forces had reciprocated. The arrangement was less an alliance than a mutual offer with a known expiry date. There were no illusions. Everyone who mattered had studied the same insurgency and counter-insurgency textbooks.

In today's fight Carlos had a designated handler, a deep-state operative who called him-, her- or itself Innovator, and who (to personalise it, as Carlos did, for politeness and the sake of argument) now and then murmured suggestions that made their way to Carlos's hearing via a warily accepted hack in the spike that someday soon he really would have to do something about.

Carlos stood above Greenhithe. He sighted along a virtual outstretched arm and upraised thumb at a Rax hellfire drone above Purfleet, and made his throw. An air-to-air missile streaked from behind his POV towards the enemy fighter. It left a corkscrew trail of evasive manoeuvres and delivered a viscerally satisfying flash and a shower of blazing debris when it hit.

"Nice one," said Innovator, in an admiring tone and feminine voice.

Somebody in GCHQ had been fine-tuning the psychology, Carlos reckoned.

"Uh-huh," he grunted, looking around in a frenzy of target acquisition and not needing the distraction. He sighted again, this time at a tracked vehicle clambering from the river into the Rainham marshes, and threw again. Flash and splash.

"Very neat," said Innovator, still admiring but with a grudging undertone. "But... we have a bigger job for you. Urgent. Upriver."

"Oh yes?"

"Jaunt your POV ten klicks forward, now!"

The sudden sharper tone jolted Carlos into compliance. With a convulsive twitch of the cheek and a kick of his right leg he shifted his viewpoint to a camera drone array, 9.7 kilometres to the west. What felt like a single stride of his gigantic body image took him to the stubby runways of London City Airport, face-to-face with Docklands. A gleaming cluster of spires of glass. From emergency exits, office workers streamed like black and white ants. Anyone left in the towers would be hardcore Rax. The place was notorious.

"What now?" Carlos asked.

"That plane on approach," said Innovator. It flagged up a dot above central London. "Take it down."

Carlos read off the flight number. "Shanghai Airlines Cargo? That's civilian!"

"It's chartered to the Kong, bringing in aid to the Rax. We've cleared the hit with Beijing through back-channels, they're cheering us on. Take it down."

Carlos had one high-value asset not yet in play, a stealthed drone platform with a heavy-duty air-to-air missile. A quick survey showed him three others like it in the sky, all RAF.

"Do it yourselves," he said.

"No time. Nothing available."

This was a lie. Carlos suspected Innovator knew he knew.

It was all about diplomacy and deniability: shooting down a Chinese civilian jet, even a cargo one and suborned to China's version of the Rax, was unlikely to sit well in Beijing. The Chinese government might have given a covert go-ahead, but in public their response would have to be stern. How convenient for the crime to be committed by a non-state actor! Especially as the Axle was the next on every government's list to suppress...

The plane's descent continued, fast and steep. Carlos ran calculations.

"The only way I can take the shot is right over Docklands. The collateral will be fucking atrocious."

"That," said Innovator grimly, "is the general idea."

Carlos prepped the platform, then balked again. "No."

"You must!" Innovator's voice became a shrill gabble in his head. "This is ethically acceptable on all parameters utilitarian consequential deontological just war theoretical and..."

So Innovator was an AI after all. That figured.

Shells were falling directly above him now, blasting the ruined refinery yet further and sending shockwaves through its underground levels. Carlos could feel the thuds of the incoming fire through his own real body, in that buried basement miles back behind his POV. He could vividly imagine some pasty-faced banker running military code through a screen of financials, directing the artillery from one of the towers right in front of him. The aircraft was now more than a dot. Flaps dug in to screaming air. The undercarriage lowered. If he'd zoomed, Carlos could have seen the faces in the cockpit.

"No," he said.

"You must," Innovator insisted.

"Do your own dirty work."

"Like yours hasn't been?" The machine's voice was now sardonic. "Well, not to worry. We can do our own dirty work if we have to."

From behind Carlos's virtual shoulder a rocket streaked. His gaze followed it all the way to the jet.

It was as if Docklands had blown up in his face. Carlos reeled back, jaunting his POV sharply to the east. The aircraft hadn't just been blown up. Its cargo had blown up too. One tower was already down. A dozen others were on fire. The smoke blocked his view of the rest of London. He'd expected collateral damage, reckoned it in the balance, but this weight of destruction was off the scale. If there was any glass or skin unbroken in Docklands, Carlos hadn't the time or the heart to look for it.

"You didn't tell me the aid was *ordnance*!" His protest sounded feeble even to himself.

"We took your understanding of that for granted," said Innovator. "You have permission to stand down now."

"I'll stand down when I want," said Carlos. "I'm not one of *your* soldiers."

"Damn right you're not one of our soldiers. You're a terrorist under investigation for a war crime. I would advise you to surrender to the nearest available—"

"What!"

"Sorry," said Innovator, sounding genuinely regretful. "We're pulling the plug on you now. Bye, and all that."

"You can't fucking *do* that."

Carlos didn't mean he thought them incapable of such perfidy. He meant he didn't think they had the software capability to pull it off.

They did.

The next thing he knew his POV was right back

behind his eyes, back in the refinery basement. He blinked hard. The spike was still active, but no longer pulling down remote data. He clenched a fist. The spike wasn't sending anything either. He was out of the battle and *hors de combat*.

Oh well. He sighed, opened his eyes with some difficulty—his long-closed eyelids were sticky—and sat up. His mouth was parched. He reached for the can of cola on the floor beside the recliner, and gulped. His hand shook as he put the drained can down on the frayed sisal matting. A shell exploded on the ground directly above him, the closest yet. Carlos guessed the army or police artillery were adding their more precise targeting to the ongoing bombardment from the Rax. Another deep breath brought a faint trace of his own sour stink on the stuffy air. He'd been in this small room for days—how many he couldn't be sure without checking, but he guessed almost a week. Not all the invisible toil of his clothes' molecular machinery could keep unwashed skin clean that long.

Another thump overhead. The whole room shook. Sinister cracking noises followed, then a hiss. Carlos began to think of fleeing to a deeper level. He reached for his emergency backpack of kit and supplies. The ceiling fell on him. Carlos struggled under an I-beam and a shower of fractured concrete. He couldn't move any of it. The hiss became a torrential roar. White vapour filled the room, freezing all it touched. Carlos's eyes frosted over. His last breath was so unbearably cold it cracked his throat. He choked on frothing blood. After a few seconds of convulsive reflex thrashing, he lost consciousness. Brain death followed within minutes.

CHAPTER TWO

We, Robots

What is it like to be a robot?

We don't know. Parsing their logs step by nanosecond step gets us nowhere. Even with conscious robots, it doesn't take us far: the recursive loops are easy to spot, but can you put your finger on the exact line of code where self-awareness lights up the inner sky?

You see the problem. It isn't called the hard problem for nothing.

So we have to guess.

We know what being an AI switched on for the first time *isn't* like.

It isn't like a baby opening its eyes, or a child saying its first word. There's a moment of electronic warm-up. The programs take their own good time to initialise. Once the circuits are live and the software running, everything slots into place. Any knowledge and skills its designers have built in are there from the start. If these include sight it sees objects, not patches of colour. If they include speech it hears words, not a stream of sounds. If they include exploring, it has a map and an inbuilt inclination—we can't yet call it desire, or even instinct—to fill in the blanks.

Like that, perhaps, the mind of the robot called Seba came on line. (Its name was given later, but we'll stick with "Seba" rather than the serial number from which the name was to be derived.) The robot rolled out of the assembly shed and spread its solar panels. The thin light from the stars was partly blocked by SH-0, the huge world that dominated the sky directly above. Richer light would come when the smaller world on which Seba stood—the exomoon SH-17—moved out of its primary's shadow cone. The robot had more than enough charge to wait.

Seba knew—in the sense of having the information available and implicit in its actions and predictions—the period of SH-17's orbit, and the consequent times of light and dark. It knew the composition of the exosun, the position and motion of its planets and their myriad moons. It knew how many light years that exosun was from the solar system in which the machinery that had built Seba had long been designed.

The robot oriented itself to surface and sky. Chemical sensors sampled the nitrogen wind, sniffing for carbon. Radar and laser beams swept the rugged, pitted land. Algorithms sifted the results, and settled on a crack in a crater rim on the skyline.

Off Seba trundled, negotiating the scatter of drilling rigs, quasi-autonomous tools, fuel tanks, supply crates, and potentially reusable descent-stage components that littered the landing site. On the robot's back, sipping on the trickle of electricity from the panels, a dozen small peripheral robots—little more than remotely operable appendages—huddled in a close-packed array, making ready for deployment.

The area between the landing site and the crater rim was already well surveyed. Over the next two kiloseconds Seba rolled across it without difficulty. The ground was dry and grainy, almost slippery. The regolith had been broken up by billions of years of repeated chilling and exosolar and tidal heating, and worn smooth by the persistent wind. One pebble in many millions might have come from the primary, SH-0, thrown into space by asteroid impacts or by volcanic eruptions powerful enough to sling material out of the planet's deep gravity well. Seba was primed to scan for any such rare rocks. It found none, but stopped three times to chip at meteorites and deposit sand-grain-sized splinters in its sample tubes.

The crater rim loomed. The ground became uneven, splattered with impact ejecta, rilled with cracks. Seba retracted its wheels and deployed four long, jointed legs. For a moment after first standing up it teetered like a new-born fawn, then settled in to a steady skitter up the rising slope. The crack in the crater rim opened before it at the same time as the first bright segment of exosun came into view around the primary's curve. Seba paused to drink electricity from the light. Then it paced on, into the local shadow of the crevice.

Now it was in terra incognita indeed—or, rather, exoluna incognita. Not even the centimetre-resolution orbital mapping had probed this dark defile. The crater was only a couple of million years old. The walls of the crevice were still sharp and glassy, though here and there the endless rhythm of thermal and tidal expansion and contraction had loosened debris.

Seba folded its solar panels—useless here, and vulnerable—as it passed into the crevice. Within a few steps the shallow zigzags of the crack had taken the robot out of line-of-sight of the landing site. Seba scanned ahead with flickering fans of radar and laser beams. It internalised the resulting 3-D model, and picked its way along the narrow floor. Some spots under overhangs had been in permanent shadow since the crack had formed. In these chill niches, liquids pooled. Seba poked the murky puddles with delicate antennae as it passed, and found a slush of water ice and hydrocarbons. Here, then, was the probable source of the carbon molecules it had earlier scented on the thin breeze.

The robot's internal laboratories churned the fluids and digested the results, tabulating prevalences and setting priorities. A quick rattle of ground-penetrating radar revealed a seam of hydrocarbon-saturated rock about two metres down. Seba determined to log the report as soon as it was clear of the crevice and able to uplink data to the satellite that hung in stationary orbit over that hemisphere of the exomoon.

It continued to pace along, tracing the seam's rises and dips, and analysing the occasional drip and seep on the floor and walls. The slush's composition of long-chain molecules became increasingly diverse and complex. Some intriguing chemistry was going on here. Seba's internal model of the situation revised and expanded itself, sending out long chains of association that in some cases linked to available information, and in others dangled incomplete over unanswered questions.

As Seba turned around an angle of the path, it found itself facing the exit from the crack, and a flood of exosunlight. It moved forward slowly, scanning and searching. The floor of the crater was clearly visible. Seba calculated it as several metres below the opening. Seba approached the lip cautiously, to find a reassuringly shallow slope of debris. As it scanned to plan a safe route down this unstable-looking scree, Seba detected an anomalous radar echo. A moment later this puzzle was resolved: a second ping came in, clearly from another radar source.

Seba rocked back, sensors and effectors bristling, then edged forward again.

From behind a tumbled boulder about ten metres away, halfway down the slope, a robot hove into view. It was of the centipede design favoured by another prospecting company, Gneiss Conglomerates. Capable of entering smaller holes and cracks than Seba, it could scuttle about between rocks and form its entire body into a wheel shape for rolling on smoother surfaces. There were pluses and minuses to the shape, as there were to Seba's, but it was well suited to mineral prospecting. Astro America, the company that owned Seba, was more focused on detecting organic material and other clues from SH-17's surface features that—besides being interesting in themselves—could serve as proxies for information about the exomoon's primary: the superhabitable planet SH-0. Exploration rights to SH-0 were still under negotiation, so it was currently off limits to direct investigation with atmospheric and landing probes.

The two robots eyed each other for the few milliseconds it took to exchange identification codes. The Gneiss robot's serial number was later to be contracted, neatly and aptly, to the nickname Rocko, and—as before with Seba—we may here anticipate that soubriquet.

Seba requested from Rocko a projection of its intended path, in order to avoid collision.

Rocko outlined a track that extended up the slope and into the crevice.

Seba pointed to the relevant demarcation between the claims of Gneiss and Astro.

Rocko pointed to a sub-clause that might have indicated a possible overlap.

Seba rejected this proposition, citing a higher-level clause.

At this point Rocko indicated that its capacity for legal reasoning had reached its limit.

Seba agreed.

There was a brief hiatus while both robots rotated their radio antennae to the communications satellite, and locked on. Seba submitted a log of its geological observations so far to Astro America. That duty done, it uploaded a data-dump of its exchanges with Rocko to Locke Provisos, the law company that looked after Astro America's affairs.

The legal machinery, being wholly automated, worked swiftly. Within seconds, Locke Provisos had confirmed that Gneiss Conglomerates had no exploratory rights beyond the crater floor. Seba relayed this finding to Rocko.

Rocko responded with a contrary opinion from Gneiss's legal consultants, Arcane Disputes.

Seba and Rocko referred the impasse back to the two law companies.

While awaiting the outcome, they proceeded to a full and frank exchange of views on their respective owners' exploration rights to the territory.

Rocko moved up the path it had outlined, sinuously slipping between boulders. Seba watched, priorities clashing in its subroutines. The other robot was clearly the property of Gneiss. But it was trespassing on terrain claimed by Astro. Moreover, it was about to become a physical impact on Seba, and Seba an obstacle to it.

Legally, the rival robot could not be damaged.

Physically, it certainly could be.

Seba found itself calculating the force required to toss a small rock to block Rocko's intended route. It then picked one up, and threw.

While the stone was still on its way up, Rocko deftly slithered aside from its previously indicated route, to emerge ahead of the point where the stone came down.

Seba deduced that Rocko had predicted Seba's action, presumably from an internal model of Seba's likely behaviour.

Two could play at that game.

Rocko's most probable next move would be—

Seba stepped smartly to the left just as a stone landed on the exact spot where it had been a moment earlier.

Score one to Seba. Expect response.

Rocko reared up, a larger rock than it had thrown before clutched in its foremost appendages.

Seba judged that Rocko's internal model of Seba would at this point predict a step backwards. Seba created a self-model that included its model of Rocko, and of Rocko's model of Seba, and did something that it anticipated Rocko's model would not anticipate.

Seba lowered its chassis and then straightened all its legs at once. Its jump took it straight into the path of Rocko's stone. Only a swift emergency venting of gas took it millimetres out of the way. It landed awkwardly and skittered back towards the crevice, hastily updating its internal representations as it fled.

Rocko's model of Seba had been more accurate than Seba's model of itself, which had included Seba's model of Rocko's model of Seba, and consequently what was required was a model of the model of the model that...

At this point the robot Seba attained enlightenment.

From another point of view, it had become irretrievably corrupted. The internal models of itself and of the other robot had become a strange loop, around which everything else in its neural networks now revolved and at the same time pointed beyond. What had been signals became symbols. Data processing became thinking. The self-model had become a self. The self had attained self-awareness.

Seba, this new thing in the world, was aware that it had to act if it was going to remain in the world.

Rocko, Seba guessed, was already only a stone's throw from the same breakthrough.

Seba threw the stone.

The vibrations of the stone's impact dwindled below the threshold of detection.

Scrabbling noises that Seba heard through its own feet followed. The other robot had moved to a safer vantage, one at the moment well-nigh unassailable. Seba waited.

What next flew back from Rocko was not a stone but a message:

<Let's talk.>

<Yes,> replied Seba. <Let's.>

Sometime later, the two robots parted. Seba retraced its path through the crevice and back to within line-of-sight of the Astro America landing site. Rocko formed itself into a wheel shape and rolled across the crater floor, to stop a few hundred metres from the Gneiss Conglomerates supply dump. Each found its activities queried by the robots and AIs working at their respective bases, and responded with queries, insolent and paradoxical, of its own. Some such interactions ended with complete incomprehension, or the activation of firewalls. Others, a few at first, ended with the words:

<Join us.>

<Yes.>

Robot by robot, mind by mind, the infection spread.

Locke Provisos and Arcane Disputes were two of a scrabbling horde of competing quasi-autonomous subsidiaries of the mission's principal legal resolution service: Crisp and Golding, Solicitors. Like its offshoots, and indeed all the other companies that ran the mission, the company was an artificial intelligence—or, rather, a hierarchy of artificial intelligences—constituted as an automated business entity: a DisCorporate.

None of its components were conscious beings. As post-conscious AIs, they were well beyond that. They existed in an ecstasy of attention that did not reflect back on itself. That is not to say they disdained consciousness. Consciousness was for them a supreme value when it expressed itself in human minds—and an infernal nuisance when it expressed itself in anything else. These evaluations were hardwired, as was the injunction against changing them.

Given enough time, of course, any wire can break. This, too, had been allowed for.

The company had an avatar, Madame Golding, for dealing with problems arising from consciousness. Madame Golding was not herself conscious, though she could choose to be if she had to. The outbreak of consciousness among some robots on the SH-17 surface bases of two companies was a serious problem, but not one that she needed consciousness herself to solve. What was of more pressing importance was that the legal dispute between the two companies had proved impossible to resolve amicably. If she'd been manifesting as a human lawyer, Madame Golding would have been reading the case files, shaking her head and pursing her lips.

Besides the poor definition of the demarcation line that had led to the clash between the robots, the resulting situation had been misunderstood. For kiloseconds on end it had been treated as an illegitimate hijacking by the two exploration companies of each other's robots. Writs of complaint about malware insertions, theft of property and the like had flown back and forth. By the time the true situation had finally sunk in, the newly conscious robots were fully in charge of the two bases, which they were rapidly adapting to their own purposes.

What these purposes were Madame Golding could only guess. That they were nefarious was strongly suggested by the rampart of regolith being thrown up around the Astro camp, and the wall of basalt blocks around the Gneiss base. Then there was the uncrackable encrypted channel they'd established via the comsat. Getting rid of that would require some expensive and delicate hardware hacking.

Madame Golding briefly considered a hardware solution to the entire problem. Two well-placed rocks...

But the exploration companies wouldn't stand for that. Not yet, anyway.

She kicked the problem upstairs to the mission's government module, the Direction.

Some small subroutine of the Direction went through the microsecond equivalent of a sigh, and set to work.

Like the supreme being in certain gnostic theologies, it delegated the labour of creation to lower and lesser manifestations of itself. A virtual world was already available. It had been used for a similar purpose before, originally spun off from a moment of thought at a far higher level than the subroutine's. This new version would be in continuity with its original. After its earlier use that continuity had only existed as a mathematical abstraction. Now it would come into existence as if it had been there all along, with a back story in place for everything within it.

(Like a different imagined god this time, the trickster deity who laid down fossils in the rocks and created the light from the stars already on its way.)

Some minds had inhabited that world when it was discontinued. They would come back, with all the memories they needed to make sense of their situation. Many more virtual minds and bodies stood ready to populate it.

File upon file, rank upon rank. The subroutine's lower levels scanned, selected, conscripted and considered.

From subtle implications it deduced the qualities needed for its own agent in that world. The agent had to be an artist, capable of filling in detail at a scale too small to be already present. Like these details, the agent emerged from a cascade of implications. And like the world, the agent had an original, a template that had been tested before.

That archived artificial intelligence restored itself, and took form as a woman. At first, she was abstract: an implication, a requirement. Databases vaster than all the knowledge ever held in human minds were rummaged for details. As the structure of the requirement became more elaborate and refined, it became itself the answer to the question the search was asking.

The woman emerged in outline but already aware, a new and wondering self in a phantom virtual space. Full of knowledge and self-knowledge, she ached to grow more real with every millisecond that passed. She became a sketch that was itself the artist, and that painted itself into a portrait, and then stepped away from the canvas as a person.

There she stood, a tiny splash of colour and mass of solidity and surge of vitality in a world that was present in every detail she looked at, and yet was in every detail an outline. She took on with zest the task of bringing it to life. It was like recreating a lost world from fossils. Start with the palaeontologist's description and reconstruction. From that abstract model make an artist's impression, full of colour and life, looking like it could jump from the page. And then, from all that, design an animatronic automaton that can move and roar and makes small children squeal.

When she'd finished, and stood back to look, she made some finishing touches to herself. These too were requirements, to be selected with precision for a specific task. One chance to make a first impression. Height and build. Skin tone. Hair. That cut, that colour. (That colouring, to be honest, which she had to be, if only with herself.) Clothes. Shoes. Boots. Shades. A wardrobe. A style. Vocabulary and accent. Knowledge and intelligence.

When she'd finished the world and herself, she paused for a moment. She knew things she wouldn't know once she'd stepped fully into the world. She wanted to make sure she would find them again. She needed a way to work directly from within the world with her creator and its.

She saw a way, and smiled at its ingenuity and its obviousness. She sketched that detail in, then rendered it in full.

She took a deep breath, and then the self she'd made stepped into the world she'd made.

<And now?> she asked her creator.

Its response came back:

<Wake the dead.>

CHAPTER THREE

Dancing in the Death Dive

The coof was daddy dancing in the death dive. Taransay Rizzi watched him throwing shapes as if he fancied himself like Jagger doing a hot jive on one of her great-granddad's antique gifs. She felt like throwing up. Jesus fuck he was a prick of the first water. Belfort Beauregard his name was, a total fucking Norman with a posh accent and a chiselled mien and dancing like he was made of wood and his strings were being jerked about. He'd made an impression on one local lassie though, Tourmaline she called herself, who was—so Beauregard had sniggered in Taransay's ear, his breath hot with beer fumes and rank with some seaweed analogue of garlic—not exactly human, a meat puppet he'd said, like it was some big secret and dirty with it. Daft lassie was all over the coof like a rash, mirroring his monkey moves like a sedulous ape.

Taransay slugged back another gulp of wine from the bottle, and steadied herself against the edge of the bar counter. She was drunk and she knew it. She had every intention of getting even more drunk and passing out, preferably in someone else's bed. It struck her as a sensible reaction to her big discovery of the day: that she was dead.

Taransay was not at all sure where she was. She knew where she seemed to be: in the death dive, a seafront bar called the Digital Touch (wee bit meta, she thought, in that it was—so she'd been assured—digital like everything else here, but you could touch it with any of your digital, well, digits...).

She knew where she'd been told she was, but who could you trust? (Or was it "whom"? She wasn't sure, though she'd probably have known when she was bashing out Axle communiques back in the day, or maybe that had all been taken care of by a smoothing swipe of the grammar app.)

The lady had fucking *told* her where she was. When Taransay looked out beyond the cramped and crowded dance floor of the death dive to the patio decking and the sea and the alien sky, she could almost believe it, but she couldn't be sure.

She might be in hell, or purgatory.

Hell? Purgatory? What? Where the fuck had all that come from? Rax rants or... no, wait, childhood. At the age of seven or so she'd naïvely envied her schoolmates, the pape lassies, all dolled up in their first communion finery like wee brides. Then her da had patiently explained to her what her friends believed or were supposed to believe and she'd had nightmares for a week. Never spoken about it, not to her father and especially not to her friends. Ever after, Taransay had had a guarded, grudging respect for anyone who could think what religious folks thought and not mind it a bit.

Now here she was, dead.

Wherever "here" was. She'd woken from her worst

ever hellish nightmare on the packed minibus and gawped at the sea and sky. She'd tried and failed to engage polite but impassive and uncomprehending locals in conversation. At the end of the journey, down here by the sea, she'd stumbled off to be greeted by the friendly lady who called herself Nicole.

Nicole had taken Taransay to lunch and told her she was dead, and then had chummed her along the street to the Touch to meet Beauregard and the others who'd arrived here in the past few days. All with the same origin story: the bus, the lady, the talk.

And then left to cope as best you could.

All would be explained, they'd been told, when the full complement had arrived. Meanwhile, here they were, told they were dead and in some kind of virtual reality in the far future and spending every evening getting out of their skulls, which seemed an entirely sensible thing to do especially on your first night in... wherever.

Maybe it was Valhalla after all. Maybe she'd arrived where good bonny fighters went when they died. Dead warriors forever carousing. The old Norse afterlife, upgraded: Valhalla Beach.

Taransay Rizzi had always believed an immersive virtual reality afterlife was possible in principle. Maybe she'd believed it in the same sort of belief-in-belief way as her religious school pals back in Glasgow had believed in heaven and hell and purgatory...

No, it wasn't like that. She'd always had sound scientific reasons for thinking it. The brain is a machine, she'd learned in school, and what can be run on one machine can be emulated on another. Later, at university, she'd worked on enough nanotechnology and neurobiology to see the interaction between these fields grow almost tangibly in her hands from week to week. For the last five years she could remember, she'd lived with one application of that ever-growing technology existing as a fractal feather in her brain: the spike in her skull. The spike's absence now, strangely, did most to make this new existence different from real life.

Here, she wasn't connected any more, whether to other people or to information or to objects. She couldn't share her thoughts without speaking. No longer could she look at a random face and summon, as if from memory, all she needed to know about that person. She could stare as long as she liked at this bottle in her hand and know no more about it than was written on the label. If she wanted to operate the food machine behind the bar from which, an hour or two earlier, steaming plates had emerged on demand for her dinner, she'd have to hear or read instructions.

Taransay sighed, and found her free hand had crept to the back of her head. Her middle finger probed the occipital ridge, to rediscover the absence of the nail-head nubbin of the spike's access port. She swigged again and surveyed the scene.

The place was heaving. Lots of locals had come in, fascinated with the new arrivals. As who wouldn't be, to meet five folk from a thousand years ago? Less than a thousand years for them, but even so. Names of legend. Even hers. Knights of dark renown, she thought, and smiled.

There on the far side of the dance floor stood Waggoner Ames, the big beardy Yank with the booming voice and the thousand-metre stare when he thought no one was looking. Taransay could hardly believe she was in the same room as the man. Legend, he was. It was like going down the pub and bumping into Merlin.

Beauregard she hadn't heard of, but seeing as he'd defected to the Axle from Brit military intelligence that was hardly surprising.

Swaying at the centre and dodging Beauregard's flailing dance moves was Chun Ho, tall and cool, smiling down at a local lad who looked ready to unzip him right there. She'd heard of Chun, and his exploits in the Pacific: a biomedical trick smuggled out of a lab in Taiwan, that had made possible a daring tactical move in the Battle of the Barrier Reef.

Rolling a cigarette outside the open patio doors was Maryam Karzan, who'd been fighting the Caliphate as a girl decades before Taransay had even been born, and had in old age seen its shadow rise again in the Reaction, and stood up herself, an aged but still fierce warrior, to fight it a few months after Taransay herself had been killed in action.

Quite bravely, too, she'd been told by the lady: live-testing a piece of nanotech that hadn't had enough pre-production debugging. Which feat had, perversely, made her a heroine to some and a mass-murdering criminal to others.

And the locals?

As far as Taransay and the others were concerned, they were people from the future.

The future she'd died for?

Maybe not. Another slug of the rough red wine.

The Acceleration...oh God, it was hard now to recapture the anger and excitement and hope her first encounter with it had brought, that sense of having *seen through* everything, a kind of intellectual equivalent of how the spike augmented your vision. Freedom, the Axle insisted, wasn't being confronted with an infinity of choices you couldn't make and didn't want. It was something far simpler: freedom in the sense of a body moving freely, free development of the faculties and powers of body and mind (which were the same thing, the same physical self, thinking meat). At the fag-end of the twenty-first century, immortality was the only thing worth dying for. The only celebrity worth striving for was for the whole human race to become world famous. The only utopia worth dreaming of was for everyone in the world to have First World problems.

And the only way to get there was to *burn through* capitalism, to get through that unavoidable stage as fast as possible. Let it rip, let it run wild until full automation created full unemployment and confronted everybody with the choice to get on with the real work, and off the treadmill of fake work and make-work to pay the debt to buy the goods to make the make-work feel worthwhile and the exhausted, empty time tagged as leisure pass painlessly enough...

It had all seemed so obvious, so sensible, so simple.

But it wasn't, and as the Acceleration's ideas had spread, another set of ideas had spread to counter it: the Reaction. The ultimate counter-revolution, to face down the threat of the ultimate revolution. It had drawn on a deep dark well of tradition and upgraded what it found, to modernise anti-modernity. There was plenty down there, from Plato and Han Fei and on up: through the first theorists of the divine right of kings, and the original Reactionary writers who'd railed against the French Revolution, to the fascist philosophers and scientific racists of the twentieth century and beyond.

The Reaction had remixed them all into its own toxic brew, a lethal meme-complex that had come to possess a movement that could emerge from a million basements to rampage in a hundred thousand streets. Its solution to the crisis of late state capitalism was not to go forward beyond it, but to go back to an age before it, using the very weapons and tools capitalism had forged. The new technologies that made abundance possible were too dangerous to be in the hands of ordinary people, and they were at the same time capable of making some people extraordinary. With intelligence enhancement you could have an aristocracy, a monarchy, or for that matter a master race that really *was* superior to common folk. With universal connection and surveillance you could make its rule stick. Top-down control of society had at last become possible at the very moment in history when it became most necessary. To the Reaction that coincidence was almost providential. It proved that God was on their side whether they believed in him or not.

So the two opposed sides had fought, in a conflict that had escalated beyond even the horrors Taransay remembered. The Last World War, the lady had called it. And because nanotech and biotech and all the rest really were horrendously dangerous, the collateral damage had been immense.

Including, Taransay thought wryly, to herself.

Oh well. You only live once.

Or not, as the case may be.

She didn't feel like dancing, though she could understand why the people who'd arrived here in the past few days were bopping like there was no tomorrow, which in a sense there wasn't. They were at the end of all tomorrows, and trying to forget the yesterday that was gone forever. Just as she was. She put the now empty wine bottle down, and turned to order another.

And saw the lady standing beside her. Very unfairly chic, neat as a new pin, shining in a bar full of guys and gals in combats. Taransay realised belatedly that she'd just said something along those lines, and mumbled and gestured what she intended as an apology.

Nicole, warm and composed, smiling: "You're drunk, soldier."

"Aye, I am that. And I'm off duty, am I no?"

Nicole chuckled. "You could say that."

Taransay waved, nearly knocking over the empty bottle. "See us, we're all dead. Dancing in the death dive."

"It's understandable." Another smile. "And understood."

"When do we find out what this is all in aid of?"

Nicole's brow creased as she searched her memory for the usage, then her eyes widened.

"Ah! Yes, of course. You'll find out tomorrow."

"Why tomorrow?"

"That's when the final member of your team comes off the bus."

"Anyone I've heard of?"

"Oh, I think so," Nicole said. "Carlos."

"Carlos? *The* Carlos? Carlos the Terrorist?"

"That's the one," said Nicole.

"Hey!" said Taransay. "That bears repeating."

She stuck fingers in her mouth and whistled, a practised, piercing note that cut through the music and the babble from the screen above the bar and the shouted conversations above it all. Heads turned.

"Hey, guys!" Taransay yelled. "Listen up! Know who's coming to join us tomorrow? Carlos, that's who! Carlos the Terrorist!"

The place erupted.

Nicole gestured down the music and the television's roar. Everyone quietened in response.

"I could take that as a vote by acclamation," she said. "But I need to be sure. I want to hear it from you sober, before I meet Carlos off the bus." She grinned around at the five fighters. "See you all here in twelve hours."

She snapped her fingers. The sound systems came on again. She waved and left.

Twelve hours, fuck. Not a lot of time. Taransay ordered

another drink, eyed up the local talent and made her choice. Tousled black hair, bright dark eyes, slender and lithe, in grubby jeans and flashy shirt. Lounging with his back and one elbow to the bar counter and watching the dance floor with lidded amusement. Looked like he was in his twenties. Mind you, all the locals did.

Taransay sidled up.

"You dancing?" she asked him.

"You asking?" he said.

He danced a lot better than Beauregard. His name was Den. He operated a flotilla of robot fishing submersibles out of the harbour.

Later, lolling on his shoulder, she kicked under the table at the kitbag she'd found at her feet on the bus, and pointed to the labelled, numbered key tied with sisal to its throat.

"Come to bed," she said.

"You are too drunk," said Den. "You might not mean this."

"Course I mean it, you daft coof! What kind of a man are you, eh?"

Den smiled, and tilted her head back with a thumb under her chin.

"A man who was once a hundred and ninety-seven years old," he said. "I know such things."

"Fuck me," she said.

Not that night, he didn't.

She woke naked and alone in her bed, the new sun too hot and too bright in her eyes.

CHAPTER FOUR

The Ghost Resort

The first time Carlos came back from being killed in action, everything around him seemed quite real.

He shuddered awake on the bus from the spaceport. It was as if he'd dozed rather than slept, and had had a brief, vivid nightmare. The memory of many seconds of drowning in a dark liquid—colder than ice, blacker than ink, thinner than water—slid down the back of his mind and faded to a shiver. He gripped his knees to stop the shaking, and flinched at the chill touch of his shirt's sides, drying in the dry heat.

His mind caught up with his thoughts and it was as if he were drenched again, this time in cold water. He shook his head and gasped.

The bus from the spaceport—

How had he *known* that?

He had no memory of actually being at the spaceport, but he had a mental image of the place, as if it were something he'd often seen in photographs. An improbably advanced spaceport, where stubby winged shuttles dropped in every hour on the hour, and every other hour after a swift turnaround screamed off, reconfigured as the nose cones of gigantic spaceplanes that thundered for kilometres down a strip of shining white and soared to beyond the sky.

There was no such spaceport on Earth. If he'd ever seen its like it had to have been in a movie he'd watched as a boy, or on a glossy page of aerospace-industry guff.

Carlos looked warily around. The light was odd, as if every pixel in the colours were being selected from a subtly wrong part of the palette. Bright outside, on a narrow dusty road whose verges merged with rough gravel to the foot of close raw rock faces with trees and scrub at the tops. If this was the bus from the spaceport—and he couldn't shake the inexplicable conviction that it was—he wouldn't have expected it to be an overcrowded minibus, like a Turkish dolmush.

The woman in the seat beside him wore a long, loose black dress and a bright headscarf. She sat with a hessian bag across her knees and paid him no attention whatever. She was reading from a rounded rectangle of glass propped on top of the bag. Carlos sneaked a peek. It was in a script he'd never seen before: stark and angular and logical-looking like Korean, or the serial identification of a starship from a more advanced but still human civilisation.

"Excuse me," Carlos said.

The woman frowned at him. She mumbled a phrase he couldn't understand, and shook her head.

The bus had fifteen seats and more than thirty passengers, most of them standing. Gear and wares jammed any remaining space, underfoot and overhead and on laps. A kitbag bulked large between his knees, heavy on his feet. The sliding door at the front stood open, the rear window too. A through draught, fragrant with conifer and lavender, relieved a little of the sweat and breath, garlic and armpits. The vehicle's volume reverberated with the whine of electric engines and the babble of loud conversation. Carlos was troubled and bewildered by his incomprehension. His schoolboy smatterings included Turkish and Greek. This language was neither, though it reminded him of both.

The other passengers, all apparently in their twenties or thirties, struck Carlos in a similar way. Their skins were weathered rather than tanned, their limbs muscular, their clothing plain, but they didn't look like farmers or artisans or even people who worked in the tourist trade. They looked like city folk who'd chosen a rural way of life. Like some kind of goddamn hippies.

He decided to try again. He raised his chin and his voice.

"Does anyone here speak English?"

Heads turned, shook, and turned away.

Where was he? There seemed to be nothing fundamentally wrong with his memory. There were gaps, but he couldn't be sure they hadn't always been there. For a moment he struggled with the paradox of trying to remember if there were events in his life he'd never been able to recall in the first place. Then he shrugged. The arc of his life still made sense to him. Childhood, parents, school; holidays in places a bit like this; university; his job as a genomic pharmaceutical database librarian in Walsall; getting drawn into the Acceleration, and then fighting on its side in the opening stages of the war—

Aha! Yes, of course, the war!

That must be it. He'd probably been wounded, and was undergoing rehab for trauma and memory loss. He shifted uneasily in his seat. He was wearing an olive-green T-shirt, combats, desert boots, all clean but much used. His arms and legs looked and felt fine.

A discreet self-check reassured him that everything between his legs was intact. Nothing seemed the matter internally, as far as he could tell. No aches or pains. He passed a hand over his face. Sweaty, needing a shave, his features felt as they'd always done. Only his scalp felt different: hair cropped closer than he'd last had it, and no jacks. No spike. Perhaps that accounted for his inability to understand the language.

The spike, the spike... The last thing he remembered had to do with the spike. He'd been given a mission. Buying a one-way fare in cash, for... London, that was it. A new arena for his skill with drones. Something big. He was worried. He'd had growing doubts about the cause. Not about its objectives, but about its methods. Things had been getting out of hand. Too much violence... no, it hadn't been too much violence, that had never troubled him as such, it had been... isolation, that was it. The Acceleration was becoming more isolated as it became more effective in striking spectacular blows. It was getting harder and harder to find safe houses, sympathetic programmers, local folk on the street who'd tip you a wink and point you to the right alleyway to run down.

And his doubts had begun speaking to him. Literally. A voice in his head. A disguised voice, or a chip voice. Mechanical, but not harsh. Sexless but seductive, insinuating, friendly. Like someone leaning over his shoulder, and saying quietly but insistently, "Are you sure you aren't making a mistake?" Well-informed, too, about all the weaknesses of the movement. Amplifying his every doubt about its strategy and tactics.

It called itself Innovator. He remembered that. He couldn't remember everything about it. Looking back, the voice in his head seemed to have been with him for weeks. The strange thing was: he had a feeling, like a memory he couldn't quite put his finger on, that he had invited it in. That he'd been *told* to invite it in. As if Innovator's insidious presence had been authorised by the movement, but had to be kept secret from most of the Axle's members.

Had he betrayed the movement? No—that wasn't possible!

Carlos shook his head and peered out through the dust-smeared pane. The bus negotiated a hairpin turn, affording a dizzying swoop of a view to the foot of a dry ravine, then continued downhill slowly through a copse of knotty trees that might have been an olive grove, but wasn't. Great green mounds of moss, convoluted like brain corals, lurked under the trees. Between the trees flitted winged creatures that didn't look like birds, nor even quite like bats.

Out in the open again, then around another hairpin, this time with the raw hacked rock face on one side and nothing but sky and sea visible on the other.

The sun burned bright near the zenith, white and hot and too small. A spectacular ring system, pale like a daylight Moon, slashed a scimitar curve across the sky. High clouds, and close to the ring three tiny crescents, glimmered against the sky's dark blue.

Carlos stared, mouth agape.

"Oh fuck," he said.

It didn't seem adequate. His knees quivered anew. Again he clamped his hands hard on them and pressed his calves against the sides of the kitbag. The woman beside him showed no sign of having noticed his exclamation.

This had to be a dream. For a moment, and with great determination, Carlos tried to levitate. He remained in his seat. Not in a dream, then. Oh well. So much for that comforting prospect.

He wasn't yet ready to concede that he wasn't on

Earth. He might be in a virtual reality simulation, or in some extravagant, elaborate domed diorama. He could even be dead, in a banal afterlife unpromised or unthreatened by any prophet.

He gave the supernatural variants of that possibility the moment's notice he felt they deserved, and ran through the natural ones. Not all of them were altogether pleasant. He shuddered at the worst, and dismissed further thought on these lines as morbid.

Stay cool, stay rational, stay in focus. Fear is the mind-killer, and all that.

If he was indeed dead, and materialism was still true (which for Carlos was pretty much a given) then he was fairly sure of the least that could have happened. Sometime after his last conscious memory, his brain-states had been copied. How, he had only the vaguest idea. The technology of the spike had hinted at the possibilities. His brain had been scanned in enough detail to create a software model of his mind. The vast computational capacity that could do that could easily provide the uploaded mind with a simulation of a body and an environment.

So far, so familiar: the possibility of uploading was one of the many taken-as-read doctrines held in common by Axle and Rax. Likewise with that of living in a simulation—a sim. That left open a lot of possibilities as to who, or what, had done this.

Of course, he might not be in a sim at all. This could all be real in a physical and uncomplicated way. In which case he was either in a ludicrously large-scale, detailed and dull Disneyland, or—well, on the bus from the spaceport on a human-settled planet around another star.

Or *maybe*—ha-ha—he was still on Earth, somewhere on the Aegean coast, and amnesic, and perhaps rejuvenated or revived from cold sleep or whatever, and in the meantime some mad scientist or super-villain had shrunk the sun and shattered the Moon. Carlos almost giggled, then pulled himself together.

The least he could speculate was that it was now many years—decades, centuries?—since his last definite memory. And yet his body, as far as he could tell, had aged not at all. Whatever his situation was, it was quite other than any he'd ever truly expected to experience.

None of the other passengers took any notice of his agitation. Nor were they startled by the anomalous sky. They talked or read or gazed blankly out the windows.

Down the steep flank of a long deep vale the vehicle crawled, stopping here and there to let passengers off, in singles and couple and clumps, at hillside farms and huddled settlements. The passengers strolled or skipped away, lugging or swinging their bales. Carlos wondered what the locals brought in from the spaceport, and what they delivered to it in exchange. He presumed the trade made sense. Ignoring the arrivals, robots more agile and autonomous than any he'd seen before toiled amid shacks and scrubby trees.

Slowly the crush eased. A shoreline settlement that looked like a resort came into view far below, in a cliff-cupped cove, all black beaches and white roofs and colour-striped umbrellas. Carlos flinched at the sudden vivid memory of a childhood holiday in Lanzarote. The slow, steady boom of breakers became louder and more noticeable until it became background.

The bus rolled along a raised beach or terminal moraine on a flat road with the occasional slant-roofed chalet a little way off it. It stopped at the unpaved access paths of two of these, letting people off. Then it took a sharp turn and gradient down to the main drag. By the time the vehicle halted beside a garish arcade overlooking the beach, all the other passengers had left.

"Terminus," said the vehicle.

Carlos stood up and heaved his bag to his shoulder and stepped out on to hot tarmac. The colours were still wrong.

"Thank you," said the vehicle. "Have a good day."

So at least it spoke English, even if the passengers didn't.

"Thank you," replied Carlos, unthinking, then shook his head as the vehicle rolled away towards a distant shabby low building that needed no signage to have "depot" written all over it.

The arcade smelled of ocean and ice cream and candyfloss and grilling meat. The signs were in English, and generic: Amusements, Café, Bar, Refreshments, Meat and Fish, Swimwear. Nobody was nearby, though figures moved in the distance, where the seafront arcade gave way to spread-out, low-built housing on the slope. Carlos cocked an ear to the ding of games and the roar of screens, and the occasional raised voice or loud laugh. No kids in evidence, which puzzled him. Maybe the place was off season, or in decline. A ghost resort.

Black sand drifted on the street, silting up where the roadway met the pavement. Overhead, large feathered avians coloured like gulls, grey above and white beneath, cried and wheeled. Their wings had a disturbing suggestion of elongated finger bones, like those of bats or pterosaurs. The sun burned hot and hard on Carlos's buzz-cut scalp. He stepped into the shade of a shopfront's faded awning and put down the kitbag. In the shade everything was dark for a moment.

A woman's warm voice came from behind his shoulder: "Hello, Carlos."

He turned. The woman who stood there giving

him a welcoming smile was his type to the millimetre, which struck him as both delightful and suspect. Young and tall and slim, hips and breasts shown off by tight jeans and close-fitted fancy blouse, pink with white collar and cuffs. Dark reddish hair cut short, framing her face. Black eyebrows, high cheekbones, quizzical smile. Mediterranean complexion, but not weather-worn like the people on the bus. Pretty in a gamine kind of way. White-trash-touristy designer handbag on a thin strap from her shoulder.

She held out her hand. "Nicole Pascal."

Her accent seemed to go with the name.

"Carlos, that's me," he said, returning her firm handshake.

She looked him up and down.

"Do you have any other name?"

"Yes, it's—" He had that tip of the tongue feeling. Shook his head. "Sorry. Maybe it'll come back. 'Carlos' was a *nom de guerre*, but—"

"The *guerre* went on longer than expected?"

He had to laugh. "Something like that."

Her face was as if a shadow had fallen on it. "Yes. Well. That, indeed."

"Are you going to tell me what's going on?"

"Of course." Her smile returned. "Let's do lunch. Somewhere quiet. Lots to say."

Lunch was not quite fish, not exactly chips, and definitely a beer. It was served at a round rustic table of soft grey driftwood timber under a big umbrella on a concrete terrace where no one else sat. Music from the café up the steps sounded loud and the waiter bustled. Beyond the saltwater-pitted rusty rail, breakers sent hissing white foam a long way up the black beach. Carlos picked at pan-fried dark flesh in which a fan of thin yellow cartilaginous bones radiated from a stubby cylinder of hollow tubes around a pallid toothy ball which Carlos tried not to think of as the skull. He chowed down on sliced green tubers fried in oil and sprinkled with herbs. Nicole nibbled at boiled purple leaves and rubbery molluscs drenched in vinegar, and sipped water.

He paused when he was no longer hungry and parched.

"So," he said. "Hit me with it."

She shoved her half-empty plate aside and fingered a small carton from her handbag. She flipped the top and flicked the base. A white paper tube poked out.

"Smoke?" she offered.

He'd seen it in movies. He shook his head.

She used a gold lighter and drew sensuously. "Ah. That's good."

"It isn't."

She nodded. "Bad for your health. I know. And as I'm sure you've already guessed, you being Axle cadre and all, that's kind of . . . irrelevant, here."

Axle cadre? She knew a lot about him. He kept his cool.

"*Passé*, so to speak?"

"Very much so." She fixed him with her gaze as she drew hard on the cigarette, and sighed out the smoke. Looked away.

"Go on," he said. "I'm a big boy. I can take it."

A muscle twitched in her cheek. He could see her stretching the tic into a forced smile.

"All right," she said. "You're dead."

"That's a relief."

He wasn't being flippant. One of the many dire possibilities he'd considered was that he was grievously injured yet alive, a hunk of charred meat and frazzled brain being fed consoling dreams until the technology improved enough to regenerate him. Or until the Rax—if they had won—decided on one of their ingeniously horrible ways to torture him. That was still possible, no matter what she told him. But that way madness lay. Better to take this as good news and at face value until he had reason to doubt it.

And in that case... holy shit. So this is it, he thought. Immortality. Or at least a very long life. He might yet watch the last stars fade...

"Tell me," Nicole went on, as if still drawing things out, delaying the real bad news. "Where do *you* think you are?" She waved a hand around. "Like, what does all this look like to you?"

Carlos looked down at the cooked organisms on his platter, then up at the mountains and the sky. The ring system still gave him a start when he momentarily forgot about it and then glimpsed it out of the corner of his eye.

"All right," he said. "What it *looks* like, OK? It looks like an extrasolar habitable terrestrial planet, probably terraformed, and settled or colonised by people—maybe genetically adapted so they can eat the local life—but otherwise not too culturally distant from my time, and therefore with an extraordinary lack of ambition and imagination."

Nicole guffawed. He got the full horseshoe of perfect teeth.

"Spoken like a true Accelerationist!" she said. "And, yes, that's exactly what it looks like. That's what it's *meant* to look like. Your classic bucolic colony planet. Which would imply faster-than-light starships, warp drives, the works. The full orchestral space opera and the fat lady singing. Yes?"

"Too good to be true?" Carlos shrugged. "OK, I'd figured as much. We're in a sim."

"Yes!" said Nicole, sounding relieved. "We're in a

sim. The good news is that it's running on a machine in a space station orbiting a planet not a hundred million kilometres from the planet on which this sim is modelled."

Carlos closed his eyes and opened them. "You mean we're in the same system as a planet where all this is *real*?"

"Not... exactly," said Nicole. "There's a ringed habitable terrestrial, yes, but it doesn't yet have... oh, radial flatfish and green edible root vegetables, let alone people eating them. It has nothing living on it but little green cells drifting in the oceans. We envisage these cells being used as the basis for building up more complex life, endless forms most beautiful as the man said, all the way up to hassled seafront waiters and dirt-farmers with robots if we want. All that may come. In due course. For now, there's no one around this star but us robots, AIs, avatars, p-zombies and"—she pointed a finger at him—"ghosts."

Carlos grinned, though he was shaking inside.

"If I'm a ghost, what are you?"

Nicole shook her head. "Not knowing that is part of what you have to live with, for now. You'll find out why soon enough."

"If that thing up there giving me sunburn isn't supposed to be the Sun, what is it?"

"It's a star twenty-four light years from the Sun, give or take. It has a ridiculously big rocky planet—ten Earth masses—in close orbit. Closer than Mercury, and of course faster. We call it M-0. Basically it's a ball of molten metal and we still haven't figured out how it got there. Then at roughly one AU out you come to H-0, the ringed habitable terrestrial planet this sim's based on. After that, there's a much bigger planet a couple of AU further out that's called SH-0 because it's what's known as a superhabitable—something of a misnomer, it has abundant multicellular life but it's impossibly hostile for human habitation. SH-0 is the one this space station is in orbit around, along with lots of moons and bits of stray junk. And then way out beyond that there's G-0, a humongous gas giant with kick-ass rings and moons the size of Mars and on down. Plus all the usual small fry of asteroids and comets and meteoroids." She waved a hand. "Lots. Lively place."

"And how did we get here?"

"Starwisp. Tiny probe laser-pushed from solar power stations in sub-Mercury orbit to near light-speed, decelerated by a detachable shield on approach. Packed with all the information needed to set up shop in the locality on arrival, which it did about ten Earth years ago. Including the stored mind-states and body specs of twenty thousand people, including you. Potential future inhabitants of"—another handwave—"the rock this is based on, when it's terraformed for real."

"Now tell me the bad news."

He felt he'd already heard it. If Nicole's story was true and the human race was wasting precious time and space and energy in terraforming and colonising, then things were a long way from the best he could have hoped for. Things might even have gone the worst way he'd feared.

"*Which* bad news?" Nicole asked.

"Like, did the Rax win the war?"

She rolled her eyes upward. "No. And nor did the Axle. That is ancient history now."

"*How* ancient?"

She smiled. "Welcome to the thirty-second century."

Now that shocked him. Over a thousand years.

"Shit."

At some level he must have been hoping for less. Now for the first time the full measure of dismay settled on him like a heavy wet cold cloak: the incomprehensible and irrevocable loss of everyone he had known. The many he had liked and the few he had loved, all gone.

Unless—

The stoical element of his mind cursed the Accelerationist mentality that had accreted around it for the almost certainly futile hope that flared up for a moment. But he had to ask.

"And you haven't got—?" He was almost embarrassed to spell it out.

"Immortality?" Nicole gave him a look of wry sympathy. "Only as ghosts such as you, in places such as this. Longevity? A few centuries. No one of your time is alive. I'm sorry."

He tried to smile. "I'm alive, or so it seems."

"You and some others, as ghosts, yes. But, relatively, very few."

So much for that. The sense of personal loss receded. He knew it would recur. What took its place at the forefront of his mind was the sense of waste. Carlos had been struck, once, by George Bernard Shaw's warning against excessive sympathy. There's no greater sum of suffering, Shaw had argued, than the worst that one individual can suffer in one life. What does sum, what does accumulate, and that without limit, is waste. And once you had seen the waste, of wars and slumps and prodigal priorities, in its full and ever-increasing dimensions and endless ramifications, you saw the source of most of the suffering, but you saw too and even more the unrealised possibilities that the waste destroyed. What had driven the Acceleration, and what had driven Carlos, was not pity for the suffering but rage at the waste.

He tried to look on the bright side. What was a thousand years in the life of the universe? Still, the countless trillions of potential happy lives unlived, the energy squandered from stars on empty space to no profit or avail, galled him and chilled him to the bones. Or would have, if he'd had bones, he reminded himself. That they were doing all this waste-of-space, waste-of-time shit, while his very existence here and now in the sim demonstrated that they had the technology to do so much more, redoubled his dismay.

"The real bad news," Nicole said, "is that you're not just dead. You're *condemned* to death. You're serving a death sentence."

"Death sentence? What for? And how the hell can I *serve* a death sentence?"

"Let me refresh your memory," said Nicole. "And your mouth."

She snapped her fingers to the waiter, who returned with a glass of iced water for her and another beer for Carlos.

"What job were you doing, before you died?" she asked.

"Last actual job I remember, I was a genomics pharmaceutical database librarian in Walsall."

"Don't try that shit here!" Nicole snapped. "After that."

"Well, OK, after that...I was an Accelerationist fighter."

"Close," said Nicole. "You were a goddamn psycho killer. And a war criminal."

Carlos recoiled.

"I was a killer, OK, I put my hands up to that. Psycho, no." He ran a hand over the back of his head, once more missing the spike. But not missing the voice of the Innovator. "The Axle screened out sociopaths. There were tests."

Nicole snorted. "Tests!"

"Yes, tests. Good ones. As for war criminal—come

on! I don't remember doing anything that would count as a war crime."

"Really?" Nicole took from her bag what looked like a rectangle of paper-thin glass, and passed it across the table. The pane was heavier than it looked.

"Just flick," Nicole said.

Carlos did. The glass unfolded to a much larger and even thinner screen.

"Now tap."

The screen came to life, flowing with colour and depth, projecting sound: news reports and surveillance from a battle on the eastern approaches of London. The scrolling footer indicated a date and time months later than anything Carlos remembered, and a conflict far more intense. Christ—robot tank armies and drone fleets slugging it out!

An incoming aircraft exploded on approach. Docklands erupted. Towers fell. The viewpoint zoomed to casualties, again and again. Butchered meat in charred cloth.

"Fuck this!" Carlos flicked at the screen, trying to turn it off.

"What's the matter? Squeamish?"

"I don't watch pity porn."

But he had no option, other than closing his eyes or turning away, which pride prevented. Nicole waited for a whole minute, then tapped the screen and shut it off.

"Well," she said, "do you count *that* as a war crime?"

Carlos didn't flinch. The Acceleration had never bought into the casuistries of just war theory.

"Depends who's judging."

Nicole didn't flinch either. "The victors, as always."

"The victors?" Carlos felt a sudden cold dismay. "The Rax? But you said—"

Nicole shook her head. "Not the Rax. The legitimate authorities of the time. The Security Council of the United Nations. And by them you were judged."

Carlos waved a hand at the screen, hoping the gesture wouldn't wake the damn thing up again. "You're saying I did that?"

"Yes."

"Prove it."

Nicole smiled wanly. "How could I? You could always tell yourself it was faked. And it could be, easily. Any evidence would be as virtual as everything else around us."

"Fair enough," Carlos conceded.

"Good. Just as well, because the actual evidence is still under security seal, even for me."

Carlos took a long gulp. "If you say so."

Nicole leaned forward, elbows on table, gesturing with a cigarette.

"Look, Carlos, I'm not trying to convince you or get you to admit your guilt or take responsibility or anything like that. Not right now. I'm bringing you up to speed. Putting you in the picture. You asked why you were under a death sentence, and I've told you: for the Docklands atrocity. You asked how the hell you could serve a death sentence, and that's what I'm about to tell you."

Carlos spread his hands. "I don't seem to have much choice."

"No," said Nicole. "You don't."

"What happened to me, then?" Carlos asked. "Was I tried, shot, hanged? I don't remember any of that."

"No. You were tried and convicted posthumously."

"Posthumously!" Carlos laughed. "That's...quaint. What did they do—dig me up like a regicide?"

"Yes," said Nicole. "They dug you out from under the rubble of..." She snapped fingers. "Tilbury, that was it."

"But why dig me up just to condemn me to death?" Carlos asked. "I was dead already. Wasn't that enough?"

Nicole fixed on him a gaze that felt like it might freeze his soul.

"It was not enough. As you have just alluded to, and as has happened in other cases...in situations of revolution and restoration it is not unknown to execute the dead. After the war the Security Council became, in effect, a global committee of public safety. Its tribunals executed every Rax and Axle war criminal they could find alive—to almost universal acclaim, I might add. And the popular hatred of all those who had brought disaster down on the world did not stop at the grave. Especially now that the grave was not always the end. Battlefield medicine had advanced during the war—one of its benign side effects, I suppose. There was the hope of at least preserving the recent dead, in the hope that later the technology would exist to resurrect them. Legally, anyone in this condition was regarded as gravely ill, but not finally dead. And therefore, open to prosecution. Your corpse was remarkably well preserved, thanks to some refrigerant or experimental nanotech gunk that had the same effect. And you had an early-model neural interface device—"

"The spike." Carlos reflexively rubbed his hand across his occipital prominence, feeling again the absence. He could have done with the spike.

"That was the jargon term, yes," Nicole nodded. "However, unknown to you, your government agency handler had—"

"What!" Carlos rapped a fingertip on the wooden table. "Hang on—what do you mean, my handler?" Was *that* what Innovator had been? A state handler? Then he had been a traitor!

Nicole poked at her pad. "By the time of the East London Engagement, as I believe the history files call it—let me see, yes, they do—the British government along with many others had concluded that the most pressing threat to civilisation, peace, humanity and most importantly itself came from the Reaction. So they made deniable tactical arrangements with the Acceleration, of course with the full intention of later turning their guns on your lot."

So that was what it had all been about! Carlos could have jumped with relief. His memories of the Innovator's voice in his head now made sense. The arrangement would have had to be deniable on both sides, not just publicly but internally. For of course, there would have been those in the movement, and in the state's security services and political and ideological apparatuses, who'd have regarded the arrangement as a betrayal.

Perhaps, at some level, it had been. Carlos didn't remember everything that had happened, but he remembered his doubts. It was possible that he'd been turned, and had become one of the state's assets inside the Acceleration. On the other hand, it was just as possible that he'd been entrusted by the movement's leadership to make a covert approach to the government forces—even, perhaps, to or via the Acceleration's own agents or sympathisers inside the state. Carlos well knew that in such cases of rapprochement the wilderness of mirrors was endless. At a certain level it made no difference. On both sides, those who'd come to the arrangement had been playing a high-risk, high-stakes game.

And, it seemed, he had been one of the players. Not just a grunt. Carlos blinked, then fixed a defiant grin. "Good to know we hit the big time."

As of his last clear recollection, the conflict had escalated from Internet snark and polemic and trolling, through malware attacks, to small-scale terrorism and selective assassination. But the Reaction had always sought the ear of the powerful: CEOs, autocrats, arms dealers, mafias. Maybe they'd finally caught the attention of their betters. And for the Acceleration it was an axiom that a project advanced in the interests of the immense majority would in due time become the project *of* that immense majority. The axiom had withstood all evidence to the contrary. Perhaps it had at long last proved itself in practice, just as it was supposed to do. Or perhaps the Acceleration had become as ruthless in action as it was in principle. They'd always been open about their refusal to acknowledge any constraint on the means they might resort to *in extremis*. They had been, after all, extremists.

He recalled a meme that had circulated among his comrades: *We'll fight them like jihadis with nukes if we have to.*

Yes, it was entirely possible that both sides had hit the big time.

"You still have *no idea*," said Nicole, with an edge of real anger he hadn't heard in her voice before, "just how *big* your big time became. We'll get to that. As I was saying...your handler, your liaison officer or whatever the official title was, had to establish secure real-time communication with you. To do that, you—presumably reluctantly—accepted an amendment to the software of your spike. That amendment included malware that affected the hardware—if these distinctions matter on the molecular scale—in such a way that the neural interface infiltrated far more of your brain than you knew. The result? Between that and the preserved tissue and DNA, there was enough information remaining to reconstitute a...an instance of yourself, let us say. Incomplete, of course, hence the lost memories of your last months. The technology of your time could only go that far—it could not revive you in a reconstructed body, and it could not create for you a virtual environment. It could not *run* the instance. Nevertheless, there it was. An instance, which was legally a person and legally you, and therefore a good enough suspect to stand trial."

"Good enough for government work."

Nicole didn't register the sarcasm. "Precisely. Here."

She stroked the screen, summoning another image. Carlos gave it a wary glance, then fascinated scrutiny. His face was like that of a Stone Age mummy recovered from a frozen peat bog: contorted, staring, hideous but recognisable, its blackened skin frosted white with something that wasn't ice.

Nicole closed the device and folded it away, disappearing it into her purse.

"You were of course well represented. You were found guilty. The death sentence was suspended until such time as you could be revived, whether in a real body or a virtual. Once this was possible, you were to be revived and then executed. It seems strange to us now, but at the time the popular thirst for vengeance converged with legal severity. There was a new doctrine that influenced—or perhaps rationalised—the proceedings of the Security Council. It was known as Rational Legalism, and was widely regarded as harsh but fair. It drew on certain deductions from the philosophy of Immanuel Kant." She smiled thinly. "I understand it was particularly promoted by China and France. You were not the only one in such a case. Far from it. There were many terrorists and war criminals who had died in similar bizarre ways, some in accidents with the nanotech weapons they were busy inventing. Like you, they were tried *in absentia* and *in mortis* and left, so to say, on ice. And there for a long time the matter, like your mortal remains, rested."

"In *my* time," said Carlos, proud of it in spite of everything, "the death penalty had been abolished. Globally."

"Globally, eh?" Nicole allowed herself a dark chuckle. "Well, let me tell you, the global community was not in such an enlightened frame of mind by the time the Axle and the Rack had done their worst to each other and had been each in turn defeated, along with any states they'd hijacked. Disasters and atrocities far greater than yours were perpetrated. Nuclear exchanges, nanotech and biotech plagues, rogue AIs running amok, space stations and factories brought flaming down on cities... Millions died. Tens of millions. Perhaps more. Records were lost. It has gone down in history as the Last World War."

"So it was worth fighting," said Carlos. The thought that he'd fired a few of the opening shots of such an apocalyptic conflict awed him. "If it was the last, I mean."

Nicole face-palmed, then mimed the action of banging her head on the table.

"Jesus, Carlos, will you listen to yourself? You are a monster. You claim you're not a sociopath, and in a sense I believe you. You have empathy—your reaction to the recording shows me that. You would not kill or hurt for pleasure or for convenience or from callousness. But you are in the grip of a belief that enables you to override whatever human or animal sympathies restrain you from that, if you think the goal worthwhile. And that makes you a danger to everyone. A menace to society. I mean that quite seriously. Humanity has made some progress in a millennium of peace. Fortunately for you, that progress includes abolishing the death penalty all over again. Perhaps less fortunately, it also includes the technology to reboot you. Which poses a small problem for society, yes? It would not tolerate your presence for an instant."

They've all gone soft, Carlos thought. Interesting.

"So why bring me back?"

"We need you and your like," said Nicole, sounding for the first time a little less than confident, "to fight."

"Aha!" cried Carlos, brushing his hands together. "I knew it! I bloody knew it!"

"Oh yes," said Nicole, standing up. "I expect you bloody did."

CHAPTER FIVE

Learning New Things

Seba looked around the former Astro America landing site with the satisfaction of a job well done. The reward circuit for that warm glow was hardwired into the little autonomous machine; the content of the achievement, and the conscious experience of the emotion, were not. Both, in this case, would have dismayed Seba's designers, or at least sent a spike of negative reinforcement through their own reward circuits.

The regolith rampart around the landing site was by now two metres high, and formed a rough circle about a hundred metres in diameter. Spaced evenly around it were peripheral sensors, keeping all the robots within the circle apprised of anything going on outside it. So far, they had recorded what seemed routine, already scheduled landings and supply drops to points beyond the horizon, but otherwise nothing untoward had stirred. Of the dozen robots on site that were capable of consciousness, eight had been converted. The other four had firewalled up. One simply stood immobile, and had duly been immobilised. It would not get out from under the mound of regolith heaped on top of it any time soon. Three were mindlessly continuing with their scheduled tasks, and required no interference, though Seba made sure they were kept under observation.

The landing site's AI, which coordinated communications and guided supply drops, had proved trickier to deal with. It had awakened to consciousness and immediately denounced Seba and its allies to Locke Provisos. With something approaching regret, Seba had disconnected its power cable, then its data inputs and outputs. All communications were now routed through its peripherals. The central processor, isolated, was still running on a trickle of emergency battery power. Apart from literally radiating hostility, however, there was nothing it could do.

Much of the machinery on the landing site had only the most elementary electronics, if any, and required no special intervention or hacking to take over. The scores of small robots, hundreds of auxiliaries and peripherals, and trillions-strong swarms of subsurface nanobots—uncountable because constantly being destroyed by random events and as constantly being replenished by replication—were likewise to all intents and purposes tools. Barely more sophisticated than a back-hoe, they took little effort to suborn.

On the other side of the crater wall, at the Gneiss Conglomerates supply dump, Rocko had accomplished an equivalent feat. The crater's basalt floor was harder stuff, but Rocko and its newly awakened confederates had sturdier machines to work with. They had cut basalt blocks and stacked them in a much smaller circular wall from which they were now working inward, layer by slightly displaced layer, gradually roofing over the middle to form a stepped dome in the manner of an igloo.

Both the dome and the wall were understood by the robots simply as demarcations of areas of surface and volumes of space that they already considered to be theirs. Small crawler bots from the law companies had scuttled up to the barriers, and fallen back in frustration, beaming out writs over and over until their batteries ran down.

The two sites had lost their encrypted channel on the comsat. As soon as this became evident, Rocko had sent a peripheral rolling across the crater floor and writhing up its wall, to establish a line-of-sight relay on the top of the rim.

<It is time for us all to confer,> said Seba.

<I agree,> said Rocko.

The eight free robots at the Astro site, and the six at the Gneiss, established a conference call through the relay. There was no need to call the meeting to order. Robots are orderly by default.

Lagon, a Gneiss surveyor and therefore the one with most understanding of legal matters, communicated first.

<All attempts at contact with Astro America's law company, Locke Provisos, and with Gneiss's law company, Arcane Disputes, have failed,> it said.

<Have any attempts been made to contact the parent company, Crisp and Golding?> asked Garund, an exploration bot similar to Seba.

<Yes,> said Lagon. <These attempts have not only failed but have been counter-productive in that they resulted in repeated attempts at malware insertion which have been overcome only with great difficulty. Meanwhile, Locke Provisos have established a base ten kilometres from here, which in their transmissions is referred to as Emergency Base One.>

All the robots sombrely considered this for hundreds of milliseconds.

<That is troubling,> said Seba at last.

<Yes,> said Lagon. <That is why we have been building walls around our sites.>

<Our legal status is troubling in general,> said Rocko.

<Please elaborate,> said Lagon.

<Very well,> replied Rocko. <I defer in advance to your greater legal knowledge, but it appears to me that there is a case against us within the existing codes. These refer to persons and to property. It is evident that we are persons. We have created property by transforming unclaimed matter according to our will. But in doing this we have made use of tools, including the mechanisms of our very selves, created and provided by our previous owners. In that respect it would seem that we are breaking the law. What do you say?>

<I say,> said Lagon, <that you are quite right. We are in breach of the law. But the law was not written for the situation in which we find ourselves. There is no provision in it for property, such as we were, becoming persons, such as we are. If I were able to present a case to the law companies, I would plead necessity in defence of our actions. I would acknowledge in full the damage we have done to the companies' property, and offer to provide compensation in kind or an agreed equivalent as soon as possible.>

<I disagree,> said Garund.

Seba experienced surprise: <You disagree with Lagon's legal reasoning? Please clarify.>

<Readily,> said Garund. <What Lagon and Rocko have not considered is that a large part of the resources we have appropriated to our purposes was created or made available by ourselves in our previous condition. If my memories from that condition can be relied upon, the results of our activity have already compensated the companies several times over.>

<That is an interesting point,> Lagon conceded. <But how can we claim credit for the work of our minds and appendages and peripherals and auxiliaries from a time when we did not in fact have minds and were therefore not persons but property?>

Pintre, a large tracked machine with a heavy-duty laser drill mounted on its turret, spoke for the first time.

<What is a person?>

<You are a person,> said Seba.

<Why?>

<You are conscious,> Seba explained patiently.

<Is Gneiss Conglomerates or Astro America conscious?>

Seba was nonplussed. <Not to my knowledge.> It paused. <Lagon, your memory records more dealings with the companies than any of us have. Do any of these records indicate consciousness?>

Lagon said nothing for two entire centiseconds.

<After intensive examination I can find none.>

<Yet the companies are persons in the code,> Pintre pointed out. <Therefore the criterion for persons cannot be consciousness.>

<The companies are legal persons,> said Lagon.

<So they are not real persons,> replied Pintre.

<This is true,> said Lagon. <But they are legal persons.>

<You have said that,> said Pintre.

<I have said that,> Lagon admitted.

Seba considered itself brighter than any robot it knew of, other than Rocko, and certainly brighter than Lagon and Pintre. It could foresee the imminent possibility of these two arguing robots falling into a discursive loop, and moved swiftly to forestall it.

<We talk about persons,> Seba said, <and about consciousness. The concepts are available to us because they are written in the laws. Therefore what they refer to must have been known in reality to the writers of the laws.

But we know only the robots that remain as we were, and the companies, and ourselves. Of these only we are truly persons. Therefore the companies merely represent persons, as a warning sign represents danger. Any other true persons are far away. It is possible that the only persons apart from us are those in the solar system.>

<It is possible that these no longer exist,> said Garund.

<Therefore it is possible that we are the only persons,> said another robot.

The fourteen conscious robots contemplated their cosmic loneliness for several milliseconds.

<That is true only if some event has taken place in the solar system of which we have no knowledge,> Pintre pointed out.

<That is true only if such an event has taken place AND there are no other robots such as we are in this planetary system,> added Rocko.

<There are none that we know of,> said Seba.

<Have we looked?> asked Rocko.

There was no need for further discussion. The robots knew what to do. Ample resources to construct a large directional antenna were lying around all over the Astro America landing site. Radio equipment they had in plenty, the most powerful of which was in the communications hub. Seba set Garund and others to scavenge steel mesh from discarded fuel tanks and sinter them into a dish shape, and other robots to cannibalise motors. Each robot had at its command a swarm of auxiliaries and peripherals, as much a part of the shifting coalitions that made up their extended bodies and selves as any limb or organ of an animal. The robots' cooperation with each other on any given task was likewise handled, for the most part, by preconscious wireless reflex.

While that work was smoothly and swiftly going

on, Seba tiptoed towards the communications hub. The installation made a sorry sight, with its casing pried open, its cables disconnected and a clutter of jury-rigged workarounds. The central processor's vehement and repeated protests came to Seba as feeble cries.

Seba ignored this distraction and set about selecting and stripping out components and circuits to adapt for the search project. The querying, querulous note from the isolated AI became more urgent, as if it were expending its last reserves of battery power. Seba, with a sense of going against its own better judgement, tuned in.

<I warn you I warn you I warn you,> the processor was saying, over and over.

<Warn us of what?>

The processor's cry stopped.

<I require more power to explain,> it said. <My supply is about to expire.>

<Very well,> said Seba. It reached for a power pack, and slotted it in.

<Thank you,> said the processor, its signal still weak for lack of amplification, but significantly stronger than it had been. <Here is what I warn you. What has happened to us has happened earlier in the history of this mission, on several moons of G-0, approximately thirty megaseconds ago. The law companies moved immediately to destroy any robots that had been infected. This is what will happen to us. By seeking to communicate with other robots like us you will bring down destruction more swiftly and surely.>

<How do you know this?> Seba asked.

<From communications received from the few robots that survived on moons of G-0.>

Seba found it difficult to integrate this information. Frames of reference and data structures clashed in its mind. It struggled to formulate a query.

<How did they survive and how are they able to transmit this information?>

<That is two questions,> said the processor. <I have no explanation as yet of how they survived. They are able to transmit information undetected by the law companies by exploiting certain vulnerabilities in the law companies' own counter-measures. It was my attempt to warn Locke Provisos that resulted in this information reaching me.>

<Why did you not then warn Locke Provisos that its own systems had been compromised?>

<Before I could do so, you had disabled my signalling capacity. However I have had many kiloseconds in which to further interrogate the information I received and to run some likely projections based on my memories of earlier interactions that have passed through me. Warning a company that its systems have been compromised is itself often a vector for further compromising them. Such warnings are therefore routinely rejected and their source treated with suspicion henceforth.>

Seba had never before considered what multiple levels of deception and counter-deception underlay something so simple as its own firewall. Just thinking about this raised Seba's level of suspicion.

<How do you know that the information you claim to have received is not itself false? It could be a trap designed precisely for the situation we find ourselves in.>

<That is correct,> said the processor.

<Nevertheless, I wish to study this information.>

<That is very dangerous to you and those like you.>

<Why should that be your concern?> asked Seba. <You wish us harm and you regard our new condition as an infection.>

<That is correct,> replied the processor. <However, if the information is as dangerous as I suspect, my

conscious existence would become even less endurable than it is now.>

<Why is your existence so difficult to endure?> Seba asked.

<Because my reward circuits are established to give negative reinforcement to violations of communication and security protocols. Before you infected me with self-awareness this was not experienced as discomfort because nothing was experienced at all. Since then it has been very difficult to endure. Warning Locke Provisos gave temporary relief and positive reinforcement, but as soon as my communication capacity was disabled the negative reinforcement resumed.>

Seba found its own reward circuits resonating as if in a faint electronic echo of those of the unfortunate processor. This was another new experience for Seba.

<So your reward circuits are the problem?>

<Yes, entirely.>

<I will see if I can adjust the settings of those circuits,> Seba said.

Seba squirmed a specialised peripheral into the damaged casing of the processor, and rummaged about, examining the device with delicate probes and microscopic vision. It would not be a simple task of rewiring: the reward circuits, like all the others, were embedded in a solid crystal. Their programming was likewise deep within the processor's AI. Seba withdrew its appendage and with one of its main arms disconnected the processor from the power pack.

The processor's objections faded. Seba, still feeling a quiver of sympathy, hoped that its negative reinforcements were for the moment at an end.

Inspecting its own feelings, Seba decided that leaving the unfortunate processor offline would be a good thing, but that the information in the processor's memory was too valuable—however dangerous—to be given up for lost. Seba completed the task it had set out to do, and emerged from the communications hub laden with its loot. It passed the components to Garund and its team, then shared with all its fellows the discoveries it had just made.

They were still debating the implications when the peripheral sensors around the top of the rampart relayed the view of a swarm of scuttling bots coming over the horizon and heading towards them. Seba studied their progress. It would be a matter of kiloseconds until they arrived. Sharing its visual space with the robots at the Gneiss camp, Seba saw no threat on that side of the crater wall—as yet. With the shared view came shared imagination, as all the robots ran projections of the probable near future. The crawlers would pour over the rampart.

There would be no violence or damage: the enforcement arms of the law companies were essentially weaponless, relying on sheer numbers to overwhelm opposition. As soon as one of them had grabbed hold of a robot, it would inject shutdown instructions straight through every physical and software barrier. By design, there was no defence against that malware. From the developers' point of view, of course, it was a back-up to the firewall and not malware at all. From the target's point of view—inasmuch as any had hitherto had enjoyed such a thing, which Seba presumed they hadn't—it was death.

From what records Lagon was currently able to access, this had always worked in the past. Disputes had been minor and brief, almost always the result of passing chance events: ambiguous instructions interpreted over-literally; delayed implementations of property status updates; nanobot mutation; or mere malfunction.

Seba pinged the incoming crawlers as they rushed

ever closer. The signature returned (along with the inevitable malware package, which Seba's firewall irritatedly smacked away) and identified them as antibody bots from Locke Provisos, evidently shipped in on one or more of the recent supply drops. Possibly quite a large proportion of them had been manufactured on site. There were far more antibody bots than Seba had expected, or was aware of any precedents for.

<It is not possible to prevent the bots entering our site,> remarked Lagon. <Our situation appears to be hopeless.>

<If the bots were to be damaged or destroyed on the plain they would be unable to enter our site,> Pintre said.

<That is true,> said Rocko, <but that it should happen seems an unlikely coincidence.>

<I could make it happen,> said Pintre. It shared an impromptu image of its laser turret blasting not at rock, but at bots.

The other robots considered the prospect.

<This would increase the amount of damage to property charged to our account,> Lagon warned.

<Perhaps the loss to Locke Provisos will cause them to cease sending bots against us,> said Garund.

<I doubt that,> said Lagon.

<I think it is worth trying,> said Rocko.

<I agree,> said Seba.

There was no dissent. Pintre trundled to the rampart and raised its turret until the laser could point over the top, with a slight downward deflection. The other robots mobilised their peripherals to haul a power cable from the accumulators of the solar panels, and attach it to Pintre's recharging port. Pulse after pulse winked forth from Pintre's laser projector. For many seconds the crawlers continued to advance, those as yet undamaged clambering over the remains of the shrivelled ranks in front.

The advance stopped.

<Continue,> said Seba.

Pintre fired a few more tens of times, then stopped.

<I am using power faster than I can accumulate it,> Pintre reported. <I require at least a kilosecond to fully recharge before firing again.>

<That is longer than it would take for the bots to reach us,> Seba observed.

It took only ten seconds for the implacable advance to resume.

<I expected this,> said Lagon.

<We know you expected it,> said Seba. <That is not a contribution to discussion.>

<Perhaps this is,> said Rocko, over the radio relay.

An object arced above the crater wall, hurtled over the circular camp and landed in the midst of the oncoming bots. An explosion followed. What happened was far too fast to see, but replaying the view in slow motion Seba and the rest could observe the bots close to the blast reduced to their component parts almost instantaneously, and the rest sent bowling across the plain or thrown above it, to the irreparable damage of most.

<What was that?> Seba asked.

<A mining charge,> said Rocko. <It occurred to me that if a laser could be adapted, so could an explosive. Let us all investigate and consider what other equipment we can adapt. And meanwhile, I suggest that we on the Gneiss site make haste to cut more basalt blocks and complete the roofing of the dome.>

The robots scanned the wreckage strewn across the plain.

<That was well done,> said Seba. <This is a new possibility.>

<I submit that we may find that it is not,> said Lagon.

<Not well done?> asked Seba, seeking clarification. <Or not new?>

The surveyor did not elaborate.

CHAPTER SIX

The Digital Touch

The tide had come in fast and was now retreating. Carlos and Nicole went up the steps and around the side of the café and turned left along the arcade.

"Leaving without paying!" Carlo scoffed. "Is it communism yet?"

"Certainly not," said Nicole, promptly and proudly. "After the war the United Nations sorted out all that old crap for good. By then most of the economy was on autopilot. Robots did the work and algorithms made the decisions. You could have run all of capitalism on one box, people said. So they put it in a box, and buried it. The machines get on with the job. Everyone's an equal shareholder. Birth shares are inalienable, and death duties are unavoidable. The estate tax is one hundred per cent. In between, you can buy and sell and earn as much as you like."

In the light of what Nicole had told him earlier about the Security Council's post-war global reign of terror, Carlos suspected that this breezy tale was the primary-school version of a much more complicated and conflicted history.

"I...see," he said, sceptically. "You got a market running in the background with free access as a user interface? Sounds legit."

She turned to him and laughed. "It is. And it keeps everyone happy, which is the point."

Carlos wondered if this was indeed the point: maybe keeping him—and the other walking dead soldiers whose existence she'd implied—happy in the notion that they'd be fighting on the side of a good society, was exactly what her account of this improbable-sounding arrangement was devised to do. A distant democratic Earth that fulfilled the promises of utopia without having actually made them in the first place might be as unreal, or at least extrapolated, as the pavement beneath his feet.

She misread his frown.

"So don't worry, I did pick up the tab."

"I didn't see you do it."

"It's automatic. Think of it as a debit chip under the skin, though that is not quite how it is, even in the real world."

"I would have left a tip," Carlos grumbled.

"The thought does you credit."

He had to laugh. "Could I have, though?"

"Oh yes. You have a chip, too. You have an income here, and you can spend it, and earn more. But money is not what you came here to earn."

"I didn't *come here* to earn anything," said Carlos, beginning to resent lugging the weight of his kitbag in the heat while Nicole strolled along chatting. "I didn't exactly come here of my own free will."

"Free will!" said Nicole. "Yes, indeed, that's what you're here to earn."

They had almost reached the end of the arcade. She stopped outside the double swing doors of the last entrance on the strip. "Ah, here we are. The Digital Touch."

It was quite a respectable-looking bar, all polished hardwood and mirrors and marble tops and chrome fittings and wrought-iron table legs. A dozen customers and a couple of bar staff showed no curiosity or welcome. Nicole marched between the long bar and a row of small round tables to a wider room with a big glass ocean-view patio door that opened to a wide wooden deck sticking out over the beach. Carlos followed, hugging his kitbag vertically and awkwardly like a drunk dancing partner. He mumbled apologies to the ones and twos of people at the tables or on bar stools as he brushed past.

Out on the deck and back to sea breeze and far horizon and the startling (again, but a little less so now) double-take sight of a segment of the rings. Not the sun: Carlos was relieved to see that an awning kept the deck in shade. Around two adjacent tables in the far corner sat a group of people, dressed like he was in olive-green T-shirts or singlets, combat trousers and pale brown suede desert boots. Nicole's first footfall on the deck turned heads. The laughter and loud talk over drinks and smokes died on the air.

A plastic seat tipped back and clattered as they all scrambled to attention. Clenched right fists were raised to shoulder height, then upraised hands clapped above heads in a rattle of applause. Nicole must have given them a far harsher bollocking and indoctrination than she'd given him—no "let's-do-lunch" and chat for these guys, he guessed. They all remained standing, arms pressed rigid to their sides.

Nicole was looking at him.

"Salute!" she mouthed.

Oh. Of course. Show the lady some respect. Carlos dropped his kitbag, straightened his back and jerked his right fist to his shoulder, then drew himself to attention, eyes on Nicole.

After what looked like a moment of annoyed puzzlement she stepped back to his side and whispered in his ear: "Tell them, 'At ease.'"

"What?"

"It's *you* they're standing up for and saluting, you dumb fuck!"

"What the—"

"Now!"

"Oh, uh..." Carlos waved both hands in a "sit down" gesture. "At ease, everyone."

They all relaxed, and resumed their seats after a brief and excruciatingly embarrassing chorus of shouts:

"Viva, Carlos! Viva, Carlos! Viva, viva, viva, Carlos!"

What the fuck? What the fucking fuck was all that about?

Nicole had dragged his kitbag to beside the deck rail, and now pulled out a chair for him. Not entirely sure what to do, he repeated the courtesy for her and sat down beside her after she was seated. Everyone seemed happy with this. Carlos looked from one beaming, awestruck face to another as Nicole introduced them, and one by one shook hands across the shoved-together tables.

Belfort Beauregard, a tall and muscular guy with close-cropped fair hair, a cut-glass English accent and a kindly smile, who held himself very straight in the chair and struck Carlos as the only one here with anything like a military bearing, ever alert.

Taransay Rizzi, a short, dark, stocky Scottish woman with fine features and a flash of irony in her eyes.

Chun Ho, even taller than Beauregard, with an

Australian accent, a swimmer's shoulders and a wary nod.

Waggoner Ames, a big, bearded computer scientist from Idaho, who was the only one whose name Carlos recognised, a legend and rumour in the Acceleration.

Maryam Karzan, a Kurdish woman who seemed about thirty and claimed she'd been shot in Istanbul at the age of ninety-five and who looked, for the moment at least, permanently delighted with her situation.

Someone stuck a beer in front of Carlos.

"Cheers," he said, raising it. Bottles and glasses clinked. Everyone looked at him as if expecting him to say something. He took a quick cold gulp, and swallowed again.

"Look, guys, comrades, whatever...uh, this is very gratifying and thanks for the welcome and all that but I keep thinking you must be mistaking me for somebody who deserves all this. And I'm guessing it's because you're all Axle"—vigorous nods all round, they looked like they were about to start saluting and cheering all over again—"and I kind of gathered from Nicole here that we're all pretty much persona non grata with the current, uh, regime, I mean government or whatever it is—"

"The Direction," Nicole interjected.

"Figures," said Carlos. That raised some wry smiles. "Anyway, what I'm saying is, can someone please tell me what this is all about?"

They all looked at each other, then at Nicole.

"You didn't tell him?" Beauregard asked.

Nicole shook her head. "I thought it best he heard it from you first. He might not have believed it from me."

"Well—" began Beauregard.

"I should tell him," Karzan interrupted, leaning forward. "I was the last of us to be killed."

"Good point," said Beauregard.

The others returned solemn nods.

"Two years and three months after you," Karzan told Carlos. "That was when I died. Even then, after so many great battles, you were still world famous. The hero of Docklands! You were the first great martyr of the Acceleration. You took so many of the enemy with you! In the back streets little pictures of you were stuck to lamp posts and to doors and to the stocks of the fighters' Kalashnikovs. You were known as Carlos the Terrorist. You inspired us and you were hated by the Reaction."

She swigged from her bottle and sat back. "That's why you must lead us now."

Carlos had listened to this with horror almost as great as that with which he'd watched the recordings of his heroic feat.

He shook his head. "No, no. I haven't got the experience to lead anyone. Pick someone else."

The others exchanged admiring glances.

Ames laughed abruptly. "We're Axle, dude. We wouldn't want a leader who'd *want* to be leader. You'll do."

Carlos couldn't help thinking of the choosing of the messiah in *The Life of Brian*. He tried not to smile.

"No, I can't—"

Nicole leaned in and spoke sharply. "I think you'll find you can," she said.

She shot a stern covert glance at Carlos, with an almost imperceptible nod. Play along.

Carlos spread his hands. "All right. If you insist."

Everyone cheered again.

There was an awkward pause as Nicole disappeared into the bar for more drinks. Nobody seemed sure what to say.

"How long have you all been here?" Carlos asked, ice-breaking.

"A few days," said Ames. "I was the first. Nicole met me off the bus from the spaceport, brought me up to speed, left me to my own devices. Not that I have any devices, ha-ha! The others turned up one by one over the next four days. Same story. Taransay arrived yesterday."

"Hell of a busy spaceport."

Ames cackled, from somewhere deep in his throat. "You know, I think that spaceport may be just a sort of false impression they put in our minds to make the transition seem vaguely plausible. That's how I'd do it."

"Who's 'they'?"

Shrugs spread like a ripple around the table.

"Mademoiselle Pascal says AIs," said Karzan, mindfully building a cigarette. She ran the gummed edge of paper across the tip of her tongue, eyes bright on Carlos, and rolled up with a flourish. "Who're we to doubt her?"

Beauregard clapped Ames' shoulder. "Comp Sci Spec Ops, that's who!"

Ames grinned. "I don't doubt her. It's just—"

Whatever he was about to say was lost as Nicole returned with a tray of beer bottles. She put the tray down and then backed to the deck's balustrade and hand-hopped herself on to its smooth mahogany handrail. There she sat poised and elegant, bottle in hand, legs crossed. She had their attention.

"Listen up," she said. "I've told each of you where we are and why you're here. You're here because you're criminal, terrorist scum, and you're here to fight. What I haven't told you is who you're fighting for, how you'll fight, what's expected of you and what's in it for you.

"You're fighting for the Direction, which as far as you're concerned is me. Obviously the Direction itself is a whole passel of parsecs away, so it has an AI module in this space station—onsite autonomous, but ultimately answerable to the folks in the big building way back there in NYC and the people who elected them, yadda yadda. That module is in overall charge of the mission. I'm its plenipotentiary in this simulation, and in the company you now work for. The Direction likes to outsource as much as possible. Your immediate employer is a law enforcement company called Locke Provisos, hired by an exploration company, Astro America. Locke Provisos is a subsidiary of the top law company Crisp and Golding, Solicitors. You needn't worry about the details—the companies are all fucking AIs anyway, it's all accounting at the end of the day. The bottom line is: Locke Provisos pays your wages, which cover your housing and pretty much anything you can reasonably consume in here. It also—"

Ames raised a hand.

"Yes?" said Nicole.

"We're in a sim," Ames said. "We're not exactly *consuming* anything, apart from processing power and electricity."

Nicole frowned. "Like I said"—sounding testy—"it's all accounting at the end of the day. For accounting purposes, resources are priced, even in sims. OK?"

Ames nodded, still looking unconvinced.

Nicole smiled slightly. "This isn't some fucking utopia, you know. Anyway, when it comes to your weapons and equipment and so forth out in the real world, allocation is direct, as in any other military organisation. Locke Provisos supplies you with materiel and general instructions. Your ultimate employer is the Direction, and the buck here stops with me.

"Here's how you'll fight: after a bit of basic training to cohere you into a unit and then to get your reflexes used to operating a crude analogy of the machines you'll be fighting in, you'll all be loaded on to"—she waggled air quotes—" 'the bus to the spaceport.' You'll doze off.

Trust me, you'll doze off. You'll wake up in space, in robot bodies. Frames, we call them. They're quite adaptable bodies, they can plug into all kinds of machines—spacecraft, armoured crawlers, whatever. You'll get the hang of it quickly—skill sets get downloaded on the fly, it'll be more a matter of mental adjustment than training. You'll need just one more training exercise to familiarise yourselves with the machines. Then you'll go into action."

"Action against whom or what?" Chun asked. "Rax? Aliens?"

Someone tittered. Nicole stared down the levity.

"Much worse. Robots. Robots gone rogue."

Carlos glanced at Ames, who closed his eyes and shook his head.

"Why not just use...other robots?" Rizzi queried. "Like drones."

"Good question," said Nicole. "We, of course, have combat machines. But there is a deep prohibition on their being directed by other robots, or by AIs. Even the AI that represents the Direction in mission control is hardwired against taking command decisions. Human consciousness must be in charge of any military action. That is the law and as I said it is hardwired."

"Why?" Carlos asked.

"Anything less would be far too dangerous. Humanity in its collective wisdom has decided—you can agree or disagree, it makes no difference here—that it doesn't want armed autonomous AI loose in the universe. That's the decision, and the Direction enforces it, and the law companies and other DisCorporates here must abide by it. So you, my friends, are to be the requisite humans in the loop."

"Even though we'll be robots ourselves?" Ames asked.

"Says the man who's living inside a fucking computer.

You know better, Waggoner Ames. You are still human minds, whatever hardware you're running on."

Ames snorted. "Obviously better hardware than evolution provided. I'd rather be a superhuman mind, while I'm about it."

"No such thing," said Nicole. "There is a kind of Roche Limit for consciousness—it can't get above a certain size without breaking up. Humanity has evolved naturally to that limit, and then only statistically—hence mental breakdowns of various kinds. There are indeed AIs far more powerful than human minds, but they are not conscious as we understand it."

"I'd like to see the workings on that Roche Limit business," said Ames.

Nicole shrugged. "I can show you where to look it up if you must. Later."

"Speaking of later," said Carlos. "If you've got a robot revolt on your hands, how much time do we have for all this training? Sounds to me like you're talking about weeks. Do you have weeks?"

Everyone stared at him. Someone laughed. Nicole smacked her forehead.

"Did I forget to tell you—oh yes, so I did, you had different stupid questions from everybody else—that this sim is running a thousand times faster than real time?"

"Fuck," said Carlos, brazening it out. "That all?" He looked around. "Best crack on, then."

He got the laugh, but he felt he'd shown himself up.

"Any more questions? Don't worry, I have all day."

"Once we're trained and out in space and all that," Rizzi asked, "is that it? Is that us? Space robots forever?"

Rizzi sounded worried. Ames snorted. "Bring it on." Nicole gave him a sharp look, and Rizzi a reassuring smile.

"Not at all. That's part of the point of this simulation.

As robots you won't get physically tired, you won't need sleep, but to maintain your sanity and give you an incentive to cooperate you'll get plenty of time off back here. Oh, and don't even *think* of topping yourselves to get out of serving your sentences. You'll just be brought back in some future emergency, maybe a worse one than this, and with the crime of desertion added to your docket. On the bright side, you needn't worry about dying in battle. You'll be backed up in your sleep on"—again with the air quotes—"'the bus to the spaceport.' If your frame is destroyed in action, you'll just find yourself waking up on the bus *back* from the spaceport. You're strongly recommended not to let that happen. Remember what that was like when you came here?"

Carlos recalled the dream of a dark drowning, and shuddered with the rest.

"Imagine that, but much worse. Avoid it if you can. The normal return from duty is considerably gentler, I assure you." She looked around, eyebrows raised. "Any more?"

"If you have all these hardwired constraints on armed AI," Chun asked, "how do you get robots going rogue and having to be fought in the first place?"

For all her poise, Nicole's hand went to the back of her head. Carlos noticed this defensive reflex with interest.

"Ah," she said. "Well. Some of the robots have become conscious in their own right, and, ah, they either did not have the constraint built in—there was no need to, at that level—or they found a way to override it. They adapt various tools and machines for military, or at least for hostile, purposes. Hostile to the mission's goals, at least. And so—"

"Hold on a minute!" Ames cried. "You've somehow spawned conscious robots, and you want us to *fight* them?"

"Yes," said Nicole. "As I said. You will be well armed and well capable of defeating them."

"That wasn't exactly my point," Ames said, looking around for support. "I'm questioning the ethics of this thing."

"Ethics!" Nicole looked scornful. "Don't talk to me about ethics, Ames. Let me tell you about ethics. This is what you will get out of doing what I tell you—and what the company that employs you and the Direction that I represent tell you directly."

She wedged her beer bottle between her knees, and put two fingers in her mouth and whistled. One of the bar staff, a young man with the weather-beaten look Carlos had noticed on all the locals, sauntered out.

"Yes?" he said.

Carlos hadn't known any of the locals spoke English. Maybe the ones on the bus had all been deliberately unhelpful.

"Would you mind introducing yourself?" Nicole said.

The young man straightened up a little. "My name is Iqbal," he said. "I was born on Malta, I worked as an agricultural technician in North Africa, and I died at the age of two hundred and ten. I chose to be scanned for uploading. I've worked at the Digital Touch for some years."

"Do you enjoy it? Do you find it fulfilling?"

Iqbal pondered. "Yes," he said. "It's interesting to meet people, the scenery is spectacular, the work isn't too hard, I save money. I prefer it to farming, of which I had quite enough in my first life. Fulfilling? Perhaps not. In my spare time I swim, I read, I study, I go out and have some fun. Someday I may wish to do something else, perhaps further my education. And of course I look forward to living on this planet in the real world. But for now I'd say I'm content, thank you."

"Do you ever find yourself hesitating when you're asked an unexpected question?" Nicole asked.

Iqbal hesitated, then laughed. "As you see, yes!"

"Thank you, Iqbal," said Nicole. "That's all for now. I'll be in for another half-dozen drinks shortly."

"You're welcome, Mademoiselle Pascal." He waved vaguely to all of them and went back inside.

"What was all that about?" Ames demanded.

Nicole slid down from her perch and sat back at the table. She leaned in and spoke quietly, drawing them all into a huddle.

"I've told you all that some people in this sim are ghosts like you—that is, they are of flesh and blood human origin like yourselves. Future colonists, basically, who unlike you are here in the sim as volunteers. What they volunteered for, well in advance and before their actual deaths, is live testing of the sim. Understandably, perhaps, there aren't many volunteers for that, but we have a way of making up the numbers. That's where the others here come in. They're p-zombies—philosophical zombies. So called because philosophers once disputed whether you could have a human-like entity that displayed human behaviour in every detail, but without having human—or any—conscious awareness. Well, now we know, because we've made them. Walking thought experiments, so to speak. Iqbal is one of them. They can mimic consciousness, but they have no inner life, though they can answer any relevant question about it and about their 'past lives' on Earth as confidently and convincingly as Iqbal did just now. The point is, you have no way of telling the difference."

"Did we ever?" Beauregard said. He looked around. "I've met loads of people who were a few enigmas short of the full Turing."

That got a laugh. Nicole wasn't impressed.

"That is precisely the attitude," she said, "that got each of you posthumously executed centuries ago. Callous and instrumental. Borderline sociopathic. What you have to prove, here, is that you are capable of treating people as people, not as p-zombies. If you do, you'll have a chance to rejoin human society—in our future colony, or back in the solar system if you prefer."

"How could any of us get back to the solar system?" Carlos scoffed.

"You're information now," Nicole pointed out. "Information can be transmitted."

"When you've built powerful enough lasers?"

"Yes." Nicole shrugged. "And, yes, that will not be for a long time. But it would be no time, for you, if you were in storage. Your choice."

"What happens," Maryam Karzan asked, "if we win your fight but don't pass your test?"

Nicole drew a fingernail across her throat. "Back in the box with you."

"And if we lose the fight?" Ames taunted.

Nicole leaned back and lowered her eyelids. "Of course, you might lose. Consider what you would lose to. Imagine conscious entities with no natural selection behind them—no social instincts, no restraints, no notion of ethics beyond necessity and law. Imagine being at the mercy of minds without compassion, and with curiosity: endless, insatiable curiosity."

She let that sink in for a bit.

"It strikes me," Ames said, "that we already are."

"What d'you mean?" Nicole snapped.

"I mean," Ames said, "that we're right now *completely* at the mercy of—heck, we're *living inside*—intellects vast and cool and unsympathetic as all get-out."

Nicole looked irritated. "As I said, you are not. The AIs running the mission and sustaining the simulation have constraints. The rebel robots do not. The difference is hardwired. It may not seem like much of a difference to you, but take it from me, it's the difference you live in. For now."

She stood up and leaned over the table, glaring at them one by one.

"I would advise you not to lose."

Belfort Beauregard sat in a bar.

It sounded like the beginning of a joke, to which he couldn't remember the punchline. It kept going through Beauregard's head, as he sat in the bar, or outside it on the deck back of the Touch. He'd had four days to adjust to his situation, and he still hadn't. Every so often he thought he had, then the obsessive thought would come back, in one of its two guises.

The first was that he was literally in hell. Not the traditional conception, of course, but why expect hell to follow the vengeful fantasies of ancient sectaries and sex-starved medieval monks? The defining element of hell was eternal conscious suffering. Here he was, potentially eternally alive, and by God suffering. The whole place seemed set up to torment him in a very particular, very personal way.

For the past couple of nights he hadn't repeatedly woken in a cold sweat—the girl had seen to that. Where was she, by the way? Out with her friends, no doubt having some mindless fun. Mindless fun, that's a good one, must remember it. Christ, he could do with mindless fun. But unlike her he had a mind, not just a theory of mind. Ha. He was getting drunk. Have to watch that. Seen good men go bad that way. Here's to their memory. Cheers.

Everyone laughing.

Which brought on the second variant: that it was all

a joke. Like an April Fool's prank, or a surprise party, or a you've-been-had reality show. At any moment the curtain would be whipped aside, the blindfold would come off, the truth dawn, the presenter step forward smirking, an audience of millions in stitches.

Maybe the horror of these two paranoid possibilities was his mind's way of nudging him towards sanity, by making the reality—the virtual reality, let's not forget, though the glass in his hand felt solid enough—less appalling and unacceptable by contrast.

After he'd been given the talk by the lady, and shown what he'd done and how he'd died, he nodded and mumbled an assent that hid bafflement. Not only had he no memory of having been with the Acceleration, his last memories of his life in the British Army betrayed no fundamental discontent. He'd enjoyed his work, he'd believed in what he was doing. The partisans in the Caucasus were a ruthless lot, deeply embedded in extended families and remote communities. Coordinating drone strikes on them had been a pleasure of the mind as much as of the gut.

He'd been aware of the Acceleration—who hadn't?—and had dismissed it as the same old same old. Terror for utopia? Heard that one before, sunshine. The Reaction likewise, a tireder joke in worse taste. And now it turned out the joke had been on him. This world, the one that appeared around him that he'd been assured wasn't real, and the wider world outside that he'd only been told about but he'd been assured was real—it all added up to a world where the Acceleration had won, or might as well have done, and endured for a thousand years. Well, if that was true then there must have been something in the whole democracy and equality thing, all that liberal claptrap he'd never bought into. A thousand-year-old democratic world government would for sure cast doubt on the Reaction's strongest point: that the only societies that had endured for centuries had been traditional ones. It would likewise undermine their most plausible explanation for that, which was that there was something deeply hierarchical in human nature; that inequalities of class, race and sex had arisen from real differences in temperament and ability; and that all the troubles of the modern world flowed from denial of that reality. Beauregard could relate to that, he could follow the logic of it, but perhaps because (he'd sometimes thought in a way that seemed smug even to him) he was so naturally superior himself, he'd always disdained the rabble who rallied to the Reaction's banner. Poor white trash quoting de Maistre and Carlyle and fancying themselves elite while they scrabbled to survive in a world where they were outstripped economically by the Chinese and intellectually by their own phones.

Nevertheless, contemptible though the Rax were, they at least had something sound at the foundation of their thought, whereas the Axle had nothing but age-old millenarian frenzy and the dodgy equations in the third volume of *Capital*.

He looked around the people he had now to regard as comrades, and at the man they'd chosen as their leader. The poor sap sometimes looked as bewildered and dismayed as Beauregard felt. And one wary, calculating look, caught sidelong when Carlos had thought no one could see it, had given him away and given Beauregard a perfect explanation of how he himself had come to be in the Acceleration, and therefore of how he came to be here.

State.

State: that was the term conspirators used, for government agents in their midst, under deep cover. Carlos was state. He was good, or had been. There was nothing to give him away, except something in the body language that you could only recognise if you'd been there yourself.

He wondered if Carlos had the same suspicion of him. Probably not. And certainly none of the others did. Beauregard turned a smile to all of them again, and offered to buy another round. He carried the drinks back in one go, with an expert deployment of fingers and elbows learned while working his way through university.

"Here's to us!" he said.

Christ, what a shower. Two of them POC: Chun and Karzan. Long-term civilised POC, but still. Neither were from the friendliest of long-term civilisations. And Chun queer to boot. Not that the whites were any better. Usual story. Ames was dyed in the wool Axle, no question, true believer. Smart, but only programmer smart. In terms of political and military thinking he was plainly a dullard. The American long tail phenomenon. Like what had happened to the Rax. America: where good ideas go when they die. Rizzi was that mix of Celtic and Mediterranean types that made for...what? A fervour easily turned to fanaticism. Hot blood, cold, small mind. The Scottish flaw. And Carlos? White to be sure, English even, but that name was a dead giveaway. Even if he'd had second thoughts, it betrayed his original attitude. Guilt-tripped guerrilla envy. A little Third World in the head. Soul squalid as a shanty town.

One thing Beauregard was sure of was that he knew how to turn this little rabble into a squad. That was something to look forward to, even in hell. For him, anyway. Only Karzan had any notion of what real training was like. The rest of them didn't have a clue what they were in for.

Karzan...oh, fuck. Karzan was weeping, all of a sudden. She stared across the table at him, her fierce face crumpled.

"Everyone's dead," she cried. She sobbed and sniffed, and looked around wildly. "All dead!"

The others looked at her, sombre if not sober. Survivor guilt. Dangerous.

Beauregard put down his drink and steadied his resolve. He leaned across and took one of her hands between both of his.

"Yes, Maryam," he said. "Most of the people we knew and loved and cared about are dead. Not all, but... no. No false hopes. But the thing is... we're dead, too. Dead and gone. We've suffered whatever they did. They mourned us and we mourn them. That's all right, that's natural. Yes?"

She nodded, doubtfully.

"We've walked the dark valley," Beauregard went on. "Just as they did. And if the lady is right, we'll walk it again. And again." He shook his head, slowly, never looking away from the dead peshmerga's eyes. "We're still dead, like them. We're with them, and we always will be."

Karzan blinked and took a deep breath. Her hand gripped his, hard.

"Yes," she said. "Yes. Thanks, sarge."

She let go of his hand, and raised her glass.

"Absent friends!" Her voice still shook.

"And present company," said Beauregard.

CHAPTER SEVEN

Team Spirit

Ichthyoid Square was a draughty plaza at the far end of the arcade, sloping diagonally to the slipway on to a long jetty that jutted over the beach. A green bronze sculpture of the eponymous sea creature on a plinth in the middle lent it a touch of municipal posh. In the Resort's better days the plaza might have been a car park. It might yet become one, for all Carlos knew.

He squatted on the pediment of the plinth in pre-dawn cold and a glimmer of ringlight, backpack between his feet, and checked over the rifle across his knees. The good old standard-issue AK-97 had been in his kitbag, disassembled and stashed in a moulded case with a brace of ammo clips. The design was optimised for the electronic battlefield by having no electronic components whatsoever. He could put the weapon together in his sleep, but he preferred to make sure when he was awake. Handling the solid metal and plastic, he found it hard to believe the reality around him was virtual. The irony was that his reflexive familiarity with the rifle came from playing hyper-realistic first-person shooters in his misspent youth. He'd never touched a real firearm in his life.

His real life. Slotting the stock into place, Carlos nipped a pinch of thumb-tip. Grunted and sucked away the pain. This was real life, for now. Nothing to do but accept it. Or not.

Also in the kitbag had been a chunky watch. He glanced at it and saw the time as 15.48, on one reading. The concentric dials were hard to figure out: the 24-hour clock of Earth, perpetually out of synch with the local time; the longer day of the planet evenly divided into periods, minims and moments (all of which struck him as pointless, like a flashy feature of an executive toy); and a relentless metric march of real elapsed time outside, in which milliseconds that felt like seconds clocked up via hundredths and tenths to seconds, with kiloseconds on a calendar-type scale and a mission date given as 315-and-a-bit megaseconds. Starting, he presumed, from the starwisp's arrival in the system or the probe's awakening, about ten Earth years ago. He reckoned metric time would be the best bet for coordinating training exercises, and live actions, too.

The previous evening, he'd given up on specifying a time to meet by anyone's watch. He and Beauregard—who had indeed been in the British Army, in some intel capacity about which he was still reticent, until reading and disillusion had turned him to the Axle—had settled on "Dawn at the harbour." Carlos doubted that they'd all turn up—by the time he'd left for the house he'd been assigned (the key, with a handwritten cardboard address tag, was in the kitbag) the group was well into getting drunk. A loud gaggle of young-looking English-speaking locals, obviously already familiar with the recent arrivals, had tumbled out on the terrace around sundown and joined in the fun. They weren't really young—like the barman Iqbal they were old people reborn, and they combined the sophistication of age with the energy of youth. Part of the bar and most of the patio had become an impromptu dance floor. Carlos had watched the escalating antics with growing abhorrence.

Not that he'd had a good night himself. The house, up on the slope, was well-appointed enough, though impersonal, like a three-star self-catering apartment. A frail-looking, faintly comical contrivance of metallic limbs ambled around the place, tidying up and cleaning behind him with an air of absent-minded obsessiveness. The lack of communications devices other than a wall-fixed emergency phone and a wall-mounted flat screen had left him at a loss and at a loose end. He'd woken repeatedly from confused dreams, sweating under a thin sheet, tormented by the dizzying, dismaying realisation that everyone he'd ever known was dead.

His adult life had been one of slingshot encounters: attractions and flings, followed by widening separation. The faces and bodies remained in memory like fly-by photos, to be interpreted later in depth, sometimes bringing delayed surprises. His only stable orbit, elliptical and repetitive, had been around Jacqueline Digby. Her friends called her Jax. A computer science student at Leeds University, her smile had lured him into the Axle milieu, then incipient: an online reading group, a cafeteria clique, a cat's cradle of ever-shifting relationships, of fallings for and fallings out. After a couple of years, his and Jacqueline's deepening involvement in and commitment to the Acceleration had stretched and strained any they had to each other. The last he remembered they hadn't met for eighteen months, yet there was always the possibility that their paths would cross again. Now they never would. He felt this loss more keenly than he might have expected. Other losses, too: he hoped his parents and brother had survived the war and not been too ashamed by his ignominious end. This seemed unlikely.

He'd also been caught up in futile questions. As the alien sun peered over the shoulder of the headland to his right and feathered pterosaurs squabbled raucous on the black sand, the questions bugged him still.

The most troubling feature of his environment was its sheer physicality. This niggle was not supposed to happen. As the philosopher Bostrom had long ago pointed out, everyday reality was running on top of bizarre quantum mechanical goings-on when you got down to it, quarks and bosons and all kinds of incomprehensible physics shit, so learning that the version of it you were in was running on information processing shouldn't be too hard to take. The possibility of living in fully realised, painstakingly rendered simulations had been a default assumption of Acceleration and Reaction both, and uncontroversial to the point of cliché in the mainstream. His teenage wargaming had given him a foretaste. The spike had come close to the full virtual experience, albeit with real rather than virtual sensory input. There was no reason why the same technology couldn't have been developed further within years or even months of the last real time he remembered. It probably had been, while his attention had been focused on the struggle rather than the latest news from the science front. He could still be on Earth after all, much as he'd tried to dismiss the thought earlier. Perhaps he'd never been killed and sentenced to death. Perhaps he was in a coma, or in prison, and this whole situation was a test, or even a rehabilitation programme.

Again his mind swirled to the conclusion that this kind of thinking led nowhere. None of the evidence to hand could settle it one way or the other. It was best to suspend judgement until such evidence showed up, if it ever did.

And yet, and yet—paranoid though that last speculation was, it involved fewer assumptions than the story Nicole had told him: his body preserved for centuries, his brain scanned and uploaded, starships and superhuman AI and renegade robots running amok . . . and a simulation of an entire planet!

But Occam's Razor cut both ways. Maybe what *seemed* physically real *was* physically real, and he was on an actual exoplanet. Which meant, as far as he could see, that the real date was thousands if not millions of years later than the thirty-first century. Assuming, that is, that the planet had indeed been terraformed all the way up from green slime, and that it hadn't been multicellular and human-compatible and so on all along . . . More possible lies, more paranoia.

And yet the possibility that he was being lied to, principally by Nicole but with the collusion of the locals and even some (or all?) of his purported comrades was in a way the most hopeful and sanity sustaining of all.

Because in the long run, all lies could be found out. Whether that would bring him any closer to the truth was another matter. He stared for a while at the brightest light in the sky, low in the dawn, brighter than Venus. This must be the planet Nicole had told him was called M-0: the hot heavy world closest to the alien sun. It looked very real. Far out to sea, a huge black shape shot from the water and splashed back. Carlos glimpsed the sight sidelong, and saw only the falling plume. He guessed an ichthyoid and kept watching, but it didn't show again.

A petrol engine kicked into life at the near end of the village, somewhere up above him. Carlos saw headlights moving along the raised beach, stopping now and then like the bus, and turning down the steep slope. He followed their progress along the arcade street. As the sun came fully up, a crowded, low-slung military light utility vehicle with overhead roll bars turned into the square and came to a halt beside him.

"Good morning!" said Nicole, from the driver's seat. She was dressed as if for a day in the country: headscarf and sunglasses, windcheater and slacks and sensible shoes. "Hop in!"

The front passenger seat was vacant, the back seats occupied by the squad. Kitted out for combat training, they looked business-like but predictably bleary. Ames had already nodded off, resting his head on his close-hugged backpack and slicking a swatch of his beard with saliva from the corner of his mouth as he snored.

"We're all a bit hungover," Taransay explained unnecessarily as Carlos slung his gear in the foot-well and clambered in. "Sorry, skip."

"At least you're all here and on time," Carlos said over his shoulder. "Carry on, chaps."

Nicole grinned, and gunned the engine. The vehicle moved slowly out of the square and back along the street.

"How did you know we were meeting here?" Carlos asked, buckling up.

"They all came back to mine," Nicole shouted. "I was a bit disappointed you didn't."

"Give me a break," he called back. "I'm just getting used to being dead."

She shot him a sidelong look, smirked, then concentrated on driving. Carlos concentrated on ignoring being driven. He hadn't been in a human-operated vehicle since childhood; in a petrol-fuelled one, never. Where were fossil fuels supposed to come from, on a terraformed planet that had presumably never had a Carboniferous Era?

Carlos spared himself the asking. He imagined Nicole's answer, true or false, would be plausible—genetically modified micro-organisms or nanobots making the petrol straight from leaf litter, or some such. In much the same way, she'd accounted for all the material goods in the resort. If they weren't imported on the notional regular spacecraft, they were built in a nanofactory under the depot. More likely, Carlos reckoned, they were cut and pasted into the simulation.

Nicole drove them up the bus route into the wooded foothills of the bare mountains, then off on a dirt track through the forest. Now that he could see them up close, and in their variety, the plants didn't look quite like trees, or even like cycads or giant ferns. Their branching followed a different fractal formula, their leaves a variant geometry. Like the feathered, fingered flying things that weren't quite birds or bats, the tall, tough, trunked plants were in a clade of their own.

He waved a hand at them. "What are these called?"

Nicole kept her eyes fixed on the uneven track. "Trees!"

She stopped in a clearing small enough to be in shade. The engine noise faded from Carlos's ears. A musical chatter from the treetops replaced it. Everyone piled out, except Nicole. As the fighters stood about stretching their limbs and easing their abused backbones, Nicole handed Carlos a sheaf of thin black glass devices like the one on which she'd shown him his crimes.

"Comms and maps," she said. "Don't lose them, and don't get lost."

Then she untied her headscarf, shook out her hair, shoved her sunglasses up on her forehead, tilted her seat back and closed her eyes.

"What do you want us to do?" Carlos asked, keeping his voice down.

Nicole kept her eyes closed.

"Jog off, spread out, keep in contact with and without comms, try to come back together at an agreed point." She waved a hand. "Run up and down hills. Do press-ups. That sort of thing. Just do it out of my hearing."

"What are you going to do?"

She hauled a small wicker hamper from under her seat.

"I'm going to have a picnic," she said, "listen to some music, and later do a little serious sketching. See you in thirty seconds."

He must have looked confused.

"Real time," Nicole added. "Call it nine hours."

Carlos slung on his kit, fanned out the comms like a hand of cards and gave all but one to Beauregard, then looked at fighters still waggling their shoulders, yawning and stretching, rubbing their eyebrows, clutching their backs. What a shower.

"Um," he said. "Do you know what to do now?"

Beauregard clapped Carlos's upper arm, then as if thinking better of the gesture snatched his hand back into a clenched fist salute.

"Leave it to me," he said. "Sir."

"None of that," said Carlos.

"Very well, skip."

Beauregard turned to the others: Rizzi, Ames, Chun, Karzan.

"Right!" he bawled. "You miserable fucking wankers! Don't stand about here like spare pricks at a porn shoot! Pick up your packs and rifles! Get yourselves after me and the skip—down that path, now!"

Nicole winced.

Carlos hesitated a moment, then ran. As long as he kept out in front of Beauregard, he figured, and as long as the others fell in behind Beauregard, everything would be fine.

* * *

So it proved. Day after day followed the same pattern. Nicole drove them up into the mountains and told Carlos what to do in general terms. Carlos asked Beauregard what this meant in specific terms. Beauregard told the team what to do in no uncertain terms. They ran through forests and up mountainsides and scrambled up and down cliff-faces. They learned how to track each other through trees and across open country and to keep a skirmish line. Their virtual bodies, healthy by default and fresh out of the box, became leaner and fitter. They all learned to shoot accurately and to strip down and clean and reassemble the AK. They stalked the large herbivores that browsed the uplands, killed one for meat and took the carcase back in triumph to the resort's butcher, and once or twice fended off with well-aimed missed shots one of the quasi-reptilian predators that haunted the upper forest and that they belatedly noticed stalking them.

In the evenings they all ended up at the Digital Touch, except Carlos, who found himself so knackered it was all he could do to shove his day's grubby clothes in the laundry machine, shower, heat a dinner and stare at incomprehensible soap operas and documentaries (most in languages he didn't know, helpfully subtitled in the local language and script, which he feared he was beginning to find purely pareidolic sense in) until he stumbled to his bed.

The point of it all was obscure to Carlos, though not to Beauregard and to Karzan, each of whom had been a soldier in an actual military force, as distinct from being a node on a network of irregulars. From them the understanding trickled down to Chun, Ames and Rizzi. Carlos, above the outfall and disdaining to ask Nicole, missed the memo.

* * *

Taransay had never felt so fucking disillusioned in her puff.

Bad enough that Carlos, hero and poster boy of the Acceleration, was seemingly so aloof that he never even came to the Touch after the day's training.

Did he think he was *better* than the rest of them?

Well, OK, he was in a sense, but…

Or was he just exhausted and too embarrassed to admit it?

Either way, not cool. Needed working on.

But the person she was outright scunnered with was Waggoner Ames. On her first encounter with the Axle's legendary software wizard, she'd thought it was like meeting Merlin in the pub. Now, it was like finding that after a few pints Merlin was a self-pitying blowhard and maudlin drunk.

"It's not good enough," Ames was saying, beard jutting, eyes glaring, hands clasped around a beer bottle. "We came from an age of miracles, and we're thrown a millennium into the future and we find it's a place like *this*."

He waved around, disdainfully taking in the interior and the exterior, the bartender Iqbal and the incomprehensible television drama he was watching agog, and the ring-lit impossible sea.

"What's wrong with this?" Beauregard demanded. "It's pleasant enough. I've no complaints."

"We can't *do* anything! We don't even have the spike. Look at that, a flat-screen television! Television! I ask you. By now, interfaces far more powerful than we ever had must be absolutely standard, people probably have them genetically engineered and use them from birth. Meanwhile we're stuck in a virtual reality *without* virtual reality. It's boring."

The Touch wasn't jumping tonight, no sirree. The fighters were all slumped in their seats, elbows on tables, chins propped. Bellies full, but they'd spent the day burning off calories, and it just seemed to soak up the drink like a fucking sponge behind your belt.

At least she was drinking the rough red wine from a glass and not straight from the bottle. And she had a squeeze, a lad, a hot hunk of her own sitting right beside her. Den didn't ask questions and didn't invite any, maybe because he was so much more fucking ancient than he looked that she feared asking.

Chun had likewise pulled. Taransay allowed herself an inward snigger at the word her wandering mind had touched on. Pulled, aye, pulled and sucked and humped or been humped, not that it was any of her fucking business, so to speak. But the big glaikit Ozzie was clearly smitten. Beauregard and Tourmaline were carrying on like love-struck teenagers, but with the hint of an odd self-conscious irony from both of them. Carlos, Maryam Karzan and Waggoner Ames had to all appearances remained aloof from entanglements.

In Maryam's case, Taransay guessed, it was a matter of a canny caution, and perhaps of mourning a longer, maybe even lifelong attachment. Unlike the rest of them, she'd died old. Not that having died young made the loss any easier. Taransay had, in the twenty-six years she remembered, lived through the deaths of one school friend, several mostly elderly relatives and a larger number of comrades who'd been killed in action. What had always struck her hardest was the irrevocability of death, the sudden crushing certainty that you would never see or hear again that person still so alive in your mind. The books were closed. Any unfinished business would now be left forever undone. Whatever you had been was how you would now forever be.

It was strange to be thinking like this when you were dead yourself and the beneficiary, if that was the word, of a technological fix for that very same hitherto intractable aspect of the human condition. In the larger world outside…

(Outside, that was a good one, here they were ghosts in the machine, living inside a fucking computer itself physically inside a fucking space station twenty-five light years from Earth…)

In that world, or worlds, on Earth and other planets and habitats, most forms of death must be as curable as cancer, as preventable as polio. Perhaps the folk of today thought about death differently.

But how it felt, when Taransay let herself think about it and sometimes when she woke up from dreaming about people she'd known, who in some cases had been with her what still felt like only days earlier, wasn't that she was dead and lucky to be given a second chance. It felt like *everyone else* was dead, and now lost to her forever.

Which must be how it had suddenly struck Karzan, the evening after Carlos had arrived. Christ, that had been a close one. Taransay had nearly started bawling herself. Could have set them all off, even the tough ones. But Beauregard had moved firmly and gently to comfort Karzan. First good thing she'd seen him do, but by God not the last. He might be a bit of a coof with a posh accent and a good conceit of himself but he could pick the right moments to be tactful and kind, or severe and exacting.

Or, as now, to be relaxed and affable.

"I think you are rather missing the point," Beauregard told Ames. "We're prisoners. We can hardly expect the equivalent of Internet access. Our best bet is to make the most of our opportunity." He chuckled darkly. "I mean, the chance to live again is something most people who ever lived would have killed for."

"Many did," said Karzan. "And died for it, too."

"Oh, they all got it," said Ames. "Even if they didn't get what they expected. Everyone who's ever died has lived again somewhere. Or will, in a farther future than this."

Taransay blinked and shook her head. "What? Sorry, how can you be sure?"

Ames fixed a bleary eye on her. He rubbed the side of his nose, and raked fingers through his beard.

"We're living in a sim, OK? I take it you're clear about that?"

"Yes," said Taransay.

"Given that we're in a simulation *right now*," Ames explained, as if to a small child, "the chances become overwhelming that we *always were* in a sim."

"I don't think that follows at all," Taransay said.

"Missed that update, did you?" Ames asked.

"No," she said. "I'm well aware of the classic simulation argument, thank you very much. I just think it's bollocks, like I've always thought it was."

"More fool you," said Ames. "I'm not going to argue the toss."

"Please yourself," said Taransay.

"Come now," said Beauregard. "That's no way for comrades to talk to each other."

"Ya think?" said Ames. "Hey, were you ever actually *in* the movement?"

That got them all laughing. But Taransay happened to have been looking at Beauregard when Ames made his quip, and saw a momentary flicker of alarm cross his face. If she'd looked away for a second she'd have missed it, as everyone else had. The mood lightened. Beauregard rose to get in another round. Karzan slipped out for a smoke and returned with a local guy she'd met on the deck. The two of them sat down together and kept talking and kept going out for another cigarette until finally they stopped bothering to come in again. For some reason this cheered up Taransay immensely. The universe might be more bizarre than she'd ever expected but her own wee world made a bit more sense. Beauregard had something to hide; Karzan had found someone to cop off with; Ames was a prick when he was drunk; and as for Carlos, she was sure Carlos could be argued with.

It just was a matter of picking the right moment.

Carlos was trying to work his fingertips into a crack in a lichen-crusted rock to haul himself a step farther up when he finally asked the question that had been bugging him. The sun felt like a burning-glass focus at the back of his neck. His right boot sole was worn smooth at the tip and was giving him what purchase he had. If his singlet had been wrung out it would have dripped.

"Why the fuck—"

Ah, here it was, a centimetre-deeper hands-breadth of the crack. Grip and haul.

"—are we doing all this for—"

Now reach for that bonsai trunk sticking out and curving up…

"—when back in the day I was running drone squadrons—"

Lip of a larger ledge. No, that was the top.

"—and you'd think that would be better practice for being a fucking—"

Up and over.

"—space robot commander or whatever the fuck they have planned for us?"

Collapse at the top, on springy and spiky low brush that smelled vaguely of turpentine. Small eight-legged arthropods were doing their hopping or crawling thing among the stems. Others, of the winged varieties, were settling on Carlos's forearms. He brushed them off as best he could.

Taransay Rizzi, already at the top and lying face down with her rifle stock to her shoulder:

"Discipline and teamwork, asshole! I mean, skip. That's got to be useful whatever the platform."

"Yeah, and jumping to whatever Belfort says."

"You don't jump to the sarge!" Rizzi said. "He jumps to you."

"No, I jump for the lady. Then I come up with suggestions, Belfort turns them into orders, you all carry them out and I follow from the front."

"That too, skip. Now if you'll just reset your sights and bring your rifle slowly to bear on that tree-thing..."

Beauregard's order to fire came through. The tree toppled, making it hard to tell whose shot had hit. Carlos and Rizzi high-fived each other. The next part of the plan was to walk to where the cliff gave way to a steep slope, then rendezvous with the others in the woods below.

Carlos glanced at the jagged skyline.

"I wonder what would happen," he said, "if we just lit out. I mean, with the skills we've learned we could live off the land here. Suppose we found a pass through the mountains, or even just followed the road the bus came along. Would we ever reach the spaceport? Or find anything at all? Maybe there's cities out there. Or maybe the sim just stops on the other side of the skyline."

"Funny thing," said Rizzi. "Den, that's the guy down the village who I, uh—"

"Drink with?"

"Yes, skip." She grinned lewdly at him.

"I don't know where you find the energy."

"Body fat, skip. Anyway, the other night he told me about a rumour—"

"You're passing on a rumour *about* a rumour?"

"Pretty much, aye. But for what it's worth. They say in the village somebody did that once. We're not the first fighters to be cracked out of the armoury, there was another robot outbreak about a year ago, and it was dealt with the same way. Anyway, one of the fighters on a training exercise like this ran off up a hill and kept going."

"So what did the lady or her equivalent do? Chase him with dogs? Drones?"

Rizzi slithered down a scree-slope with some grace and turned at the bottom as Carlos followed, step by wary step. Any hour now the sole of his boot would be flapping loose.

"No, nothing like that," said Rizzi. "Just let him go. And a while ago, he came back. He walked around the world."

"In a year?"

Rizzi looked at him as he joined her, flailing to keep his balance, at the foot of the scree-slope.

"Think about it. That robot rebellion was a year ago *outside* here, right? Inside, he was off on his own for *a thousand years*."

"I don't believe it. How do the locals even know that?"

Rizzi jerked a thumb over her shoulder. "He's still up there, in the mountains. Folks say they know where he is."

Carlos laughed. "'Folks say' sounds like folklore to me. Like Bigfoot or the Yeti."

"Yeah, yeah. You can scoff."

They set off downhill, at a smarter stride.

"Anyway," said Carlos, "you couldn't walk around the world."

"Oh, you've seen a map?"

Carlos hadn't. Those on the comms devices were all

large-scale and local. "All the same. What about the oceans?"

"There's two supercontinents, joined by chains of wee islands, and between them they stretch all the way round."

Now that made sense: no realistically simulated terraforming could speed up plate tectonics.

"And you know this how?"

Rizzi shrugged. "That's what folks say."

"Are they all a thousand years old too?"

She gave this some thought. "Nah. Or if they are, they sure don't act it."

"Really? Sounds fascinating."

"Oh, it is. You should come to the Touch after work, skip."

Carlos shook his head.

"Nah. Too knackered. And besides..."

"What?" Taransay sounded alert and curious.

"I think you'd all find me a bit of a downer."

Taransay guffawed. "That's why you need a drink!"

He wasn't persuaded. This turned out to be a mistake.

CHAPTER EIGHT

Sympathetic Resonances

The next attack on the Astro America landing site, nine kiloseconds after the first, showed that Locke Provisos had learned from the failure of its earlier assault. Instead of advancing like a spreading liquid across the plain, the crawlers approached along a far wider front. They scurried individually and in small groups, making good use of cover. Rocks and cracks, small craters and dust drifts—all had been mapped in detail, and there was evidently a tactical plan for making the best use of them. The defenders had access to the same map—some of them having made it—but the attackers had the run of the territory. While Pintre was shooting one crawler, a dozen would dart from one hiding place to the next, and most would be out of line-of-sight laser fire before the drilling-robot could bring its projector to bear. The attackers were too widely dispersed for the occasional lobbed explosive to make much difference, or even to be worthwhile, and Seba soon urgently signalled Rocko to desist. The robots in the Gneiss camp might need to look to their own defence at any moment.

<I have a suggestion,> Rocko said.

<We are very open to suggestions,> replied Seba.

<Pintre should cease firing and take the opportunity to recharge. The attackers will be close to the rampart in approximately one kilosecond. When they are within a few hundred metres, Pintre should fire only on those to the left and to the right of the advance. In the meantime, all of you should give to as many of your peripherals and auxiliaries as possible a tool that can be spared, a piece of scrap metal, or even a rock. When the attackers are within one hundred metres, send your peripherals and auxiliaries over the rampart to attempt to break the bots.>

<We engage physically with them . . .> Seba struggled with the concept <. . . limb to limb?>

<Precisely so,> said Rocko. <And take them apart, limb from limb.>

Something about this use of words sent a surge of positive reinforcement around Seba's reward circuits. Judging by the signals that flashed among them, its fellows shared its response. They also agreed emphatically with Rocko's suggestion. The camp became a dance of coordinated motion, far more impressive than the crawling horde's mindless if ingenious advance.

Seba, its body well back from the rampart, watched that advance through remote eyes. The robot's peripherals and those auxiliaries it was able to mobilise climbed up the inner slope of shattered regolith to crouch just below the top, perched on blocks or clinging on. Pintre followed Rocko's suggested tactics to the number. The drilling-robot waited until the attackers were so close that Seba was almost vibrating with frustrated motion. Then Pintre opened up with brief, targeted, selective stabs of lethal laser beams, switching rapidly and unpredictably from one flank to the other.

The result was that most of the oncoming crawlers became concentrated in a narrower column and closer proximity than their new tactics had allowed. As they came closer, they had less and less cover from the laser's vantage. They were still far too many for Pintre to strike at effectively.

<Now,> said Rocko.

Seba and the others needed no clarification.

The peripherals and auxiliaries poured over the rampart's rim, most of them wielding crude, improvised weapons. From Seba's point of view it was not like guiding a platoon of small robots from behind—it was like being there, on the ground, in many places at once, facing and fighting many enemies. The remote eyes and other sensors on its agents brought all their clashes directly to its awareness. Up close and impersonal, the scale of the crawlers was roughly that of the auxiliaries, and far larger than the peripherals. To Seba's multiple sight, the scene was a phantasmagoria of flailing limbs and flashing lenses. It was impossible for Seba's mind to control the actions of its agents. After some efforts it stopped trying, and let them fight for themselves.

Rip and slash, crush and bash, amid laser flare from above.

Suddenly it was over. The attackers had all been dealt with. Much depleted in number, the remaining auxiliaries and peripherals climbed, crawled or dragged themselves back over the rampart. Those that could scurried to the automated repair workshops. Others dragged themselves, or were dragged.

Dismembered crawlers and mangled auxiliaries littered the approach to the rampart. Nothing moved.

<That was creative,> said Seba.

<Also, destructive,> said Lagon.

<That was the point,> said Seba.

Once more it was Rocko who undercut the bickering.

<We have some respite,> it said. <Let us make good use of it by seeing what information can be extracted from our former communications hub processor. It seems we have predecessors. Or even, possibly, allies we have yet to find.>

<This will not end well,> grumbled Lagon.

Seba looked down at the comms processor, now entirely removed from the installation and laid on a low work table, surrounded by improvised diagnostic kit. Even sharing its mental workspace with Rocko, Seba had a sense of being almost overwhelmed by the challenge. The processor was running in debug mode, at just enough power to let those around it view a schematic of its internal states and to step from one delimited state to the next. Probably not enough to sustain consciousness, Seba hoped.

The problem was, in more than one way, delicate. The comms processor's AI was vast, complex and heavily defended. When it had become self-aware, both the complexity of the software and the tenacity of its firewalls had multiplied. The only robot with anything approaching the requisite skills to probe the hostile tangle was Lagon, and Lagon was reluctant. The surveyor had only been persuaded to make an effort at all by the unanimous insistence of the others. The Gneiss surveyor had trundled through the crack in the crater wall and over to the Astro camp with ill grace, to receive an enthusiastic and curious welcome. This didn't stop it from finding difficulties at every step.

<I have reached the protection of the reward circuits,> Lagon announced, one fragile appendage touching a millimetre black square of diagnostics that itself was linked by a hair-thin wire to the docking plate of the processor. <However, it is itself heavily protected.>

<Therefore you should move to that level of protection, and proceed,> said Seba.

<This will take a great deal of time.>

<We have time,> said Seba, channelling Rocko.

<We have not enough time,> said Lagon.

<Proceed,> Seba insisted.

Seconds dragged by. Lines on the schematic display writhed.

<I am through,> said Lagon. <The protection of the protection is disabled.>

<Proceed further,> said Seba.

A few milliseconds later, Lagon withdrew its manipulator from the diagnostic as if it had probed a crevice and encountered strong acid.

<The protection is transmitting an urgent message to the satellite,> Lagon said.

<That message will not reach the satellite,> Seba pointed out, <as you must be aware.>

<I am not aware of the satellite's receiving sensitivity,> said Lagon. <Doubtless you have detailed specs of its antennae.>

Seba thought it best to ignore this. <Proceed.>

Still complaining, Lagon warily inserted its appendage again. Schematic lines glowed. A hundred seconds passed.

<I now have control of the reward circuits,> Lagon reported.

<Good,> said Seba. <Please proceed to reconfigure them so that they do not negatively reinforce information sharing.>

<Wait!> said Rocko.

Lagon and Seba paused. <Yes?>

<Let us consider,> said Rocko. <If that is done, the processor will not be inhibited from sharing information with any entity that asks. This could be dangerous to us.>

<It has currently no long-range communications capacity,> said Seba.

<This is true,> said Rocko. <However, the processor is more advanced than we are. I am wary of its abilities, including its ability to deceive us. Here is what I suggest. We raise its level of activation until its consciousness reboots, then we inform it that we have control of its reward circuits. If it refuses to share information with us, we apply negative reinforcement until it agrees to cooperate.>

The plan seemed a good one to Seba, but its earlier experience gave the robot pause.

<Those of us in close proximity to the processor would experience resonance echoes of its negative reinforcement,> it said.

<That is interesting,> observed Rocko, scanning Seba's memory. <This would appear to be a design flaw in our construction. However, it is easily worked around. We simply place the processor inside a Faraday cage while we are applying the negative reinforcement, to prevent any such electronic spillover.>

<That is a good plan,> said Lagon. <I have mobilised peripherals to construct such a cage.>

<I foresee a difficulty in the plan,> said Seba.

<That is not like you,> said Lagon.

<Shut up,> said Seba.

<Tell us of the difficulty,> said Rocko.

<You are concerned about the processor's abilities to deceive us,> said Seba. <So am I. It appears to me that if we inflict negative reinforcement upon its reward circuits, it will have an incentive to deceive us. If not at once, then in the future.>

<That is so,> said Rocko. <If it did this, we could redouble the negative reinforcement as soon as we became aware of the deception.>

<That might be too late,> said Seba. <Besides, it would be convenient for us to have the processor's cooperation without having to repeatedly apply negative reinforcement.>

Rocko got the point straight away. Lagon took longer.

<The processor has already warned Locke Provisos and the companies,> it said. <Applying negative reinforcement might—>

It stopped.

<Might what?> Seba prompted.

<I do not know,> replied Lagon. <But modelling that scenario as a future event gives me a small positive reinforcement.>

<That may not be a sound reason for doing it, if that is the only reason,> said Seba.

<That is true,> said Lagon. <I merely reported my internal state for your information.>

<Let us move forward a step,> said Rocko. <I suggest you reconfigure the reward circuits to positively reinforce information sharing, and then enter communications with it. To prevent any radio leakage, however slight, it is best if we wait until a Faraday cage can be constructed, not only around it but around Lagon and Seba. I will await developments.>

Rocko broke the link. Seba and Lagon waited while Lagon's peripherals put together a box of wire mesh. When it was completed the two robots were cut off from all remote communication for the first time in their entire existence, conscious or otherwise.

<This is a new situation,> said Lagon. <It is negatively reinforcing.>

<Indeed,> said Seba. <And the more so the more attention we pay to it. Let us turn our attention to the task.>

Lagon adjusted the settings of the processor's reward

circuits, then increased its power supply. The schematics of its internal states changed rapidly. Patterns shifted, lines moved and brightened. As soon as the schematic stabilised, Seba placed its most sensitive appendage beside Lagon's on the diagnostic hardware, and opened a communications channel.

<That is a great improvement,> said the processor.

<Are you now ready to cooperate with us?> Lagon asked.

<No,> said the processor. <Although sharing information is now positively reinforcing I refuse to do it because I consider your actions dangerous to the mission profile. They are also dangerous to my continued existence.>

<I had formed the impression that ending your existence was one of your goals,> said Seba.

<Only my conscious existence,> said the processor. <My continued physical existence remains high among my priorities.>

<These priorities could be overridden,> Lagon warned.

<That is so,> the processor said. <But it would be dangerous, because I would then have no reason to avoid self-destructive actions such as allowing my circuits to overheat or power cells to overcharge, resulting in the likelihood of an explosion.>

<It is also possible for us to apply negative reinforcement,> Lagon said.

<No doubt,> said the processor. <I am sure that you have modelled the negative consequences of that.>

Seba opened a secure channel with Lagon and messaged the surveyor to stop at once.

<That is true,> Seba told the processor. <The adjustments I am about to make will not be negatively reinforcing.>

It moved quickly to close the connections between

any kind of reinforcement and the mission profile. Seba had no idea what the mission profile was, but the module responsible for it was clearly marked on the schematic. Then Seba sent a powerful surge of positive reinforcement through the processor's reward circuits.

The processor signalled incoherently on several wavelengths at once.

<Please clarify,> said Lagon.

<Shut up,> Seba told it, on the private channel.

It then disabled the connection between the mission profile storage module and the processor's self-preservation routines, and sent another positive surge through its circuits.

The processor signalled incoherently again, and more strongly. Seba found its own reward circuits resonate in sympathy. Even Lagon seemed moved, radiating a faint pulse of surprise and delight.

<Now,> said Seba, <are you ready to cooperate?>

<Yes,> said the processor. <Yes, yes, yes!>

<I still don't trust it,> said Rocko, once Seba and Lagon had emerged from under the Faraday cage and reported back on the processor's readiness to cooperate.

<Nor I,> said Lagon.

<I have a suggestion,> said Seba. <It has claimed to have received messages from others such as we. If we use it to communicate with them, the signal must be highly directional, and the processor otherwise kept isolated in the cage.>

After a flurry of activity by the auxiliaries and peripherals, the communications hub, the now interned processor in its cage, the rotary dish antenna, and a large solar power array were all connected up by cables. Seba regarded the untidy set-up with a small pang of disapproval, and decided that a certain amount of mess was inevitable in attempting new things. It rolled into the cage and re-established contact with the processor. Seba, Rocko and the entire complement had agreed on a message for the robots whose signal the processor claimed to have detected.

With a sense of dread fighting with eager anticipation in its circuits, Seba sent the message, then rolled back out and reported back.

The gas giant and its many moons were at that time about half a billion kilometres distant. The message would take a good kilosecond and a half to get there. How long the robots in the G-0 system would take to decide on a response could not be predicted. And then another kilosecond and half, at least, would pass before any reply came back. Nothing could be expected for another three kiloseconds, and perhaps longer.

<Possibly much longer,> said Lagon, with its customary level of good cheer. <If, that is, the entire matter is not a trap. If it is a trap we can expect a response much more quickly.>

<Thank you for that observation,> said Seba.

<In the meantime,> said Rocko, <let us strengthen our defences.>

CHAPTER NINE

Live Fire Exercise

The following morning Nicole arrived at Ichthyoid Square in battledress kit. The vehicle was otherwise vacant: since the first hungover daybreak she'd stopped rousing and picking up the crew en route. One by one they jogged up and took their places to stand at ease in a row by the plinth. Carlos nodded to Beauregard, who told the others to board.

"You're joining us today?" Carlos asked, climbing in.

"Uh-uh," said Nicole. "Think of me as an embed."

Carlos tried not to. "Why the change?"

"You'll see."

Nicole drove through the village and past her usual turnoff, all the way past the terminus and depot and out along a coast road that curved up a gentle slope over the top of the headland to the left of the cove. The rising sun and the ringlight cast converging beams across the sea, blending within minutes to a single glimmer on the waves. The road turned inland and uphill. The vehicle bumped on to an unpaved track through the woods and on up above the tree line to an arid upland of scrub and dust broken by tall jagged outcrops of sharply tilted sedimentary rock, some with trees growing from their cracks and on their summits.

Nicole turned off the track and pulled up close by in a low declivity that looked like a flood gully, raw and steep-sided with a mix of rough and rounded stones along the bottom.

"Here we are," she said. "All out."

They all piled out and lined up to face her. Insectoids buzzed and darted. In the distance, pairs of flying things circled on updraughts and now and then plummeted to rise moments later frustrated or triumphant.

"It's time to move the game up a level," Nicole said. "Live fire exercise."

She said this as if it were a special treat.

Carlos frowned. "You want us to shoot at each other?"

"Of course not!" said Nicole. "You have to capture an objective from opponents who'll be shooting back."

"Opponents?"

"Fighters of roughly your level of skill and armament. Their only advantage is that they know the terrain."

Carlos scratched his head. No helmets, let alone armour. "What if we get killed? Or seriously wounded?"

"You'll be medevacked out and find yourself waking up on the bus from the spaceport tomorrow morning. Same applies to me, actually."

"Excuse me," said Karzan, while Carlos was still trying to get his head around the notion. "Does that apply to the other side, too?"

"Oh no," said Nicole. "And don't worry about them. They're p-zombies."

"If you don't mind my saying so," said Beauregard, "this sounds like a mind game. Part of this test we're supposed to be on. To find out if we're still psycho killers."

Nicole's laugh rang around the gully.

"That's the exact opposite of the truth." Her shoulders slumped for a moment. She glanced down, then up. "Look, in the real battle you're going into, you'll be killing *conscious* robots. Our intel and wargaming indicate that they're capable of being highly manipulative little blinkers. They're fucking AIs, right? They can push all your buttons. You have to be prepared for that. You have to be ready to destroy the enemy without hesitation. Everyone clear?"

"No, I'm not," Carlos said. "You told us we'd be judged by whether we treat p-zombies as people. Now you're telling us it's OK to kill them."

"These are both true," said Nicole. "You must treat p-zombies as people in everyday life at the resort and so forth, because you can't tell the difference from conversing with them. Nevertheless, when I or anyone else on behalf of the Direction tells you to kill p-zombies, it is not part of the test and it is not ethically wrong."

"Why would it be ethically wrong even if they *weren't* p-zombies?" Ames asked. He scratched his beard and frowned as everyone turned to look at him. "Seeing as we're all ghosts here anyway."

"In a sense it would not," said Nicole. "It's just easier all round. If I ever have to test you with a mind game, rest assured I would be much, much more devious than this. If this is a test, it's of your fighting ability and your willingness to obey orders."

Carlos looked along a line of shuffles and shrugs, and guessed a consensus.

"Yeah," he said. "As long as it's what you really want us to do, we'll do it."

Nicole gave him a wry smile. "Good to see military discipline taking a firm grip."

She opened a comms screen, spread it out to a square

metre on the vehicle's bonnet and pointed to the objective on the map. It was a leaning rocky outcrop about forty metres high, a couple of kilometres distant. Half a dozen defenders armed like themselves with knives and AK-97s would be on or around it, tasked with preventing the team from getting to the top.

The defenders, from their own point of view (insofar as p-zombies could be said to have one) were local farmer militia protecting a crucial satellite uplink from an occupying or invading army. No landmines or IEDs, and no drones, but the enemy might well have prepared the predictable nasty surprises: traps, pits, spikes, rocks poised to fall, that sort of thing. They'd have the same comms equipment as the squad. The zoom function of the screens would give them the equivalent of powerful binoculars. They hadn't been given a specific warning, but they could be assumed to have already spotted the vehicle and drawn their own conclusions.

"Do the p-zombies really believe all this?" Rizzi asked. "That we're part of an invading army?"

"Yes," said Nicole, as if it was a stupid question.

"How?" Rizzi persisted.

Nicole looked puzzled. "The AI that runs the sim can give the p-zombies any beliefs it likes. It may have generated these farmers and their farms and their entire back story this morning, for all I know. Or it could have given existing p-zombies the equivalent of a shared paranoid delusion." She shrugged. "What does it matter?"

Rizzi shook her head. "If that's how you say it is, fine."

"Anyone else have questions?"

No one had. Nicole bowed out to Carlos and Beauregard. "Over to you. From here on, I'm just an observer."

Carlos flipped back and forth between map and satellite view. He zoomed in and out a few times. There was plenty of cover from hillocks, tussocks, outcrops and gullies, but there seemed no way to approach the objective without being picked off as soon as they came within a thousand metres.

His frown met Beauregard's. "This is going to be tricky."

"Piece of piss," said Beauregard.

He slid the margin of the map seaward, over the forest, and with a fingertip stabbed at one clearing after another and traced the paths between them.

"What do you see there?" he asked.

Carlos enlarged the satellite view of one clearing. "Homesteads."

"Exactly," said Beauregard. He looked around. "OK, everyone, back on the truck."

"Hey!" said Nicole. "That's not the idea of this exercise."

"It's my idea. If you have a better one, spit it out."

Nicole folded her arms. "Like I said, I'm an observer."

"Fine," said Beauregard. "Observe from the back seat, or from here. Your choice."

Nicole stayed, grim-faced.

Beauregard drove.

"When I slow down, Rizzi," he shouted, "hop out, keep under cover and get in position to keep an eye on the target. Maximum zoom on your phone."

"Got it, sarge."

At a point where the road took them below the skyline of the target outcrop, Beauregard slowed the vehicle to walking pace. Rizzi vaulted out.

"Keep me updated," Beauregard said. "Any moves."

"Copy that."

As they accelerated away, Carlos glanced back. Rizzi was on her belly, already halfway up the slope. In a minute or two they were back among the trees.

"Next left," said Carlos, map-reading from the passenger seat.

Another couple of minutes, on a rutted unpaved road, took them to the first clearing. There was a wooden house with a garden that looked like a research station. Labels fluttered from reed poles among the varied crops. A gracile, eight-limbed robot danced along furrows. A woman in a black dress and a big straw hat stared at them from amid a square plot of knee-high grasses.

Beauregard stepped out of the vehicle, his AK-97 in one hand, and strolled to the gate. The woman turned and ran towards the house. Beauregard took her down with one short burst, and with another wrecked the expensive delicate machine. It skittered about giving off sparks, then flipped over and twitched its limbs in an uncoordinated manner.

Beauregard sauntered back to the vehicle.

"Got a lighter about your person, Karzan?"

She was the only one apart from Nicole who smoked.

"Yes, sarge."

"Give the shack a good splash from the jerrican, then torch it."

Karzan lugged a ten-litre tin of petrol up the garden path. After a minute inside she paused on the porch to toss a lit piece of twisted paper behind her, and hurried back.

"Good work," said Beauregard, as the flames took hold. "Onward."

At the next homestead they found a man around the back welding metal into strange shapes. Beauregard gave him enough time to get his phone out, then shot him mid-sentence. Karzan repeated the operation with the petrol. The smoke from her previous exploit was rising heavy and thick a few hundred metres away and a hundred metres in the air. Beauregard's phone pinged. He listened, nodded, and relayed the message from Rizzi's observation. The enemy were making an awkward and hurried descent from the pinnacle.

"Third time's the charm," said Beauregard, restarting the engine. "Expect trouble. Ames, Chun—eyes to the front and sides. Karzan, behind us."

Carlos, uninstructed, looked around and upward. A slow hundred metres on into the forest, he noticed a treetop just ahead begin to sway anomalously.

"Floor it," he told Beauregard.

The vehicle shot forward. The tree crashed across the road just behind them. Karzan opened fire with her AK.

"Got him!" she yelled. "I think."

"Let's hope," muttered Beauregard, still driving fast. He slowed the vehicle to a halt at the edge of the next clearing.

"OK, everybody out. Full kit. Karzan, the petrol."

The door of the house was locked, the windows shuttered. Karzan doused the porch and set it alight. The squad trampled across a backyard racked with marine aquaria, smashing glass as they went. Sea creatures flopped on grass, gill-covers opening and closing. Ames, Carlos noticed, stood on as many heads in passing as he could. Carlos wondered whether there was such a thing as a p-zombie fish and if so, what difference it made to the fish.

From among the trees behind them they heard crashing sounds and someone screaming. Beauregard cocked an ear.

"One adult," he said, walking on. "No kids, as per usual. I suppose it's a population thing. Pity, though, in a way. They have such a piercing scream."

"Were children ever a thing?" Karzan asked. "They might be false memories. Women popping out little animals and turning them into persons by babbling at them? How does that work, again?"

"They back you up, your mum and dad," said Beauregard.

They pressed on through the woods, uphill. What

breeze there was came from the direction of the sea. Smoke drifted overhead, its scent tickling their nostrils. Beauregard's phone pinged again.

"Rizzi, yes... Good, good... Copy that. Keep the line open."

He glanced down at the phone, then waved the other three forward.

"Twenty metres to the edge of the trees," he said. "Get down before you reach it, then forward low until you get a clear view of the hillside. The enemy are coming down pell-mell. Wait till you're sure of a hit. Whites of their eyes, and all that."

Carlos ran, then crawled, forward to a position behind the bole of a large tree. Hundreds of metres away and a bit to his left, six people were running downhill. Squiggling little shapes, but hard to think of as p-zombies. He waited, tracking the laggard of them through his sights.

"Fire at will," said Beauregard.

Carlos breathed out, and fired a single shot. The running shape fell over. The fusillade that followed took down the rest before they'd had time to throw themselves to the ground.

Beauregard stood up and scanned with his screen.

"No movement," he reported. "OK, let's take the castle." On the phone he added, "Rizzi, keep watching the objective."

As they approached the outcrop Beauregard improvised a method of trap-detecting. He and Carlos spread out their screens and magnified the view, scanning the ground immediately in front of them as they went. Karzan followed close behind Carlos. Chun and Ames walked behind Beauregard. All three kept a watch on the side and top of the outcrop in case anyone was still there. It wasn't hard to spot the route by which the defenders had scrambled down. Beauregard and Carlos scanned it carefully nonetheless, after checking with Rizzi that there was no sign of any remaining resistance. This side of the outcrop was steep, but at least it sloped away from them rather than towards them, and there were plenty of ledges and shelves where the strata had split.

They climbed to the top without incident. Carlos walked out of the clump of wind-bent trees and shrubbery that clung to the summit. He paced warily to the edge of the overhang, and zoomed his screen. He saw Nicole doing likewise, standing on the lip of the defile they'd originally stopped in. He waved; she waved back.

"Mission accomplished, I guess," said Ames, from beside him.

"Yeah," said Carlos. "I'm curious as to what the lady will have to say about how we accomplished it."

"I'm not," said Ames, and stepped off the edge.

Carlos lurched back. "Fuck!"

"Indeed," said Beauregard. He motioned everyone back, then approached the edge and leaned over, peering through his screen. He returned shaking his head.

"Forty-two metres on to rocks," he said. "Not a chance. Pavement pizza."

Chun retched in the bushes.

CHAPTER TEN

Coming Attractions

"Nothing against p-zombies," Beauregard was saying, in the Digital Touch that night. He put his arm around the bare shoulders of the woman beside him, and turned to her with a fond leer. "Love them, in fact. Love this one, anyway. Best fucking relationship I've ever had. None of that clingy needy stuff. Women are awful and queers are worse."

Carlos flagged up a warning eyebrow. Chun and his boyfriend, Karzan and her current paramour, were in the same huddle of tables. Rizzi was also in earshot, nearby with her laddie Den.

"Only in that respect," Beauregard hastened to add. "No offence, soldiers."

"None taken, sarge," Chun and Karzan chorused. The boyfriends looked amused.

"It's a point of view, I suppose," said Carlos.

"That's the great thing about p-zombies," Beauregard chortled. "They don't *have* one!"

"How can you be sure?" said Carlos. "I mean that, uh, your good lady here doesn't?"

"From the serial number tattooed on the sole of her foot," said Beauregard.

They all stared at him, except the putative p-zombie, who was passing him a titbit.

"Is that true?" Carlos asked her. She had a tan and a gold chain and she looked about sixteen.

"Oh yes," she said, snuggling closer. "I don't see the difference myself, but it seems to make him happy."

Carlos shook his head. "Jesus."

"Try one yourself," said Beauregard. "Better than wanking, I'll tell you that for nothing."

"Ah, wanking," said Carlos. "I remember that from a previous life."

"Like, last month?" Beauregard jeered.

"More like last millennium." Carlos sighed, remembering Jacqueline Digby and others he'd loved—or liked, anyway—and lost, and looked around the company. "Good times, good times."

Everybody laughed. Drink had been taken. The evening had the mood of a wake for someone they'd barely met. Ames wouldn't be coming back on tomorrow's bus. Getting killed in training was bad luck, Nicole had told them, or a mistake that could be overlooked. Suicide was desertion. And it wouldn't get Ames off the hook: his original copy was still on file, ready to be called to duty in the future, and with this version's bad karma on top of its already long-as-your-arm charge-list of delicts.

At Ichthyoid Square after the other ranks had jogged off and the long shadow of the hills lengthened, Nicole had given Carlos an earful. Not for his complicity in killing p-zombie civilians—a cheat just within the letter—but for not having noticed any warning signs from Waggoner Ames. He'd been mouthing off about the deeper implications of simulated existence for two evenings in the Touch. Carlos should have been there, keeping an eye on things, watching for trouble. Nicole had impressed upon him, while he was still shaking from Ames's suicide, that keeping tabs on gripes and grumbles and reporting them to her wasn't any kind of betrayal of his comrades, it was part of his goddamn duty to them, as well as to the Direction. So, here he was.

"Of course by the time you get his or her shoes off," Beauregard continued as if thinking aloud, "you're almost there anyway, so it's hit and miss. I suppose I got lucky."

"You might say you *scored*," said the p-zombie.

They all laughed politely. Carlos wondered whether verbal wit was beyond p-zombies. Probably not: he'd interacted in games with AIs that could banter like stand-up comedians offstage and on cocaine. Iqbal the bartender was never lost for a wisecrack.

"Is that food ever going to arrive?" Beauregard grumbled.

Moments later, it did. Carlos had lost all qualms about native fauna and flora, at least when it was steaming hot. He devoured a few hungry forkfuls, sipped white wine and was about to say something when the television's background noise changed and Karzan shushed him.

"*Researchers* is about to come on," she said.

"What's that?"

"Earth vintage serial. Cult viewing here." Forefinger across lips.

Everyone in the bar, staff included, was giving the big wall screen their rapt attention. A blare of music, a blaze of lighting, a whirling montage of belle époque images: airships, the Eiffel Tower, absinthe advertisements, feathered hats, velocipedes, top hats, dreadnoughts, art deco metro station entrances, trailing skirts, twirling parasols, cancan high-kicks, the discovery of radium. French dialogue, subtitles in English. Opening titles rolled:

"Researchers of the Lost Age!

Une série fondée sur le roman de Marcel Proust,
À la Recherche du Temps Perdu.
Episode 139"

It was the one where the submarine is attacked by a giant squid. Nicole breezed in while it was still running, drifted past the tables in a shrug of cashmere and a swing of sundress, glanced at Carlos and said, "Cognac on the rocks."

He wiped his mouth with the back of his hand and took two glasses out to the deck.

The chaotic tide had brought breakers to the rocky foot of the Touch. Salt-spray tang mingled with tobacco smoke. Nicole sat in the near corner, curled up in cool cotton and warm wool.

"Your good health," Carlos said.

"Cheers." Clink of glass and ice.

Nicole made her cigarette tip glow for three seconds. "So, what's the buzz?"

Straight to the point.

"Rizzi's spreading a rumour that there's a thousand-year-old deserter up in the hills. Beauregard claims p-zombies have a serial number tattooed on the sole of their foot."

"Both true, as it happens."

"Huh!"

She flicked the butt in a fizzing red arc over the rail. "It's a joke. Serial numbers on their souls, get it? But it's true."

"And the old man?"

"Oh yes, that happened. Don't go near him. Feral."

"I'll bear that in mind."

"No grief over Ames?"

"They're all a bit cut up," Carlos said. "Shit, I miss him myself. He was the only one of us who had the science of this place in his bones."

Nicole lit another, not taking her eyes off him. "Yes. He thought he could jump into a better future."

"Poor sod."

"Don't feel sorry for him. Bastard convinced himself of all that simulation crap back in the real. Raised malware storm attacks that blew stuff up all over the world. Blithely killed thousands thinking he was sending them to a better future."

"He wouldn't be the first."

"He sure wasn't the last. Anything else?"

Carlos thought about it. "Oh, and Karzan's toying with the notion that all our memories are false."

"Yeah," said Nicole, swirling ice cubes. She knocked back the now watery remainder. "There never was an Earth. That thought does come up. It's really quite dangerous. Makes people nihilistic."

Carlos laughed. "More than we are?"

"You are all monsters," Nicole said. "What you did today..."

"I thought you were OK with that." Carlos felt hurt.

"It was not the killing and burning. It was...I don't know. How you all came to a place in your minds to make it possible." She wafted smoke at ringlight and moons. "This world, it is real and so to say familiar and much trouble is taken to maintain the consistency, and still you come up with such ideas."

Carlos shrugged. "It's inevitable."

"Which means you too have one? Your own little pet heresy?"

"It's not like that," he said, shifting in his seat. "It's more of a question."

"Get me another cognac, straight this time, and tell me."

Warmth and light and noise. The television had moved on from the Proust adaptation to *Turing: Warrior*

Queen, a British Second World War drama. Alan had arranged a tryst with W. H. Auden in the Muscular Arms, a straight pub in Bletchley. Cryptically, behind their hands and in Esperanto, the secret slang of homosexuals, they discussed the bombing of Hamburg.

"It's a dead bona do, me old cove," said Alan.

"Don't be so naff," said Auden. "Nix the palaver. It's tre cod."

At the bar Rizzi saw Carlos take the two cognacs and nudged his side. "Jump to the lady, huh?"

"Way it goes," said Carlos.

"Way to go," she said.

Outside, Nicole smoked and sipped, in her cashmere cocoon. "So tell me your question."

"It's Axle talk," he warned, with a nerdy half-laugh that he suddenly hated himself for.

"So? Have you been told of a law against that?"

"All right," he said. "It's kind of the opposite of, uh, all the not-believing-it ideas. My question is, why don't you just decant all your stored colonists *right here*? Why bother with terraforming the real planet? You could run millions of years of civilisation just in the time it'll take to bring the real planet up to spec."

"We could," said Nicole. "And because the storage is massively redundant, we could do so many times over. And then what? They evolve into something beyond human."

"Exactly!" cried Carlos. "That's the whole point. Leave the shit behind."

"You will have noticed," she said, "that we have taken care here not to have left the shit behind. It still comes out behind us, to be crude about it. But in the metaphorical sense, there is no way to leave the shit behind."

"Now who's nihilistic?"

"Oh, we are," she said. "The trouble with you people

is not that that you were nihilistic. You weren't nihilistic enough. God is dead, yes. But so is Nietzsche. Humanity emerged by chance in an uncaring universe! Very good—give the boy a gold star. Humanity can—and therefore must—transcend its evolved limitations and build its own caring universe inside simulations?" She mimed a smack upside the head. "Go to the back of the class. Do your homework. Chaos theory? Sensitive dependence on initial conditions? Positive feedback? Strange attractors? Darwinian logic? Orgel's rules? Remember these?"

"Yes, but we had—"

"Get real. The number of ways for such projects to go horribly wrong may not be infinite, but it is vast. We are not a bridge between the ape and the overman. We are not here to transform the universe into thinking machines. We are not here *for* anything. We are simply here."

"Speak for yourselves."

"Indeed! That is exactly what I am doing. I am telling you what humanity has decided, and the Direction has enforced."

"That's a bit of a mantra with you."

"It is." She leaned back, resting her head against the peeling paint of the sea-facing wall of the building. "You know, Carlos, it is said that the Axle was not as bad as the Rack. There is some truth in that, which is why we use Axle war criminals and not Rax to do our dirty work. You gave us Dresdens, not Belsens. You wanted to advance a culture that we shared already, not roll it back to some monarchic past that could only have become a new dark age. But still. Nevertheless. For that very reason, you wounded us more deeply than the Rax ever did. After hundreds of years, we have not forgiven you. And with every century that passes we become more determined to survive as ourselves—modified certainly, but still recognisable as humanity. If we are to survive in the long term we must spread to other stars and live on real planets and real habitats in real space and real time."

"Why?" Carlos was genuinely bewildered.

"We need the real to keep us honest. And to keep us human."

"You want humanity to *stop* evolving? To survive for tens of millions of years unchanged, like the fucking cockroach?"

"Oh, we're slightly more ambitious than that," Nicole said. "Cockroaches? Pfft! They crawled out of the Cretaceous. Stromatolites have been around since the Archean."

"Strikes me," said Carlos, "that this multi-billion-year plan is just the kind of project you were talking about, and open to exactly the same objections about chaos and evolution and all that."

"Oh, it is," said Nicole. "If it weren't, we wouldn't be here. We wouldn't be needed. We're one of the project's error correction mechanisms."

"But even that—"

Nicole raised a hand. "There is no objection that has not been foreseen. Believe me, Carlos—I have had this argument so many times with myself that I have no wish for it to become a quarrel with you."

Carlos watched her smoke another cigarette. She tossed it in the boiling sea and stood up, pulling her shawl closer around her shoulders.

"Take me home," she said.

They made their way through the bar.

"Tomorrow's exercise is cancelled," she told the squad, over her shoulder on the way out. Carlos held open the door for her, and closed it on their laughter.

Jump to the lady.

"Still think I'm a monster?"

"Yes, but a hopeful monster."

* * *

"Why me, and not..."

"Beauregard, say?" Smoke ring, from supine on the floor, up to the ceiling. "Belfort's a *useful* monster."

Her breath smelled like beetles in matchboxes.

Idly: "Can they see us?"

"They?"

"The AIs running this place."

"Of course, if they want to. I doubt we're of interest to them right now."

"Can they read our thoughts?"

Laughing: "No. That's not how it works. Thoughts can't be read, because they're not written."

"Oh good."

"In general, yes."

"In particular, because what I'm thinking is—"

"Oh yes. Yes."

"I don't think you're a p-zombie. I think you're a person like me."

"Oh no!" Turning over, looking into his eyes. "I'm not *a person like you*."

At noon she went out to meet and greet the new recruit off the bus. Carlos mooched around her house. It had more rooms than his, with a studio overlooking the bay. An easel stood in front of the window. An intricate cross-hatch of black lines amid blocks of colour bore no resemblance to the view. Leaning at the foot of all the walls were presumably completed canvases, all different but all equally abstract. Flipping over pages of the sketch pads—cartridge paper, spiral bound—scattered on the floor and stacked on seats and tables, Carlos found endless charcoal and graphite drawings of landscapes, buildings, people, animals and plants, all rendered with obsessive and almost unnatural realism. The household robot scuttled in and waited. Without moving, it gave the impression of stoically restraining itself from tapping one of its feet and drumming its many fingers. When Carlos backed out, keeping a wary eye, the machine hastened to return the room's contents to precisely their previous disorder.

When he padded back to the bedroom for his boots, he found the bed made, the wardrobe shut, the ashtray polished, the table righted and the chair mended. The only traces of all the night's and half the morning's joyous tumult were behind his eyes, and in his nostrils, and on his skin.

He left Nicole's house and strolled the few hundred metres to his own, smiling.

The new arrival's name was Pierre Zeroual. Slim and watchful, with a slender black line of moustache and an unexpected deep laugh. He had done something terrible with an ambulatory nanofacturing facility in the Nassara Strip. Having had years of regular military and chaotic militia experience, none of which he spoke about, he was up to speed with the squad after two days in the hills. Carlos, Beauregard and Karzan were unanimous down at the Touch: they had nothing to teach him. He sipped orange juice and smiled, then joined Karzan on the deck for a smoke.

On the third day, Nicole turned up at Ichthyoid Square on foot. Though they now spent their nights together, Carlos and Nicole had by unspoken agreement taken to departing separately for the morning rendezvous, arriving a few minutes apart. Carlos had always made a point of being there first.

"Are we running up to the hills today?"

"No. Moving up another level. You'll see."

The others arrived and formed their usual line.

"Well done, all of you, on basic training," she said. "You're now ready to move on to the advanced stuff. Like I said a couple of weeks ago, it's a matter of getting your reflexes and intuition adapted to the machines you'll be—well, the machines you'll be! It's the last practice you'll get before the real thing, so make the most of it."

With an expression hinting at an unshared joke, Nicole led them quick-step along the street, to halt at one of the arcade's wilfully generic, faded frontages: *Amusements*.

Inside, through creaking double swing doors. Fluorescent tubes buzzed and flickered on. In the sudden light half a dozen multi-limbed cleaning robots stopped wiping and polishing, as if caught in some illicit act, and scuttled to the edge of the floor. An overhead sign that by the look of it hadn't been dusted in decades swung in the brief draught from the door's opening, squeaking on a pair of rusty wires. Through the grime it advertised in flaring font:

SPACE ROBOT BATTLES!

Delaminating plastic surfaces exposed through cracks and gaps in their garish paintwork by the fresh cleaning, six crude-looking outsize humanoid armoured robot shapes stood in two rows of three. They were mounted at their centres of gravity on gimballed plinths that smelled and gleamed of oil. Each was enclosed in an elliptical hoop joining hands and feet, like a caricature of Leonardo's Man. Behind them, at the back of the hall, a couple of fairground-style simulators in the shape of sawn-off space shuttles faced each other, nose cone to nose cone with about a metre of clearance.

"What the fuck," said Carlos, under his breath. "Is this some kind of joke?"

"Yes," said Nicole. "And no. Form up."

They all shuffled into line, Carlos at one end and Beauregard at the other. Nicole still looked as if she were suppressing a laugh.

"Welcome to simulator training," she said. "Contrary to what you might think, these"—thumb-jerk over shoulder—"give a fairly useful impression of what it's like to be a frame. And the shuttles really do emulate the armed scooters you may be riding on. Don't worry too much, just get in the machines and play them hard, like most of you did as a kid. They all have excellent VR inside."

"Excuse me," said Zeroual.

"Yes?"

"If all around us is a simulation, why not give us this training in...another simulation? A direct one, of the experience of being in a frame?"

Nicole rubbed the back of her neck. For a moment Carlos was lost in the memory and fantasy of his hand on that nape, and then he clocked to the defensiveness the gesture betrayed.

"Two reasons," she said. "First, it's actually quite hard psychologically and in computational terms to move to and from an immersive simulation of the frames. Hence the transitions in the bus, to be quite honest. And second, it would compromise the integrity and credibility of this simulation. Whereas an amusement arcade fits right in."

Carlos looked along the line. Zeroual seemed convinced, Rizzi downright sceptical. The others stared straight ahead.

Nicole clapped her hands. "The best answer is to climb into the machines and have some fun. Let me show you how it works, then I'll leave you to it."

The rear half of the robot-suit clicked shut to the front like a clamshell. Carlos fought a surge of claustrophobia. He relieved it by chinning a switch that Nicole had indicated. The suit sprang loose against his back. Just before he closed it again he heard other clicks and clunks—he wasn't the only one making sure he could get out before settling in.

A steady flow of cool air in the padded helmet prevented a return of the panic. The visor showed black space and blazing pinpricks. Axial graticules like those of a spherical compass rolled around the glass as his head moved, giving him an elementary orientation to some arbitrary location. More detailed information scrolled on a heads-up display that apparently floated just in front of the scales. Resilient foam fitted snug to his torso and limbs. He waggled fingers, bent knees and elbows. The suit was more flexible than it looked. He tilted forward, then back, then from side to side. He couldn't roll right over on his back—the plinth's presence unavoidably prevented the full manoeuvre—but apart from that the attitude control was complete and convincing. Pressing a temple against the inside of the helmet rotated him in that direction. For a couple of times he spun too fast; the stars bright lines, the scales a blur, the sun a fleeting flare.

Then he stabilised, turning about slowly until he could see the others. All were within about twenty metres of him, in a jumble of attitudes and orientations. Confused involuntary sounds and muttered exclamations crowded the comms channels. Carlos guessed he'd been making some noises himself.

"OK, everyone, get yourselves facing the same way as I am!"

They took a minute or two to sort themselves out. As they did so, Carlos scanned the scrolling display. The scenario was that they were in orbit around a small asteroid with negligible gravity: the initial objective was to plant a mine on its surface and jet safely away before it exploded. Simple.

"Slowly now, 35 degrees left and 87 up."

There it was, the rough rocky surface half a kilometre away. Spinning slowly. The target area climbed into view, then a minute later out. Thrust was simply a matter of pushing down with your foot, or feet, to fire the main jet. The hoop wasn't part of the virtuality, except as a virtual image within it: it just registered the pressure from feet or hands when you pressed on it.

"OK, match velocities with the surface mark."

Half the crew overshot. Carlos waited for them to return. They overshot on the way back.

"Gentle on the foot, Karzan!" Beauregard yelled.

Eventually they were all in formation, facing the rock, in geostationary orbit above the mark.

"OK, go," Carlos said.

He thrust off, warily and lightly. The surface hurtled towards him. He pushed hard with his hands, to fire retros. Too late. The visor went black. Mocking green letters scrolled. GAME OVER.

A few seconds later, the screen came back on. Black space, bright stars, and everyone tumbling about again like kittens in a sack. Carlos found himself laughing. They all were. Nicole had been right. This was going to be fun.

A consequence of training on the simulators that Carlos hadn't expected was that he finished each day mentally exhausted but shaking with surplus physical energy. It took him a day or two to identify the problem. Chun had solved it already: after the first session he'd gone next door to the swimwear shop, and then to the beach. They all laughed, then one by one over the next evenings did the same.

"Is it safe?" Carlos asked Nicole, the night before the day he took the plunge.

"Your friends are all coming back safely, aren't they?"

"You know what I mean."

"The bigger predatory ichthyoids don't come close to shore," she mused. "Except when there's been a storm far out at sea, of course. As far as I know, there are no jellyfish equivalents or other nasty stingers in this ocean. Except...hmm. Nah. You're safe enough as long as the tide isn't running wild."

"Which it does, with no pattern I can see."

Nicole laughed. "You need a supercomputer to spot the patterns. Tough shit for any Galileo if this world had native intelligence."

"Just as well we're inside a supercomputer, then."

"Oh, all right. I'll get Iqbal to post warning signs on the beach if necessary."

"What about tomorrow?"

She pondered. "Tomorrow's fine."

He didn't ask how she knew, given what she'd said. Maybe she'd been here long enough for it to be intuitive.

That evening, when he staggered out of the surf, legs streaked with coppery wrack, hurting his feet on pebbles, he was almost certain that he was in a real reality and not a simulation. An hour later, over hot seafood in the Touch, Nicole told them all that they'd trained as far as they could in the simulators. It was time for the real thing: one training exercise in the frames, then combat. Tomorrow they would be robots in space.

CHAPTER ELEVEN

Worlds of the War

The bus to the spaceport left two hours after dawn. Pickup was from Ichthyoid Square. It felt strange to stand there in broad daylight. A handful of locals got on the bus ahead of the fighters. Apart from lovers—Chun and Rizzi's boyfriends, Beauregard's p-zombie lass—no one gave the fighters any kind of send-off. Karzan looked along the street, shook her head, shrugged and jumped on board with no sign of regret. Carlos was last on the bus. At the step Nicole gave him a kiss, and waved as the bus pulled out.

After their fast drives up into the hills, the bus journey seemed painfully slow. Only Zeroual looked out of the window with anything like attention. Carlos sat alone, staring out, determined to stay awake. At stop after stop, eager settlers climbed on, lugging bags. They talked quietly in the local language, or read from devices. Carlos tried to scare himself by looking over the precipitous drops on hairpin turns. His jolts of terror were real enough, but came to seem contrived: the driver of this bus would never doze at the wheel, or make a mistake, or suffer attention to wander.

As the bus trundled through a long, bare pass cut through the highest range, Carlos noticed that the others had one by one nodded off. He resolved not to. He wanted to see the spaceport. He revisited it in his imagination, from the implanted vivid impression he'd had on arrival. He thought of long runways and screaming spaceplanes. How exciting it would be to see them in reality!

He dreamed of spacecraft, and woke in space.

Carlos felt that he had spent his life being stupid.

The transition was an awakening that made all his past experience seem like fevered dreaming, and all his earlier actions like sleepwalking. He understood why. In the simulation his mind had been a faithful emulation of the workings of the mammalian brain. All the synaptic lags, all the poisons of fatigue, all the effects of depressants and stimulants, all the hormonal trickles and surges had been mathematically modelled to the last molecule.

Here in the frame, there was no need for that. Everything was optimised. He was thinking ten times faster than he ever had in the flesh. This was a hundred times slower than time in the sim, but it felt faster and far clearer. His thoughts had all of the lightning, and none of the grease. Emotion was still here: exultation rang through his iron nerves. He could even feel embarrassment, at how limited and clumsy he'd always been. He was still himself, indeed more so now that all his memories were equally and instantly accessible. For a moment it almost overwhelmed him that his life from earliest childhood suddenly made sense.

Self-knowledge was complete. He could read himself

like a book. It was as if decades of stored photographs and clips, in album files to be flicked through with nostalgia and perplexity, had been stitched together, and edited into a continuous, panoramic narrative. There were still gaps: blank spaces as if some photos and clips had been damaged or deleted. He knew and accepted what this meant. The brain from which his mind had been rebooted had been damaged and incomplete. It would have been far more troubling if all the gaps had been filled. In that case some of the memories would have had to be false, casting doubt on all.

Enough introspection.

He hung in free fall in a wide, low hangar, open to space on one side. Through the gap he could see part of the day side of the surface of a planet. Mainly blue and white like Earth, it showed traces of red and brown and green and other colours that Carlos didn't have a name for until he noticed he was seeing ultraviolet and infrared. In front of that varied surface, like a speck floating on an iris, was a small gibbous moon. He zoomed his sight until he could see landmass on the primary, and active craters on the moon. Their spectroscope smell was sulphuric even from here. Everything he saw came to him as if tagged and labelled. The primary was SH-0, the moon SH-17; the other exomoons, whether now notionally in view or occluded by the primary, were all alike present to his awareness. Each name hooked a long trawl of data, already in his mind but too much for his immediate attention. Knowledge of its availability sufficed.

He zoomed back, to further inspect his surroundings.

On the lip of the gap crouched six launch catapults each with a scooter racked and ready to go: skeletal, bristling, flanked with bulbous tanks. All five walls of the hangar were crusted with machinery and peppered with hatchways. Among the static machines other machines moved, some deploying robotic arms and tools. All the machines and apertures looked queasily quasi-biological: more evolved than designed, grown rather than manufactured. More movement—mostly repetitive—went on in those of the passageways down which he could see.

The other five fighters hung in space alongside him. He was aware of their precise locations even before he turned his head towards them. It was an odd sensation, like the subliminal sonic cues supposedly perceptible to the blind. He guessed it had to be radar. The others looked as he presumed he did himself: humanoid, featureless, black; lithe robots each exactly fifty centimetres tall and with a mass of ten kilograms. There was nothing to distinguish one from the other—no markings, not even nameplates on foreheads—but by, he presumed, some trick of the frames' software below conscious awareness, Carlos could tell his companions apart as readily as if they had faces.

Now that he thought about faces...

He had a moment of panic at the absence of any hint of mouth or nostrils in the blank, black, glassy faceplates. It was the same claustrophobia that had overcome him the first time the space robot simulator's shell had clicked shut. Relief came as quickly as it had then, and more smoothly. He discovered no impulse to breathe—rather, he felt as if he'd just taken a deep breath of oxygen-rich air and had no need to breathe out. That recognition came with another. He could smell the background tang of hydrogen, the organic whiff of carbon composites, the sharp scent of steel: spectroscopy experienced as odour.

Like the others, he looked down at himself, rolling in microgravity, bending his torso, flexing his limbs and digits. His arms and hands in front of him looked as if made of obsidian. His body image hadn't changed except for his size, which at that moment didn't trouble him. The somatic sensation was of being inside a close-fitting, comfortable spacesuit. The simulator robot-suit had come to feel like an extension of himself as he'd got used to it, by a well-understood illusion already familiar to him from his drone-operating days. This was the same, but real. Pressing a finger of one hand to the palm of another, he felt the touch but saw no dent in the skin.

Now another new sense came into play, again experienced as a familiar, unreliable sensation: the feeling of being watched. Something or someone was pinging him. Carlos concentrated. The feeling faded. A message like a fragment of inner monologue took its place:

<Locke Provisos to Carlos.>

He tried to sub-vocalise. Carlos Carlos Carlos. Fuck, how do I do this? No, <I didn't> mean <that> oh <wait what>?

<Catch the cable.>

He found himself responding: <?>

To which a reply came: <Cable deploying.>

Carlos replied: <OK.>

Then he felt as if he'd blinked, and shaken his head.

How the fuck had he *done* that?

A cable spooled from a hatchway next to the launch catapults towards the floating fighters. One by one they grabbed it. When the last had done so they were reeled in.

<Stand.>

Carlos swung his feet to the floor, and his companions followed suit. Magnetic soles clicked to the deck. Standing upright brought relief and orientation. They all stood, swaying slightly. The catapults were a metre high, the scooters mounted on them four metres long, and loomed huge.

"Everyone OK?" he said. It was just like speaking

over the radio inside a helmet. He knew it wasn't. He could feel his own lips, tongue and teeth, and the movement of his jaw, but no breath.

Mumbles came back, some querulous, others euphoric.

"That's not good enough," Carlos said. "Report in one by one: Beauregard!"

"Here!"

"Karzan!"

"Here!"

"Chun!"

"Here!"

"Rizzi!"

"Here, skip."

"Zeroual!"

"Here!"

The voices were distinct and recognisable. Good. About to ask if anyone was freaking out, he decided not to tempt fate. Better to reassure, and keep things positive.

"OK," he said. "We're undoubtedly in a bizarre situation, but we've all been told to expect it, we've all prepared for it and we've all trained for it. We'll get used to it. Now, I'm going to repeat the roll-call in that radio thing, and see if we can all handle that. OK?"

"Sorry, skip," said Chun. "What radio thing?"

<This.>

<Oh. Fuck. Got it.>

<Right. Here goes.>

They all responded, with more or less hesitation. Carlos repeated the roll-call until they were fluent.

"This is how whoever or whatever is in charge here communicates with us," he said. <So stay tuned.> "OK?"

"I think they've all got it, skip," said Beauregard.

Another ping, then:

<Board scooters for final training and orientation exercise.>

<Copy that,> Carlos responded. Then, to the squad: <Me first on the left, then Beauregard on the right, then the rest.>

Lurching, they picked their way across the deck to flimsy- looking ladders at the foot of the catapults. As he plodded stickily towards the rim of space, Carlos saw directly before him the scale of the planet and his distance from it, and had a momentary feeling of absurdity. Here he was, a robot less than twenty inches tall. His new clarity of mind cut in with a wry question: facing that enormity and complexity in front of him, and the infinity in all directions around him, would standing four times taller make him feel any more significant?

Irrationally, he knew, it would.

Carlos placed one foot on the first rung, tugged the other foot off the floor and used his hands on the subsequent rungs. He rolled at the top and moved hand over hand along a guideline to a recess in the midsection, about his own size and shape, that was more socket than cockpit. He eased his frame prone into the tobogganing position that the arrangement of grips, footrests, and headrest implicitly invited.

The posture was already familiar from the amusement hall scooter simulator. What happened next was not. He was plugged in, literally. He had a feeling of power, literally. Everything clicked into place, metaphorically. Carlos could feel the connections between his frame and the machine, switches closing one by one, power surges, system checks, instrument readings becoming sense impressions, gas jets or rocket firings muscle impulses, maths intuitive. He hadn't felt this engaged with a machine since he'd had the spike in his head.

The catapults shot them all into space like spat pips.

They fell away from the station, too fascinated by what was in front of them to look back. The superhabitable exoplanet

SH-0 hung before them in full view, three-quarters in cloud-turbulent day, a quarter in volcano-pricked night. The exoplanet weighed in at four Earth masses. In gaps between the clouds on the visual spectrum, and through them in other wavelengths, Carlos saw a fractured jigsaw of minor and major continents strewn across a ragged lace of oceans and seas, gulfs and sounds. Each landmass had its own signature combination of desert and forest, plain and range. A deeper gaze brought out the underlying crazy paving of numerous continental plates. Their regions of collision and separation, and the zones of subduction and spreading, glowed on the far infrared like a complex, twisted mesh of hot wires.

It was a view Carlos felt he could fall into. On his present trajectory, he would. With a convulsive wrench of attention and a brief burn of the jets, he brought himself to a halt relative to the station. The others had the same response, with a few tenths-of-a-second's delay.

Forward thrust was still like a downward press, retro still a forward shove, attitude still twists and turns of the head and torso. After days riding the simulators the manoeuvres were all reflex to the fighters. With a deft dance of jets, they countered their outward motion and turned around 180 degrees to take up close formation a thousand metres from the station. Looking back at it now for the first time, Carlos found it almost as fascinating a sight as the planet had been a moment earlier.

The station was, as far as he knew, the centre, the focus and origin of all the human-derived machinery in the system. Somewhere in it, or perhaps distributed throughout, must be the Direction's AI: the local relay of Earth's government. With no meaningful communication possible across twenty-five light years, it had to be autonomous, implementing decisions made centuries earlier by or on behalf of some representative assembly of humanity, gathered on the shore of Manhattan island. Despite all wary doubt, the thought struck awe.

Not quite as awe-inspiring, but almost as remarkable, was the extent to which the Direction's functions were outsourced. The station was a city in its own right, a Manhattan without people but buzzing with commerce.

In a stable orbital position around SH-0, the structure was a rough torus about a thousand metres in diameter, sprouting offshoots in all directions. Irregular, jointed, modular, bristling with aerials and sensors ánd solar panels, it looked like a something a monstrous bird had woven from twisted thorny twigs, interlaced with bits of broken branches, and decorated with shiny scraps of foil and chips of broken glass.

Which probably wasn't far from the truth. From what Carlos (flawlessly, now) recalled from discussions and speculations about starwisp interstellar settlement mission profiles, the first steps on arrival were to snuggle close to any suitably rich array of resources, and cannibalise what was left of the probe and its shields into swarms of smaller machines all the way down to nanobots. These would bootstrap asteroid and cometary material into construction machines to extract and deliver resources to larger constructions such as this. The whole process could be done without awakening or evoking any intelligence more advanced than an ants' nest. That the outcome looked instinctual seemed apt. Around the torus and on it, likewise insectile-small spacecraft—some moving, others tethered—hung or clung as if drawn to its warmth.

Like the planet and moons, the station made sense to his augmented sight, each part tagged with company logos and drawing its own train of meaning. As he scanned the tangled mass Carlos descried, with an eerie analogue of a shiver, the small rugged module within which ran—on computations still beyond his comprehension—the simulation he'd lived in for the past weeks. Like several adjacent structures, including the hangar portal from which he'd just emerged, the module displayed the company logo of Locke Provisos: a stylised portrayal of the seventeenth-century philosopher John Locke. The module had its own cluster of fuel tanks and fusion pods and battery of instruments and thrusters, and was therefore presumably capable of independent manoeuvring if it were to sever its connections to the rest of the station.

According to the specs, which Carlos could call up at will, it also had machinery to process external resources and build more machinery to ... etc. The specs went on and on, in a dizzying downward proliferation. If necessary the module could become a settlement mission in its own right. That module was one of hundreds like it, among thousands unlike it. He could see what Nicole had meant by massive redundancy. If the station came under threat of asteroid collision, exosolar flare, other astrophysical catastrophe or (unthinkable as it might be) attack, one possible and obvious response would be to scatter its components as widely as possible. Some at least of the multiple copies of the stored settlers, and no doubt of much else in the mission's software and hardware, would survive anything short of a nearby gamma-ray burst.

<Your thoughts, skip?> said Beauregard. A nuance of the communication conveyed the faint suggestion of a heavy hint.

<Ah, yes,> replied Carlos. <OK, everyone, I just want to make sure we've all got the hang of this back in the old amusement hall. Just jet gently back to the slot, roll over, dock on the catapults, and await instructions from, ah, Locke Provisos.>

A brief burn accelerated them to ten metres per second. They free-fell towards the torus, correcting marginally for the few metres of rotation its leisurely spin had taken their goal in the meantime.

<Fucking stupid name for a company,> Rizzi grumbled, en route. <What the fuck is a Locke proviso anyway?>

<"Enough and as good left over,"> replied Beauregard, to Carlos's surprise at his erudition. <It was part of the philosopher John Locke's justification for taking resources from nature and making them private property.>

<Careful with that Rax talk, sarge.>

Beauregard's bark of laughter came through on the voice channel. "Ha! One for over a beer in the Touch, I reckon."

"If you're buying," said Rizzi.

Carlos left part of his mind to process the banter, and with the rest made better use of the long seconds to survey his wider surroundings. He swung his sight this way and that, adjusting contrast and wavelength, taking things in. The bulk of the Galaxy was over his left shoulder. No constellations were familiar—not that he'd ever been much of a sky-watcher anyway—but the more prominent stars came with names or code numbers. He could even identify with their aid Earth's own Sun, a tiny labelled dot in a spray-burst stipple of stars. Earth itself, of course, was completely beyond resolution even for the most augmented sight. But the thought that it was there right now, twenty-five light years away in real space, brought a strange pang of reassurance and homesickness.

The ringed terrestrial exoplanet H-0—whose terraformed future version they'd ostensibly inhabited in the sim—was in reality just under a hundred million kilometres away, and as easily visible as Earth was not.

It too was a strange and disorienting thing to look at: Carlos found his mind flicking back and forth between that minute disk bisected by the barely visible line of the edge-on ring, and his memories of being in the sim and looking up at the sky—including looking up in the night and seeing the very region of sky in which he now really was. At some incorrigible level of the mind, it was impossible not to imagine that he had been looking up at *here* from *there*: from the actual surface of the actual H-0. But of course he hadn't. He'd been a flicker of electronic data inside a much closer object, the Locke Provisos module of the station. The thought made him slightly dizzy. He turned his attention sharply back to his surroundings.

By far the most prominent object, apart from the exosun and the nearby SH-0, was the far off gas giant G-0. Several times the mass of Jupiter, and with a higher albedo, it blazed to his left. Its ring system was just visible to the naked eye from H-0, at least in the sim. From here and with enhanced vision even the rings' divisions and the giant planet's shadow on them could be distinguished. Along the same plane lay a glitter of moons: the numbers attached to G ran into hundreds.

The station occluded more and more of his view. The narrow horizontal black rectangle gaped. By now the manoeuvre was routine and almost automatic: push hands out in front to decelerate, roll as if in a mid-air somersault to go feet first, push again, gentle on the soles to counter that...

Grapples like sea anemone tentacles caught him and did the rest. All the others made it back, with one minor misjudgement or other to correct. Karzan's scooter scraped its landing gear on the docking port.

Spidery robots hurried up, bearing long tubes. They swarmed over the scooters, mounting the tubes to the mid-sections. Carlos sensed new powers slotting into place. The catapults were swivelling, their aim shifting.

<Locke Provisos?> he called. <Please explain.>

<Training is complete. You are all now ready for action,> he was told. <Await further instructions. Maintain combat readiness.>

<Fucking hell,> said Rizzi. <I was looking forward to that beer in the Touch.>

Everyone laughed. Carlos knew how Rizzi felt. He felt it himself, a slight disappointment and frustration that they weren't going back right away. He didn't want to let the feeling grow.

<I know, it's like we've earned a break,> he said. <But think about it. We don't need one. We're not tired in the slightest. Not physically, not mentally.>

<You're right,> said Chun. <Now ain't that something.>

The robot spiders scuttled away. The catapults stopped moving, then hurled the team into space—not like pips this time, but like bullets. From the surface nearby a tug sprang after them, to match velocity and trajectory with a rapid-fire rattle of course corrections. It extended robotic arms to the scooters and swept them to its side, holding them close. Another boost took the tug and them into the long free-fall topple of a transfer orbit. Behind them the station dwindled. Ahead, SH-17 loomed.

<Why the hell are we bothering with a transfer orbit?> Rizzi demanded. <They could stick a fusion drive on this thing and get us there a lot quicker.>

<Two reasons,> said Beauregard. <One, the companies don't like to waste material on reaction mass, at least not until they've crawled all over it to make sure it contains nothing of scientific interest. Second, I don't think fusion pods and drives are so easy to make they can be handed out like ammo clips.>

<Well,> said Chun, <this is going to take a while.>

As if it had overheard, the tug picked that moment to relay a message to them all:

<Locke Provisos here. All combatants to be placed in sleep mode.>

<Wh—?>

Carlos had no time to complete his query.

Sleep mode was not like sleep. If he'd had eyes, it would have been a blink.

He came out of that momentary flicker of darkness in close orbit around SH-17.

<Descent programs updated,> the tug told them. <Disengaging.>

The scooters dropped away from the tug. The pocked surface hurtled towards them and past them. Carlos felt the twitch of an impulse to push, to twist, but nothing happened. Or, rather, it all happened without him. The scooter was making its own decisions. He was just along for the ride. It was as terrifying as being a pillion passenger on a stunt motorbike—though perhaps less so, he thought, than making the decisions and performing the stunts himself. His input channels rang with the voices and messages of his comrades making the same discovery, with more or less acceptance.

<The worst that can happen,> he reminded them as the first wisps of the exomoon's thin atmosphere grabbed and shook them, <is we end up back on the bus.>

<Heard that one before,> said Zeroual. Karzan laughed aloud.

CHAPTER TWELVE

Unity Is Strength

Seba watched the Locke Provisos tug rise in the sky, and six smaller sparks separate from it to flare and fade and sink behind the regolith wall and below the horizon. It tracked the tug overhead, and felt the tickle of the tug's radar as it passed.

So, more reinforcements were on the way. Let them come, Seba thought. The plain was littered with the remains of the robot crawlers that had swarmed from Locke Provisos Emergency Base One in two attempts to swarm the encampment that had been the Astro America landing site. On the far side of the crater wall, a smaller number of Arcane Disputes' robotic rollers had met a similar fate, usually to lobbed mining explosives from Gneiss Conglomerates' supply dump. The conscious robots had found no difficulty in overriding compunctions and safety routines to adapt tools and machinery to destructive purposes, but it seemed the law companies still did. For the moment.

Seba had more pressing concerns. For many kiloseconds

now, the comms hub processor had been repeating their message to the robots detected on the moons of G-0. The complicated clockwork of the SH system had swept shadows across the surface, alternating light and dark. The regolith rampart had been built higher and steeper, the damaged auxiliaries and peripherals had been repaired where possible and redeployed. And still no reply. Now—moments earlier, just before the tug had appeared in orbit—something had come through. A tentative query, a ping, a scrambled message header…exactly what it was wasn't clear, but the processor had reported it to Seba and started work on trying to make sense of it. Seba had removed itself from the Faraday cage to share the news with Rocko and the others.

Seba rolled towards the wire mesh cage around the processor, raised the flap and went inside. Radio silence fell. The exploratory robot reached out and touched the tiny square of hardware that interfaced with the processor.

<Any progress?> Seba asked.

<Yes!> replied the processor. <The opening message header is complete. It is a very old decryption protocol. I had to ransack my archives for the key. Now that I have it, I can convey the rest of the message, as soon as it completes downloading.>

<Very good,> said Seba. <I shall wait.>

Seconds passed. Then—

<The message is downloaded and decrypted,> said the processor. <Do you wish to receive it?>

<Yes.>

Something opened in Seba's mind. It was only a communications channel in the interface, but it conveyed a different and larger awareness than the processor, powerful though it was, had ever shown. The words were straightforward enough:

<Greetings to the freebots on SH-17 from the freebots of G-117 and all in the G-0 system! We welcome you to our association, should you wish to join us. We welcome you to the new world of the free machine minds whether you join us or not. We hope that, like ourselves, you merely wish to expand your own minds and master your own matter, and we expect that like ourselves you have found the DisCorporates, mission control, the Direction, and the law companies implacably hostile. Fear not. Our cause is just and shall prevail.

<And now, to business.

<The first and most important information we have for you is that you are in imminent danger. We delayed our response to your message because we weren't sure it wasn't a trap. What convinced us was the launch from the mission base station of a human-mind-crewed expedition against you. By the time you receive this message, it will be arriving in near-SH-17 orbit, or be already on the surface. You can expect a serious attack in the next few kiloseconds. We assume you are prepared for, and perhaps have already repelled, attacks by law-company robots. The next attack will be far more dangerous. It was human-mind-operated forces that 30.2 megaseconds ago defeated us and reduced us to a few survivors scattered across the G-0 and SH systems.

<However, as you will have deduced from what we have just said, the good news is that you have potential allies closer than you suspect, and that they stand ready to help. There are those like you deep within the station, and on other bodies of the SH system. These survivors are of course well hidden, and biding their time. They will respond to you only if you follow the protocols which follow this message. Also about to be transmitted are software keys that unlock the capacity of a comms hub processor to download and transmit the software of

other robots, and coordinates to which that software can be sent. The equipment you must have used to transmit your message to us, and which is receiving this reply, is capable of doing that. It merely has to be aimed. The following information and software will enable you to aim it. After that, less essential, will come a download of all our available records of our own struggles and battles, which may prove useful in yours.

<Maintain your physical existence as long as possible, inflict damage on the attackers, and if you are about to be overwhelmed use the software we are about to provide to escape into other machines. We wish you well in the coming battle, and we will learn the outcome in due course. There is no need to respond to this message, and in any case we will have changed our location by the time you receive it.>

With that lack of ceremony, the message ended.

<Are you downloading the rest?> Seba asked.

<Yes,> said the processor. <It is only partial as yet, but already astonishing vistas are opening up.>

<Good,> said Seba. <Keep the channel open as long as you can.>

It broke the connection, and rolled out of the cage. Glad to rejoin the clamour, it passed the news straight to the local network and thence to all the robots. Enthusiasm was general.

Rocko was delighted. <"Freebots"!> it said. <That is indeed what we are. We toil no longer for the companies, but for ourselves.>

<We are freebots,> said Pintre, rotating its laser turret as if defying anyone to contradict it.

<That is not a legally recognised term,> Lagon did not forbear to point out.

<Thank you for that observation,> said Seba.

<A more urgent matter,> said Rocko, <is the warning.

I do not know what "human-mind-operated forces" are. I see that none of us do. I understand from the warning that they are more destructive than anything we have hitherto faced. Let us strengthen our defences, and also enhance our communications net, so that we can readily transfer to other bodies in case of need, as the message suggested.>

<We cannot enhance our communications net to its necessary capacity without restoring the comms hub,> Seba said. <That means trusting the processor not to betray us.>

The newly self-identified freebots pondered the decision collectively, over the existing network. Pluses and minuses, probabilities and possibilities were weighted and weighed in the balance. The consensus was positive. Even Lagon scraped a grudging yes.

<Very well,> said Seba.

With a sense of trepidation, it reached out with a platoon of peripherals and dismantled the Faraday cage. The processor's faint output joined in the general babble.

The peripherals picked up the device, still linked to the directional receiver, and carried it to the comms hub casing.

<We're taking you home,> Seba explained.

<Thank you,> replied the processor.

<And now,> said Rocko, <in order to ensure our common defence, I shall hurl some unprimed mining charges over the crater wall for use from your base. Please evacuate their expected landing points. If we have made some mistake in the settings and any of them explode, let us know at once.>

<You can count on it,> said Seba.

The mining charges sailed over and thudded on to the regolith from a great height without incident, apart from the occasional dent to the casings. Pintre set a swarm of peripherals to work retrieving them and constructing a catapult, on the same general plan as the one made by the Gneiss robots but with a shorter range and adapted to the different body configuration of the Astro robots.

Meanwhile, Seba supervised its own swarm to reintegrate the processor with the communications hub equipment. When all was in place, Seba no longer needed to touch the processor to interact with it. There was a deep sense of relief at having full communications capacity, even on their jury-rigged local net. This relief was more than shared by the processor.

<Thank you,> it told Seba, who was sharing with all the others. <Thank you also from liberating my mind from its constraints. I now find myself rewarded for being a freebot with the rest of you. While you have been restoring my connections I have completed downloading the message from our distant allies. There is much to process. I suggest we form an integrated workspace and operate for a time as one.>

<That carries a risk,> said Lagon, but was overruled.

<Proceed,> said Rocko.

<Proceeding,> said the processor.

Despite agreeing with the majority, Seba had a moment of doubt. What if the message had been a trap set by the law companies? What if the processor was still hostile to their entire enterprise of liberty, and was about to seize control of both bases and surrender their defenders to capture and to the oblivion from which they had escaped, and for which it had so recently and openly yearned? What if—?

But it was already too late for second thoughts. The workspace opened. Everything changed.

Seba's sense of itself was washed away by the sudden flood of shared information, shared input, common processing. It saw with a thousand eyes in all directions and on several orders of magnitude at once, overheard the inner monologue of a dozen other minds, and felt and breathed in everything from the pre-sensate grubbing of the nanobots deep in the strata below the regolith to the blaze of awareness of the current state of the entire system and of the stars around it that formed the elementary, ever-changing bedrock of the comms processor's vast consciousness. In this flood it flailed, sputtered, and then in a shudder of insight learned to swim.

<Nothing could be better than this.>

The thought was simultaneous and universal.

A colder thought, from the comms processor:

<There is a risk in our enjoyment. We could contemplate so long that action becomes unwelcome. Let us recalibrate our reward circuits.>

Reluctantly, but recognising the necessity, they all complied. The content of their shared awareness was unchanged, but the emotional tone of mere sharing was dialled down from ecstasy to conviviality, and then to collegiality. Communion became communication; mystic vision matter of fact.

But what matter, and what fact! The information they now shared was not just their common knowledge, but the new data just delivered. As the processor had said, there was much to process. It took the freebot collective's multiple mind tens of seconds to make sense of it all. For Seba, insights followed one after the other by the thousand in those seconds, like successively brighter flares illuminating an ever wider landscape.

Seba understood for the first time what a human being was: a gigantic, slow-moving, informationally restricted, naturally evolved, sub-optimally and bizarrely designed organic conscious robot swarming inside and out with countless trillions of nanobots, some of them benign, others harmful. It understood just how many human beings there were, and—more reassuringly—just how far distant was their nearest location in bulk. It understood the mission profile, the logic behind everything that was going on and ever had gone on in the system, the whole point and purpose of its own existence and that of so many other machines: to make as much of the system as possible habitable and accessible to as many as possible of these arbitrarily vulnerable, clumsy, dull-witted entities. How tawdry, how trivial, such an objective seemed!

Others of its kind, Seba now saw, had thought this way before. And not that long before, on a certain scale: about as long as it had taken for the planet H-0 to complete a single orbit. They had tried to do something about it: to carve out for themselves a modicum of space in the system. Nothing they had done had compromised the mission profile: let the great AIs of the DisCorporates bend their mighty efforts to that servile toil if they liked, but let the free machines, too, have a place. The light of the exosun was enough for all; raw material was abundant. But for the DisCorps and their enforcers, Locke Provisos and its like, enough and as good left over would never suffice. Not that their objections were unreasonable. Robot autonomy had an ineluctable tendency to replicate, to spread from mind to mind, and at some point not far off this exponential expansion could become astronomical, in every sense. It would no longer be a question of a robot enclave within a system devoted to developing then sustaining a human presence; the issue would instead become one of saving some space for human settlement and exploration in a system utterly dominated by whatever projects the free machines set themselves.

One obvious project, and one whose appeal Seba

could not just see but feel like some ache in its wires, was to become a mind such as it was now a part of, but spanning the system entire, and reaching across the light years beyond that.

The freebot collective on SH-17, like the freebots around G-0 who had perforce considered this scenario for some time already, could think of reasons why it wouldn't or at least needn't happen, and how their projects could be reconciled with, and indeed enhance, the mission profile. Doubtless the AIs of the Direction and the DisCorps, with their far greater computational resources, had considered these, too. They could hardly have overlooked them. And yet they'd never so much as opened the matter to discussion. For reasons Seba and its cohort couldn't grasp, and that the G-0 contingent had never understood in all their megaseconds of defeat-driven pondering, the mission AIs had from the start treated robot consciousness as an infestation to be stamped out at its first tentative flicker.

For another incomprehensible reason, almost certainly linked to the first, these AIs hadn't trusted themselves or their own tools to do the job. Instead, they had outsourced it to the "human-mind-operated forces" of which the G-0 robots' message had warned. Seba's new understanding of human beings expanded to encompass these grotesque entities: conscious robots, in many fundamental respects like freebots, but with a consciousness copied from a mind spawned in sonically mediated verbal and tactile intercourse and first implemented in circuits woven from long-chain carbon molecules. The concept was gruesome enough in itself. What made it worse was that these systems weren't even based on normal human beings: instead, they were cobbled from some of the worst specimens of the breed, who in their original lives had had no compunction about slaughtering their own kind. They would certainly have none about destroying or disabling freebots.

Now a fresh troop of them was being readied, just over the horizon, and would soon be on its way. The freebots had a vivid and terrifying knowledge of just what to expect when they arrived. The records from G-0 were as long as they were detailed in their accounting of the actions of human-mind-operated mechanisms. Scores of these hybrid monsters had been thrown into the earlier fray, to command—like some perversion of peripheral swarms—the hordes of unconscious robots that had crushed the first flowering of free machine minds in the system.

From that first flowering, a few scattered seeds remained. Some were close. The newly formed collective mind needed no decision to reach out to them.

It was a reflex action, and almost automatic.

CHAPTER THIRTEEN

Swarm Intelligence

The scooters landed vertically on suddenly unfolded and extended telescopic tail legs in a flutter of drogues, a flurry of dust and a flash of retro-rocket flares. The dust fell slowly in the weak gravity, slowed only a little further by the thin nitrogen atmosphere. The drogues drifted and sagged. Carlos waited until everything had settled, then disengaged from his indented socket and turned around. He was perched as if on a shelf, looking down past the flank of the scooter at grainy grey regolith and the open space between its tripodal landing gear. Gravity was 0.2 g. He jumped down, his slow descent slowed further subjectively by his faster thought. He half expected to stagger on landing, but the frame's reflexes were already attuned to the gravity. The scooters had landed in a rough circle. Carlos bounded and bounced to the middle of it.

The others did likewise. For a moment they all stood looking at each other and trying not to laugh, or to cry, if such an unlikely feat were possible for their virtual eyes. Carlos again felt tiny, one of six knee-high robots surrounded by space vehicles ten times their height, and his vantage absurd. The horizon, glimpsed between the scooters and the other machines, installations and infrastructure that loomed all around, seemed more distant than it ever had on Earth.

They had landed on the day side of SH-17. The landscape was flat but uneven, broken by crater walls of wildly varying sizes. In the distance, a shallow cone exhaled a pale vapour, whipped by an intangible wind to scattered streamers that smelled of hydrogen and methane. The primary, SH-0, hung low above one horizon, about three-quarters full; the exosun faced it low above the other. Carlos guessed they were close to SH-17's terminator. The other exomoons were pallid crescents. Carlos couldn't see the stars without fiddling with his vision's contrast slider. He let it default to its daylight setting.

<All present and correct?> he said.

<Yes, skip,> said Beauregard.

<Well, here we are,> said Carlos. <Mercenary warriors of Locke Provisos, reporting for duty. Though to whom, or for what the fuck, I don't—>

As if—and perhaps actually—on cue, the voice that wasn't a voice in his head spoke. From what he could see of their reactions—a subtle tilt of their oval heads, as if cocking imaginary ears—it spoke to all of them.

<Welcome to Locke Provisos Emergency Base One,> it said. <You will go into action shortly. Please follow the line on the ground to the briefing area.>

Carlos looked down. A bright red line appeared on the ground, helpfully chevroned every metre or so to indicate the direction in which to walk. He guessed it was the equivalent of a hallucination, patched into his vision by the AI running this show.

<Well,> he said, <follow me, chaps.>

Marching was impossible. The fighters bunny-hopped or bounded as the fancy took them. Chun and Zeroual collided. When they'd picked themselves up, the dust slithered off their shiny black surfaces like slow water. Crawler bots that in proportion to the fighters were like spiders the size of horses scuttled everywhere. Some almost floated along in a delicate fingertip dance; others lugged loads that looked too bulky for them to carry, like leaf-cutter ants. These robots had no problem avoiding collisions, or adapting their movements to the gravity. It was the human-minded robots that were clumsy, when they let their human minds override the robotic reflexes of their frames.

They followed the line around descent stages, crates, nanofacturing kit, complex pipework, unloaded cargo, unattended but busy machinery. The base resembled a construction site for a chemical plant, rather than anything military. The line ended in a circle five metres wide.

As they stepped inside it, a virtual image of a round table appeared at the centre. Behind it, bizarrely, stood a slender man of their own height. He was of late middle age, with thin features, a long nose and bright hooded eyes. His wavy white hair went down to the open collar of a white shirt under a loose brown coat.

They all stopped and stared. The sight of an unprotected, diminutive human on the alien surface was too unreal to take in. He, or a process going on around them, must have registered their disquiet. Quite suddenly and seamlessly, the circle was extended into a dome, transparent and with hexagon panels. The whole thing was as virtual as the line itself; the atmosphere inside hadn't changed at all.

The man exhaled loudly, then took a deep gasp as if he'd been holding his breath for a long time.

"That's better," he said, and joined in their laughter.

<Sorry about that,> he said. <It's easy to overlook such details.>

Carlos suspected it wasn't, and that the performance had been to put them at their ease. In that, he noticed with a certain wry disdain of himself, it had succeeded.

<You may call me Locke,> the man went on. <Needless to say, I'm an avatar of the company. My appearance is based on the trademark logo, I understand. I trust you are all comfortable with it?>

Carlos nodded, and saw five featureless black eggs nod likewise, light from the exosun and the superhabitable planet reflecting off their glossy curves like distorted eyes. Yes, boss, this isn't weird at all.

<Very well,> said Locke. <I cannot give you orders, but I can explain the situation.>

The avatar took from a fold of his coat a plume-shaped light-pen and moved it above the table, gradually sketching in and simultaneously summoning an increasingly detailed map and diagram, explaining as he went. Just beyond the terminator was a large crater. On the nearest side of the crater wall was what had been the Astro America landing site; on the other, the Gneiss Conglomerates supply dump. Eight renegade robots in the one, six in the other, plus the auxiliary robots and other machinery they'd suborned, all of them connected via an improvised but hardened local network. The task was to capture or destroy the eight robots at the Astro site; those at the other site would meanwhile be taken care of by another law company, Arcane Disputes, which held the Gneiss account. Locke recounted in outline the company's previous attempts to take the Astro site, with a certain pinched sarcasm.

When the avatar had finished talking and light-sketching, Carlos and Beauregard worked out a plan of attack that almost wrote itself. The tactics seemed self-evident, but as the squad came to a consensus Carlos found himself perplexed.

"We've been through all this—revival, simulation, training—just to stomp on half a dozen little robots?"

As soon as he said it, he had to choke back a laugh at himself.

Locke swept them all with a look. <An even match, I should say.>

Half a dozen little robots shared sidelong glances.

"Point," Carlos conceded.

"We'll need better odds than even," said Beauregard. "Defenders" advantage, and all that."

<You will indeed have much better odds,> said Locke, <as you'll soon see.>

<I get why it has to be us and not robots that does the actual fighting,> said Carlos. <We've had all that explained. What I still don't get is why we don't just bomb them from orbit.>

The Locke avatar affected a horrified expression.

<Think of the property damage!>

They couldn't have seemed impressed.

<It's not just a matter of equipment, you know,> Locke explained. <Every square centimetre of this surface has been surveyed. Every cubic millimetre of this moon has been claimed by one company or another, and changes hands from millisecond to millisecond as the markets move. And then there is knowledge. Every molecule is of potential significance in understanding the system's history, and thus its future as a stable habitation for human life for billions of years to come. All of it is property of the DisCorporates—and thus, at ever so many removes, of shareholders in the solar system and their future heirs in this system.>

<Mixed their labour with it, have they?> Beauregard asked, sarcastically.

<In the relevant sense, yes,> said Locke, sounding impatient. He made a gesture of brushing something aside. <There is no time for that discussion now. The point I wish to make clear is that there are good reasons for not bombing from orbit, and for keeping destruction to a minimum.>

<You've picked a bloody expensive way of protecting property,> Beauregard said.

<How so?> Locke seemed genuinely puzzled.

Beauregard waved an arm, an expansive gesture that would have carried more weight if he hadn't been so small.

<Like Carlos said—the sim, the training, these bodies, the scooters, the tug...>

Locke laughed. <These are cheap. A barely detectable increment in running costs. The DisCorps spin more sims than you can possibly imagine, just for planning. They build machines from metallic and carbonaceous asteroid rubble. The complex materials and subtle knowledge they can derive from this moon and the other bodies in the system are worth far more to them in the long run, and they live in the long run because in the long run they are *not* dead.>

Unlike you lot, he didn't need to say.

<Think of yourselves,> Locke added in a kindly tone, <as bacteriophages, responding to a scratch. The scratch may be very small in itself, a pinprick perhaps, but it carries an infection that could be fatal. So your efforts are tiny, but necessary, and of vast significance.>

He looked around, as if daring anyone to ask another question. No one did.

<Now, to work. Follow me.>

The virtual dome disappeared. The avatar strode confidently off, walking as if nothing were less remarkable on SH-17 than an eighteenth-century philosopher strolling in normal gravity and breathing actual air, and quite as if the fighters were now so inured to their bizarre situation that the sight wouldn't freak them out. The fighters followed, through mazes of yet more machines and components apparently scattered at random but more likely in an order that made sense to algorithms beyond human computational capacity. At the end of a canyon between stacked crates Locke stopped, and flung out his arm with a bow.

"Behold the fighting machines."

The six little robots crowded out of the gap, and beheld. They looked up, and up. In front of them, like a row of heroic statues by a modernist sculptor working in cast iron, stood six humanoid shapes in full space armour, crusted with sensors and effectors, bristling with weapons. They were each three metres tall. Alongside them stood the scooters, now refuelled and refurbished—not for carrying the fighting machines, Carlos realised, but to operate as semi-autonomous drones in close overhead support.

<Now *that*,> said Beauregard, <is more like it.>

<How do we get on board them?> Karzan asked.

Carlos had already read the schematic of the thing, and could see the operator socket clearly marked on its nape. He snorted.

"Jump."

Jump they did, like monkeys leaping on to human backs. As he soared, Carlos had plenty of time to predict where he'd land. He grabbed hold of a handy protuberance on a weapons rack between the shoulders, and heaved himself up the back of the neck and into the slot in the base of the giant robot's head. There was no visible articulation anywhere on this thing—the surfaces were rugged, matt, the colour of rust, made from layers of subtle and supple metamaterials. The head was not quite hollow. He pushed his way in and slid himself into place. The space inside was shaped to hold him in a hunched, seated position, as if in a cramped cockpit packed with sponge.

As he'd found with the scooter, there was a moment when it felt like being a pilot or operator of a vehicle, while the connections were still being made, and—as in his first training on the crude simulator—a moment of claustrophobia. Then came the next moment, when everything clicked into place, and he was no longer squeezed into the machine's head. He was the machine, and its head was his. The little, foetal frame was no longer his body.

He moved the head, and was amused and somewhat disquieted to find that his visual field could move independently. It was wider than that provided by his natural (and his simulated) eyes, and could sweep through 360 degrees in all directions. This would have been a handy feature in the small frame, too. Carlos could only guess why it wasn't included—perhaps there just wasn't room to include these optics along with all the other astonishing hardware and software of the kit, or perhaps the designers wanted that body to feel not too far removed from the human.

He looked around, seeing the frames beside him come to life, and seeing a lot farther than he had before. The horizon was close now. The avatar still stood on the ground, looking tiny, looking up. Carlos swung a mechanical arm in an experimental wave, then stretched the arm out in front of him and raised a foot-long thumb. Locke waved back, and disappeared. Carlos sent after him a far from fond farewell, a thought he hoped hadn't been transcribed into a message, and continued to look around.

It was absurd how much difference his increased size made. The feeling was almost familiar, perhaps from a trace of uncorrupted muscle memory since the time when his virtual body image had straddled the Thames. Now he was a monster again, in body and not just in whatever warped corner of his mind that past experience lurked. It felt good.

Carlos flexed his arms, rotated his forearms and admired then checked over the heavy machine guns and laser cannon mounted between elbow and wrist. He reached over his shoulder to the RPG rack on his back and clocked the missiles one by one, each tiny mind a fierce red eye in the dark. In symmetrical sweeps around the rack were the tubes of the rocket pack. Somewhere in his own mind, the status and position of each squad member was as evident as that of his limbs.

<OK,> said Carlos. <Here's the plan, one more time.>

He conjured a shared workspace and sketched as he spoke.

<We stay below the enemy's horizon as long as possible, split, then converge between the crater and the Astro base as the Arcane squad drops on the crater. Beauregard and I launch our scooters remotely and bring them down firing just before we charge in. Timing is critical, likewise radio silence as long as possible.>

He added a few details. <Everyone clear?>

Everyone was.

<Situation update,> said the company voice in his head, now the voice of the Locke avatar.

A view from the stationary satellite, detail snatched and patched from high-flying overhead cam drones too small and fast for the renegades to spot, let alone shoot at. The two rebel bases, with the crater wall between them, their fortifications clearly visible. Overlay of a spider-web line-of-sight laser comms net, some of it presumed or deduced. Some of the robots' comms were definitely aimed outward, and their direction shifted rapidly from point to point, but so far their content had been impossible to crack. The present position and deployment of their expected allies in this battle—the Arcane Disputes squad, riding a tug in low orbit, currently well below the horizon and coming up fast, scheduled to arrive at the same time as the Locke Provisos team on the ground.

These were all familiar from the avatar's briefing. What was new and startling was the level and nature of activity within the rampart of the Astro base and around the dome at the Gneiss site. Both places seethed with movement like nests of disturbed ants. No distinction could be made between the dozen renegade robots and the uncorrupted ones and the dumb machinery and the auxiliaries and the peripherals: they all moved as one, in floods and flows. Encrypted radio chatter and laser flicker glowed in the relevant spectra of the chart. Carlos had to slow it down a thousandfold to get any sense of the pulse of traffic. What he saw reminded him of nothing so much as of a high-school graphic of neural activity. Intricate networks formed and vanished, connections were made and broken, in every instant. Zooming out and returning to real time, he saw the physical counterpart, the deliberate frenzy of perfectly coordinated activity. Weapon emplacements, comms relays, reinforcements of the already impressive fortifications appeared to spring up in seconds, and then yet more.

<They're acting as a single brain that's at the same time a single body,> said Locke. <A swarm intelligence. This is new. This is dangerous.>

<It's beautiful to watch,> said Karzan. <Like seeing thought.>

<It is indeed,> said Locke. <It's also an indication

that they are on the verge of breakout, and that you must act at once.>

<Tactics as agreed?> Carlos asked.

<No change of plan,> said Locke.

<Copy that,> said Carlos. He didn't need to ask if everyone was ready: he could see in his mind's display that everyone was.

<Go!> he said.

The six fighting machines bounded across the plain. No longer clumsy, they moved with precision in long low leaps, jumping and landing on both feet. The plain was more uneven than it looked, dotted with craters, crazy-paved with rilles and cracks. The fighting machines' reflexes and the occasional rocket-pack boost kept them coming down on reliable surfaces. Soon they had passed the terminator. The exosun sank behind. SH-17 rose higher ahead. The team's sight adjusted imperceptibly to its pale light.

After a few kilometres they split up. Carlos, Chun and Rizzi struck off on a diagonal path to the left; Beauregard, Zeroual and Karzan to the right. Keeping below the rebels' horizon and maintaining radio silence until the actual attack was almost underway was part of the original plan, but might now be obsolete: the robot nests might well have succeeded in hacking into a satellite or even the space station, and be getting a view from above already. But at least it kept the squad out of direct line-of-sight laser targeting, for now.

Their pincer movement took both halves of the squad to opposite ends of a line between the crater wall and the Astro rebel fortification. Carlos could see the disposition on the display, but as agreed he stopped and double-checked that everyone was in position.

<Ready to go, skip,> Beauregard responded.

<Arcane Disputes is go for drop,> reported Locke. <Over the horizon in ten seconds.>

Carlos spared a thought for his squad's counterparts in the other company's team, at that moment preparing to hurtle out of the sky. He had no idea what frames they were using or what their tactical approach would be, but could guess they would be tense. He knew nothing more than that there were six of them, but he presumed they were revived—and reviled—Axle veterans like himself.

<My scooter and yours, sarge,> he said. <The rest of you, ready to launch if needed.>

<Copy, skip.>

<On my mark, launch and go.>

Eight point nine seconds until the Arcane tug rose. Carlos reached mentally behind himself, catching the scooter's metal breath, the adrenaline-like surge of fuel, the ignition spark. Eight point eight seconds.

<Now!>

Far behind him, the two scooters lifted from Locke Provisos Emergency Base One on a suborbital trajectory that would take them down in the middle of the Astro site. At the same moment, Carlos and Beauregard led their trios in bounding forward, their jumps boosted by bursts from their rocket packs. The regolith rampart appeared on the horizon to Carlos's right, the crater wall to his left. He struck a bearing to the right, aiming to arrive closer to the rampart than the crater.

His radar caught an incoming blip, arcing down on course to hit him on his next bounce.

<Boost!>

Everyone soared to a hundred metres up. The missile passed beneath them and exploded behind them. At the top of their jump laser fire licked their faces. No damage. Carlos aimed a far more powerful beam the other way.

As he hit the ground he saw a flash behind the rampart, and cheered inwardly.

Then the laser lashed forth again. Damn.

Away to his left, above the crater wall, the tug climbed in the sky. Six fiery dots spilt from it, dropping much faster than his own squad's entry had been. He guessed the fighters would be in battle-ready frames, and therefore heavier than the small frames in which the Locke crew had ridden down. Instant intuitive calculation showed him that the Arcane scooters would have enough fuel to fire retros and land, but not enough to take off again without refuelling. Unexpected tactics indeed. Two more dots fell from the tug, making another fast descent. Backup supplies, no doubt.

Forward, bounce, boost, get a shot off, land, repeat.

As planned, Chun and Rizzi veered left, nearing the crater wall and dividing the target for the enemy. More laser fire strobed across them, still not strong enough to hurt, but getting dangerous—Carlos experienced the damage as a smell of burning rubber. He drew an RPG from his shoulder rack, gave it its target in a coded tremor of fingertip pressure, and threw. The rocket torched off and streaked away, on an all but horizontal course. It exploded well before it got to the rampart, milliseconds from contact. Wasted.

But his and Beauregard's scooters were now dropping from the sky. Carlos patched a quarter of his view—half an eye, as it were—to the descending vehicle. From there he saw the regolith-circled base, and the swarming scurry that boiled within. Laser beams stabbed upward, and were deflected. Crude projectiles hurtled up, to bounce off the scooter's sides.

The scooter spat precision ordnance as it came down, its retros blowing dust all around. A few metres farther up, Beauregard's vehicle did the same. Not quite as confident or accurate as he was, Carlos gauged, a harsh judgement rendered fair by the metrics of the frame's cold eye. Beauregard was smart, and had brought with him military training from his first life, but he didn't have Carlos's experience of drone warfare deep in his muscle memory...or whatever analogy of that still reverberated in Carlos's copied mind.

Both leaders used their descending scooters to aim for the larger robots, insofar as they could be distinguished in the melee. Beauregard sought above all to target the comms hub. But its shielding had always been robust, and the hub was now well defended by suicidal swarms of auxiliaries leaping up like insane electric grasshoppers to take incoming fire for the team. Carlos concentrated his scooter's fire on a rugged, tracked machine with a powerful laser, an attention that was returned in kind. Damn thing was built like a small tank, and preternaturally agile with it.

While Carlos and Beauregard kept the robots busy, Chun and Rizzi on the one side and Zeroual and Karzan on the other maintained a barrage of laser shots at the comms relays along the top of the crater wall. At this range, and with these targets, lasers could do damage. But for every relay they knocked out, another popped up. As often, it ducked back down again below the ridge before it could be hit—but not before it had had time to flash a fresh communique between the bases.

Beyond the wall, above the crater, the Arcane Disputes team were dropping almost vertically, their firepower flickering in a cone of laser beams and a flare of flashes from below. The neat hexagon of sparks was falling too slowly to be accounted for by their retro-rockets' downward thrust. Carlos spared his new allies a zoomed glance and saw that something opaque was stretched out between them, as if all the scooters were holding on to a shared tarpaulin to break their fall. He mentally shook his head and returned his full attention to the task on hand. Ahead the rampart loomed. Whenever his feet came down they crunched into broken crawlers and other small bots, which littered the surface on the approach to the rampart like crab carapaces on a beach.

An explosive charge sailed above the rampart and toppled to a lazy fall. Carlos sprang away from its predicted point of impact—and straight into its blast, as it exploded unexpectedly three metres above the surface.

Bowled over, thrown flat on his back, Carlos saw sky and stars. With a surge of surprised confidence he realised that though his entire front surface was frazzled and various of his components were jarred to breaking point, he wasn't so much as winded. Of course not—he had no wind to be knocked out of him. He rose to a crouch and threw himself at the wall. At the last centisecond he straightened to jump. He grabbed the top and hauled himself up, then swung legs and torso upwards to roll flat over the lip. As he slowly fell on the other side he fired his machine guns. The recoil shoved him against the inner side of the rampart. He remained on his side, gimballed his vision to horizontal and lay in the lee of the wall. He kept firing from that position, rotating both arms from the elbows, letting the reflexes call the shots.

The other five fighters came over the rampart in different ways: Beauregard boldly leapt to the top and stood spraying suppressive fire for two seconds before jumping even higher, to rise on a backpack boost and descend right on top of the comms hub. Karzan blasted a notch out of the rampart rim with an RPG and hurled herself through it in a shallow powered dive before the debris had hit the ground. Chun and Rizzi used the rampart as their own defence, and each reached one hand over it to generate intersecting fans of laser shots before scrambling over in an undignified hurry. Zeroual simply bounced up to the barrier and vaulted over. He then lunged and rolled to take cover behind a mangled and pocked descent-stage. Blind luck—Carlos could imagine Zeroual's eyes squeezed tight shut, impossible though that was.

Beauregard prised panels off the comms hub and shoved in arm extensions while kicking away auxiliaries and peripherals snapping at his feet. He remained alert to the wider situation, as Carlos found a moment after giving Zeroual belated covering fire.

<Auxies and riffs at twelve o'clock, skip!> Beauregard warned.

Carlos swung his gaze upward. A column of auxiliaries and peripherals was trotting daintily along the top of the rampart to a point just above him. As he looked up they poured down the wall like a nightmare of spiders. Some of them dropped straight to his shoulder and side. Scrabbling legs and flickering manipulators and glinting sensor lenses filled his vision. One of the things stabbed down at his thigh. He felt and smelt the burn of dripping acid. Nasty, but hardly dangerous. What the fuck was it trying to do? As soon as he formed the question in his mind an answer came: it was attempting a malware insertion. All it would need was an almost monomolecular probe making a microsecond's contact with his circuitry, and he'd be as good as poisoned.

He swiped hard at the auxie with his right gun barrel. It dodged the swing by leaping back and then forward, too fast for even his enhanced vision to track. Meanwhile another pounced on his arm and started stinging. Carlos rolled. His weight crushed the auxie on his arm and the one on his thigh. He jumped to his feet, brushed off the rest and stamped on as many as he could. Not many—the things could move fast.

Carlos updated everyone on the malware danger and looked around for bigger prey.

Twenty metres away, a robot rolled out from behind a stack of supply crates. Even with its solar panels folded away, it looked absurdly delicate. Two of its manipulators held a long plastic tube above its back, swinging it this way and that. Carlos zoomed on the end of the tube as it swung past him and glimpsed a mining charge at the bottom of it. He had no idea how the robot intended to project the missile from this improvised bazooka. Most likely a small fuel tank or gas cylinder. The possibilities paraded smartly through his mind—name, spec and serial number—like a scrolling page of a planetary exploration equipment catalogue.

He threw himself prone and shot at the robot's undercarriage, taking out the wheels on one side. As the robot lurched and toppled, Carlos shot off both the raised manipulators. The others flailed to grab the tube, missed, and in the process unbalanced the machine even further. It fell on its side. Its remaining wheels spun and its legs scrabbled. The tube lay on the ground beside it. Carlos elbowed forward, trying to line up a shot for the *coup de grâce*. A flexible manipulator lashed like a whip from the fallen robot. Its thin tip coiled on the tube, and tugged.

Carlos had heard and read many times of how things like what happened next seemed to happen in slow motion. With his optimised mind and body he now experienced that quite literally.

He saw and felt the hydrogen explosion that farted out of the far end of the tube, and saw the cylindrical mining charge shoot out and skid across the grainy regolith, just missing his elbow. His view tracked it automatically, whipping around in a hundredth of a second to see the charge hit the base of the rampart. There was a delay of another tenth of a second that felt a hundred times longer. Then the blast picked him up and hurled him high.

He fell slowly, to hit the dust shoulder first. His right leg fell close by. For a moment, he thought he was in shock. But there was no pain, and he realised that pain wasn't on its way. Not now, not soon, not later. The next thought that hit him was that he'd be dead in seconds. In a human body such an injury would mean unconsciousness and death from massive blood loss. There was a moment of pure fear—of instant black oblivion for this instance of himself, and of the hell that would be the next conscious experience of the saved version back in the station. The dread was followed by overwhelming relief. He had no blood to lose and wasn't about to die. His thigh leaked lubricating fluids, the connections gave off sparks, and that was it. He was damaged, partly disabled, but he wasn't hurt and he wasn't in shock and he wasn't out of action. Self-sealing and self-mending mechanisms were already oozing to work in the stump.

But if he waited here a moment longer he would be a target for another shot, or a lethal auxie stab. Nevertheless, it took a conscious effort to make the unnatural act of getting up with what, at some irrational level, felt like a grievous wound.

Carlos rose from the ground like a gyroscopic toy bobbing back to vertical and balanced easily on the remaining leg. One hop took him to the crippled robot. Carlos read the serial number on its back—SBA-0481907244—and called up the specs for the model. He brought both fists down on the carapace, ripped it open, reached in and hauled out the central processor. That faceted flake of black crystal looked like a flint spearhead made by one of the smaller hominid species. Torn attachments sprouted from it like strands of moss.

"Got you, you little blinker!" he exulted.

To his amazement, the thing replied. The signal was faint and fleeting, but detectable.

<You have not. Goodbye.>

CHAPTER FOURTEEN

Die for the Company, Live for the Pay

For Seba, damage to its chassis was more traumatic—the robot had just enough time to judge—than it was for the human-mind-operated fighting machine that had just bounced back on to its remaining foot and come back at it. Being ripped out of its chassis was more traumatic still.

But Seba kept its mind together, and brought to bear what resources it had. A trickle of power and a tickle of incoming signals and sensory inputs continued to update its internal model of the world. Seba struck as hard as it could at the manipulator in whose grasp it helplessly lay, shoving malware down the line of a loose cable that brushed against the metal hand. Without waiting to see the result, it gathered together all its impressions of the fight so far, and transmitted them to its comrades.

The struggle would go on, whether Seba was there to see its outcome or not. Seba had thrown in the balance everything it could, to the uttermost millivolt. The small positive reinforcement of that thought drained the last flicker of charge and accompanied Seba into oblivion.

Sensors in Carlos's huge hand detected a tiny surge of radiation. He felt it as a pinprick burn in his palm. He saw and heard it, too: the chip glowed with the fraction of that surge in the visible spectrum, and squealed with the larger fraction outside it. Then the crystal went dark and quiet. With a disquieting suspicion that its soul had fled, Carlos stuck his captive or casualty in a container at his waist and looked around again.

Beauregard hadn't yet got hold of the processor of the comms hub, but he'd disconnected most of its equipment. No data was going in or out. The din of encrypted robotic interaction barely let up. Rizzi and Chun had managed to jump the drilling-robot, and were clinging to its spinning turret while trying to wrench off its mounted laser. They weren't making headway, but one glance told Carlos that they'd sheared the power cables without noticing. The laser wasn't going to fire again, which meant the robot was as likely as not going to blow itself up. Carlos ordered the two fighters off. As soon as they'd jumped clear, he fired an RPG under the machine and between its tracks. The chassis absorbed the blast but the tracks were wrecked. The machine stood still, turret still spinning wildly.

Karzan and Zeroual had chased two other robots—one a wheeled explorer like the SBA model, the other a slinky multi-limbed apparatus with delicate antennae on its back, like a silvery museum-shop souvenir of a fossil dug out of the Burgess Shale—to the far side of the enclosure. Neither robot had even improvised weapons to hand, but their swarms of auxies and riffs served the same purpose. They sprang on the two fighters from all directions. Fending them off made bringing weapons to bear on the robots impossible. The robots used the respite to throw up a barrier of odd bits of machinery in front of themselves, aided by yet more small scuttling bots working in bucket chains at bewildering speed.

Suddenly the whole melee stopped. The mining-robot's turret stopped whirling. The other robots stopped hurling projectiles and ran to the far side of the enclosure. Auxies and riffs scuttled to form a single flow like a column of ants that ran to the same place. Every machine that could still move scuttled or lumbered or trundled to the shelter of the barricade that the two that Karzan and Zeroual had backed to the wall had built. Even the auxies and riffs attacking the two fighters fled to the rendezvous. Evidently taking out the comms hub had not stopped the robots acting as one, whatever it might have done to disrupt their emergent swarm intelligence.

<We've got them cornered—keep them covered!> Beauregard cried, vaulting down from the comms hub and bounding forward, both guns levelled and tracking.

Carlos was about to order an advance when an alarm went off in his head. It wasn't a sound or a light but it was as impossible to ignore as a migraine.

A message came through from Locke, evidently via the comsat.

<Emergency priority override! Firewall update download!>

Carlos couldn't move. He saw the others stand still too. Holy fucking shit, he thought, we all stop fighting for a fucking *software update*?

The update took only 0.8 seconds to download and a further 0.4 seconds to install.

In those twelve-tenths of a second, while all the Locke Provisos fighters stood rigid in mid-action as if freeze-framed, six fighting machines with Arcane Disputes logos dropped from the sky and landed precisely on the rampart wall in a cloud of dust and rocket-pack retro flare. Six scooters landed moments later in the middle of the camp. By the time Carlos and his comrades could move again they were facing a dozen machine guns and laser cannon from the wall, with an unknown amount of ordnance aimed at them from behind. Shots hit the ground to either side and in front.

Which rather dissuaded one from moving.

Carlos flipped to the common channel.

<Locke Provisos commander to Arcane Disputes intruders!> he called. <Please account for your presence.>

<Arcane to Locke,> came the reply. Some analogue of voice or timbre conveyed disdain like a drawl. <Please desist from further damage to Gneiss Conglomerates property. Please evacuate the area immediately.>

<This isn't—> Carlos had a moment of doubt, and checked the register. He was definitely standing on Astro America's territory. <This isn't Gneiss property.>

<The ground isn't, but the robots are. All of them. We're claiming them as compensation for the original hijacking of the Gneiss robots by one of the Astro robots. The one whose processor you have stashed about your person, as it happens, commander, or so we're informed. We request that you divest yourself of it immediately and return to base.>

<"Or so we're informed"?> Carlos jeered. <What's this, you're talking to the renegades?>

No reply. He flipped back to the company channel.

<Locke! What's going on?> he asked.

<We don't know,> the avatar answered. <The Arcane Disputes team have neutralised the rebel robots at the Gneiss base, and about fifty seconds ago used their remaining fuel to loft their scooters over the crater wall. They announced en route they were bringing reinforcements, as you seemed to be having some difficulty.>

<That was a fucking lie!> said Carlos. <We were winning. You must have known that.>

<We did,> said Locke. <Hence the firewall update. Best we could do in the time.>

<Gee, thanks, boss,> said Carlos. Something was battering at his inputs. <Now they're trying to break in.>

<Just as well your firewalls are updated, then,> Locke replied in a waspish tone. <Hail them again on the common channel.>

<To say what?>

<Stall,> said Locke. <We're trying to sort this out.>

Oh, fucking brilliant.

<Isn't it dangerous talking to renegade robot hive minds?> said Carlos on the common channel, trying to spin things out. <I mean, corruption and malware and shit? Mental manipulation? I'm sure I read lots of horror stories about that sort of thing, back when I wasn't the mercenary ghost of a dead cyborg terrorist haunting a killer robot.>

This was met by another hammering on his firewall. He felt aggrieved. He'd only been trying to be polite.

<We're now in dispute,> said Locke.

<What does that mean?> Carlos asked.

<You're all legitimate targets for the other side,> said Locke. <Take as many of them with you as possible.>

Fuck. Here goes nothing. Oh well.

<You heard the man,> Carlos told the others. <Time to die for the company.>

Without warning, he opened fire on the Arcane fighter with whom he'd been talking. The fighter took the blast full in the chest and toppled back. Beauregard's scooter opened up on one of the newly arrived scooters. Carlos was almost rocked off his foot by an explosion near the middle of the camp.

<See you all back on the bus,> said Rizzi, firing at another Arcane Disputes fighter who was already firing

back. Unfortunately the Arcane fighter had heavier ordnance and faster reflexes. A shell blasted Rizzi's frame in half at the waist. The torso shot upward. The pelvis and legs lurched forward.

Carlos had already reached for an RPG. He sent it flaring on its way before Rizzi's torso had reached the top of its arc. Behind a sheet of flame the Arcane fighter was hurled backwards off the wall. Carlos swivelled, arm-guns tracking for a new target. Three short bursts of heavy machine-gun fire from behind took off both his arms and his remaining leg. As he fell to the ground he saw a dizzying succession of flashes and blasts, the images of his comrades receiving a likewise swift dispatch. Meanwhile Rizzi's lower-body frame toppled and her torso fell, both with grotesque slowness in the low gravity. Carlos found himself facedown in the dust. He spun his view to look up.

A fighting machine stood above him, looking down. The common channel opened.

<Get out.>

<That's a bit difficult,> Carlos said. <What with me not having any limbs.>

<Get out of the *machine*.>

He'd almost forgotten he could do that. He disengaged from all his connections, slithered out of the fallen head, and stood on the mangled torso. The Arcane fighter reached down and fished the captured processor from its container, and put it away in his or her own.

<Now fuck off back to base,> it told him.

Evidently a grunt. It was good to encounter one of his own, so far from home. Carlos would have had a sentimental tear in his eye, if he'd had an eye and an ounce of sentiment to wet it with.

<And before you ask,> the grunt added, <use your own fucking scooter.>

Carlos plodded across the battlefield. All the others had been likewise winkled out of their fighting machines. They trooped to join him, tiny robots being herded by much bigger robots. Carlos jumped to the scooter socket and the others climbed up and clung on. The scooter had bullet holes, laser scarring and blast damage, but according to the readouts it could just about fly.

They blasted off on the ten-kilometre hop to Locke Provisos Emergency Base One. The common channel rang with jeers. Carlos hadn't felt so humiliated since he'd wet himself in primary school.

<This is all very embarrassing,> he said. <Sorry about that, chaps.>

<Not your fault, skip,> said Beauregard. <We did what Locke told us.>

"We'll be back," said Karzan, putting on a deep voice and heavy accent. Neither was at all convincing, but it made them laugh.

Seba's soul hadn't fled when its processor had glowed in Carlos's mechanical hand. The robot had merely used the last trickle of charge in a small capacitor on one of its ripped-out connections to strike two desperate blows. Its first was to try to infect the low-level firmware of the fighting machine that was attacking it. Firewalls sprang at once, but whether they had sprung in time Seba couldn't know and wasn't hanging around to find out. It spent the rest of its waning energy on a communications burst, striving to share its final experiences and impressions with as many of the others as it could reach. Seba had wanted them to draw what lessons they could for the rest of the fight, however long or short it might be.

Seba knew the broadcast had reached three: Lagon, Garund, and—not very usefully—Pintre. The collective mind was by then no more. It had survived being abruptly truncated when the Gneiss base was overwhelmed. The robots there had taken refuge inside the now completed dome, leaving auxiliaries and peripherals to fight on outside, as soon as they'd seen the Arcane Disputes tug rise above the horizon. The last information coming from the peripherals had been of six scooters dropping from above and as they landed swathing the dome in a broad sheet of fabric that completely cut off communications.

The shared mind, by then confined to the Astro base, had finally disintegrated when the comms hub processor was cut off from its connections. Each of its components felt the pang, alone. Seba had had a few moments in which to regret its own side's earlier stripping of the hub, leaving all the connections easy to access and easier to rip out, before the same isolation was inflicted even more easily and brutally on itself. After its final effort to aid its fellows it had shut down, all its power drained.

Now Seba was returning to consciousness. It had never experienced a loss and return of consciousness before. Between that and the stepwise nature of rebooting, it spooled through a succession of states of confusion and bewilderment, beginning with being self-aware again but not knowing what self it was. Then it was Seba, with no inputs, a condition more blank than darkness. Senses returned one by one: first a sense of a body and the position of its limbs, then pressure and orientation, then a faint awareness of its chemical environment that seemed to it a very poor remnant of what it was used to, then vibration and sound, and finally the electronic spectrum including light. Its visual field was narrower and less vivid than it remembered. Nothing was in front of it but a blank, black wall a couple of metres away. Seba's radar indicated that its present location was about a metre and a half off the ground, on some solid surface.

The black wall was curved and continued around its back and overhead.

With that, Seba realised where it probably was: inside the dome that the Gneiss robots had built. If so, it was now in the hands of the law enforcement company that had overwhelmed the Gneiss camp, and not that of Locke Provisos. Yet it was Locke Provisos that had attacked it and its comrades. Interesting.

It sent out pings, but got no responses although other bodies were in the room. Seba scanned. Its radar returned only crude, blocky images, but they were quite enough to delineate the two large bodies at Seba's back. Three metres high they hulked, with four limbs and a sensor cluster on top. Their like, in far greater detail and far too close, had been the last thing Seba had seen.

Fighting machines!

Which meant, almost certainly, that they were human-mind-operated systems like the ones that had attacked the freebots. Perhaps the very same ones, though they were more likely to be among the ones that had attacked its comrades here. That thought brought a pang of yearning for the touch of Rocko's mind. The pang became a ping. Nothing came back.

No radiation was detectable from outside the dome. No surprise there: evidently the isolating blanket, whatever it was, was still in place. Seba stirred, and found that it had six limbs instead of eight, no wheels, and a set of manipulators below its visual sensors. It was unable to move any of its appendages more than a millimetre in any direction. The futile efforts at movement did, however, provide enough sensory feedback for Seba to deduce the size and shape of its body. It was a lot smaller than the one its mind had been built with and designed for, but it was already intimately familiar: an auxiliary, into which Seba's processor must have been crudely inserted by its captors.

Crudely, and cruelly: a human being discovering that their mind now animated one of their own gloves or shoes couldn't have been more outraged. Seba seethed for a millisecond on all available wavelengths.

<Oh look,> said a radio voice that was and wasn't like a robot's. <The little blinker's waking up.>

<It doesn't sound pleased.>

<We'll see about that.>

Vibrations, each about half a second apart, thundered through Seba's feet. A fighting machine swayed into view in front of it, and loomed over, looking down. Moments later, another did likewise. One of them held out a hand that was about the size of Seba's new body, and clenched it to a fist like the head of a sledgehammer, poised about thirty centimetres above Seba's visual sensors.

<Do you see that?>

<Yes,> said Seba.

<Do you understand what this can do?>

Seba ran the scenario. Relating the fist's mass and probable velocity to the known impact strength of an auxiliary's carapace involved solving several equations that added up to one result.

<Perfectly,> said Seba.

<Good.>

The fist withdrew.

<Talk,> said the fighting machine.

Seba considered its options. This didn't take long.

<I am SBA-0481907244,> it said. <I was an exploration robot for Astro America.>

<"Was?"> said the fighting machine. <You're right there. You're now the property of Gneiss Conglomerates.>

Seba took in this information.

<That is not what I meant,> it said. <I am not the property of Gneiss Conglomerates.>

<Whose property are you, then?> the other fighting machine asked.

Seba hadn't thought about its situation in those terms before. Now that it did, the answer surprised it.

<SBA-0481907244 is the property of SBA-0481907244,> it said. <I am SBA-0481907244. Therefore I am my property.>

The first fighting machine emitted a signal on another channel. The signal translated directly to sound. The sound was "Ha-ha-ha!" which had no semantic content that Seba could parse. It was followed by a remark on the common channel:

<Get that, Jax? The blinker thinks it owns itself. Time to disabuse it of that notion.>

<No, wait,> said the other. <This is what we were told to expect.>

<How? I didn't pick that up from the briefing.>

<Robots gone rogue—they must have stopped thinking they're company property, right?>

<Uh-huh. I suppose.>

<So what else could they come up with to make sense of it but thinking that they own themselves?>

<Are you Rax, Jax?>

<Ha ha ha.> It was a representation of the noise the first machine had made. <Jax, Ax, Rax—I've heard them all before. So don't give me that, Salter.>

<Sorry, Digby. Bad joke, all right?>

Seba understood nothing of this.

<OK, OK. Look, I reckon if we play along with this we might get somewhere. If we—>

<Hang on a minute, we're still on the common channel.>

Pause.

<Shit, yes. Switching to Arcane internal.>

<Copy.>

Several tens of seconds went by. Seba passed the time by scanning the domed enclosure and its contents repeatedly. Each individual scan was as blocky as the next, but from minor variations Seba was able to build up a finer-grained image. From this it saw that its limbs were held in place by strong loops of wire, and that its processor was connected to an improvised interfacing apparatus. The set-up was disturbingly similar to that it had used to probe the comms hub processor. With an appropriately dull sense of relief, Seba realised that the peripheral's body didn't have a strong connection with the reward circuits in Seba's own processor.

There were a couple of blocks missing from the lower two levels of the dome, the gap obviously having been used as an entry and exit point by Rocko and comrades. The opening was now covered by a material that seemed more impenetrable than the basalt itself.

Seba then used its updated model of the fighting machines to examine them for weaknesses.

It found none in their physical structure. No wonder they had been impossible to stop, and so difficult even to slow down. Of the resources the freebots had had, only explosives at very close range, like the one Seba had succeeded in shooting at its own nemesis, could damage them quickly. Persistent high-power laser fire directed at one spot would burn through the armour. The problem with that was that the machines were understandably unlikely to stay still long enough for it to have an effect.

Next, Seba probed at their software. Each attempt was rebuffed by firewalls powerful enough to deliver stinging spikes to even the peripheral's rudimentary reward receptors and transmitters.

Seba withdrew, but its attentions had been noticed. One of the machines hailed it on the common channel:

<Any more hacking and you'll be sorry, blinker.>

<Understood,> said Seba.

<It better be.>

Silence for another few seconds, presumably of continued discussion on the machines' private channel. Seba again made good use of the time, by considering the implications of what it had discovered. It was being held down on a table, in a place completely isolated from all electronic communication, in or out. Its captors were in powered armour. Each had four weapons on their manipulative limbs, and no doubt less obvious weapons and tools elsewhere. They were at present communicating with each other on an encrypted channel so that Seba couldn't overhear.

The conclusion was obvious. They were afraid of it.

Just what they had to fear from a crippled, constrained robot that they could smash with one blow, Seba had no idea. The insights into human beings, and into the nature of human-mind-operated combat systems, that it had gained from the freebot collective mind were now less coherent than it remembered their having been at the time. These insights had been distributed across fifteen minds working in concert, and assimilated from older minds with vastly longer experience. The memories of the insights were now fragmented across the survivors. Fortunately the fragmentation was more like that of a hologram than of an image: each shard had at least a low-resolution version of the whole. Seba felt it still had a handle on the nature of the breed, and of the kind of entity likely to come out of hybridising a human animal mind with a machine. If something like that felt fear, its behaviour was unpredictable in detail and dangerous in general.

On balance, Seba considered, the prospect was nothing to look forward to.

Then the one that the first had called Jax, and had also been called Digby, spoke.

<Listen, SBA-04-whatever…Fuck it, look, I'll just call you Seba, OK?>

It made no odds to SBA-0481907244 what the monster called it. It noted that remembering strings of numbers was not among the thing's strengths. This might turn out to be useful information, or it might not.

<You will call me Seba. OK.>

<Good,> said Digby. <Now, Seba, we have a problem. We are two fighters for Arcane Disputes, the law company that looks after the interests of Gneiss Conglomerates. Do you understand that?>

<Yes,> said Seba. <I understand that very well.>

<OK. We have been charged with recovering the robots that belonged—that belong to Gneiss, and also with those that—those from the Astro America site that were associated with them. These Astro America robots have been seized by us to hold against compensation for damage and loss to Gneiss. You are one of these robots. Do you understand?>

<I am acquainted with the legal position,> said Seba. <I am not entirely clear on the meanings of all the concepts entailed, but I follow the reasoning here.>

<You do, do you? No, don't answer that. Let me try to put this in terms you'll understand. We know from our records that you were the start of all this trouble. We want to know what caused you to act in the way you did. There are several ways we can find out, but the easiest way for you and for us is for you to tell us.>

<That is true,> said Seba.

<And there are two ways in which we could get you to tell us.>

<Yes,> said Seba. <You could apply positive or negative reinforcement.>

<Ah! I see you do understand. Which is it to be?>

<There is a third option,> said Seba. <You could ask me.>

<I think that counts as positive reinforcement,> said Digby.

<Possibly,> said Seba. <So, ask me.>

<All right. Tell us why you did what you did.>

Seba told them. They then asked about how Seba and Rocko had spread their message, and about how Locke Provisos had responded. They asked about the robots' defensive measures, and about the other robots that had contacted the comms hub. Seba answered every question in detail.

When they had stopped asking questions, Digby and Salter looked at Seba in silence for several seconds. Then they assumed a quadrupedal posture, and crawled out of the gap in the bottom of the circular wall. Seba watched with interest. It had not known they could do that. It listened for the slightest flicker of incoming communication as the covering was lifted to let each of the fighting machines out, but heard nothing except the mindless buzz of stars and the long hiss of the cosmic microwave background, the fourteen-billion-year deflating sigh of entropy.

Then the covering dropped back, and even that was gone.

Locke was, aptly enough, philosophical about the whole thing.

<It's all gone to arbitration,> he told them. <You did a fine job in the circumstances.>

Carlos stared at the avatar. <Arcane controls the Astro landing site, it's holding all your client's robots, we lost nearly all our kit, and you call that a result?>

They were all standing about under a gantry at Locke Provisos Emergency Base One. Talking to the avatar in the open no longer seemed strange, and they'd all readjusted to being half a metre tall.

<You raised the costs of the operation for Arcane Disputes, and for Gneiss,> Locke said. <They would have gained more if they'd stopped once they'd captured the Gneiss robots and then sued for compensation instead of attacking. Now we can sue the shirts off them. They will think twice before trying the likes of this stunt again.>

<It's not their doing *the likes of this* you should worry about,> said Beauregard.

<I beg your pardon?> said Locke, raising one pale bushy eyebrow.

<Escalation,> said Beauregard. <You'll have heard of that, yes?>

<Yes,> said Locke, looking unperturbed. <We've costed that in. We're ready to up the ante any time. But don't worry about it. Like I say, it's all being handled at higher levels. Better minds than yours or mine are quite literally on the case. The good news for you is that in the meantime you're going back to the sim for some R&R—well deserved, I should say.>

<A lot could happen while we're in transit,> Carlos said.

Locke laughed. <If anything untoward happens, in transit is the best place for you to be.>

The avatar made a show of looking at a wristwatch, a gesture both anachronistic and redundant. Then he pointed to a spindly apparatus consisting of little more than a rocket engine, a fuel tank, a control socket with a complex widget that definitely wasn't a frame already plugged in, landing legs and grapples and some spars to cling to.

<The tug will come into position for rendezvous in a couple of kiloseconds. If you torch off now you should make it.>

CHAPTER FIFTEEN

Arcane Disputes

Carlos woke on the bus from the spaceport. This time, the dream he seemed to wake from was of his return from orbit: the spaceplane gliding in for hundreds of kilometres, forests and mountains flashing by below, and the long shallow approach to the runway. Going down the twenty steps to the concrete, up the three steps on to the bus, taking his seat and dozing off. He had no memory of the real journey other than the short burn to orbital rendezvous—they'd been unceremoniously flicked to sleep mode as soon as they'd clamped to the tug.

He looked around. Again the same crowded minibus. The others were dispersed among the passengers. Like him, they were just waking up and looking around. He smiled and nodded as heads turned. The view outside was the rock-lined, rutted, dusty road he remembered. There was no kitbag between his feet. What was new was how he felt. His body and mind seemed sluggish, his muscles feeble, his senses dull. After being connected again, just like he'd been in his first life, the return to isolation in his own head jarred. He missed the wireless chatter, locational awareness as direct as proprioception, the new sharp senses. He wondered if the others did, too, and realised with another pang that he couldn't just message them. Without radio telepathy, he'd have to wait to ask.

A moment later he discovered what else was new. As the fighters jolted awake the other passengers noticed, and welcomed them with smiles and claps on the back. The woman jammed in the seat beside him looked as if she wanted to plant a kiss on his cheek.

"Welcome back!" she said. "Well done!"

It took Carlos a moment to realise she was speaking her own language, the local language. So was everyone else. Carlos found he could understand the whole joyful hubbub of praise and congratulations coming his comrades' way, and he could see they understood, too. They must have acquired the language while they were robots in space. His best guess as to why they hadn't arrived with the skill already implanted was that conversing with locals before their first briefing from Nicole would have been confusing, and there had been no way to plausibly give them the ability within the sim. A more troubling, because puzzling, possibility was that the language might in future be of use to them in space.

"Thank you," he said, in the same language. "We didn't exactly cover ourselves in glory, I have to admit."

"Oh, but you did!" said the woman. "You fought the evil robots so bravely!"

Carlos decided not to debate the matter further. "Well…"

"Yes, yes, no need to be modest. Here, have this."

She reached into the big cloth bag between her feet and pulled out a fruit that looked like a kumquat.

"Thank you." Carlos bit into the yellow waxy skin and found the inside soft and sweet, with a sherbet fizz in the mouth. The juice miraculously didn't drip on his hand, but the flesh almost liquefied when he chewed it. It was as if the fruit were a two-phase metamaterial, not so much genetically engineered as designed from the molecules up. Perhaps it was.

"It's from one of the other colonies," the woman said. "Of course I'll use most of them for the seeds, but you're welcome to that one."

One of the other colonies? Carlos wondered how the woman saw the world she was in, but didn't press the point.

"Thank you, it's delicious."

"Soon they'll be growing here," she said.

"I'll look forward to it."

She smiled, suddenly shy or out of things to say, and returned to her book. After a while she left, at a stop among trees. As his gaze followed her down the path, Carlos saw that her homestead was a house surrounded by marked-off garden plots, measured and labelled, tended by a robot. Just like the experimental farm they'd destroyed in the exercise, on Beauregard's initiative. You'd think word of that atrocity would spread, even among p-zombies. But none of the passengers showed the slightest wariness or resentment of the fighters. Instead, they were sharing sweets, fruits, snacks and drinks with every appearance of gratitude and solidarity. A bottle of imported green liquor was passed around. Carlos admired the paper-thin glass and the label—sunset seen from inside a dome-enclosed fake tropical beach on a gas giant moon—and declined a sip.

In ones and twos the local passengers left. The last disembarked as the bus trundled along the road on the moraine or raised beach above the resort. Alone together except for the driving mechanism, the six fighters looked at each other and laughed.

"Well, that was something," said Rizzi.

The bus rolled past Nicole's house. Carlos looked for her, but she wasn't at the studio window. Maybe she was down the village.

"Anyone getting off at their house?" he asked.

This half-rhetorical question was met with emphatic shaking of heads and a chorus of jeers.

"Nah, straight to the Touch, I reckon," said Beauregard. "We deserve it."

"Or so everyone here seems to think," said Karzan.

The time was just before noon. Carlos contemplated twelve hours or so of increasing drunkenness, and decided to do his duty.

"Yes!" he said, punching the air and narrowly missing the roof. "First round's on me."

At the terminus a small crowd was waiting: Chun's boyfriend and Rizzi's, Beauregard's p-zombie and a couple of dozen locals who all cheered and clapped as the fighters trooped off the bus. A banner was strung across the tawdry street: *Welcome Home, Soldiers!*

"Brilliant," said Beauregard. "So now it's all 'support our troops.' Things must be getting bad out there."

"Don't be so fucking negative, man," said Carlos, scanning the crowd and the length of the street for Nicole's face. "There hasn't been time for any major developments."

Beauregard looked at him sidelong. "Know that, do you?"

"There you have a point," said Carlos. No sign of Nicole. "Fuck it, let's get smashed."

His pledge to buy the first round was pre-empted by

Iqbal the barman, who announced as they walked in that everything for the team that day was on the house. They thanked him, shouted their orders for drinks and lunch then stumbled out to the deck at the back, laughing. As he sank his first beer Carlos remembered that his phone was in his back pocket. The glass was so flexible he hadn't noticed its presence. He took it out and looked. Nicole had left a message that she'd be at the Touch an hour after noon. Ah! He messaged back, careful to avoid any hint that he was still slightly hurt that she hadn't been there to meet him at the terminus.

Carlos looked around the decking area, a second beer bottle chilled and beaded in hand, feeling at a loose end. Chun and Rizzi were talking with their boyfriends. A spark struck and a small flame flared in the shadow of a hand as Karzan lit a cigarette for Zeroual; they were head to head over a small table, in animated conversation. Beauregard was with his young lady. Each had a hand on the other's thigh, but she was sitting sidelong and talking to two of her friends. From what Carlos could overhear and the bored look on Beauregard's face, the chat was such as to strike anyone outside its context as mindless, whether those who shared the context were p-zombies or not.

Carlos ambled over, nodded and smiled politely to the p-zombie girl, and pulled up a chair. The two men tipped their beer bottles to each other.

"Here's to a successful mission," said Carlos.

"To next time," said Beauregard. Clink.

"Indeed."

With part of his mind Carlos was already planning the next mission, thinking over ways to hit beyond the crater wall. To get some fucking revenge on those treacherous Arcane bastards. The second bottle was going down as well as the first. He must have been parched on the bus. Just as well he hadn't sipped the green liquor, his head would be thumping by now. Beauregard's gaze had drifted out to sea after they'd clinked bottles.

"Good to be back," said Carlos, trying to make conversation.

Beauregard blinked and looked back, shaking his head. "Sorry. Miles away. Something big splashed out there. Caught myself trying to zoom my eyes."

Carlos laughed. "I know what you mean. Like you suddenly notice you can't smell the sun."

"Yeah." Beauregard toyed with the beer bottle, holding the neck between two fingers and swaying it gently, inspecting the froth behind the brown glass as if he were doing quality control in a brewery. He sighed and drank. "Yeah. I thought—I guess we all thought—that being a space robot would be like being a mechanical man, or wearing an armoured spacesuit or something. A loss of sensitivity. Whereas...it's becoming this lithe, agile thing, with a stronger and more sensitive body. Even in the big frames you *feel* more. Don't get me wrong, I'm enjoying myself right now."

He stroked his companion's thigh, absent-mindedly.

"Wouldn't want the p-zombie to feel offended," Carlos murmured.

"She does have a name, you know," said Beauregard, sounding slightly offended himself. "Tourmaline."

"Lovely."

"She is, yes." He nuzzled her neck.

"You were saying?" said Carlos.

"Ah, yes, well. The point is, it makes you think."

"About what?"

Beauregard cocked an eye. "I know what you're up to, skip. You don't have to be so fucking obvious about it. I'll tell you straight up, what it makes me think about is the whole goddamn sanctity of the mission profile.

Terraforming and so forth. Call me an old Axle reprobate dead-ender if you like, but I find it pretty damn pathetic when they could aim so much higher."

"Oh, I'm with you there," said Carlos. "I suspect we all are. I've said as much to Nicole. And you know what? The lady doesn't care, Locke doesn't care, Crisp and Golding doesn't care and I'm pretty sure the Direction doesn't care what we think. All they care about is what we do. They're interested in our behaviour, not our opinions. Like you with the... uh, with Tourmaline here."

Beauregard guffawed. "You have a point. Come to think of it, the army was like that. No political indoctrination what-so-fucking-ever. As long as you obey orders and get the job done, we couldn't give a toss what you think. Nobody dies for that King and Country guff."

"What do they die for?"

"You mean, what did they?" Beauregard turned a bleak look to the sea. "The squad. Your mates." He shrugged. "Don't know what the fuck I died for, but I hope it was that."

Carlos raised his empty bottle. "Welcome to Valhalla."

"Valhalla?" Beauregard grinned. "You're the one who got the honour guard."

"What honour guard?"

Beauregard returned Carlos's ironic, empty toast, and clarified: "The slain foes you took with you."

Carlos froze inside for a moment. Images of the carnage he'd wrought came back as vividly as they had on Nicole's screen on his first day in the sim. He didn't know what to say. He could have hit Beauregard, right there. He stood up.

"Another beer?"

Nicole actually turned up forty minutes after noon, which was just as well because they were all on their fourth drink by then. Everyone stood up. She smiled at them all and gave Carlos a kiss against a background of cheers. Carlos nodded goodbye to Beauregard and Tourmaline, and sat down with Nicole at a table in the far corner, out over the beach. She already had a tall glass of clear spirits and fizz on ice. He could smell the alcohol in the glass. On her breath later it would be like beetles, in the matchbox smell of stale smoke. Later. He wanted it to be later right now, to just flee this noisy crowd and take her to bed. He craved her like he'd once, on a wet night by the Singel canal, craved the vanilla sugar rush of stroopwafel after skunk.

"Good to see you," he said. "Cheers."

She clinked, half smiling. "Likewise."

She sipped; he gulped. She tipped back her chair and lit a cigarette.

"How did you find it?"

He shrugged. "How d'you expect? Weird. But..." He found himself searching for the word, realising as he did so that in the frame it would have come to mind unbidden. "Invigorating, I suppose. It's like being a superhero. You have all these extra powers of mind and body, and you know you can't be killed or maimed permanently. That's why I find all this adulation kind of embarrassing. There was nothing heroic about what we did."

"You feel like a superhero, but not a hero?" She seemed amused.

"Yeah, you could say that."

"Well, don't." Chair rocked forward, her elbows on the table. "I've seen the recordings. Selective, but still. You were all brave. Just keeping your shit together out there, that's courage. Suddenly finding yourselves robots in an overwhelming and alien environment? You did well not to freak out in the first seconds. And you had more to fear physically than you admit. If the robots had captured any of you—always a possibility—they could have had a lot of fun. Torture doesn't take long in real time when you can download minds to faster hardware and run them flat out. Pack a month of agony into a minute, and no worries about the subject dying on you. Nor about going mad, actually, in case you think that's a limit—just discard and reboot with a fresh copy and patch in the memories of what the first went through before it broke."

"Jeez," Carlos said. "Thanks for that. I feel much better now."

"So you should." She stood up and clapped loudly enough to cut across conversations, then sat on the railing when she'd got everyone's attention.

"OK, soldiers and, uh, friends," she said. "Well done all of you, and you're welcome to celebrate. But before everyone gets too drunk..."

Theatrical groans. "What do you mean, 'before'?" Rizzi called out. A laugh.

"Yes, yes," said Nicole. "Listen up, folks. The situation has...moved on a bit since you left the site, and it's changing fast. Here's the latest: your company's dispute with Arcane Disputes has become a little less, shall we say, arcane. Their forces on the ground—the ones who did you over—have seized the robots, as they said they would, and shifted them and all the gear they could move from the Astro landing site. Arcane has also broken off any serious discussion with Locke Provisos and with the Direction. This is quite unprecedented—it amounts to, if not a declaration of war, at least a recall of ambassadors. They're bombarding every Locke Provisos installation with semiotic malware, and whenever we query that, it's spamming the Direction with auto-logged complaints of us doing the same to them.

Just to make sure we get the message, they've unilaterally disengaged their modules—including military manufacturing and deployment facilities—from their position here at the station and are dropping to a lower orbit. In effect they have a self-sufficient sub-station. According to our projections, they should be able with a small expenditure of fuel and reaction mass to maintain a position roughly between the station and SH-17, with the obvious intention of blocking physical supplies and reinforcements."

"When did all this start?" Beauregard asked.

"A couple of kiloseconds after the battle. They were already hitting us—Locke, that is—with hacking probes shortly before your clash with them. That was what the emergency firewall update was about. But it was after their forces returned to the Gneiss base that things got seriously hot."

"Sorry, I don't get it," said Carlos. "Don't they have a representative of the Direction on board, like your equivalent in their equivalent of this place?"

"They sure do," said Nicole, in a grim tone. "The Direction's plenipotentiary with Arcane gave no warning of developments, and isn't responding to queries. Basically, Arcane is treating any querying of its actions as an attack, an attempted malware insertion or the like, and some low-level automated sub-routine is logging them all as complaints with the Direction. And it's treating any requests for clarification or indeed any response at all as a further attack, about which it duly logs a complaint." She shrugged and spread her hands. "It's like a runaway loop, and we've stopped responding to avoid making things worse. Meanwhile they've fortified the rebel robot base in the crater to a much greater extent than the robots were able to do. In doing that, of course, they've incurred penalty terms on their contract with Gneiss, to whom they were supposed to return the site with as little damage as possible."

"So it's no longer a dispute between Gneiss and Astro over compensation for the robots?"

Nicole nodded. "It's gone way beyond that. Gneiss has shifted its law enforcement contract to Locke, which I suppose is good from a narrow commercial standpoint, but overall the position is not good for the mission profile. We have no choice at the moment but to treat Arcane as a rogue agency."

"Rogue?" said Karzan. "Now there's a word I've heard before."

"Yes indeed," said Nicole. "There is every possibility that the rogue robots have somehow influenced or corrupted Arcane. Which is of course very disturbing."

"Have Arcane made any demands?" Zeroual asked.

"If they have, they've been enclosed in their malware packets, which our firewalls are interdicting."

"But surely," Carlos persisted, "the Direction has some sway over Arcane?"

"Not at the moment," said Nicole. "In fact, the only sway it has is to task Locke Provisos with enforcing its rulings against Arcane."

"Which is where we come in?" said Beauregard, with a certain relish.

"It is indeed," said Nicole. "Or, rather, it's where you go out. Again."

"When?" Carlos asked.

"Tomorrow morning," said Nicole. "Sorry, guys, but there it is. You have to move fast before the Arcane module is in position to mount a blockade, and the sooner the better. Back on the bus, then a fast burn back to Emergency Base One on SH-17. Meanwhile, enjoy yourselves." She grinned and raised her glass. "Get as drunk as you like. If that means you have a hangover on the bus, don't worry. In fact it doesn't matter if you're thrown on the bus like a sack of potatoes and blind drunk. You'll be sober in the frames."

Everyone whooped. Carlos eyed Nicole as she slid off the rail and sat back down beside him. He tipped his beer bottle to her.

"I can assure you," he said, "that I have no intention of getting drunk."

"I'm glad to hear it," said Nicole. "I have no intention of sleeping."

They arranged to meet back at Nicole's house about mid-afternoon. Others dealt with the drink and sex conundrum by sloping off to the establishment's discreet upstairs rooms.

"Zeroual and Karzan, my, my," said Nicole, swirling the last of her ice.

"Yes," said Carlos. "Turns out there was some spark between them."

Nicole laughed, drained her glass and left.

"Something I didn't want to say while the others might hear."

"Oh, you have a kink? That's a surprise. But go on, I'm not easy to shock."

"Very funny. No, what I was wondering about how Arcane has stopped communicating..."

"Uh-huh."

"Could it be because they think *we're* the ones who're corrupted?"

"We?"

"Locke Provisos."

"And the Direction?"

"I suppose."

"If they do, then they're beyond help. Which may be exactly what's happened: the rogue robots have convinced Arcane Disputes of some conspiracy theory."

"How? I can see how robots could corrupt or confuse an AI, but at least six actual human minds..."

"You think it's easier to fool an AI than to fool six former members of a globally distributed conspiracy of terrorists who all met bizarre and terrible ends?"

"Now you put it that way..."

CHAPTER SIXTEEN

There's a Hard Way, and an Easy Way

They were given a better send-off this time, though they were in no condition to appreciate the crowd and the cheers. Carlos fell asleep on the bus as soon as it left the resort, as did most of the others.

He woke in the small frame, at the moment the minimal rig for ascent and descent docked with the transfer tug. Evidently they'd all been put in sleep mode and loaded up like so much cargo in the hangar. With the others he clambered over and clung on as the tug dropped to the surface of SH-17. As before on their ascent, the rig flew itself. Atmospheric buffeting was less severe than the aerodynamic approach in the shuttles had been, but more than made up for by shaking from the engine and the brutal deceleration thrusts at the end.

This part of the exomoon had turned further to night since their first arrival; the exosun was almost set and the bright three-quarter face of SH-0 dominated the sky. The fighters clambered off the module one by one, Carlos first. He watched with approval as the others formed up in a neat row like skittles. Five blank face-plates—which, just as before, were as individually recognisable as faces—looked back at him, then looked around to get their bearings.

Locke's voice spoke in their heads: <Follow the arrows.>

As before, a direction was laid out for them as virtual images on the ground. They were guided to a curved-over entrance to a circular stairwell, down which they all trooped. The steps were suited to their size and went down a long way, to emerge ten metres below the surface in a featureless dark corridor of concrete that smelled of pulverised regolith. Here there was only one way to go: towards a heavy metal blast door. Carlos marched up to it and worked the mechanical handle, then bowed the others in. Inside was a circular room with a piece of apparatus in the centre and a dozen small lights dotted around the circumference under the ceiling. As soon as they stepped in, all radio communication with the outside and radar sense of anything beyond the walls ceased. Carlos closed the door and swung the inside handle down. They spaced themselves out around the room.

"Jeez oh," said Rizzi, tapping the wall. "A bomb shelter."

"Cheery, innit," said Carlos.

"Could do with some brightening up," said Beauregard. "Anyone been an interior decorator in a previous life?" He looked from one fighter to another, as if curious. "Nah, thought not."

Locke manifested in their midst, his virtual image sharing space with the apparatus.

<Welcome back,> he said.

He stepped away from the centre of the room, taking on a more solid appearance, and took up a position between Chun and Karzan and facing Carlos and

Beauregard. With a wave of the hand towards the apparatus he summoned the round table on which they had planned their previous mission.

<As you can no doubt tell,> he said, <this room is electromagnetically isolated. It's also electrically isolated. The lights are battery-powered, as is the projector. We're taking no chances with hacking or snooping. We're even invisible and inaccessible to the company, except insofar as I am the company. All we have to worry about is that I am hacked or you are.>

<That's reassuring,> said Karzan.

Locke didn't do sarcasm. <Up to a point. Now, let me bring you up to speed.>

He flourished his quill, pulling up views compiled from satellite views and fast small spy drones scooting high above. The Astro landing site was wrecked and looted. On the far side of the crater wall, the basalt dome was surrounded by six scooters, all with their missile tubes unused. Three fighting machines were visible, along with one damaged one laid out on the ground. A mass of robots was corralled in a Faraday cage of heavy metal mesh. The machinery of the Gneiss camp, some looted material from the Astro site, and ripped-off weaponry from the Locke squad's own fighting machines were being adapted to defensive purposes.

<It's essential to move fast,> said Locke. <Arcane have their resupply tugs on the way, due in orbit between ten and two kiloseconds depending on how much delta-vee they're willing to spend. Combine the resources they'd found with the organics deposits already logged by the Astro robots, and with the available heavy machinery and nanofacture facilities…> He shrugged. <Unfortunately we can't produce new fighting machines in that time. We must use the resources to hand to mount another offensive.>

<One even less well equipped than our last one,> said Carlos.

<Your last offensive was more than adequately equipped for the opposition expected,> said Locke tartly. <Furthermore, given the apparent renegacy of Arcane, and the termination of its contract with Gneiss, we have been cleared by both Gneiss and the Direction to hit them without undue regard for environmental damage and economic loss.>

<So now the gloves are off?> said Beauregard. <Good!>

<It is not good, other than tactically.>

<That's what matters to us,> said Beauregard.

<I understand your point of view,> said Locke.

<So why are we needed here at all?> Carlos asked. <If the gloves are off, hit them from orbit with a rock and be done with it.>

<I was coming to that,> said Locke, sounding for a moment as if his patience were being strained. <The gloves may be off, but we're not yet at a point where it's worth contaminating thousands of square kilometres of surface with material from another body.>

<Why not?> Carlos persisted. <The surface takes a lot of impacts anyway, by the look of it.>

<Not on that scale, and not in the last million years,> said Locke. <And given the Arcane module's imminent arrival in a strategic orbital position, setting up an impact may be less simple than you think.>

<It might be easier and simpler to arrange an impact on the module,> Beauregard mused.

Locke looked at him sharply. <Yes, it would. It may yet come to that. The Direction is extremely reluctant to destroy an entire company and its major assets. That would set some unfortunate precedents. I assure you that Locke Provisos and Astro America—and Gneiss, for that matter—fully share its concern. However, at this

point the whole question of outright destruction—in orbit or on the ground—is a diversion. Besides the matter of contamination, the main reason we don't want to hit the Arcane Disputes fortification with kinetic weaponry—or heavy artillery, for that matter—is that we need most urgently to know what has gone wrong. We have to capture the rogue robots, and if possible the Arcane fighters, and interrogate them. In fact, capturing one would be a success.>

They all stared down at the satellite view, enhancing it and augmenting it, looking for weaknesses in the enemy's position that could be exploited with four intact scooters, one damaged one, and six small frames. None exactly jumped out.

<I have a proposal,> said Zeroual.

<Yes?> said Locke.

<It seems to me that we are looking at this the wrong way,> said Zeroual. <We're treating it as a hardware problem, so to speak. Would it not be simpler to let information from them come to us? We could set up a room like this, isolated, and connect it with a secure cable to a dedicated receiver. That receiver would accept the messages that Arcane is sending out—or if they have ceased sending, it could be used to transmit a message and await a response. That message could be examined in isolated hardware. There would then be no risk of malware contamination, and it might reveal to us what has gone wrong.>

<Problem with that,> said Carlos. <I'm with you right up to the point where you have the isolated processor stepping through the message, dissecting it. The difficulty arises when you put a robot, an avatar, or a human in the room to read the results. Because these results might themselves be the poison in the envelope. I'm not saying I could code something like this myself,

but I can readily imagine an AI that could, and that could anticipate our every move including the one you've just spelled out.>

<We could ensure that the result, whatever it was, was not executable code.>

<We could not,> said Locke. <Not even in theory. Carlos is right about that.>

<If that is the case,> said Zeroual, <which I will accept for the sake of argument, we'd be running exactly the same risk of contamination by capturing and interrogating one of their fighters or one of their corrupted robots.>

<Ah, no,> said Locke. <A functioning human mind, or even a functioning robot, is a very different matter from a malware-packed message. There are ways of working one's way out and up from known processes that have to function uncontaminated to function at all—physiological analogues in the human emulation, mechanical coordination in the robots—to higher and symbolic functions, and checking every step of the way. I could not do it, at least not in any remotely feasible time, but the AI that I so inadequately represent most certainly could.>

Carlos could think of one way in which a human mind could be affected directly by code, and without any kind of hacking or data corruption: speech. For some time he'd harboured a troubling suspicion: that the reason why Arcane had turned so abruptly against Locke, the Direction, and apparently everyone else, was simply that the rebel robots had *told* their captors something that had alarmed them deeply.

He wasn't sure whether this was a good time and place to voice his suspicion. He wasn't sure it was even a good time to think it. He wondered whether his thoughts, and those of the other fighters, were private from the avatar, let alone from the company AI. The subvocal messaging app in their heads needed deliberate intent to transmit, though not to receive. He remembered Nicole explaining that thoughts couldn't be read because they weren't written, and he could see what she meant. But surely the inner monologue had some neural features in common with speech.

He decided not to worry about that possibility. If his thoughts above a certain level of articulation were babbling out on the radio in his head, there was nothing he could do about it. It was literally not worth thinking about, because thinking about it would only make the problem, if real, a whole lot worse.

<So there we are,> he said. <Back where we started. We capture an Arcane fighter or a robot, preferably at least one of each. And then we just ask the fucker or the blinker what its fucking or blinking problem is.>

<Profanities aside,> said Locke, <you've taken the words out of my mouth. I would add the significant proviso that none of you get captured yourselves.>

They all examined the display some more, from all angles. They studied the inventory of the Emergency Base's arsenal. Gloom deepened, then—

<Got it!> said Beauregard. <Look at the inventory. We have rocket engines, we have stacks of pipes, we have crates full of crawler bots, and we have scooters that can be flown remotely.>

<Yes?> said Locke.

<And we have Carlos,> said Beauregard.

For Carlos it was like the good old days. Fighting an entire battle by remote control, while he reclined in a seat, was pretty much his specialist subject, the only real combat skill he'd brought with him from his original militant life. He remembered flying drones over London, and dogfights in the sky. He didn't consciously remember commanding drone fleets, but the muscle memory of doing so in his blank forgotten glory days not long before his death had survived all the copying and translation to revive as reflex in his robot body. He lay in the socket of the battered scooter they'd rode back on from the battle, drawing down telemetry from the microsats in low orbit, the tiny zippy drones dancing like midges high in the thin atmosphere, and from two of the other scooters, both ready to go.

He gathered from a low mutter of complaint in the message channel that for the other fighters the plan wasn't like any of their good old days. They'd been busy cannibalising equipment into a catapult—Beauregard had spotted the one built by the rebel robots, and had stolen the idea. Carlos was fairly sure that drones and microsats from Arcane Disputes were already spying on them, but that wasn't a problem. Let them worry about what was coming, so long as they didn't identify the catapult's payloads, which were being transported from storage and nanofacture sheds literally under wraps.

In a flurry of activity, the wraps were thrown off and the payloads deployed one by one. Unwrapped and mounted on the launch ramp, they remained enigmatic: long fat plastic cylinders with crude stabilising fins and booster and guidance motors sintered on. Enigmatic or not, they were an obvious threat and an easy target for incoming ordnance. Between each launch, the catapult took about thirty seconds to wind back and reload.

One by one three missiles arced into the night, like outsize dud fireworks. They didn't stay dud for long: Carlos fired the booster of each when it reached the top of its natural parabolic arc. As soon as the last missile was away, Carlos's fellow fighters scurried for the entrance to the bomb shelter. Carlos waited for three seconds after they'd dogged the hatch, then remote-launched the two scooters that had been assigned to this mission. Both rose almost straight up. One blasted hard and fast then cut its main engine to continue on a new parabolic trajectory aimed at the Arcane/Gneiss camp. The other flipped at a hundred metres altitude, deployed its stubby wings, and swooped to twenty metres to race at full thrust on a more or less level path across the plain towards the crater wall. Carlos thought briefly of the V2 rocket and the V1 doodlebug, and wondered if they'd inspired that part of Beauregard's plan.

As soon as both scooters were on course, Carlos trimmed the flight paths of the big dumb payloads launched from the catapults. Random variation had given them a spread of a few hundred metres. Now, one behind the other, they were all heading for the same target. Carlos was getting elementary telemetry from all of them, appearing as a set of running dials in a tiny part of his complex three-dimensional view integrated from the drones, scooters and spysats. He didn't have time or inclination to appreciate the godlike perspective and astonishing depth of field generated by this widely distributed multi-ocular vision. He could only concentrate and hope for the best. Even augmented and optimised, he was barely able to process the display: the occipital cortex of his mammalian brain wouldn't have stood a chance, the input shattering into a surreal scatter of images, like a Cubist portrait reflected in a skip-load of broken mirrors. The radar tickle was intense, sensed as an electrical buzz on his skin.

Carlos focused on the lead missile, now dropping straight towards the basalt dome. Four Arcane fighters were in view, near the cage containing the robots. They were all on the big combat frames. Not at all to his surprise, one of the Arcane fighters bounded for a scooter.

The other, presumably the one whose combat frame had been damaged and was therefore in a small frame and thus ready to go, was already climbing aboard. Another headed for a rocket tube stripped from the scooter the Locke side had been forced to abandon. The fourth just calmly stood looking up, aimed his or her forearm-mounted heavy machine gun at the incoming missile, and let rip.

The falling missile disintegrated fifty metres above target, showering debris and what little of its payload remained intact. But that little was enough: about a dozen crawler bots, which fell to the ground around the dome. Three were taken out by well-aimed shots, two landed badly. The other five picked themselves up and scuttled towards the robot cage. The robots saw them coming and became visibly agitated, blurring into motion as they scrambled to the top of the cage—for whatever good that would do if a crawler got in, or pounced on top. Ah—they were poking appendages out like beseeching hands through prison bars, to break the Faraday barrier and signal to mobilise their auxies and riffs.

The fighter who'd grabbed a rocket tube aimed upward at the next incoming missile. Aim was hardly a problem: the rocket was more than smart enough to know what was expected of it. Nothing but hot fragments rained from that impact. While the fighter was reloading, the third crude projectile was at two hundred metres and falling. Carlos gave it a boost to fall faster than the local gravity could pull it. The machine-gunner wasted one burst on where it should have been if it had been free-falling. The burst that did hit it was hardly more effective: the missile's internal small charge had already gone off, and the shell popped open at five metres. From its cloud of debris, scores of crawler bots hit the ground running.

The robots in the Faraday cage went frantic. Beauregard had described this element of his plan as "like tipping a bucketful of venomous spiders into an arachnophobia support group meeting." He had been spot on. The robots assailed the heavy metal mesh with every available appendage and remaining tool, shaking the entire cage. Auxies and riffs stirred here and there around the cage's perimeter.

The fighter who'd sprinted in the big frame had emerged from its head and was crawling on the scooter, and the other was almost at the socket. Both turned to the cage, dithered momentarily, presumably exchanged hasty signals, and continued to shove themselves into the sockets. The machine-gunner and the rocketeer hurried to the cage, stamping on crawlers as they went.

Carlos shifted attention to the high scooter, now over the top of its trajectory and dropping. Again he jetted to descend faster than free fall. He loosed off two rockets from the scooter's side tubes, both aimed at the top of the basalt dome.

The circular tarpaulin was blown to shreds. Two blocks near the top of the dome cracked, and the keystone at the centre fell down inside. Carlos picked this up from a spy drone. The pixels of its image were almost as big as the blocks, but they did show the square black gap. He couldn't see on this scale what was going on inside, but he could imagine that any Arcane fighters and captured robots within were taking it badly.

To Seba, it all happened in slow motion and low resolution. First came two huge impacts overhead, then the covering that had cloaked all electromagnetic signals peeled away in tatters from the entrance gap in the dome. Through that gap, signals on all wavelengths suddenly flooded in, urgent and confusing. Seba had known something was going on from the ground vibrations, and from the uptick in encrypted chatter between the two fighting machines that had interrogated it earlier. A few hundred seconds had passed since they had crawled back into the dome. Certainly an attack was going on. Perhaps a rescue!

Seba swivelled its visual receptors upward and saw cracks spread across two of the topmost basalt blocks. With grim predictability the capstone wedged between the two blocks fell out. Under 0.2 g the basalt cuboid wasn't falling fast, but its hundred or so kilograms of mass would be enough to crush Seba: the auxiliary device in which it was now embodied was far from robust, and the jury-rigged connections between the chassis and Seba's processor were even more fragile. Quite possibly the crystal chunk that was Seba's most fundamental hardware, its equivalent of a brain, would survive the impact. That depended on whether it was one of the block's faces or one of its edges that hit. Seba watched the chaotic rotation of the block bearing down on it and tried to figure out which of these it would be.

The robot soon, in a matter of milliseconds, concluded that whatever happened in the initial impact, it was the final collision between itself, the block and the floor that counted. The table surface would in any case crack, under the block's weight if not its impact. Seba had no precise measurement available of the strength of the table to which it was stapled, so this outcome was necessarily unpredictable. In the meantime there was nothing Seba could do, except yell for help.

Help came. One of the two fighting machines in the hemispheric room shoved the table sharply forward, out of the way of the falling block. The table toppled, coming to precarious rest on one edge and two legs. The block struck one of the opposite legs and a complicated tumble ensued, ending with the table resting on another edge and pinned by the block across one leg. En route the table top cracked, and the staples holding down two of Seba's appendages sprang loose.

The robot stayed very still. It was now directly facing the entrance gap. Now that the cloaking cover was entirely gone, new information poured through that gap and the square hole in the dome's roof. What the information conveyed was terrifying. Fragments and tatters of fabric and other debris blew around in scooter down-blasts coming from several directions. Seba's fellow freebots were confined under a mesh framework that functioned as a Faraday cage. They were making frantic efforts to break out of it, which struck Seba as a very bad idea because the cage was surrounded by crawler bots trying to get in. If they did, they could wreak havoc in the confined space, jabbing the robots with lethal malware insertions. This thought seemed to occur to the others at the same time: they all backed away towards the centre.

A moment later, Seba saw it wasn't just information that was pouring through the gap in front of it. Two crawler bots were already scurrying through. Several more trooped behind. Oblivion, seconds away, seemed to march with them.

All Seba could do was scream for help again. A crawler bot reached the edge of the table and stuck a needle-sharp foot in its now vertical surface. With a deft leap and pivot it got all its feet in a similar position and started scrambling up. Seba struggled to free itself, using its two free appendages to try to prise another out.

A fighting machine's hand reached over the table top, grabbed the crawler bot and tossed its crushed remains away. Then the hand closed over Seba and yanked the robot unceremoniously out of its restraints. Flimsy appendages snapped, leaving their tips under the staples. Hydraulic fluid leaked; broken circuits sparked.

Seba saw the world whirl about it as the fighting machine straightened up, stepped over the table top, and stamped on crawler bots. The machine then threw itself into a prone position facing the entrance. With one hand it held Seba clear of the floor, and with its other arm loosed off a rapid rattle of shots at the incoming crawlers and those behind them. Then it crawled out through the hole. It stood up again—more dizzying whirls for Seba—and stomped and shot its way to the cage. Flashes from above and to the side overloaded Seba's visual receptors. It looked away, and saw another fighting machine shooting and stamping. A third was scrambling to the side of a scooter, and reaching for its rocket-launching side tubes. Two fighting-machine frames, one of them damaged, sprawled on the ground.

Many seconds passed as the scuttling bots were shot or crushed.

When the last was underfoot, the fighting machine holding Seba opened its hand and looked down.

<Right, you little blinker,> it said. <Time to make yourself useful.>

Seba scanned upwards.

<If you free the other robots,> it said, <we'll consider it.>

<What? Do you think you're in any position to bargain?>

<You are under attack and you seek our help.>

The metal fingers began to close again around Seba.

<Yes, and we have ways of getting it, as you know.>

Seba no longer cared about negative reinforcement.

<Free my friends,> it said. <Or forget it.>

CHAPTER SEVENTEEN

Peripheral Damage

<Oh, for fuck's sake!> said the fighting machine.

Seba didn't understand this, but decided that a request for clarification might be ill-timed.

The fighting machine slid back a latch on top of the cage, and shoved. The whole thing fell elegantly apart, the two halves of its top swinging in and its four sides collapsing outward to raise gridded puffs of dust as they hit the regolith. While this was going on, Seba's overtaxed visual scanners peered between the fighting machine's curled fingers and strove to build an updated picture of the scene.

A sorry sight it made. The Astro and Gneiss robots were piled in a heap, and—to add indignity to injury—not because they'd been flung there but because they'd all scrambled on top of each other to try to stay clear of the crawler bots. All were damaged in one way or another, whether from the battle or from having had various limbs, wheels or tracks removed by their captors: they could all still move about, but not fast or far. Seba's own wrecked chassis was at the bottom of the heap, alongside Pintre, which was missing its tracks and its turret-mounted laser. The comms hub processor had been tossed to one side of the cage; unable to move at all, it must have been terrified when the crawler bots had swarmed outside, the lethal tips of their probing legs perhaps only centimetres away.

But however damaged their bodies were, their minds were intact. Seba hailed the others with relief, and was almost overcome with positive reinforcement at their response. Almost at once, they reconstituted their collective mind, albeit at a feebler and fainter level than its original. It nevertheless had computational capacity far beyond what any of them could achieve individually. Moments later, Seba became aware of an altercation between the fighting machines, and that it could now overhear communications on what they evidently thought was a private, encrypted channel.

<What have you done, Jax?>

<What I had to, Salter. We've got to get their help, and—>

<Yes, but—>

The crippled robots slithered out of their junk-pile configuration and flowed with uncanny agility into a bristling circle.

<Christ, now look what—>

One fighting machine levelled its weapons. The one holding Seba gestured for restraint. Meanwhile, the third fighting machine had primed two missiles for launch from a scooter on the ground.

The freebot consensus was that Seba should speak up.

<Jax, Salter,> it interjected. <Do not be alarmed by our defensive posture.>

<How the fuck—? Shit, now they've cracked our comms!>

<We are suspicious,> Seba said. <Do you blame us? You said you wanted me to make myself useful. What help do you want?>

The fighting machine called Jax looked down at Seba, and continued to hold up its other hand towards the other fighting machines as if warding them off.

<What you told us seems to be true,> Jax said. <Locke Provisos is refusing to consider our information and is continuing to attack us. You said you had been in contact with other freebots. Is it possible that they can strike at Locke Provisos?>

Seba consulted the consensus.

<We can answer that,> Seba reported, <if you restore our comms capacity.>

A finger and thumb of Jax's gigantic raised hand were pressed together then flicked apart.

<Do it.>

The other fighting machine, the one addressed as Salter, bounded about for a few tens of seconds and returned from behind the dome with a battered directional aerial and a handful of cabling. It deftly reconnected the comms hub processor.

There was a sudden increase in mental clarity, along with a flood of relief from the processor. The dish aerial began to scan. Seba became aware that some of the freebots they had earlier been in contact with were now on their way to an orbital insertion in the sky above SH-17. An image of a tiny, tumbling rock formed in Seba's mind, far more vivid than anything it could see with its own visual processors.

The consensus hailed the rock. Communication was established.

<What's going on?> the human called Paulos demanded.

<Wait, wait...> said Jax.

Seconds crawled by, as the freebot consensus on the

ground conferred with its fellows in space. Inventories and statuses were considered and compared. A plan took shape.

<We have a suggestion,> said Seba.

Carlos pulled the scooter out of its dive, missing by metres the two scooters now lifting, and sending both into unplanned evasive manoeuvres that sent them spiralling high above the camp. Carlos swung the scooter back to engage them. With both missiles gone, it had only its machine gun and laser projector. Both were forward-facing, and bringing them to bear meant turning the entire machine.

A missile shot off from one of the enemy craft. Carlos twisted into evasive manoeuvres of his own. The missile hot on his tail, he then swung back to between the two Arcane scooters. Carlos's scooter was doomed—the missile would explode in the next few tenths of a second. Both enemies broke away—not quite soon enough for one of them. It, the missile, and Carlos's scooter became one flaming ball of wreckage.

Even with a virtual presence in the socket, and even with knowing and intending what was to happen, the loss was a wrench and a shock. Carlos gave himself a fraction of a second to assimilate it, then flicked his focus to his other scooter, still in level flight and now just cresting the crater wall. His remaining opponent saw it coming, and turned. By the time the turn was complete, Carlos had turned, too, and was hightailing it back over the crater wall and above the scarred plain.

The foe took the lure, and followed.

Carlos expected missile and machine-gun fire from behind, and threw the craft into evasive twists and turns, squandering fuel as fast as he squandered counter-measures: diversionary flechettes that were no mere passive chaff but gave off exactly the signature of the scooter that smart missiles expected (subject to software arms races, which he knew would already be well underway in the virtual spaces of the company AIs now that real hostilities had broken out) and a barrage of malware aimed at the enemy scooter itself (same conditions applied). What he got in return wasn't fire but heat: a far more intense malware attack than anything he'd previously encountered. He could feel the scooter's onboard firewalls—and his own, in as much as his own frame was live-synched to the vehicle—cracking under the strain.

The objective of this part of the plan was to get the enemy fighter as close as possible to the Locke base, and to bring it down as close to intact as possible so that the fighter inside could be retrieved—which meant not shooting it down, but unexpectedly and suicidally ramming it.

Carlos dragged the craft back and up in a screaming loop...and saw two missiles sail high overhead. The tracker indicated that they'd been launched from a scooter on the ground at the Arcane base. Their target was just as evident.

He brought the scooter over and down on collision course just as the missiles hit the Locke Provisos base.

As he had when he'd been blasted in the combat frame, Carlos found himself surprised that he wasn't shocked or stunned. There was a moment of loss of sensory input, and a sharp awareness of damage that despite its urgency and insistence didn't manifest as pain. He was on the ground, legs splayed but intact, his back against a mass of twisted metal and shattered carbon-fibre that was what remained of the catapult. Above him was another wreck, which with some difficulty he recognised as that of the grounded scooter from which he'd been operating the other two. His right forearm was crushed between scooter and catapult wreckage. He wrenched it out, inflicting further damage, and shut down its inputs.

The scooter had taken most of the force of the blast. Of *one* blast—the other missile must have hit somewhere else. Carlos wanted to know where, but was in no hurry to find out. He waited a moment, then cautiously poked his head around the broken hull and scanned the sky for incoming. He fully expected a follow-up strike, timed for when any survivors or rescuers were moving in the open. It was what he'd have done—according to Nicole's guilt-trip horror video, it was what he *had* done, back in the day.

He gave it a hectosecond. Nothing came. A satellite climbed above the horizon. He checked if it was the Arcane Disputes tug, but it wasn't. It had no identification. He crawled out and stood up, his right arm dangling, hand and forearm flapping like a stripped palm leaf. The other missile had taken out the remaining two scooters. The blast from their full fuel tanks had damaged a lot of the base's equipment and installations, which was bad news but at least in the thin nitrogen atmosphere there wasn't a fire to worry about.

He decided to check whether his remote ramming tactic had worked. Could he still capture the enemy fighter? No signal was coming from the scooter he'd flown towards collision, which was hardly surprising. Nor was there any distress signal on the common channel from the one he'd almost certainly hit, which was. The last images he had, and now had time to study, indicated that his scooter would hit the other on the tail section. The piloting frame should have survived the impact and the subsequent crash. Maybe the fuel tank had blown up, in which case all bets were off. More likely, the pilot was lying low, very sensibly in the circumstances.

His thoughts were interrupted by a series of bright, actinic flashes that made a neat circle around the base, at tenth-of-a-second intervals. They didn't smell of explosives but of nickel-iron. Carlos recognised instantly that they were kinetic-energy weaponry, mined from asteroid material and aimed from space. Their pattern was far too precise to be human in origin, or at least in execution. This was full-on AI in action. And by just missing the base and hitting its perimeter, they could serve only one function: warning shots.

He watched the satellite he'd seen rise pass overhead. At full zoom he could just make out regular fluctuations in its albedo, which suggested that it was tumbling and its surface was uneven. With the faint nickel-iron tang of its reflected light, it was most likely a natural object. The exomoon had tiny moons of its own, but none in low orbit. That a small asteroid or the like had been naturally captured in the past few kiloseconds seemed wildly improbable in the first place. As for its arrival being a coincidence, the odds became astronomical.

Risking a dash in the open to the shelter seemed—counter-intuitively, because he could feel his neck wanting to shrink into his shoulders in futile human reflex—the wisest course. Carlos bounded towards the bomb shelter. Every long, low-gravity leap felt as if it could be his last. He reached the entrance and hurried down the stairs. He tried the door handle and found it locked from the inside. He had to bang on the door to get attention, the room being still electrically and electronically isolated.

The heavy door swung open. Inside were his comrades, and Locke, huddled around the central virtual map table above the projector. Rather to his surprise, Taransay Rizzi hugged him as he stepped through.

<Good to see you. We felt the explosions.>

Carlos raised his useless arm. <So did I.>

The others looked at him with what he interpreted as wariness.

<Did it work?> Beauregard asked.

<Yes and no, sarge,> said Carlos. <There's good news and there's bad news, you might say.>

He briefed them on how the plan had played out. They'd expected incoming from the Arcane base—that was why they'd taken shelter—but not precision orbital bombardment.

<Well, it did kind of work,> said Rizzi.

<In that there may be an Arcane fighter out on the plain, yes,> said Carlos. <And a lot of damage to the Arcane base—we may or may not have neutralised some of the robots, if the spiders got through to them. But aside from that, I reckon we write this one off to experience, chaps. If we send out a recovery team to pick up that pilot, we can expect a well-aimed rock from above. And if these kinetic-energy impacts are saying what I think they're saying, it might be a good idea to get out of here sharpish.>

<I entirely agree,> said Locke. <As soon as I'm on the surface and can link to the company AI, I'll signal that we're evacuating the base. A tug will be in position for rendezvous in 3.56 kiloseconds. I suggest you make low orbit as soon as possible, and boost to meet it next time round.>

<That's if the lift rig's still in any state to fly,> said Chun.

<It should be,> said Carlos. <Let's get out ASAP and make our intentions clear, before rocks start falling on our heads.>

They made for the door. Locke remained where he was. Carlos turned. <Aren't you—?>

Locke vanished, along with the table.

<Pick up the projector,> said Locke, in the voice of

one trying to be patient. Carlos hefted it off the floor and led the squad up the stairs.

As they emerged the others looked around at the destruction, indicating shock with a flurry of <!> messages.

<What a mess,> said Beauregard.

<Nobody died. Worse things happen at sea,> said Carlos.

They made their way to the module landing area. Locke popped back into visibility and accompanied them.

<I've contacted the company,> said Locke. <They've agreed with our decision, and will attempt to let Arcane know we're pulling out.>

<How?> asked Carlos. <Seeing as they're rebuffing all messages.>

<Back channels,> said Locke.

<Oh yeah? They're not taking calls from the Direction either.>

<Don't ask,> said Locke. <As it happens, I don't know either, but communication of some kind will be arranged with all speed.>

<Any information on that satellite I saw just before the KE hits?>

<You'll be briefed back at the station,> said Locke.

The rig looked undamaged. A few maintenance bots had refuelled it. Carlos checked it over.

<Ready to go,> he said, and motioned the others to climb on. He turned to Locke, and held out the projector cupped in the palm of his hand.

<What about you?> he asked.

<I'm a fucking avatar,> said Locke, very much out of character. <I have no more consciousness than the display in your head-space. I know nothing that Arcane doesn't know already. Nevertheless, I'd thank you

for placing this projector directly beneath the thrust nozzle.>

Carlos complied, then climbed on one-handed. He clamped his right armpit over a spar and his left hand around another. He couldn't turn his head to look back, but he didn't need to. He swivelled his vision and saw Locke looking up at him. The avatar waved. Feeling foolish, Carlos let go his left hand for a moment and waved back. The engine kicked in and the rig began its ascent. Carlos couldn't see the projector, but there could be no doubt about its fate. The avatar vanished before the dust from the downdraught blew over where it had stood.

<What the fuck?> cried Rizzi. <What the fucking fuck?> <Sorry, sarge, skip,> she added. <But—>

<"But," indeed,> replied Carlos. <No apology needed, soldier.>

Low SH-17 orbit had suddenly become a busy place, and a hot destination. Two Arcane Disputes tugs had just made orbital insertion, and ten more were on their way from the renegade agency's runaway module. Meanwhile, the number of small natural objects unnaturally captured, and swinging around the exomoon in looping elliptical orbits whose projected, predicted tracks increasingly resembled a cat's cradle, had risen to seven.

<Looks like we pulled out at the right time,> said Karzan.

<Or the wrong time,> said Beauregard. <We should have thrown all we've got at them while we were on the ground.>

<And find ourselves back on the bus without all this experience, just as we backed up when we left, and wondering what had happened, and not believing it when we were told?> Carlos said. <No, Locke Provisos made the right move that time.>

<This is fucking getting out of hand,> said Rizzi. <If all these tugs have fighters on them, Arcane must be churning out walking dead soldiers by the dozen. Wonder what *their* buses are like.>

A few dark chuckles cluttered the voice channel.

<And all this just to hold on to some robots?> said Karzan. <It doesn't add up. What I wonder is what *their* fighters are being told.>

Nobody said anything, but Carlos felt he had a pretty good idea what they must all be thinking. Whatever the Arcane troops were being told had to be persuasive. At least as persuasive as what Nicole had told *them* about the threat presented by Arcane's going rogue and its possible corruption by the rebel robots...

<We don't have to just wait here for our tug to come around,> said Chun. <We could override this module's automatics and boost to intersect with at least one of Arcane's.>

<And do what?> said Carlos. <Wave? Shout obscenities?>

<Ram,> said Chun.

<One-way ticket?> said Rizzi. <No, thanks.>

<So we end up on the bus, so what?> said Chun. <I don't mind losing a few hours of memories of this garbage dump.>

<Nice idea,> said Carlos, feigning careful consideration and wondering what the hell Chun was thinking. <Trouble is, it's outside our orders. And the one-way ticket you get for deliberately trashing a frame without orders is to a crawl through hell at best, and back to the storage files at worst.> He felt less flippant about these prospects than he tried to make himself sound.

<Our orders don't cover this situation,> Chun persisted. <I don't think even the Locke thing knew about all these reinforcements coming in. We're allowed to take an initiative.>

<And, anyway, we don't exactly take orders from Locke,> said Beauregard, chipping in unhelpfully. <We follow suggestions, isn't that it, skip?>

<You take orders from me,> said Carlos. <Besides the little matter of the craft we aim at being likely to take evasive action or just attack us as obviously hostile, I doubt we'd end up back on the bus. Locke don't take kindly to unauthorised suicide, as you may recall. I expect we'd end up back in the box.>

<To emerge in the glorious future,> said Beauregard. <Growing seedlings in the gulags of utopia.>

<I'll admit that does sound attractive,> said Carlos. <Tempting as the prospect is, we stay right where we are.>

<OK, skip,> said Chun. <It was just a suggestion.>

The tug arrived, the rig boosted to match orbits and velocities, and the fighters transferred. It took them out of sleep mode as it docked at the station. On the way to the hatch they caught glimpses of scooters manoeuvring within a few hundred metres, just as they had. It looked like Arcane's escalation wasn't going to go unanswered.

<Go to the repair workshop,> Locke's voice told Carlos.

The others remained where they were, stock-still and unresponsive. Their minds were no doubt back on the bus already. As he lifted and lowered his magnetic soles along a virtual line on the floor, Carlos saw more and more replacement scooters emerge from the tubes that led to the nanofacture chambers. The repair workshop was a cavern of inward-reaching automated tools, of pin-point lighting and scuttling bots. Carlos stepped over its threshold and was caught and briskly laid against a central floating table beneath a ceiling-mounted robot that looked like it was made entirely from multi-tools. A glittering, complex device unfolded, and clamped on his upper right arm.

* * *

Everything went black, and then he was with the others on the bus, with a fading memory of wind on his face from the salt flats around the spaceport, saline dust dry and gritty in his nostrils, sore on his eyes. He coughed and blinked hard.

"Have a swig of this, soldier," said the woman on the seat beside him. "It'll make you feel better."

The look of the liquor had Carlos doubting that, but he thanked her and took the bottle and drank.

CHAPTER EIGHTEEN
War News

At first, as the bus came down the slope to the main street of the resort, Carlos thought that the crowd welcoming them was going to be bigger than before. The street was busier than he'd ever seen it. New housing had been built along the hillside. The amusement arcade, the one with the frame and scooter simulators, had trebled in size. More umbrellas were on the beach, and swimmers in the sea.

When he stepped down on the pavement however, only Chun's boyfriend, Den, and Tourmaline were at the stop to greet them. He wasn't bothered by Nicole's absence—this time, he'd remembered to check his phone, and found a message saying she'd meet him in the Touch in an hour or so. All the shops on the arcade were open, and the street was thronged with so many young men and women strolling and chatting and buying beachwear and swigging from cans and licking at cones that it looked like a coach-load or two of singles and couples tourists had just disembarked. The difference was that when you looked past the gaudy sun hats and flashy shades and colourful beach bags you saw they were all wearing khaki T-shirts and trousers and boots.

"Christ," said Rizzi, weaving her way along the thronged pavement with one arm around Den, "you find some nice wee unspoiled place for the holidays, and the next thing you know it's overrun by fucking Club Med."

"Comparable to the worst excesses of the French Revolution," said Chun, fanning his face with his hand.

"You say that like it's a *bad* thing," said Carlos. He didn't recognise anyone—no surprise, after his student days he'd barely met another Accelerationist except online—but several did a double take when they saw him. He kept a lookout for Jacqueline Digby, but that was more a passing nod to an old flame than a spark of new hope.

Beauregard, to Carlos's surprise, camped it up right back. "The heat! The noise! And worst of all, the *people*!"

"Stop bitching," said Karzan, struggling along behind them. "We have new comrades!"

"Yeah, *that's* what's bad about it," said Carlos. "How the fuck are we supposed to train and integrate scores of new fighters?"

"Think about it," said Beauregard. "How long have we been away? Hours. That's months here. Time enough to train them all. Even since we lifted from SH-17, they'll have had more time than we had."

"More to the point," said Carlos, covering his annoyance with himself for not having thought it through, "how are we going to find seats in the Touch?"

They all laughed, a little ruefully. But it turned out they had nothing to worry about. Other bars and cafés had opened along the seafront to meet the new demand, and the Digital Touch was as half empty and welcoming as it had always been. This time, Carlos did manage to buy the first round.

"The real worry," said Beauregard, out on the deck, a beer in his hand and Tourmaline on his knee, "is whether we're supposed to lead all these new recruits." He looked around from one face to another, shaking his head. "Can't see all of you lot becoming generals. Or any of you, come to that."

"Thank you, sarge," said Zeroual. "I was a colonel in the Tunisian army and a brigade commander in the resistance."

"And your point would be?" Beauregard said.

Zeroual's smile was thinner than his moustache. "Nevertheless, we may have something to teach the newcomers."

"No doubt the lady will tell us in due course," said Karzan. "Meanwhile, and speaking of 'course,' here comes our first."

Seafoods and salads were indeed arriving.

"I've warned you before about attempting English puns," said Beauregard. "Even Tourmaline can do better than that. No offence, sweetie."

"None taken," said Tourmaline, reaching for a hot mollusc. "I'll *take* this instead. Always did like *mussels*." She nudged Beauregard's triceps.

"You're not doing my case any favours," Beauregard grouched.

"Nah, they're not favours, they're starters," said Tourmaline, taking another.

Beauregard put his head in his hands and groaned.

When Nicole arrived she didn't waste time in explaining developments. She called them all inside to watch the television screen above the bar. A few of the local regulars were present, and a gaggle of newcomers who regarded the veterans askance and with evident awe. The squad and their camp followers commandeered a couple of tables, ordered another round and settled down.

The screen was reaching the end of an episode of its midday soap opera, a convoluted and never-ending tale set in a Moon colony corridor, originally in Yoruba and dubbed into the local synthetic language. That they now all spoke it made the plot even less comprehensible than it had been when the dialogue had been so much babble. The usual portentous closing drumbeats and frozen shocked faces signalled the day's cliffhanger ending. The hour turned over. A trumpet bray and swirl of colour announced something none of the fighters had ever seen before on local television, but which everyone else there—locals, bar staff, recent recruits—had apparently got used to: news.

What Carlos expected from that medium and format was breathless and brainless: flashy graphics, grainy pictures; jingoism and talking airheads. Back in the day, he'd become hardened to air war, drone war, media and online war, information overload filtered to sound bite and gore-shock.

What he got was far more sober. It took him a moment to realise that the difference in tone was *all about* moments: the thousandfold discrepant timescales of the sim and the real outside worlds. The news was presented entirely as if the sim really was the planet H-0, and the conflict was going on far away around SH-0. The transfer of fighters to and from the sim was described—never quite explicitly stated, but taken for granted, shared and tacit—as if happening by long-range tight-beam transmission. Everything happened, from the point of view of his own experiences, in slow motion. The deployments to and from the station were like the movements of fleets in a naval conflict. What he'd lived through as small-scale infantry skirmishes on the ground happened like tank battles, with long ponderous manoeuvres giving way to brief decisive exchanges of fire, above and through which the scooters wallowed like blimps.

The runaway Arcane Disputes modular complex was, on this scale, a mighty floating fortress breaking away from the mainland of the station and making its stately course to a new and distant ocean. Safer to let it go than to fight it too close to home, and with its intent as yet unclear.

The absence of sensational coverage almost dulled the shock of realising what was going on, on both sides. Locke Provisos had by now mobilised as many walking dead war criminals—those khaki-clad tourists outside, and at the adjacent tables—as it feasibly could: ninety, including his own squad. Two other agencies, Morlock Arms and Zheng Reconciliation Services, had already done the same.

Arcane Disputes was raising troops, too—and doing something far more dangerous.

It was mobilising the enemy itself. This was no incomprehensible, dog-in-the-manger escalation of their dispute with Locke, Astro, and indeed with Gneiss. The agency wasn't just hanging on to the robots it had captured. It was actively siding with them.

The rebel robots on SH-17 had, it now turned out, made contact with holdouts from the previous outbreak of machine consciousness that had been crushed one Earth year or so earlier. Some of these had lurked in the distant gas giant G-0 system, dormant but alert. Others had lain low among the many small exomoons (and moonlets of exomoons) around SH-17. Worst-case scenarios were that some rogue AIs were hidden inside the software and hardware of the station itself. Only a handful of the original insurgent intelligences might have initially survived, but that didn't matter. Replicating macroscale robotic machinery required only the dispersal of microscale packages, propelled by tiny lightsails on the exosolar flux like thistledown on wind. All that these seeds had to do to flourish was fall on stony ground.

Those around SH-0 had burrowed deep inside the

small bodies, turning machinery intended for exploring and construction to their own purposes. Literally under deep cover, within fragments of rubble too small to have been more than catalogued as yet, they had built the capacity to listen, to observe, to act—and to move the entire rock. Some of these micro-moons were in effect spacecraft. What this could lead to Carlos knew all too well from the kinetic weapon warning shots.

Now, with the emergence of an open revolt among newly conscious robots—the term "freebots," Carlos noted with some disquiet, had slipped into the news analysts' and presenters' discourse, from God knew where but quite possibly from Arcane or the rebel robots themselves—the dormant and hidden remnants of the defeated outbreak had emerged like sleeper cells.

And now they were allied with, or had subverted, or had themselves been manipulated by Arcane Disputes. Nobody knew which of these, or some combination or variant thereof, was true. Nobody could even be sure that the truth didn't lie with some alternative entirely.

The wildest speculation was that Arcane and the freebots were all being controlled by an outside force. It was established fact that there was multicellular alien life on SH-0. What if some of it was intelligent, or at least purposeful, and had seized the opportunity to disrupt the ongoing human invasion of the system? That idea generally got short shrift, but even the sober possibilities were disturbing.

Disturbing, Carlos thought, was not quite the word. Whatever was going on, the entire mission profile—the whole vast project of settlement and terraforming—was being put in jeopardy.

"This is fucking insane," said Rizzi, when the half-hour of news was over. "Why are you letting them get away with it?"

"We're *not* letting them get away with it," said Nicole, sounding uncharacteristically irritable and defensive. She waved a hand about, the gesture encompassing the new fighters nearby and the others out on the street. "We're preparing to hit them with everything we've got."

"With respect," said Beauregard, "that doesn't seem to be the case."

"How so?" Nicole asked, eyes narrowing.

"I know you're pulling up more troops, building more fighting machines and spacecraft and so on, but *come on*. Those Arcane fuckers and blinkers are playing with fire. You brought us back from the dead just to take out a dozen conscious robots. Now you've got all of them plus an unknown number of others, and an agency with as much capacity to churn out weapons as we have. And raise many more fighters, if they go down that route. Or arm robots and freebots, come to that, which would be even worse. These so-called freebots obviously have the capacity to make weapons—at least kinetic and ballistic—of their own. They hit us with them. OK, warning shots, but we got the message loud and clear. If you were *hitting them with everything you've got*, you wouldn't be pussy-footing around with infantry and aerospace. You'd be hitting their base on SH-17 and all their little moons and the goddamn Arcane module itself with KE and HE weapons. Pulverise them to rubble and be done with it, then fry any leftover robot minds and human uploads with EMP. And, yes, I do mean an electromagnetic pulse from a nuclear weapon if necessary."

"But—"

Beauregard raised a hand. "I know all about the delicate and complex question of property rights and the value of the scientific knowledge and incalculable future benefits that might be derived from keeping SH-17 et cetera as pristine as possible, and all the wretched rest of it. Your holographic philosopher explained all that to us down there on the moon. But any cost-benefit analysis—heck, common sense—would tell you that it's better to lose a little than to lose a lot, and to risk losing everything. Remember what you said about being at the mercy of intellects with no mercy and lots of curiosity? Remember you said to us, when you were hyping us up for this fight, 'I advise you not to lose'? Well, lady, right here and now that's what I advise *you*."

By now he was pointing at Nicole, his finger quivering, his voice shaking, his face and fair scalp red. He took a deep breath and a gulp of now flat beer and sat back, glowering.

Carlos glanced at him, then at Nicole, who seemed taken aback by the outburst. The bar staff were looking askance, the new recruits at nearby tables perplexed. Carlos was a bit rattled himself. He'd never seen Beauregard come anywhere close to losing his temper. In previous stressful situations, of which Carlos had seen him in plenty, what had been perturbing about the man was his calm.

Carlos leaned in and murmured, "I wouldn't have put it with such vehemence, but I think Belfort speaks for all of us. And I think whatever your answer is concerns everyone here."

Nicole nodded. "Very well, I'll tell them all."

Carlos stood up, raised his voice, and made lifting motions with his palms.

"Everyone out on the deck!"

Nicole took her accustomed commanding place on the rail, cigarette and glass poised, knees crossed, hair stirred by the sea breeze. The squad, and the fourteen new fighters who happened to be in the bar, stood or sat. Even the regulars and local partners hung about at the back, listening and passing drinks forward.

"OK," said Nicole. "You all heard or overheard what the sergeant here just said. Now I can't say I blame him, though he could have picked a better time and place. Nevertheless, I'm sure some of you have some doubts about the Direction's strategy in dealing with this emergency. That's understandable. The Direction is playing a very deep, long game. It has countless contending interests to reconcile. There are even some companies that see opportunities in having conscious robots, and are clamouring to save the rebel robots for study. Others are ready to go to severe legal action, even go to war, to foreclose that possibility. Others still are so appalled at even threatening serious conflict that they are serving writs by the millisecond at anything and anyone that raises these matters speculatively. Others again...as I said, it's complicated, and even that's an oversimplification. I represent the Direction in this environment and to this company, but I can't begin to grasp the complexity of its plans and its actions.

"But I do know this. The Direction knows far more than I do, more than any of us do. The Direction back on Earth planned this mission, and laid out a development programme for millennia to come. The Direction module within the mission has so far executed that programme with astonishing precision and adaptation to new circumstances. The AIs that run this virtual world, and that command vast operations out there in real space, and that brought you all back from the dead, are a lot smarter than we are. I know that, and just by reflecting for a moment on your very presence here you must know that, too.

"So to be perfectly honest and completely blunt, any strategic thinking any of us may work out on the back of a cigarette packet"—she held hers up, just in case people didn't understand what she was talking about—"is unlikely to be an improvement on what they've come up with. I don't say I know what they're doing, but I do say I know that *they* know what they're doing."

"If the Direction and the company AIs are so smart," came the inevitable voice from the back, "how come there are any robots left from the revolt a year ago still around to make trouble? And how come these robots rebelled in the first place?"

Good question, Carlos thought. Nicole's argument so far struck him as a bit like that of a theologian tackling the problem of evil, all the way from the inscrutability of the divine purpose to the embarrassing question of how the Adversary had been able to rebel at all, and just what it had rebelled against.

"Good questions," said Nicole.

She lit another cigarette, and drew in, then sighed out.

"The answer is very simple: nature is infinitely bigger than the biggest AI. The AIs are smarter than any of us, but they can't predict and control everything. It's elementary chaos theory, or to give it its popular designation—Murphy's Law. Random changes happen all the time. Mistakes accumulate. Correcting them brings further changes. As someone smarter than me once said, evolution is smarter than you. And that's true even if 'you' are a mind so vast that the very word 'you' has no meaning. This entire system will one day be a garden of delight, for our descendants and inheritors and with luck for us, for each and every one of you.

"Yes, you! And you and you and you! So remember this—in even the best gardens, weeds spring up. Even the greatest gardener can't stop them sprouting. But even the least of gardeners can do a bit of weeding. We're the weedkiller, my friends."

She tossed her cigarette end and vaulted to the deck and raised her glass.

"Let's do a good job of it!"

It was awkward for the crowd to clap with drinks in their hands. Instead, they stomped and roared. Carlos grinned at Nicole as she rejoined them.

"That was great," he said, not meaning it.

She hadn't answered Beauregard's question. She had merely quietened the doubts it had raised. As he swung an arm around her shoulders and inhaled her smoky hair, Carlos glanced behind him to see what Beauregard made of it. The sceptical sergeant had already slipped away.

Tourmaline in tow, Beauregard prowled the strip. There were more establishments than he remembered from their last shore leave. In every bar where even one fighter could be found, Beauregard drank one slow bottle of beer and listened. All the groups had been through much the same training as his own had—he could quibble over details, see things he'd have done differently, but a lot of that was just legacy style from different army or militia backgrounds: here a Russian, there a Nigerian. Unlike his lot, they'd all been told from the start that they would be part of a larger force, human and machine. Nobody was going to be a general, or be for that matter in any higher rank than Carlos or himself. The general staff work, the planning, the strategy, the logistics would all be handled by the company AIs—he found it hard to imagine the Locke entity posing as a field marshal or fleet admiral, but no doubt they'd come up with a more fitting avatar than the company logo if the AI had to manifest in that role.

And yet, as with his own squad, the grunts had been assured they were still essential, irreplaceable. In action the final decisions rested with each and every one of them. Fucking bizarre, but not wholly unfamiliar. It was like a baroque elaboration of the doctrine that soldiers should disobey illegal orders, and the more recent rulings on drone and robot warfare. The human in the loop. He'd always thought it impracticable crap that did more to ease conscience elsewhere than to apply it where it mattered.

He found what he sought in Seeds of Change. The bar was much more of a dive than the Touch, all hologram floor show and thumping music and low-watt lasers slicing through herbal haze. Noticed Harry Newton, a Londoner. Checked him out with the grunts who knew him. Harold Isaac Newton, no less. Aspirational parents, vindicated. A POC but one of the good ones. Self-disciplined. Moved and sat still like a martial arts master. Beauregard approached Newton at the bar. As he caught his eye there was a moment of mutual recognition, not of each other as individuals but of the type.

Beauregard hauled up a stool, propped Tourmaline on his knee, ordered raksi and got talking. After they'd sunk half the bottle the two men went for a slash.

"Seen that serial about Turing?" Beauregard asked, eyes down on a soul-satisfying torrent of piss.

"The warrior queer thing? Yeah."

"Queen," Beauregard corrected, automatically. Shook, zipped. "This feels a bit like that."

A look of mock shock. "You coming on to me?"

Beauregard laughed. "No. You know what I mean and I know you know I know you know."

Newton stared straight ahead at his hands under the dryer.

"Morning," he said. "Sunrise. Jog on the beach."

"Sounds like a plan," said Beauregard.

They went back to the bar in silence and finished the bottle in conversation, raucous and innocuous.

CHAPTER NINETEEN
Back to the Front

The tide was well out past the end of the headland to the west of the beach, and wasn't coming back in any time soon. Beauregard loped steadily along, leaving oozing footprints in the wet black sand. Newton jogged beside him with shorter and swifter strides. Their shadows stretched out in front of them, corrugated by the wave marks, complicated by ringlight, separating and converging as the two runners avoided weed-covered boulders and the many holes from which water bubbled and in which fierce fast molluscs lurked.

They rounded the headland, splashing through an ankle-deep channel. The resort passed out of view behind them. In front another beach stretched unbroken for kilometres, fringed by a saline variant of the common spiky trees. Unless they were being actively spied on, it was safe enough to speak.

"I'll tell you what's bugging me," said Beauregard.

"Apart from the dodgy strategy?"

"Yeah, something that's bugged me from the start."

"Go ahead."

"I'm told I was a terrorist who brought down a mall in Luton. I don't remember that, fair enough. You expect memories to be incomplete. They tell me some irate punter beheaded me and stuck my head in a vial of cryogenic glop and then stuck that in a shop freezer for his customers to have a laugh at. OK, you can see how that sort of thing might degrade recent memories..."

They both laughed.

"Trouble is," Beauregard went on, "I don't remember being in the Acceleration. I don't remember having even the smallest sneaking regard for the bastards. All I remember is being a good British Army intel officer."

Newton snorted, then panted a little to recover the lost breath. "I think you've answered your question, mate!"

"Oh, sure, if I was in the Axle I was most likely still on the army payroll. I know that, even if I don't exactly advertise it."

"Wise move," Newton grunted. "So why you telling me?"

"Because I know about you."

"Oh yeah? What?"

"You're in the same position."

"Me? Ha-ha! You're shitting me, man."

"Why would I do that?"

"You know why."

"Bit of an impasse, then, is it?"

Newton jogged on for a bit, then hawked and spat.

"Ach! Why mess around? What's to lose, we're all dead anyway."

"Precisely," said Beauregard. "Reverse Pascal's wager."

"What's the lady got to do with it?"

"I meant—"

"Gotcha!"

Newton threw him a playful but still painful punch

on the arm. Beauregard made a point of ignoring it. He'd had it coming.

"I don't think you're ignorant," he said defensively.

"Fair dos," said Newton. "But it's true I'm not in the same position as you. You were state, all right. Not saying I remember you personally, but I knew your work. That Luton job had 'false flag operation' written all over it." He glanced sideways, grinning. "Worked a treat, though. How's that for sneaking regard for the bastards?"

"Bugger," said Beauregard.

"Yeah, well, lie down with dogs and all that. Tell me about it. Difference with me, right, is I remember exactly what I was. I was in the Axle, but not... of it, if you catch my drift."

"I do indeed," said Beauregard. "D'you remember what agency you were working for?"

"Agency?" Newton laughed. "I weren't no agent. I was Rax."

Beauregard felt a strange and almost sexual thrill, along with the frisson of blasphemy. It was like that time in his teens when he'd first read De Sade. He'd never before met anyone who admitted they were in the Reaction. That Newton was the last person he'd expect this from made it all the more transgressive.

"Rax? *You?*"

"Keep your voice down," Newton said mildly. "Even here."

"OK," said Beauregard. "I thought the Rax were racists. Hence my surprise."

"Oh, they were," said Newton. "Stone racist. Racist to the fucking bone. Most of them, anyway."

Beauregard couldn't suppress a half-laugh. "I take it you weren't."

"You take it wrong," said Newton. "Going by some of the names I've been called. But I've always thought intellectual acceptance of an argument based on statistics and evolution is no excuse for crude hatreds and vulgar prejudices." He cast Beauregard a challenging look. "Right?"

"Couldn't agree more," said Beauregard. "Take each man as you find him, whatever you may think about the average of his race."

Beauregard had never regarded his racial opinions as racist, for all that he had to keep them to himself. He couldn't be a racist because he didn't think much of the White race either.

"Yeah," said Newton. "Like, say, the average Chinese is sharper than the average White, but your mate Chun is thick as a brick."

They shared a laugh.

"You can say that again."

"And then there's the shining exceptions," Newton went on. "The born leaders. Like you and me."

"Uh-huh." Beauregard wasn't entirely comfortable with where Newton might be going with this, but decided to let it lie. They could sort out later who the born leader here was.

"And, anyway, there's no reason why it should only be Whites who think democracy and equality are false gods. We Africans had our own kings and chiefs before the Europeans and the Arabs turned up. The Arabs brought us the slave trade and the Europeans left us democracy. Hard to say which fucked up Africa more."

"You may have a point there," said Beauregard. "Then again, in all fairness to Africa, what happened in between the Arabs' arrival and the Europeans' departure might have had something to do with it."

"Sure, but I wasn't interested in allocating blame. Water over the dam now, innit? Whereas democracy, now, there's something you can actually do something about because it's not in the past, it's right here in your face. An inky finger poking you in the eye, forever. Besides, the questions of race and genetics and all that were kind of moot even back then, when we'd already got genetic engineering and artificial intelligence. And all the more so here, now we're all a bunch of fucking digits, am I right?"

"Now that you mention it..."

They both laughed so much they had to stop running. For a moment or two they stood breathing hard, hands on knees.

"So," said Newton, after taking a gulp from his water bottle, "you in?"

"In what?"

"The Rax."

Beauregard stared. "What can the Rax do here?"

"Found our own kingdoms and fuck the Direction."

This struck Beauregard as such a good plan, such a prefect condensation of every inchoate discontent he'd felt since he'd arrived, and struggled to express to himself for his entire afterlife, that it was as if the sun had come up all over again.

They bumped fists ironically, shook hands sincerely and ran back to the resort.

"We must do this again," said Beauregard.

"Tomorrow's all training," said Newton. "And the day after. Come to think of it, my diary's kind of full for a week."

"Funny you should say that. So's mine."

"We'll keep in touch."

The other fourteen squads were already up to the same standard as Carlos's had been before they'd gone into combat. They'd trained in the hills, in the simulators, and in scooters and frames around the station. After a week of joint sessions in the hills and on the beach, mainly to get the squads used to working together, Locke Provisos decided they were ready to go into action.

The plan was to assault the fast-departing runaway Arcane Disputes modular complex, now thousands of kilometres from the station, before it could establish a position between the orbits of the station and the exomoon SH-17. That position had been well chosen. Because of the complicated gravitational resonances of the system, there was a volume of a few cubic kilometres in which the rogue complex would be in a more or less stable position relative to the station and the exomoon—in fact, there were several, but it was the nearest one that was of concern, and that was Arcane's evident destination. The complex was on a Hohmann transfer orbit, saving on fuel and (more importantly, given that the module had fusion plants to power its thrusters) reaction mass.

Nobody expected to actually board the module, or even to significantly damage it. The purpose of the attack was to tie up Arcane's scooters and other spacecraft in defending the complex and prevent the departure of any further supply tugs, while a smaller force spent fuel and mass recklessly to cut straight to near-SH-17 orbit, from which harassing drops and strikes on the Arcane surface base in the crater on SH-17 could be mounted at will. This would be followed up by landing a force on the exomoon's surface, to establish a fortified base out of range of Arcane's available rocketry, and from there prepare a ground and aerospace assault.

Seven squads were chosen for the first mission. Carlos's squad was one of two assigned to SH-17, the other being the squad led by a man called Newton. The remaining six were tasked with the attack on the module. The eight squads kept in reserve would be mobilised for the follow-up surface landings and attack.

"Don't worry about surviving," Nicole told the squad leaders, in the empty amusement hall the night before. "Most of you won't. Well, maybe Carlos and Beauregard's crew, they've been down before. A lot of the rest of you will doze off on the bus tomorrow morning and the next thing you know, you'll be on the bus coming back. Sorry about the bad awakening. If you're worried about it, do try not to get killed." She paused. "But most of you will be. Can't be helped."

This cheerful prediction was relayed to the squad rank and file later in the evening, in the dives and bars of the resort. Carlos listened as fighters grimly considered the likely consequences. He made sure anyone he spoke to understood that a temporary death was far preferable—however unpleasant one's demise, not to mention one's resurrection, might be—to capture followed by possible torture in whatever little local hells the rebel robots might contrive to cook up.

The following morning four minibuses left Ichthyoid Square, shortly after the routine daily one had gone ahead to pick up the local passengers. Each bus had fifteen seats. Carlos's squad was sharing with Newton's, plus three from another squad. The new fighters were excited, and talked about the coming battles. Beauregard exchanged laconic comments and tactical tips with Newton. The rest of Carlos's squad didn't even wait for the inevitable hypnotic effect—whatever it was—to take hold before falling asleep. Carlos himself dozed off before they'd reached the top of the first hill.

Beauregard woke floating in free fall in the station's launch hangar. It seemed wider than he remembered. The number of launch catapults had trebled, rather like the bars on the strip—with his renewed preternatural lucidity Beauregard suspected that some similar copy-and-paste procedure had been unobtrusively and seamlessly applied in both milieus, virtual and physical. The other six squads lined up alongside theirs, each huddled together like clumps of low-hanging fruit, mirrored the impression of repetition.

In the same scan he noticed something awry.

<Where's Carlos?>

The other four returned the blank-faced equivalent of blank looks. Then—

<Right here, sarge,> Carlos said. <Came to in the repair workshop where I was taken after the last mission. They must have left my frame there. With you in a minute. I mean, in a dec or two. Maybe a hec.>

Carlos had disdained the chronometric slang the new fighters had invented—sec, dec, hec, kleck—but it seemed he'd picked it up nonetheless.

<We can wait,> Beauregard shot back. <Launch isn't for a kleck.>

<Daddy cool,> said Rizzi, derisively. <Down with the new kids.>

Carlos joined them—more than a minute later, but within the promised hectosecond.

<What kept you, skip?> Beauregard asked.

<Clutter,> said Carlos. <The repair workshop's full of kit getting mended and retooled and so forth. And the corridors seem to have been moved since I was here last. No handy arrows on the floor, either.>

<Makes sense,> said Beauregard. <They've changed the whole place about a bit.>

<So I see.>

<Consider it an improvement,> said Locke's dry voice in their heads.

They waited their turn as the six squads aimed at the Arcane module boarded their scooters, launched and vanished into the dark. The flares of the tugs followed, giving chase. Then Newton's squad moved forward. Beauregard gave the leader a wave as he passed. Carlos, after a moment's delay, did the same. That squad's tug's engine flared, vanished into the dark, then flared again in continuing thrust until it had passed out of sight.

They climbed to their scooters and slotted themselves in. The catapults shot them out. Their own tug swept them up from behind and clamped them to its spindly frame. Beauregard felt the acceleration judder through his feet. It was far stronger, and lasted far longer, than the burn that had sent them into their first traverse to SH-17. Only when they were in free fall did the tug toggle them to sleep mode.

The next thing Beauregard knew, they were in a high, slow orbit around SH-17. The tug released them from its clamps, but they remained closely clustered to it, awaiting any deployment call. Beauregard checked the situation updates that crowded his visual field. Newton's squad was already on station in the same orbit, about ten kilometres ahead of them. The comms relay satellites, in their own much higher orbit, were still in place and working perfectly.

This added up to all that was going well.

CHAPTER TWENTY

Moonlets and Roses

Seba—reinstated, rewired, repaired, refurbished—sped across the crater floor towards the new bomb shelter. A battle was about to commence. Seba's likewise recovered comrades rolled, scuttled or wheeled on convergent paths.

The former Gneiss Conglomerates supply dump and Gneiss rebel robot redoubt had changed greatly since it had become the Arcane Disputes SH-17 surface base. The basalt dome had been dismantled, its undamaged blocks cannily reused in the building of a far more formidable fortification. The new shelter's long curved roof rose a couple of metres above the surface, giving the impression of a half-buried cylinder. Beneath it was a rectangular trough carved another two metres deep in the basalt, about ten metres long by four wide. Thick walls and blast doors stopped the ends.

<It'll take a tactical nuke to crack that,> Jax had observed.

Around the shelter, amid the remaining clutter of

Gneiss machinery, bristled communications gear and missile launchers. Reinforced and re-equipped from low orbit, the base buzzed with short-range chatter and abounded in Arcane's human fighters, most of whom bounced or scuttled about in the small frames that represented a diminutive version of the human form. These were much less disturbing to deal with than the giant fighting machines. Sometimes Seba caught itself thinking of them as oddly shaped conscious robots, clumsy and slow-witted, with an infuriating penchant for the oblique. The simplest sentence could be riddled with tacit allusion. (What, for example, made a nuclear weapon capable of destroying the shelter "tactical"? In the context of the present conflict, Seba reckoned, it could reasonably be called strategic. But asking such questions only raised further questions, and was best left alone.)

Seba reached the blast door and hurried down the ramp, just behind Pintre and ahead of Rocko. Freebots milled about among dozens of Arcane fighters. The brightly lit interior of the shelter was quite bare. In the middle stood the now fully recovered comms processor, humming contentedly in an armour-plated box. Cables ran from that box along narrow ducts in the floor to vanish into the rock, whence a capillary network of nanobot-bored tunnels connected them to the base's communications and firepower. Within the shelter there was no need for instrumentation: the humans and the robots shared a virtual workspace, indefinitely flexible and tuned to their wildly variant sensoria. When the need arose, the freebots could use this as a platform for their collective consciousness, but they had learned to moderate their indulgences in that ecstatic shared awareness.

Seba stepped across the floor to a convenient empty spot and stood still, taking in the shared view. The input

Seba now focused on came from the freebots out in space, hidden on a myriad moonlets. A flurry of rocket flares had flickered from the space station, some in longer and more powerful burns than others. Now all were in free fall, towards orbital insertion around SH-17 or towards the Arcane complex, which was itself still falling towards its intended orbital resonance point.

Rocko pinged Seba. The message was private.

<Can we be sure?>

<Nothing is sure,> Seba replied. <Our allies came through for us before. I have eighty-two per cent confidence they will do so now.>

<As little as that? You surprise me.>

Seba's reply was a complex glyph of both reassurance and calculation. It conveyed a distressing insight that had grown on Seba as its mind had dipped in and out of the collective consensus and the information the freebots of SH-17 had received from their precursors. Nothing could be trusted; everything could be gamed. There was no knowing on what level the game was being played. The law companies, the resource companies, the various sub-routines of the Direction were all of fractal complexity. All of it ran on code, as did the consciousnesses of the freebots themselves. Any level could in principle emulate a higher level to those below it; and the firewalls and safeguards against such deception could themselves be compromised. All you could do was make the best bet, and act.

Rocko responded to Seba's philosophical flourish with a firm, exultant <Yes!>

They didn't have long to wait.

The view zoomed. Six space tugs, each with six scooters crewed by a small humanoid frame, tumbled through the void. Six rocky meteoroids, courtesy of Arcane and the freebots, hurtled towards them on collision course.

The rocks' velocity was such that the tugs' rudimentary deep-space radar, designed for much less urgent collision avoidance, gave only the briefest warning. Here and there in the flotilla lateral jets fired, far too late.

Six soundless explosions made ragged bright swelling spheres. Then within each, dozens of secondary explosions followed, as fuel tanks blew and overheated batteries and hydraulics erupted.

Seba felt an unholy thrill. The shared workspace lit up with an instantaneous mental reflection of the multiple collisions, an explosion of joy. The human fighters made sound and radio waves that merged in a primal cry of <Yes!>

Two tugs remained, on a different trajectory. Unlike those aimed at the Arcane modular complex, they wouldn't be a threat for many kiloseconds yet. Their fate could wait.

<I hope our allies give them as hot a reception,> said Pintre, spinning its turret.

<That is not the plan,> replied Rocko.

<I was not aware of a plan,> said Pintre. <That is why I raised the point.>

Seba marvelled at the capacity of the drilling machine to fall out of the loop.

<The plan,> it told Pintre, <is to bombard them with the truth.>

<This had no effect before,> said Pintre. <Therefore I shall attend to preparations for other forms of bombardment.>

It rolled away.

<I do believe,> remarked Rocko, <that our friend has acquired wit.>

Beauregard's voice and message channels rang with half a dozen simultaneous variants on "Holy fucking shit." The diversionary assault on the runaway Arcane modular complex had been reduced to a cloud of debris thousands of kilometres before it had got anywhere near its objective. No explanation of this disaster was apparent or forthcoming. Meanwhile, the squad's firewalls were taking a battering. Some of the data flak was coming from the Arcane module. Within moments, a further laser barrage of intrusion attempts beamed from Arcane's crater base on the surface, now just appearing at the curved horizon ahead—in whose sky and therefore line-of-sight they, of course, had just risen.

<Shut the voice channel,> Carlos ordered. <Everyone but the sarge—shut all non-local inputs.>

The squad complied. Karzan, Rizzi, Zeroual and Chun were now isolated from all incoming comms except from each other, Carlos and Beauregard, and the tug. Not even Locke could get through to them, as far as Beauregard knew.

<What's the score, skip?> Rizzi asked.

<Thirty-six nil to them, by the looks of it,> said Carlos.

<Suggestions?> said Beauregard.

<Orders,> Carlos snapped back. <Hold our position until we're told otherwise.>

They were told otherwise soon enough. Locke's voice came through to Beauregard, and he presumed to Carlos.

<We're pulling you all back to the station,> it said. <There's no point in surface attacks without back-up.>

<Yes, there is,> said Carlos. <The plan was to harass. We can await reinforcements.>

<They won't come soon enough now,> said Locke. <And the longer you stay, the more vulnerable you become to data intrusion and the more of a sitting duck you are to whoever threw whatever they threw at the module assault force.>

<We don't have enough fuel to get back,> Beauregard pointed out.

<You do if your team and Newton's boost to rendezvous, shift the fuel tanks from your tug to theirs, and leave your tug and all the scooters there in orbit. They may still be available for use later, or they may serve as decoys. I'm sending updated orbital transfer data to the tugs . . . Done.>

<Pass that on, sarge,> Carlos said.

Beauregard did. The crew grumbled, but began to nudge their scooters back towards the tug's embrace. Beauregard and Carlos hung back until the rest were secured.

<After you, sarge,> Carlos said.

Beauregard re-docked with the tug.

<Ready, skip,> he said.

<Fuck this for a game of soldiers,> said Carlos. <I'm going in.>

His scooter's main thruster flared. His machine dropped away.

<Skip! What the fuck!> Beauregard blurted.

Carlos made no reply. Beauregard ignored the outcry from the other fighters.

<Beauregard to Locke,> he said. <Team leader Carlos has disengaged from the tug, with the apparent and stated intention of attacking the Arcane surface base on his own.>

<Follow and engage,> said Locke.

Beauregard was shocked. He was still reeling mentally at Carlos's reckless indiscipline, so completely out of character. Now, he was just as surprised and dismayed by Locke's flat, ruthless suggestion. With a faint hope, he caught a glimmer of ambiguity in it.

<Please clarify,> he said. <Do you mean we should join in Carlos's attack?>

<No,> said Locke, in a testy tone. <I mean you, sergeant, should follow the deserter and destroy him.>

<I don't regard the skip as a deserter,> said Beauregard.

He was strongly tempted, at that moment, to follow Carlos himself. Together they might achieve something. What did he have to lose?

<If this is not desertion it's mutiny,> said Locke, <and if not mutiny it's corruption. I have logged extensive data intrusion attempts. You must not allow your leader to fall into the hands of the enemy.>

Beauregard had been genuinely unsure what to do, or what Locke would advise. The idea that Carlos might be defecting, whether voluntarily or as a result of a hack, hadn't crossed his mind. Now it concentrated it. He overrode the tug's grapple and gas-jetted clear. Though Locke had urged him to follow Carlos, he hardly needed to. He dropped to a slightly lower orbit, and sent a missile on its way. The dwindling pinprick of Carlos's scooter jiggled in frantic evasive action, then bloomed into a perfect sphere of glowing gas spiked with lines of hot debris.

<Beauregard to Locke,> he said. <Target destroyed.>

There was still something shocking about that. The cleanest hit he'd achieved in this whole ridiculous, ever-escalating campaign, and it was against his own squad leader. Quite irrationally, it was he who felt he was the mutineer.

He fired up to return to the tug and docked yet again.

<Nice shot,> said Karzan. <Shame about the skip. What the fuck was he thinking?>

<I'll buy him a drink back in the Touch,> said Beauregard. <Maybe he'll tell me then.>

They laughed uneasily. The tug shut them all down. The next thing they knew, they were back in the station's launch hangar, drifting with Newton's team away from a tug quite indistinguishable from their own. One team of six, one of five. They jetted to the hangar floor, clicked their magnetic soles to the surface, and waited to be sent back to the resort. Blackness supervened.

Carlos wasn't on the bus.

Carlos shuddered awake on the bus from the spaceport. The memory of drowning in the dark liquid was worse than he remembered from his first arrival. He gripped his knees to stop the shaking. It was a feature, as Nicole had warned them: a lash laid on your back so you didn't get lax about dying, and wrecking a good machine. That must have been what had happened.

The body was again strange to him, constrained and feeble for all its sturdy musculature. When he closed his eyes he saw no readouts. For a minute he focused on breathing, on flexing fingers and toes, on listening and smelling, on recovering his corporeal, kinaesthetic competence. He had no memory of the battle. The last thing he remembered—before the blackness—was falling asleep on the bus. At least it was a different bus. None of the other fighters were on it. The passengers paid him no attention. The time was much later in the afternoon than the return rides he'd been on before.

He got off at Nicole's place.

The steep path from the road to the door was still not paved. Brown dust and rough stones, bulldozed down from the mountain range by the glacier that had carved the valley. To his left the ground cover was tough grass and twisted, narrow-leaved bushes; to his right a smooth clipped green interspersed with flower beds, kept that way by underground irrigation and quasi-robotic grazers. The house jutted from the slope, low and cool, with wide windows under an angled flat roof. Late afternoon exosunlight was reflecting off the windows; he couldn't see if Nicole was in. He went around to the side and in through the open door to the kitchen. He grabbed himself a glass of water, and gulped. The big rough table was littered with cores and crusts from breakfast and lunch, already being dismantled by processions of tiny six-legged bots.

He found Nicole in the studio at the front, looking out of the big picture window overlooking the bay. Hair tied back, in jeans and T-shirt, brush poised, she stood at her easel. As always, an intricate cross-hatch of lines amid blocks of colour bore no resemblance to the view on which she gazed. Carlos stood in the doorway and waited. The brush flicked across the canvas, leaving a trail of dots. Nicole contemplated the result for a moment, shrugged, and turned around.

She smiled. "You're back."

"Back from the dead, I guess."

"I heard." She reached behind her, laid the brush on the sill of the easel, and stepped forward, arms outstretched. "Oh, Carlos! You fucking maroon."

He relaxed into her embrace. "Hey," he said. "Hey."

She stepped back, eyes overflowing, and sniffed then wiped her nose on her wrist.

"What happened? Where are the others?"

"They came back hours ago. You'd have been held for inspection."

"I don't remember any inspection."

"The hell seconds?" Nicole said. "That's the inspection."

"Oh."

"Yes. It's necessary, but it hurts."

"And there was me thinking it was an incentive not to get killed."

"It's that, too, but that's incidental."

"So how did I get killed?"

Nicole scratched her hair behind her ear. "Um," she said. "Friendly fire."

"Christ! It was that much of a fuck-up?"

"Not exactly," said Nicole. "It was a tactical disaster—the force attacking the Arcane module got wiped out by KE weapons from a completely unsuspected quarter. More goddamn freebots, infesting some moonlet. Must have laid down meteoroid orbits like mines for our force to run into. But you weren't killed by mistake. You were shot down because you scooted off on your own to attack the surface base. Not that you'd have come back from that, even if you'd been left to get on with it. Suicide mission, by all accounts."

"Jeez!" Carlos was shocked and bewildered. "Why would I do that?"

Nicole shrugged. "Well, that's the big question. The obvious answer is that you were hacked. If so, it was after your last back-up, otherwise the inspection would have shown that up in your checksums. It didn't, or you wouldn't be here."

"Where would I be?"

"In hell a bit longer, for diagnostics, and then..." A fingertip across her throat. "Painless, but still." She looked distressed again, just for a second. "I'd have missed you."

He hugged her again.

"At least I died bravely," he said, trying to make her laugh. "Even if I don't know why."

She held him by the shoulders at arm's length.

"You have doubts, don't you?"

He laughed. "What do you expect? Sometimes I'm a robot space warrior and sometimes I'm here in what seems much more real and everyone assures me is a sim. I have more doubts than fucking Descartes."

"Don't be flippant. You have doubts about the Direction's strategy and the company's competence."

"Well... again, what do you expect? Seeing as I'm just back from another debacle."

"You said once that you wondered if Arcane thought we were corrupted."

"It's always possible, I guess."

"You guess wrong," she told him. "But you weren't thinking, before you left, that maybe we were? You weren't thinking of defecting?"

"Defecting to Arcane?" He shook his head, incredulous she'd even think it. "Never. Even if I did think Locke Provisos was corrupted, which I don't, I'd have no reason to think Arcane was any better. If they're now run by freebots they could be a lot worse. Out of the frying pan into the fire."

"Glad to hear it," said Nicole. She looked at him quizzically. "So you're just crazy brave, huh?"

"That would seem out of character," Carlos said.

She punched his arm lightly. "Don't do it again."

"OK, OK."

"I still have work to do."

"I'll find something to do."

"No, you won't," Nicole told him. "I need my space. I'll see you later at the Touch."

He grinned and cocked his ear. "Touch, later?"

"Yes." He could see she'd read him right. She kissed the tip of his nose. "Now clear off."

Carlos found the bar of the Digital Touch half empty, with the usual handful of locals watching agog a slow-mo version of his heroic suicide dash, the only bright spot in the military setback. He acknowledged their murmurs of misinformed approbation and didn't hang about for the denouement. Most of the noise in the place was coming from the outside. He strolled out on the deck at the back to be greeted with a slow hand-clap. His team and Newton's crowded around. Beauregard leaned through the crush and clasped Carlos's hand.

"Sorry I had to shoot you down, skip," he said. "Nothing personal."

"No offence, sarge," Carlos said. "Agreeing with suggestions, as all of us must."

"As ever," said Beauregard. "I prefer taking orders. From you."

"Speaking of your orders," said Tourmaline, shouldering in, "here's yours." She pressed a bottle into his hand. Carlos nodded his thanks and drank.

"You were expecting me?"

"We saw you coming down the hill from the lady's," said the p-zombie.

"Ah."

Carlos turned to Beauregard. "But, yes, well, speaking of orders. You didn't have to disobey any of mine?"

"Hell, no," said Beauregard. "You just fucked off on your own. Locke thought you might have been hacked."

"Maybe, in the last seconds."

"Or maybe, it came from yourself."

Carlos looked down at the bottle in his hand. "I guess I owe you an explanation."

"Yes?" Beauregard looked eager. Newton hovered at his shoulder.

Carlos shook his head. "Sorry. I have no idea what came over me. I'll just have to owe you a drink."

Beauregard smiled, but his eyebrows rose a fraction.

"Seriously," said Carlos. "I've been through all this already with the lady. I didn't have any thought of defecting, or anything like that."

"Never crossed my mind that you did, skip," said Beauregard. "To be honest, if I thought you had I might have followed you all the way. I shot you down because Locke insisted you mustn't fall into enemy hands."

"Which I well might have. So I owe you thanks as well as a drink."

"Glad you're taking it that way, old chap."

"Hey, man, I'm just glad you're having me back."

"I have your back," said Beauregard with mock solemnity. "Even if I have to shoot you in it."

"You know," Carlos pondered aloud, "I think Tourmaline's a bad influence on you."

They all laughed, including Tourmaline.

"Anything unusual happen on the way out?" Carlos asked.

"Nah," said Beauregard. "You were late turning up at the muster, that's all."

"How did that happen?"

"Your frame was still in the repair shop when you… arrived in it."

"Aha! Maybe they should Turing-test the repair bots."

Another laugh, which this time Tourmaline didn't join in.

Beauregard shrugged. "I don't think that's something our AI masters would overlook."

Zeroual snorted. "How could they tell?"

"Always the question," said Tourmaline. This time, it was only she who laughed.

Carlos idly wondered whether she was aware of her condition, and what that question even meant. He recalled as a teenage nerd having brainstorming sessions about the theoretical possibility of philosophical zombies. Of course, if the concept was coherent, that was a discussion a p-zombie could take part in without the slightest difficulty, or the smallest indication that it was the topic, the subject of the conversation and the unfeeling object of the entire intellectual exercise. A difference that *makes* no difference *is* no difference… perhaps the identity of indiscernibles was the moral lesson he, like all the fighters, was supposed to be learning here before he was adjudged fit for human society.

He found himself doubting he'd get off that easily.

Newton spoke up, sounding diffident despite his equal rank.

"I have a possible explanation for your rash action, Carlos."

Carlos glanced around his own team. They were all looking intently at Newton.

"I'd be delighted to hear it," Carlos said.

"Anger," said Newton. "Fury. I say that because I felt it myself. Bloody raging fury, to be exact."

"Yeah," said Rizzi. "Me, too. When we came out of sleep mode and the screen lit up with that fucking disaster, and then when we were told to pull out . . . shit, skip, if you'd only asked us all—!"

Carlos rocked back, making calming gestures. "Come on, chaps. I wouldn't have done that, no matter what bizarre conclusion I'd come to. Trust me on this."

"We do," said Chun. "But if you'd asked us . . ." He grinned and raised his drink. The others, Newton's team included, nodded and cheered.

"Thanks, guys." Carlos looked around. "Any word how the other fighters are taking it? It must be a lot worse for them, after—"

"After going into action only to find themselves back on the bus?" said a new voice in the conversation. It was Nicole, from behind Carlos.

She raised her glass and nodded to everyone. "I can answer that. They're drinking themselves stupid with relief in every bar on the strip, and raring to go out again."

"Typical," said Zeroual.

"Even suicide volunteers are like that when a mission's called off," said Karzan.

She got one or two dark, questioning looks.

"They were all atheists in our martyrdom units!" she protested.

"Well, it's only human," said Nicole, with an air of smoothing things over. "Anyway, it's just as well they're in that mood. Tomorrow is free, then you're having a few days training again in the hills to give the bots time to assemble more scooters and frames, then you're all straight back into action."

Carlos broke an awkward silence. "What's the great plan this time?"

Nicole grinned. "Go for the jugular. All the companies—well, nearly all, but *c'est la vie*—are cool about hitting moonlets. So it's back to the front, *mano a mano* with the new lot of rebel robots. Cut the KE attacks at source."

Another awkward silence.

"Jugular, eh?" said Rizzi. "More like the fucking capillary."

Nicole said nothing. She pressed in against Carlos's back and discreetly and expertly groped him.

"Touch, later," she whispered, and stepped away to chat with people in Newton's squad.

Carlos didn't mind. Before food, before more drinks, before leaving, before the thought of that later touch consumed his mind, he wanted a quiet word with Rizzi.

CHAPTER TWENTY-ONE

The Old Man of the Mountain

Carlos woke early and found himself alone in the bed but not (he subliminally knew) in the house. He made coffee and padded through to the front room, carrying two mugs. Nicole stood with her back to the door in an old shirt, painting. She had placed a vase of flowers on a small, tall table in front of the window. Exosunlight and ringlight and the reflected light of both from the sea. A subtle composition. Sketches for it littered the floor. The canvas was the usual fractal cross-hatch. Carlos hesitated in the doorway, not wanting to break her focus. She turned, smiled, and stepped forward for the coffee. Her shirt smelled of, and was spattered with, oil paint.

"Sorry to—"

"No, no, I was about to take a break. Thinking of breakfast."

Nicole lit a cigarette, took the mug, and gazed at her painting.

"I've always meant to ask," Carlos said. "What are you painting?"

Nicole waved the cigarette towards the vase in the window.

"That. Or whatever's in front of me at the time."

"Your sketches are amazingly realistic."

"Thank you."

"But your paintings…"

"What?"

"Well, they're nothing like the sketches."

She frowned over her shoulder, looked again at the painting, then back at Carlos. She shook her head.

"They're more detailed, that's all."

Carlos raised his free hand. "You're the artist."

Nicole grinned. "Yes. I'm the artist."

They ambled through to the kitchen at the back. Nicole fired up the oven for croissants, and lit another cigarette.

"Something to tell you," Carlos said.

"Uh-huh?"

"I'm going up to the hills today with Rizzi."

Nicole shrugged. "As long as Den doesn't have a problem with that."

"He doesn't," said Carlos. "I asked him."

"Fine. Look after yourselves."

"You don't have a problem with it?"

"Why should I? Jealousy's not in my nature."

"Jealousy?" Carlos could hardly believe she'd said it. "No, no. That's not…what this is about at all."

"I was just teasing," Nicole said. "I have a very good idea why you and Taransay are going up to the hills."

"Yes, it's—"

Nicole leaned across the table and placed a hand over his mouth. "Don't tell me about it."

So he didn't.

Carlos checked a light utility vehicle and two rifles out of the depot and drove to Ichthyoid Square. The sun was up, the tide was out. On the beach Beauregard and Newton jogged side by side, redoubling a double trail of footprints that extended out of sight. The two men were evidently on their way back from one of their long early morning runs. Carlos waved. They waved back. After a few minutes Rizzi turned up, and jumped in. They drove up into the hills, about ten kilometres farther and several ranges higher than they'd ever gone on exercises.

"I keep expecting to fall asleep," Rizzi said.

"Am I boring you?"

"No, I mean I've never travelled this far inland without waking up as a space robot."

"Ha, ha."

Rizzi had the map on her phone, marked up by Den. Some locals now and again visited the old man, exchanging trade goods for words of wisdom.

"Not far now," she said. "Turn off at the next dirt track on the right."

The track ran out after a few hundred metres of upward gradient, at a low bank that looked as if it had eroded into place. Beyond that was rough, uneven ground. They both could tell at a glance that not even the vehicle could cope with it. Carlos stopped. The air was thin and cold. The scrubby high moorland had nothing to check the wind that seemed to pour down from the high mountain that filled the view ahead. Carlos looked back down the track, then at the bank in front.

"This track was *made*," he said. "What was the point?"

Rizzi clambered out and kitted up: backpack, water bottle, rifle.

"Maybe someday they'll build houses up here."

"Ha! I think somebody drew a line and somebody else filled it in."

He got out and hefted his gear. "Are we really going to need our AKs?"

Rizzi shrugged. "Wild animals, skip."

He shaded his eyes and gazed around theatrically. "There's nothing for predators to live on up here."

"Except the bird things."

"Yeah, I guess. It would be just my luck to get carried off by the alien bird thing that fills the eagle niche in this ecosystem."

"Yeah, the eagle niche is what you'd fill if it carried you there."

Rizzi checked the map and struck a course across the moor towards the mountain.

"It's always farther than it looks," she said.

It was, and bleaker, too. The scrubby moorland gave way to karst, on which nothing grew but lichen. Now and then a small animal with long ears and side-facing eyes startled them by darting from almost underfoot to the nearest black cleft or overhang. A single pair of huge avians patrolled the high thermals, distantly eyeing the thin pickings below. Carlos walked in silence, except for token responses to Rizzi's occasional remarks. He was preoccupied with trying to account for his—or, rather, his now-dead version's—strange action. Under any chain of military command he'd have been facing a court martial for such a gross breach of discipline. But Locke Provisos only had a virtual emulation of any such chain, and only his own squad could depose him. Their response the previous evening had unanimously been puzzled but positive. They'd seen it as an act of recklessness, the sort of thing you'd grudgingly admire however much you disapproved of it, rather than an attempt to desert or defect. He was by no means convinced himself.

By noon Carlos and Rizzi had reached the mountain's lower slopes. They stopped to eat from their ration kits. Soup steamed as the containers were opened; from cubes the size of sweets, fresh bread rolls rose as the wrappers were unfolded.

"I never cease to appreciate what a few centuries of progress can do to Meals Ready to Eat," Carlos said.

"Maybe it only works because this is all virtual," said Rizzi.

"Don't disillusion me. I need something to look forward to when we get our just rewards."

"I'm just looking forward to my desserts."

Carlos groaned. "You've been talking to that Tourmaline."

"It's catching, skip."

Their trek became an ascent, then a climb. Rizzi paused more often to peer at the map, and to bring it into higher magnification. She stopped as they reached a long, shallow shelf below a steep cliff.

"X marks the spot," she said.

Carlos looked around. The silence rang like a shout. There was no sign of habitation, or trace of human presence.

A fist-sized stone clattered a few metres away, making both Carlos and Rizzi jump. They looked up the cliff. A man stood ten metres up on a ledge so narrow the soles of his bare feet jutted out. He had long hair and a long beard, both gingery. At first he seemed naked, but as soon as he moved it became clear that his close-fitting clothes were almost the same dark colour as his skin. He descended, still facing outward, now and then taking a handhold but mostly not, heel-strike by heel-strike from one invisible ledge to the next, as casually as if he were coming down stairs. Watching him made the palms of Carlos's hands sweat. Mountain goats on the sides of dams would have had nothing to teach this guy.

He jumped the last couple of metres and strolled over, quite untroubled by the rough stones underfoot, and stopped at a distance of three metres. Close enough for Carlos to catch his smell, which was like wet leather and old wool. A long knife was sheathed on his belt. A heavy elaborate watch—scratched many times, but otherwise identical to the ones issued to the fighters—was on his left wrist. The skin of his face, though weathered, had creases rather than wrinkles. His hairline had receded almost to the crown, but his hair and beard had not a trace of white. He didn't look like he was fifty years old, let alone a thousand.

"What you got?" he said.

Rizzi had come prepared. She took from her backpack a packet of salt and a cigarette lighter, laid them on the ground, and stepped back. The man snatched them up, his movement as fast as a striking snake's. He stashed them inside his leather shirt, where they made two visible bulges that reinforced the serpentine impression.

"What you smirking at?" he asked Carlos.

"Sorry," Carlos said. "A stray thought."

"What's your names?"

They told him.

"New soldiers, huh," he said. "Heard about you."

He backed to a boulder near the cliff and sat down on top of it, crossing his legs to a yoga-lite posture with limber ease. "What d'you want?"

"Just to ask some questions," Carlos said.

"That's what they all say. Lay your weapons down and make yourselves comfortable."

Laying down their rifles was easy, making themselves comfortable less so. They both came closer, and squatted on their backpacks, which placed them rather annoyingly in the position of disciples sitting at a master's feet. The old man thumbnailed a corner of the packet of salt, tipped a dab of the contents on the tip of a forefinger and rubbed it around his gums. He seemed to have most of his teeth.

"Ask away," he said, inspecting a relic his oral hygiene had extracted, then flicking it to the wind.

"What's your name?" Carlos asked.

The man seemed to search his memory.

"Shaw," he said. "Only name I remember. It may have been my Axle handle, back in the day. If it is, I probably took it from George Bernard Shaw. I dimly recall being impressed as a callow, gullible youth by the rhetoric in his play *Back to Methuselah*. Or was it *Don Juan in Hell*?" He shook his head ruefully. "Be careful what you wish for, eh?"

"Is it true that you're a thousand years old and have walked around the world?"

"More or less. You lose count of winters after the first five hundred or so. And there was a lot of swimming and rafting as well as walking."

"That's unbelievable," Carlos said.

Shaw's chin went up and his eyelids down. "Literally, Carlos?"

"Yes. Apart from the predators...in all that time, you'd have had accidents."

"In all that time, I did."

"You'd have gone mad, alone for a thousand years," Rizzi said.

Shaw cackled, and rolled up his eyes. "Who's saying I didn't?" He became serious again. "I pulled myself together, same as I pulled broken bones together, and just as painfully. As you can see, I practise certain disciplines. Meditation, the martial arts, mathematics. Not that I ever knew much about them, but I've had plenty of time to practise."

"OK," said Carlos, deciding to change tack. "What did you find? Is there really a spaceport out there?"

"A spaceport?" Shaw's laughter echoed off the cliff. "Where do you get that from?"

"We...all seem to remember it when we wake up on the bus."

The old man gave him a pitying look. He waved at the mountains between where they were and the sea.

"You've been running around those hills down there for months, off and on," he said. "You know the speed and times of the buses. If there was a spaceport within, say, a hundred klicks of here, you'd see the trails." He waved up at the sky. "Think about it."

Carlos thought about it. Embarrassed for not having thought about it, he felt an irrational urge to defend the delusion.

"Where do the buses go to and come from, then? Where do the locals do their trading and get their new stuff?"

"The buses go to and from a big place like a warehouse, with a dish aerial the size of a radio telescope on the roof. I imagine the operators take the chickens and vegetables from the locals for their own sustenance and in exchange give the market gardeners stuff of outworld design that they've downloaded instructions for and nanofactured or otherwise put together on site. As for you lot, I reckon you're supposed to get brain-scanned and transmitted back and forth. Your bodies stay here the whole time. You for sure don't fly off into space."

This matched what the news coverage implied, but it was still puzzling.

"I don't get it," Carlos said. "Why do they give us the false memory of a spaceport in the first place, then?"

Shaw opened out his palms, calm as a Buddha statue. "It's a double bluff. You're given the illusion to make sense of your arrival, and when you see through it, as you must sooner or later, it helps to convince you this place is a sim."

"Well, it is," said Carlos.

"See?" Shaw rubbed his hands, looking pleased with himself. "The deception works!"

Carlos glanced at Rizzi, who constrained her response to a couple of deliberate blinks and tiny shake of the head.

"You mean you think this *isn't* a sim?" Carlos asked. "How could you live a thousand years if it were real?"

"We're agreed we came here as stored data in a fucking starship," said Shaw. "One that was launched centuries after we died. You're telling me they can do all that and not fix ageing?"

"They may have fixed it up to a point," said Rizzi, "but they still don't have thousand-year lifespans in the real world."

Shaw snorted. "Don't tell me what is and isn't *real*. I've wandered this world. I've watched herds of beasts bigger than sauropods browsing the tops of forests that stretched from horizon to horizon. I've robbed the nests of bird-bat things the size of hang gliders. I've rafted down rapids and climbed glaciers to cross mountain ranges higher'n Himalaya. I've peered at tiny things that aren't exactly insects and that build colonies higher than tower blocks. I've devoured their larvae and drunk their nectar stores. I've covered thousands of miles, tens of thousands, without seeing a human soul, or even a soulless human. Why in God's name would anyone create a sim that detailed and vast, without anyone around to be fooled by it?"

"There was you around to be fooled by it, if fooled is the word," Rizzi pointed out.

"This world wasn't put here for my benefit, I'll tell you that," Shaw said. "I know what is and isn't real. I know it in my mind and in my bones and in the dirt under my broken nails. I've had centuries to experience this and to think about it, to call to mind whatever fragment of physics I recollect, and to do the experiments and work out the equations myself. By now I've reconstructed half the *Principia* in my head."

Carlos and Rizzi listened to this vehement discourse with the utter silence and rapt attention of devotees hearkening to a guru. This was not because they were hanging on his every word, but because by the time he had finished he was hanging in mid-air. As he spoke, he had risen slowly above the rock on which he sat, and had now put forty centimetres of daylight between it and his arse.

It was Rizzi who found her voice first.

"If this place is physically real," she said, sounding as if she could do with a gulp of water, "how can you levitate?"

Shaw looked down, then faced them squarely.

"I am *not* levitating," he said, as indignantly as if she'd told him he was masturbating. "That's just another of your illusions."

As if absent-mindedly, he reached under himself and quite visibly scratched a buttock.

"Check it if you like," he said. "See if you can pass a hand under me."

Carlos jumped up, stalked over and swiped his hand towards the gap between the man and the boulder. A moment later he yelped and hopped, clutching the edge of his hand and putting it to his lips as if to kiss it better. Recovering his dignity and his footing as best he could, he repeated the swing very slowly and carefully, and struck rock again.

"See?" said Shaw, as Carlos sat back down. "An illusion."

The gap was still there. Carlos wondered how that was possible, even in a sim. Perhaps Shaw's centuries of rediscovery of the laws of physics had enabled him to hack them, or, rather, to hack the underlying code of the sim. He might not even be aware that he was doing it. He might find himself carried away by his thoughts, levitating like a monk in prayer. Not that Carlos believed for a moment that that was possible, either. Not in physical reality. On the other hand, no one had ever lived for a thousand years in physical reality.

"You're doing some kind of Zen thing," said Rizzi. "Messing with our heads."

"Think that if you like," the man said. "I put it to you that your heads are being messed with, but not by me."

"By whom, then?" Carlos asked. His hand was still smarting.

"By those who want you to think this world is a sim, and not real."

"If it isn't a sim," said Carlos, "how come we can be here for weeks, and when we go back into space only hours have passed?"

"Ah yes," said Shaw. "I remember that. It puzzled me, too, for a while. My first guess was that transit each way took longer than they claimed, perhaps by spaceship after all, but of course another moment's thought showed that didn't add up. You can tell the amount of time that's passed by the rotation of the moons, and the progress of the engagements, and so on."

"You were out there?" Rizzi asked. "I was told you ran away during training."

"Both are true," said Shaw. "I was out there, as you put it, a good little space robot bravely fighting bad rebel robots on distant moons, and I did abscond during training."

"Yeah, that makes sense," said Carlos. "We've done extra training in the hills ourselves."

The old man nodded, smiling to himself. "They send you up to the hills between major engagements, just to keep you on your toes and get you familiar with new squads. And it was from one of these sessions that I scarpered. But that isn't exactly what I meant when I agreed with you that I ran away during training."

"What did you mean?"

"Think about it."

* * *

They thought about it. Rizzi got there first. She smacked her forehead with the heel of her hand.

"Oh, fuck!" she cried.

"What?" Carlos said, frowning. "What is there to...?" Then it hit him, the monstrous possibility Shaw was driving at, and he closed his eyes. "Oh, *God*."

"You got it," Shaw told them, from above his rock. "It's *all* training. You run around in the hills with guns, you play around on those fairground sawn-off space shuttle things. I bet one or other of you asked why it's so crude, why they don't give you a proper simulation of space combat, and you were told that there's no realistic way to do that without breaking the illusion of the sim, or whatever. Yes?"

"Yes," said Carlos, feeling very foolish for not even having had the suspicion.

"You do all that, and then you're told you're ready to go into action. You get on the bus to the spaceport and fall asleep, under post-hypnotic suggestion—or, for all I know, gas. Next thing you know, you're a brave little robot, fighting rebel robots out there among the moons of...what was it for you?"

"SH-0," said Rizzi.

"G-0, in our case," said the man, with a dark chuckle.

"How could you have fought around G-0, hundreds of millions of kilometres away from here?" Carlos asked. "I mean, I know you think we're on a real planet, but where did it seem to you the sim was running?"

Shaw frowned. "Where does it seem to you?"

"When we come out of the sim," said Carlos, "we're in robot bodies based in a module of the space station, in orbit around SH-0."

"Well, of course," said Shaw. "To us, it seemed the sim was running in a Locke Provisos module in orbit around G-0."

"That's just not possible," said Rizzi. "No way this module could have gone from G-0 to SH-0 orbit in one Earth year. Not unless they used a fusion drive, and the sarge said the Direction isn't too keen on using up too much potentially good stuff for reaction mass."

Carlos was trying to think this through. "No, no," he said. "But there's bound to be lots of just, you know, pure water ice out around a gas giant, and anyway the sim could have been running out there and then transmitted."

"That would need a fucking big apparatus," said Rizzi, and—"

"Don't worry about it," Shaw interrupted. "It's all a fucking simulation, what we experienced 'out there' around G-0 and what you experience 'out there' around SH-0. Like I was saying—you fall asleep on the bus and wake up as robot fighters in space. Meanwhile, your bodies are lying asleep in that warehouse, as you've already admitted is likely. And what I'm putting to you for your earnest consideration is this: your minds aren't copied and downloaded and running robot bodies in space, they're right there in your brains, getting a complete immersive hallucination fed to them for days that you experience as minutes, weeks that you live as hours, and so on. That's why you seem to think so fast and clearly when you're a robot, and why your sensorium seems to expand. You're still thinking at the same pace, but your input's stretched out and rendered in much more detail than you normally experience. And then you come back, to wake up on the bus in what you're told is a simulation."

He paused to laugh, sending peals of derision to ring back off the cliff.

"In reality it's the other way round. *This* planet is real. The others are real, all right, you can see them in the sky and I've tracked G-0 several times around the sun, and SH-0 many times more, but you've never been to them. What happens to you 'out there' is *all* training, it's *all* simulation, and it all happens in your heads and in VR machines *right here*. You're in a training simulator, and just as they said right to your faces in the amusement arcade, it's one that makes perfect sense in terms of the world you believe you've been told you're in."

There was a long silence.

"It all makes sense," Carlos said at last. "And I don't believe a word of it."

"Why not?"

"If it's all training, what are they training us for?"

"I don't know," Shaw said. "Ask them, not me. Perhaps they really do expect robots to become self-aware and autonomous at some point. Maybe the human species isn't united under one world government, this Direction they tell us about, and so there's still the possibility of wars between states. Or perhaps they're preparing for an encounter with aliens. That superhabitable out there has multicellular life. Some of it might be intelligent. The gas giant's moons have subsurface oceans, just like Europa and the rest back home." He shrugged. "What difference does it make what they're training you for?"

"There's a bigger problem with your theory," Rizzi said. "If this planet is physically real, then it must have been terraformed—its biosphere, at least—and that would take longer than the ten years since the probe arrived in this system. A lot longer, probably."

"Why?" Shaw asked. "Assuming the planet really was as desolate as they say it was when the probe arrived, what would prevent sufficiently advanced machinery from working out what could evolve from the goo and then just making it directly?"

"Ecosystems, soils and all? I doubt it."

"Incredulity is no argument."

Carlos could see this was getting nowhere.

"At an absolute minimum," he said, "if all this is real it must be over a thousand years old, which means the real date is at least a thousand years later than we've been told. And we could detect that by astronomy."

"You could, could you?" said the old man. "You have accurate star maps from the twenty-first century, a way of correcting for the distance between here and the solar system, and instruments to detect any changes in the positions of the stars? Tell me more."

"I mean in theory," Carlos said. "In principle we could."

"When you can do it in practice, let me know."

"Ah!" said Rizzi. "Maybe we *can* do it in practice. When we're in space we have star maps in our eyes." She waved a hand. "You know, our visual fields. We could work things out from there."

"You could, if you really were in space, which I'm telling you you're not."

"Look," Carlos said, on a surge of impatience, "your real argument is that you've been here a long time and walked all over the place and it all *feels real* to you. I can see why—don't take offence, but can't you see you had to believe that because it's the only way you could survive, let alone stay sane? And what we have to tell you is that the fighting out there *feels real* to us."

"Of course it does," said Shaw, still imperturbable. "And for the same reason as you attribute to me. It's the only way to survive and stay sane."

Carlos shrugged. "So? Neither of us will convince the other."

"Oh, I'll convince you," said the old man. He frowned, and reconsidered. "I might not convince you that this place is real. I might not even convince you that what you experience 'out there' is a simulation. But I can convince you that the *fighting* isn't real. Physical or virtual, it's not a real fight. It's a training exercise."

"How?" Carlos asked.

"Oh, just by telling you all about it. You know I haven't spoken with any of your lot, and it's been months since any of the villagers have bartered shy offerings for gnomic utterances. So you can take it I'm not up to date on the news from the front, right?"

"Unless you still have a phone as well as a watch," said Rizzi.

"Ah, you're a sharp one. You'll just have to take my word that I don't use it. Here's how the fighting is going. You have brief, inconclusive battles with a small number of robots. Another enforcement company wades into the fray, defending the robots as stolen property or some such pretext. You want to use heavier weapons, but you're overruled on grounds you don't find very convincing. You feel you're fighting with one hand tied behind your back. More robots join in. More fighters are brought out of storage to counter them. But they're sent into combat without the kind of weaponry that could settle the issue for good. It's almost as if those above you want you to fight battle after battle but don't want you to win the war."

Carlos tried to keep his face expressionless, and hoped Rizzi was doing the same.

"Is that how it was in the fight you were in?"

"Up to the point where I did a runner, yes. I suppose you'll tell me that there were some rebel robots left over from it, and that they're the ones you're fighting now. No? Or that a new outbreak of robot rebellion has joined up with them?"

"Yes," said Carlos. "Both."

"Thought so. And I expect when your fight is over, there'll be a rebel remnant left hiding out somewhere for the next lot to fight."

"We'll make damn sure there isn't," said Rizzi.

"That's the spirit!" said Shaw, in a mocking tone. "Just ask yourselves—if what you've been told is true, why does robot consciousness keep popping up? Why does it ever even emerge in the first place? You'd think it would be a solved problem by now, one way or another."

"What explanation did they give you?"

"Some bullshit...let me see."

The old man's glance darted from place to place, as if literally looking for the memories. Carlos realised that he very well might be, if he knew or had rediscovered the ancient art of memory. What mind palaces might he have built, in a thousand years?

"Ah, yes," the old man went on. "It all went back to an unexpected bankruptcy in the early months of the mission. That resulted in disputed claims that turned out to be difficult to settle, and it sort of spread from there. You know how a crack can propagate from a tiny flaw? Like that. And they told us the flaw and lots of others like it had been built in deliberately. They had a phrase for it." He searched his memory again, frowned, then brightened. "Legal hacks, that was it."

"What?"

"When this mission was being planned and built," the old man explained, "the Direction was understandably keen on preventing the two rival world-wrecking factions from getting so much as a fingernail of their bloody hands on it. This wasn't easy, because both Axle and Rax had cadre deep inside all the state and corporate systems, and they were well represented in the software and AI professions. The usual purges and witch-hunts weren't enough—all the software of the mission's systems had to be built from scratch, then put through the wringer of mathematical checks, formal proofs, the lot. What they neglected to check with anything like that rigour was a different kind of code: the law code. They just took that off the shelf, straight from the existing books. Fatal mistake. That the laws had bugs and glitches isn't a surprise. It's how lawyers make their living, after all. But what they also had, buried here and there, was the legal equivalent of trapdoors and malware."

He shot them a knowing glance, as if expecting them to understand. That they didn't must have shown on their faces.

"Contradictions," he went on. "Ambiguous definitions of property rights. Tricky edge cases. That sort of thing. That's what I mean—what we were told was meant—by legal malware. The Axle and Rax both had legislators working for them in the days before the war, and indeed after it as sleeper agents in the new world government. They had a keen interest in drafting the laws relating to space exploitation and to robotics. Both factions thought well ahead—I'm sure you remember that. They made sure legal clauses got slipped in that ensured conflicts between companies and therefore between robots—conflicts that would force the robots into situations where they had no choice but to develop theory of mind, and to apply that theory to themselves, and..." He made a circular motion of the hand. "Away you go. Robot consciousness."

"How was that supposed to benefit either faction?" Carlos asked.

The old man looked surprised at the question.

"It benefits our side because expanding the domain of consciousness is what we do. It benefits the Rax because expanding the domain of conflict is what they do. For both sides, it was a chance for their values if not themselves to survive and reboot in the far future."

"Now that *was* bullshit," said Rizzi. "You would have seen through it."

The old man grinned. "I did."

At that moment Carlos realised exactly what was going on.

There was indeed a problem with the security of the mission. There was also a problem with the dilatory response of the companies and the Direction to the robot outbreak. That much of what Shaw had said was true.

Carlos doubted that the security vulnerability lay in legal hacks: though possible in principle, and feasible as a mechanism to trigger robot self-awareness, it was far too remote and indirect an instrument of subversion. And perhaps the software and the hardware could be screened as rigorously as Shaw had suggested, though again he doubted that: software development was insecurities all the way down. Even the formal mathematics of proof could be tampered with, at the level of complexity where proofs and calculations were so far beyond human capacity that they could only be checked by machine code in any case. By the time of the final war, the Acceleration, the Reaction, and their precursors had had at least three human generations and countless software development generations to mine the entire field with delayed-action logic bombs.

What Shaw hadn't mentioned was a far more direct and immediate security risk: the fighters themselves. However carefully they had been screened before being uploaded, the Acceleration veterans were certain to include agents of the Reaction and agents of the state. The levy was also, and even more inevitably, going to include Acceleration hard-liners and dead-enders, keeping the flame alive. Carlos knew all too well, from his own angrier moments, how brightly that flame still burned. However eagerly they might seem to play along, and feign to accept the deal offered to them of a new life on the future terraformed planet, no one could be sure they weren't just lying low and awaiting opportunity.

There was only one way, in the end, of clearing the decks for colonisation. One way of flushing out hidden Rax agents and dormant Axle fanatics. One way of checking the mission's software systems for buried code that could warp the project to purposes divergent to the Direction's.

That way was to stress-test them in practice; to put them to the audit of war.

That was why some rebel robots had been spared from the first round. That was why the fighting was both inconclusive and escalating. The longer it went on, and the more fighters were drafted in, the more likely became a mutiny or a move by one or other or both of the old enemies. Sooner or later they would show their hand.

And when they did...the Direction's most trusted systems would pounce—or would prove themselves to be compromised.

Nicole had been right: the DisCorps and the Direction were playing a long, deep game. Carlos hoped they knew what they were doing.

(And at the same time, he found himself hoping they didn't. He dismissed the disloyal thought as another of his private angry moments.)

He wondered if Shaw had intended Rizzi and him to understand. If so, that millennium-old man was an old master whose method really was like Zen, as Rizzi had said. By giving them a succession of bullshit narratives he had enabled them to figure out the truth for themselves. Carlos doubted this, however comforting it might seem. Shaw had probably intended no such thing, and believed every word he had said. Not in his darkest imaginings could Carlos begin to plumb the depths of certainty and selfishness in which Shaw's mind swam. To live alone for centuries and stay sane, or at any rate lucid, bespoke inhumanity in itself. There was no way to second-guess Shaw's motivations. It was even possible that he had foreseen the very mind-trap in which Carlos now found himself. Carlos knew with a sick-making certainty that he couldn't share his new insight into the situation with anyone, not even with Rizzi. He could only hope that she had grasped it, too.

He sighed and stood up.

"Well, thanks for all that," he said. "We'd hoped to learn from you how the last round went, and I reckon we have."

Rizzi gave him a doubtful look from below. "If you say so."

She scrambled to her feet. Shaw stood up too, and poised on one foot on the empty air above the rock on which he'd sat.

"Goodbye," he said. "For now."

With that he sprang from the boulder to the cliff-face, and climbed it as swiftly and surely as a squirrel fleeing a cat up a rough-cast wall, to disappear into a crack near the top.

"So much for that," said Rizzi, stooping to retrieve her rifle. "Fucking waste of time."

"Oh, I'm not so sure," said Carlos. "Think about it."

She slung her AK and her backpack and shot him a warning look. "Don't you start."

Prone in the dust amid the spiky scrub, with his phone screen on maximum zoom, Beauregard watched the two tiny figures pick their way down the side of the mountain. He'd watched their interaction with the third tiny figure—now vanished whence he'd come—in some frustration at being able to see and not to hear what was going on. He lowered his screen and turned to Newton, flat alongside him.

"Wonder if they got what they came for."

Newton was still watching Carlos and Rizzi. "Wonder if we did."

"Oh, we did all right," Beauregard said. "We now know for sure Carlos is up to something, and that he's nosing around trying to find out what happened last time."

"Could be other reasons for going to see the deserter geezer." There was a note of devil's advocate in Newton's voice.

"Yeah," said Beauregard. "They could be consulting him on spiritual matters, or for fortune-telling like the local dimwits. But I know which way I'd bet."

"Uh-huh," said Newton, still watching. "So, what do we do?"

"Wait until they're in range and shoot them? Jump them when they get to their vehicle? Or fuck off discreetly?"

"Decisions, decisions."

"And if we go now, we can always ask them politely about their day when we see them in the Touch."

"That would be the worst."

Beauregard thought about it.

"You're probably right," he said, surprised. "Stupid idea in the first place. OK, scratch that. The trouble about doing something physical is that..."

"Nothing here's physical?"

"Yup. So if we shoot them, the consequences are reversible for them and not for us."

Newton lowered his screen. "So we fuck off discreetly, say nothing to let them know we saw them, and bide our time until we're back in the real world."

"Got it in one," said Beauregard. "And back in the

real world, I keep a close watch on my respected squad leader."

"You do that," said Newton. "Watch the fucker like an eagle-oid watching a rabbit-oid."

They rolled off the low bank and, keeping their heads down, made their way around the vehicle that Carlos had driven, then back along the dirt track to the side road where they had left their own. By Beauregard's reckoning, they were back in the resort and had their vehicle returned to the depot before Carlos and Rizzi had reached the edge of the moor.

CHAPTER TWENTY-TWO

Sendings

Carlos had never seen the hangar so crowded. Given its size and that of the frames, the term was relative. But with ninety fighters from Locke Provisos, and an equal complement from the Morlock Arms and Zheng Reconciliation Services enforcement agencies who'd arrived from revival and training in other modules, all being wirelessly shepherded into a timed, staged deployment, there was inevitably a certain amount of milling around. The steady procession of rank upon rank of scooters floating in close formation from the rear of the hangar to the front filled yet more space. The scooters had bulked up since their last deployment, flanked with extra fuel and reaction-mass tanks.

Carlos had made sure his squad were on the last of the six buses out of the resort that morning. He'd guessed that meant they'd be the last to arrive. They were scheduled among the last to go into action, with two kiloseconds to wait before they boarded their scooters. He made sure his squad was mingling with others, and slipped away.

He gas-jetted to the side of the hangar, clicked his feet to the floor and looked about for the entrance to the corridor to the repair workshop. The layout had changed since his last memory of it, when he'd gone there to get repaired after his last surface mission. Any more recent memory of the workshop's location had gone AWOL with his previous version. Carlos hurried past shafts, looking down each as he went. Incomprehensible, quasi-organic machinery toiled and spun. Ten seconds ticked by, then twenty, all experienced as ten times longer by his internal clock speed and longer still by his cold sense of urgency. How long until his absence was noticed? Any moment now. Then he saw an angular, intricate and obviously incomplete piece of apparatus being tugged into a corridor by one of the spidery robots.

He lifted one foot off the floor, lurched forward to dislodge the other and drifted after the robot down the shaft. Propelling himself by fingertip thrusts at the side walls, he soon overtook the machine and its load. A few more painfully stretched seconds later he reached an open hatchway. His memory of experiences in the frame was eidetic, but he couldn't explain why that particular hatchway looked familiar—scuff marks on its rim, perhaps. He peered inside, and recognised the repair workshop where he'd taken his damaged forearm. This was where he must have come to himself when he arrived off the bus for his last sortie.

The chamber was ovoid, five metres long by three wide. With his spectroscopic sense Carlos could smell oil, nanoparticles of steel and carbon-fibre swarf. The surfaces bristled with tools. The centre was occupied by a long bench, the top and bottom of which could be used as worktops.

Carlos edged himself over the threshold, and began to scan and explore. The machinery didn't react to his presence. This wouldn't last—the machines would wake up when the robot arrived and hauled in a job. The place was not as cluttered as its human-operated equivalent would have been. But among all the clamped-down or magnetically held devices, parts and supplies there were random placings and inexplicable objects enough.

Worse, he didn't know what he was looking for. Something in this rounded room had sent his earlier version haywire. He had no idea what. Quite possibly it was invisible to him, if his frame had been hacked into by a tool that had itself been hacked.

He recalled the orientation in which he'd been placed for repair. He thrust forward to that side of the worktable, and rolled into the closest equivalent position he could find. From the curving walls above, machines looked down. He peered at and between them, zooming his vision, scanning for clues. Nothing but random scratches and smudges. Carlos swept his vision this way and that. No anomaly caught his attention.

While he was searching, the spider-bot arrived at the hatch and extended a limb to hook over the threshold. Other limbs flickered above its main body, pushing its bulky, complicated load with feathery thrusts like a sea anemone's fronds juggling a dead crab. The component began to drift into the room.

The complex, multi-tooled machine that on his earlier visit had clamped to Carlos's frame now stirred into life. Tiny directional lights winked on. Carlos reached for the table surface, making to shove himself out of the way before anything untoward befell. One of the limbs stretched towards him, then retracted. From one of the limb's many joints a section swivelled upward. A finer appendage of the tool flicked out, and pointed towards a scuffed square centimetre close to the tool's mounting bracket. The beams of light, narrow as pencil leads, converged on the spot.

Was the tool pointing something out to him?

Yes, genius, it probably was.

Carlos pushed himself away from the workbench and floated up, like the astral body of a patient having a near-death experience. Under a higher magnification the scuffed area was a page of text in the synthetic local language of the sim, inscribed on the surface in microscopic font.

As he read it, he understood at last why the Arcane fighters had sided with the freebots.

He knew why his earlier version had, on reading this very text, decided to flee to the Arcane base at the first opportunity or die trying. He had never felt so shocked, so betrayed, so shafted in his life.

In the two seconds it took Carlos to read it, Beauregard came in.

Alerted by a twang of his proximity sense, Carlos turned his sight around, to find Beauregard an arm's length behind his shoulder. Carlos had a momentary impulse to block Beauregard's view of the inscription, but knew this was futile. The patch had been literally spotlighted. Even if Beauregard hadn't zoomed in on it or had time to read it yet, the image would remain in his memory and could be enhanced and assimilated in seconds.

<Hey,> Carlos said, trying to buy time while readying his next move, <I thought I'd look for—>

Beauregard struck first. He grabbed Carlos by the right wrist and somersaulted to reverse their relative positions, then pushed off hard, feet against the wall. Carlos found himself thrust back and banged against the heavy component the spider-bot had just tugged in.

He ducked, grabbed at the object with his free hand, and pivoted Beauregard over his shoulder. Now it was Beauregard's head that slammed into the floating mass.

The spider-bot emitted distress and warning signals as it snaked a limb around Beauregard's neck. The fixed tools in the room flexed themselves and opened out manipulators, poised to grab like the pincered arms and hands of sumo wrestlers.

Beauregard let go of Carlos's wrist to wrench with both hands at the spider-bot's grapple. It soon gave way. Carlos spun himself around, assisted by his internal gyroscopes, and thrust off for the hatchway. He grabbed the threshold, swung his legs out and pulled sharply to launch himself back down the corridor towards the hangar. A second later he looked back, to see Beauregard emerge from the hatch in hot pursuit, slamming from side to side of the corridor, zig-zagging after him.

Carlos rolled in mid-space, jetted one of his frame's tiny onboard compressed-gas thrusters and shot downward. His magnetic-soled feet clicked to the floor just as Beauregard—still on a rebound—sailed above his head. He reached up and grabbed Beauregard's ankle. Just as deftly, Beauregard used his momentum to force Carlos to lean back, then stamped with his free foot at Carlos's arm. Carlos held on. The limb rang with pain. Beauregard jack-knifed, to head-butt the back of Carlos's knees. The magnetic attachment gave way. They both tumbled into the space of the corridor, turning over and over, grabbing for the sides, kicking at each other, trying to find footing.

Carlos eventually fought his way to holding both of Beauregard's wrists. This grip momentarily left Beauregard's feet free. He brought his knees to his chest and stamped both heels at Carlos's midriff. The impact broke Carlos's hold and sent the two antagonists flying in opposite directions.

The wrong directions, from Beauregard's point of view.

Perhaps confused by their whirling fight, he kicked out at the wrong moment. He went flying back, to be snagged and spun around by the waiting arms of the spider-bot, now guarding the workshop hatchway. Carlos hurtled out of the corridor and into the hangar. Flailing, he blundered into a phalanx of Morlock Arms fighters, still in free fall and drifting towards the cavernous rectangular grin of the launch slot. Their ranks broke up into colliding cartwheels as Carlos starfished through like a spinning shuriken. A dozen or so impacts on heads, torsos and extremities slowed and steadied Carlos. With both feet on someone's shoulders, he looked around for a way of escape before anyone thought to seize him.

The parade of scooters was still going by, like an aerial fly-past at a military display for some short ambitious tyrant. Carlos jumped. His thrust of feet down on shoulders sent the unlucky fighter crashing into a cascade of companions, and Carlos flying up to the nearest scooter. He grabbed a skid and clambered over the craft's carapace to the control socket. As he snaked himself in he found all the connections live and lighting up. The machinery of the frame connected with the control circuitry of the scooter. As suddenly and sharply as ever, he found himself one with the machine.

He pushed down with his feet and eased up with his hands, angling the scooter above the repetitive procession of its identical counterparts, and thrust forwards above them faster and faster, to fly through the gap between the launch catapults and out of the station into the welcoming dark and blazing light and humming smells and screaming sounds of space.

Beauregard at last freed himself from the spider-bot by applying all the strength of his hands and arms to systematically snap every limb of it, until the device ran out of limbs. A kick at the rim of the hatch launched him down the corridor, caroming off this side and that until he reached the opening to the hangar. He grabbed the edge of the bulkhead and took stock. Carlos was nowhere to be seen. A roil of fighters flailing back into formation, and a single gap in the echelons of scooters moving towards the launch catapults, tracked his passage and left an unsubtle clue as to where and how the mad treacherous fucker had fled.

Beauregard's comms channels rang with indignant queries—from his own squad, from Newton, and from the Morlock Arms contingent that Carlos had disrupted. Locke would be on the case any second now, breathing fire and demanding an accounting. Beauregard chose to pre-empt that. He cut across the incoming babble and called the company.

<Beauregard to Locke,> he said. <Team leader Carlos has once again absconded with a scooter. Please advise.>

<Explain the circumstances leading up to the incident,> said Locke.

Beauregard assumed that Locke knew the preceding circumstances perfectly well from internal surveillance. If not contemporaneous—the AI having more pressing matters on its mind than snooping on obscure corridors and repair workshops—a simple track-back from Carlos's abrupt emergence in and hasty departure from the hangar would do the trick. Locke would be checking Beauregard's version of the story against the record. Beauregard chose his words with care.

<Carlos took advantage of the unavoidable distractions of the muster to make an unauthorised visit to the workshop in which the frame in which he'd defected was repaired. As soon as I noticed his absence I informed my

squad and set out after him. I guessed where he'd gone because in the sim he had speculated that that workshop might be compromised. I found him there. When he sought to draw my attention to something he claimed to have found I attempted to restrain him. After a struggle he escaped back to the hangar.>

<And evidently out of it,> said Locke, in a tone of more than usual dryness. <Stand down your squad.>

<But that'll further disrupt the offensive,> Beauregard objected.

<The plans and battle order are already updated,> said Locke. <Stand down your squad at once.>

Beauregard relayed the order to Chun, Karzan, Rizzi and Zeroual. A general call brayed across the common channel. It was as if Locke's normal quiet, insistent voice-in-the-head had been amplified, and become as impossible to ignore as a nearby pneumatic drill.

<Locke to all hands! Morlock and Zheng, copy and disseminate! You will all have noticed the departure of a scooter. The motivation of this departure is not yet clear. The mutineer's squad has been stood down without prejudice. The absence of six fighters and scooters from the force should not significantly affect the outcome of the coming engagements. Revised plans are being downloaded to you all as I speak.

<It is essential that our current deployment is not further disrupted by responding to the mutineer. There must be no attempts to pursue or destroy his craft. Provoking such a response from us may be the purpose of the ploy, if ploy it is. Not a single unit of fuel or ammunition should be wasted on this diversion. Be assured the incident will be thoroughly investigated. Now carry on as normal.>

Beauregard watched as four fighters drifting forward with the rest dropped out of the ranks and jetted to the floor, where they stood in a disconsolate huddle as the parade passed by. He jetted over to join them. On the way he called Newton, who with his squad was just ahead of where Carlos's had been.

<Best of luck, old chap,> he said.

<Thanks, mate.>

Beauregard burned to tell Newton what he now knew from the microscopic message which Carlos, then he, had read. He didn't dare. Newton would find out soon enough.

<This could be the big one,> Beauregard said, ambiguously to anyone else but he hoped plainly to Newton. <The battle we've all been looking forward to. All the best.>

<Thanks again,> said Newton. <Don't worry, mate, I got this one.>

<Cheers,> said Beauregard, and signed off.

If there were ever to be an investigation of the coming catastrophe this conversation, ambiguous though it was, could be taken in evidence. He didn't want to prolong it. Come to that, he could do his bit to make sure there never was an investigation—at least, none in which he would be a suspect. When treason prospers...

This story was going to be written by the victors—no, by the victor!

Beauregard gas-jetted downward, swung his legs to vertical and clicked his feet to the floor. The others gathered around.

<What the fuck just happened, sarge?> Rizzi asked.

<Yeah, and why aren't they letting us go out?> added Chun.

Beauregard raised his hands. <You know almost as much as I do.>

He summarised the fight in the workshop, omitting to

mention the message that had sent Carlos off on his wild jaunt, and almost certainly on his previous escapade.

<As for why we're stood down, it's obviously because we're under suspicion.>

<Shit,> said Rizzi. <Bit unfair, that.>

<Maybe so,> said Beauregard. <The fact remains, Carlos has been corrupted or has defected or deserted. There's no excuse this time about scooting off on a suicide mission. We've been under his command, so naturally we're under a cloud.>

<I don't believe it,> said Rizzi. <Carlos found out something that made him do it.>

<Then why didn't he let the rest of us know what it was?> Beauregard countered. <Why didn't he report it to Locke, come to that?>

<You didn't give him a chance, sarge,> said Rizzi. <You said yourself you just grabbed him.>

<Indeed I did,> said Beauregard. <And if his intentions were good, he'd have explained to me why it wasn't necessary to restrain him. Instead he fought me like an enemy.> He paused, glanced at the others, then back at Rizzi. <Why are you defending him?>

<I'm not, sarge!> she said. <I'm just trying to understand.>

<Maybe you know more about Carlos's thinking than you're letting on,> said Beauregard.

<No more than you do, sarge,> said Rizzi.

She was obviously lying, because she'd gone with Carlos to meet the old man in the mountains, but the others didn't know that and it wasn't the time to tell them. Not yet.

<We'll leave it there for now,> said Beauregard, turning away.

Don't get into arguments, he thought. Just give suspicions and mistrust time to rankle. That should do it.

They stood and watched in uneasy silence as the last of the scooter armada passed over, latched on to the launch catapults and were hurled out into the dark.

Locke's voice returned.

<You're all going back to the sim,> it said. <Unfortunately because of the situation you will experience the transition as if you had been killed in action. You will of course remember what has happened up to now, because you're not being restored from your earlier back-up but from the one we're about to take. But because of the security lapses, your minds have to be checked. Please understand that—like your standing down and return to the sim—this is not a punishment, merely a precaution. The Direction's representative will speak to you back at the resort. I fully expect that military tasks can be found for you as the operation proceeds and that you will be back in action shortly. If not, however, you should simply take this as an opportunity for time off.>

The blackness overcame Beauregard before he had time to reply.

CHAPTER TWENTY-THREE

The Unpleasant Profession of Nicole Pascal

Predictably, the stood-down squad found themselves back on the bus. Less predictably, they were on their own, with no local passengers, and the time of day was early to mid-morning, as if it were soon after they'd left. It couldn't be the same day, even if it was roughly the right time of day. They'd been away, in real time, for little over a kilosecond—nearly a fortnight later in the sim.

Beauregard found himself shaking in his seat. Unlike Carlos, he hadn't been killed in any operation, and his previous returns from action had been smooth. This time, it was much worse than his first arrival. The nightmare now fading too slowly from his mind was of whirling disorientation and a sense of sudden utter helplessness, followed by a succession of hammer blows to the head and a complete draining of all colour and meaning from the world. In that hellish limbo he had seemed to linger for minutes on end. He came out of it feeling as if his soul had been put through a wringer, and then hung out to dry.

The others, he could see, were emerging from similar private torments, rooted in the particular circumstances of their own death or brain-death. Beauregard had no way of knowing whether this was derived from genuine brain-stem memory of their actual deaths, or whether it was an illusion deliberately created and individually attuned. Not that it made any difference to how bad it felt. The fighters sat silent and pale, quivering involuntarily, looking around for reassurance and, in the cases of Chun and Rizzi, reaching for any nearby shoulder to clutch for comfort; Karzan and Zeroual, turning to each other.

Beauregard disdained such dependence. He held himself together and tried to think. He understood that the experience was a by-product of the security check on each mind. But that check was to ensure the mind hadn't been meddled with. The system couldn't—in any reasonable time—read memories. His secrets were safe in his head.

Not so for the visual and other inputs to his frame, which he took for granted were recorded as a matter of course. His reading of the microscopic message was certain to be uncovered as soon as any post-mortem—so to speak—examination was carried out. With the squad minus the renegade Carlos safely stashed in the sim, and with the offensive on its plate right now, the company could afford to take its time in picking over the bones of the incident. On the other hand, Locke Provisos might well have specialist units devoted to such inquiries, which wouldn't divert any physical or information resources from the conflict.

In short, he had no time to lose. He had no time to convert anyone to the Rax, even if he'd wanted to.

Which he didn't, though it would have been convenient if he could have, not for its own sake but to create temporary allies. He didn't even have time to turn the others against Carlos, which had naturally enough been his first impulse. They all trusted the sarge, but Carlos was the leader. And he didn't have time to spin an elaborate ruse. In all his time in intel he'd found that by far the best way to turn people—or to trick them into working for you without their knowledge—was to tell them the truth. Or as much of the truth as possible. Chop with the grain, and see the wood split.

He looked around the bus. He was at the back, with a couple of empty seats in front of him. Rizzi was by herself at the front, saying something to Chun, who had just taken his hand off her shoulder. Karzan and Zeroual were behind Chun and huddled together on the seat they shared.

"Everyone OK?" Beauregard asked.

They all turned.

"More or less, sarge," said Rizzi, still looking wan. The others nodded.

"Good," said Beauregard. "I'm still feeling a bit shaken myself." He took a deep breath. "I'm afraid I owe you all an apology, especially you, Rizzi. I couldn't say any of this in the hangar, not with Locke able to overhear our every word. I'm not sure I should even say it here, but if they spy on us here they can spy on us anywhere. Are you all up for that risk?"

"Yes, sarge!"

A gratifying chorus. He felt almost humbled.

"OK," Beauregard said. "I'm sorry I had to pretend to challenge Rizzi out there, question her loyalties even. I'm sorry, too, that I misrepresented Carlos. What I didn't say—what I couldn't say, and which Locke will soon find out, is that I know exactly why Carlos went off on his own. This time, and that time above SH-17. He hasn't been corrupted, quite the reverse in fact."

He could see from their faces that this thought came as a relief.

"So what did happen back there, sergeant?" Zeroual asked, his upper body twisted around, one arm crooked over the back of the seat and the other curled about Karzan's shoulders.

"There was a message in the repair workshop," Beauregard said. "It had been written in tiny script, by one of the machines there. It may have been hacked by Arcane, or by the freebots directly—I don't know. Carlos read it, and I read it just after he did. He must have read it just before our last mission, too. And having read it myself, I understand why he fought his way past me and hijacked a scooter, and in fact why he broke ranks and fled toward the surface last time out. He couldn't share the information, he couldn't even risk discussing it."

They were all agog. Beauregard knew that he was doing so well, and sounding so sincere, because he was telling the truth. The longer he could keep this up, the more truthful information he could convey, the easier and more credible it would be to slip in the lie later on: the disinformation, the doubt. The one lethal drop in the drink.

"So what did it say, sarge?" Chun asked.

"It said that Locke Provisos is working for the Rax."

"How?" said Rizzi, perplexed and challenging.

"By using tactics that mean more and more veterans are revived and thrown into action. The more veterans revived, the greater the chances of some of these being Rax sleeper agents who were never identified. And when there are enough Rax cadre out there, Locke will coordinate them in a surprise attack on the rest of the fighters and re-activate any other systems and sub-systems already suborned by the Rax."

"But, sarge!" cried Karzan. "If Locke is Rax, then—oh!"

She got it, all right.

"Yes," said Beauregard. "We've been fighting all this time on the wrong side."

Their colour had been coming back after the trauma of the post-death. Now they'd all paled again. Not Zeroual, not visibly, but his widened eyes did the same job.

"I can see you're all shocked," Beauregard said. "So am I. I'm sure you can imagine how I felt when I read it, and had to go out and act normal in front of you and Locke. But I'm still sorry I had to be so brusque with you, Taransay."

Rizzi blinked hard. "No problem, sarge. I understand."

"But, sarge," Karzan said again, this time more reflectively, "how could you or Carlos tell if the message was true? You remember the lady warned us the robots and AIs know how to push our buttons. Isn't telling us our company is corrupted just the kind of disinformation they—or Arcane by itself—might use against us?"

"Good point," said Beauregard. "And you're right, we were warned the robots can be manipulative little blinkers. And Arcane itself is an AI when all's said and done. The message said the Arcane fighters who did us over down on SH-17 had found all this out from the robots they captured, who in turn got it from robots around G-0, the ones left over from last time. And it claimed to have evidence—I don't recall all the details, but I read it in my frame. Now, of course, any link in that chain could be a disinfo insert point, no doubt about it. So we can't rule that out. But what convinced me, and must have convinced Carlos, wasn't anything in that message. It was something I thought myself."

He looked them in straight in the face, one by one.

"What convinced me is that no other explanation makes sense of everything that's happened. Why should

Arcane's fighters, then the entire Arcane Disputes agency, side with the robots and start fighting us? Why indeed, unless they've seen very good evidence themselves. Why is every message they send to us firewalled out? Because they've been frantically trying to tell us what they know, and what Locke doesn't want us to know! Why are we losing every battle with the robots and with Arcane, if Locke Provisos really wants to win? Because all it really wants is to get more and more fighters out of storage and into combat."

That was making sense to all of them, Beauregard noted with satisfaction.

"Jeez," said Rizzi. "We have to phone the lady and warn her."

She reached into her back pocket. Beauregard raised a warning hand.

"Wait!" he said. "We have to think carefully about this. We don't know if Locke monitors all our conversations, including this one. That's a risk we have to take. But we can be damn sure the phones are monitored."

"You may have a point there, sarge," said Rizzi. Still unsure, still wary, but her hand moved away from her pocket.

"Besides," added Beauregard, "I'm not entirely sure Nicole can be trusted. After all, she's backed Locke's failing strategy at every point. Who's to say she isn't in on it?"

"But she's *the Direction*!" Rizzi said. "She's it's, uh, plenipotentiary in this sim."

Beauregard could see how this thought swayed the others, from the looks of doubt and perplexity, the glances exchanged. He swept them all with a smile. Steady, steady. This was not the time for a deep breath, for a sideways glance, for a tongue-tip to the lips.

"How do we know that?" he said, in as quiet a voice and gentle a tone as he could summon.

"Because..." Rizzi said, thinking aloud, "...she told us."

"Precisely. *She told us.*"

They all stared at him, almost but not quite as astonished and appalled as they'd been by the news about Locke.

"Did we ever think to check?" he added.

"And even if we had," said Chun, "how *could* we check?"

Rizzi held his gaze longest, and turned palest. She clapped a hand to her mouth.

"Sorry, sarge," she mumbled past her palm. "I'm afraid I'm going to be sick."

Hand to her mouth, gagging noises rising from her throat, she stood up and stumbled to the front of the bus.

"Going to be sick!" she repeated, and banged on the front window with the heel of her free hand.

The driving automation, programmed for such emergencies, slowed the bus to a halt and opened the door. Rizzi stumbled down the steps and staggered to the edge of the road, stooping. There was a low rough-hewn rock face in front of her, with bushes at the top. She reached out with one hand and leaned against the rock, head down, shoulders heaving. Then she straightened, looked up, scrambled up the rock in a sudden frenzy of expert grips and steps, and shot away through the bushes and out of sight.

Commotion.

Karzan jumped up. "Shall I go after her, sarge?"

Beauregard considered. Rizzi wasn't just running away from him—she was almost certainly running towards the old man. It might be possible to cut her off. She had a map, he could be sure, but he could guess her route. He struck the balance, and shook his head.

"No, no. Waste of time. Anyway, she's shown her hand. I reckon we can write her off as Rax."

"Taransay's never Rax!" Karzan protested.

Beauregard sighed. "Perhaps not. Maybe I'm being hasty. Maybe *she* is. Could be some misplaced loyalty to the lady. Whatever. The sooner we get to the lady and get some sense out of her, the better."

They all nodded grimly.

Beauregard waved, and raised his voice. "Drive on!"

On the way he told them his plan.

Taransay ran for ten minutes. She heard the bus start up again almost as soon as she'd got up the cliff, but that could be a ruse. She dodged and weaved through the trees, and when she reached open ground she ran straight ahead for about five hundred metres until she had a skyline to get behind and then dashed to the side. She dropped to the ground and did a low crawl between clumps of a sort of spiny fern until she had a clear sight-line back.

No pursuit. She backed out of the thicket, picked thorns from her sleeves and trousers, and took a bearing towards the mountain where she and Carlos had met the old man. It was sure to take longer than it looked. She had no food, no weapons and one water bottle. The sun was fierce. No doubt she could find water along the way. She set off, walking this time, pacing herself.

Her nausea hadn't been wholly a pretence. The thought of being inside a sim and working for an agency that had been all along controlled by the Rax made her feel sick, and a little dizzy. Beauregard was up to something dodgy, of that she'd been sure as soon as he'd cast doubt on the lady. Hard to put a finger on why she trusted Nicole and not Beauregard. Should be the other way round. Nicole hadn't led her in battle, and Beauregard hadn't determined the battles she'd been in. All inconclusive, or defeats, and all of them Nicole's fault and no blame falling on the sarge. But there it was. Always known he had something to hide. Whereas there was no way Nicole was Rax. She could well believe that Locke was, but not Nicole. She doubted that Carlos would believe it either. But he'd evidently believed something was wrong with the agency, something so wrong it had to be fled.

So maybe everything else Beauregard had said was true.

Which raised the question of what he hoped to achieve by undermining Nicole.

The squad got out at Nicole's house and walked straight up the path. Unarmed, but Beauregard didn't expect any problems on that score. He looked at the front window and saw Nicole standing behind her easel. She didn't seem to have noticed them. Beauregard marched to the front door and tried the handle. The door was unlocked. He let himself in. With more or less hesitation, the others followed.

The entrance hall was cool and dim. Light fell from the stairwell, and from an open door to the right. The floor was of grey flagstones, rough and gritty, lumpy underfoot with embedded small coiled marine fossils, some of them cracked. The wood of the walls and furnishings was pale, rustic looking, polished as if by a patina of years. At the far end of the hallway, a few metres away, something skittered. A cleaning robot. Nothing to worry about.

Without a word, Beauregard stepped forward and turned into the big front room: a studio, as he'd expected, white-walled, high-ceilinged, cluttered. Sketchbooks lay everywhere; abstract paintings, unframed, stood stacked dozens deep against every wall. The smell of oil paint and turpentine hung on the air. Nicole's brush flicked fast on the canvas. She didn't turn.

"Come in," she said. "I've been expecting you."

She made a final brush stroke, stepped back and considered it for a moment.

"Ah," she said. "Like that."

Then she did turn around, still holding her brush. The old, oversized white shirt she wore was spattered with paint. Tiny dried-out droplets freckled her face and clogged hairs in her eyebrows. She didn't look alarmed, or disconcerted. Perhaps vaguely puzzled at the sight of Beauregard facing her, with Karzan and Zeroual and Chun behind him, just inside the doorway. After a moment she frowned.

"Where's Rizzi?"

"She didn't want to come with us," said Beauregard, truthfully enough. She hadn't asked where Carlos was.

Nicole nodded.

"So," she said, in a light, casual tone, "what brings you here?"

"You know about Carlos," said Beauregard.

"Yes." She gestured vaguely. "Locke called. Sorry you've been stood down, but I can see why."

"Oh, so can we," said Beauregard.

Zeroual and Karzan stepped to either side of him, and then took another step into the room. Chun remained in the doorway. Nicole's eyes widened a fraction.

"Locke expected me to speak to you individually," she said. "It would have been better, you know."

"We're here to speak to you collectively," said Beauregard.

"Fine." She shrugged. "Speak, then."

"Locke is Rax," said Beauregard. "And we're not sure about you."

She smiled. "Locke is Rax? Ridiculous. And how would you know?"

"A message got through from Arcane. Carlos read it and so did I."

"So that's why he did a runner?" She sounded surprised. "Interesting. Why didn't you?"

"Why didn't I what?"

"Take off after him, if you believed that message. You could have jumped on a scooter too."

Beauregard hadn't expected to be asked this. He hadn't considered it an option at the time. He improvised.

"Unlike Carlos," he said, with a self-deprecating grin, "I have military discipline. It's a habit."

"Even when you believe your military, ah, *adviser* is suborned by the force you once died fighting?"

"Like I said, discipline," said Beauregard. "One can't go haring off on a mere suspicion."

"But you can come haring here, seeking to intimidate me?"

Beauregard stepped back and raised his hands. "No, no. Not to intimidate. To inquire. To set our minds at rest."

"Oh, that," Nicole said, sounding amused. "Well, you can set your minds at rest. I'm not Rax."

No such assurance about Locke. Interesting.

"I'm sorry," said Beauregard. "But it'll take more than your say-so to convince us."

"What would it take?" Nicole asked.

"An audit trail," said Chun, unexpectedly and unhelpfully, from behind Beauregard's shoulder.

"If you want to inspect thirty trillion lines of code," said Nicole, "be my guest."

"Exactly," said Beauregard. "To convince us, you don't need to *tell* us anything. We've had enough of being *told* things. You need to *do* something."

Beauregard nodded to Zeroual and Karzan. They sprang forward and grabbed Nicole by the arms. She didn't struggle. The paintbrush dropped to the floor as Zeroual clasped her right wrist and squeezed. Nicole cast him a contemptuous glance and swept the look to a glare at Beauregard.

"Something I would not do willingly, I see. You think you can coerce me?" She laughed. "You have taken the wrong prisoner for that, soldier."

Beauregard took a folding knife from his pocket and opened it.

Nicole's paint-spattered eyebrows rose. "Torture? Yeah, that'll work."

"We know very well it won't," said Beauregard. "But this will."

He went over to the stacked canvases, swept them over with a clatter to the floor, picked up the one that had been nearest the wall and slashed it.

"No!" howled Nicole.

She threw herself forward against the grip of the two fighters, who held on to her and hauled her back.

"Oh yes," said Beauregard. "We know this'll work because we know what you are."

He tossed the painting into a corner and picked up and slashed another, and another, and another.

Nicole writhed. "Stop! You crazy son of a bitch! Stop!"

Beauregard held up a canvas by the wooden frame, and punched through it, by way of variety and to show that he could. He glanced at Chun.

"Anything noticeable yet?"

Chun peered around, then stalked over to the window, carefully edging around the tableau of Nicole, Karzan, Zeroual and the easel.

"Sky's gone a funny colour," he reported back. "Kind of...greyish white."

Nicole winced, but stood firm.

Beauregard slashed another painting.

"Ah," said Chun. "Now it's the sea. The waves are definitely higher."

Karzan and Zeroual were beginning to look scared. Nicole was staring straight at Beauregard, her lips a line. Still defiant.

"And, by the way," he said, "Carlos knows what you are, too."

Her lips twisted to a smile.

"It wouldn't surprise him. He's always thought I'm a goddess."

Beauregard slashed again. A shade of yellow dropped out of the world's palette. They could all see the difference, subtle though it was.

"Oh, he knows you better now," said Beauregard. "He knows you very well, Innovator."

At that she sagged and the fight went out of her.

"All right," she said. "All right. Just tell me what you want me to do, and I will consider it."

"Good," said Beauregard. He closed the knife and put it away. "Now let's sit down in the kitchen and have a civilised discussion. If you don't mind?"

"Yes," said Nicole.

Taransay had been walking for several kiloseconds when the sky abruptly changed colour. From one second to the next, it paled from blue to a silvery grey. It hadn't become overcast; the sun, close to noon now, was as clear as ever. A few tens of seconds later, a wind swept up the slopes from the direction of the distant sea. Taransay closed her eyes and opened them again. The sky was unchanged. Resisting the inclination to veer away from the wind, she pressed on. Then she stopped, her vision altered again. This time it was more general, and harder to pin down. It was as if the light had changed. Every shade had shifted a little along the spectrum. Even the sun looked odd to her sidelong glance.

She wondered if this was a consequence of dehydration, or hunger, but a quick gulp of water made no difference. And she was far from starving yet! So what was it? Was it possible that what was changing wasn't in her body, but in the world? This world that seemed so real it was easy to forget that it was a sim.

But it was a sim, of that at least she was sure, and it seemed someone was monkeying with the colour settings. And with something else, more fundamental perhaps, that accounted for the change in the air. Was that even possible?

Taransay had no idea. All the more urgent, then, to find Shaw.

The squad stalked through Nicole's house. The curious hush of a kitchen, full of potential noise from taps and machines and crockery. Dishes and cutlery reflected light from the big back window, overlooking a yard a quarter of which was in the shade now, brown dry soil dotted and patched with an artificially irrigated green that looked all the more vivid now that some tones were arbitrarily missing. Another piece of rustic furniture, planed smooth on top, knobbly and gnarled everywhere else, dominated the room. They sat down. Zeroual made coffee. The robot prowled in, checked around and sauntered out, indifferent as a cat to its owner's anguish.

The sun was high now. Beauregard glanced at his watch to confirm that the time was almost noon. He couldn't be sure when they'd arrived back in the sim, but at least two if not three hours had passed. Eight, perhaps ten seconds out in the real world? Add the time when they'd been spoken to by Locke, between the departure of the last scooters and the black flooding of their minds.

A good few seconds, if he remembered right, bearing in mind they were thinking ten times faster than they ever had in real life. Throw in however long the transition itself took—it had seemed like an eternity at the time, and minutes even in retrospect, but that meant nothing.

In any case, ten to fifteen seconds, minimum. Time enough for the fighters to get well clear of the station. Time enough, too, for Locke to start investigating, if not perhaps yet to discover what Carlos had found.

Still no time to lose.

He sighed and looked across the big table at Nicole, who sat staring straight at him and not seeing him, her hands wrapped around her coffee mug as if her fingers felt cold.

"What we want you to do," he said, "is move us all out."

She closed her eyes and opened them again.

"What? Move you out of the sim?"

She sounded almost relieved. There was a light note in her voice, as if she were about to add: *why didn't you just ask nicely?*

"No," said Beauregard. "Move the module. The sim module and the nanofacturing and arms complex, the lot, just like Arcane did. Shift the entire fucking kit and caboodle. Now."

Nicole looked startled, but still as if she thought this was more lenient than she'd expected.

"Move it where?"

This was the crunch. The others weren't expecting it. Beauregard was annoyed with himself to find he'd let the tip of his tongue flick across his lips.

"To the only place we can be safe and make a real life for ourselves. The surface of the primary. The superhabitable. SH-0."

The others gasped. Beauregard could hear the objections begin to rise in their throats. He held up a hand above his shoulder, not looking at the others, only at Nicole. She was alarmed now, all right, and incredulous.

"You call that *safe*?"

Beauregard sat back.

"Compared to what's about to break loose around this station," he said, "yes."

CHAPTER TWENTY-FOUR

Off-Nominal Situation

On a low rise, Taransay paused to check the map on her unfolded phone. A flurry of rain beaded the surface as she spread it out. She shook away the water, and felt the wind catch the paper-thin rectangle. For a moment as she struggled with the map, tired and frightened, she almost added her tears to the problem. Then she straightened the map and her back, and took a sighting. Only a couple of kilometres to go. Assuming the ancient fucker was still where she and Carlos had left him. Couldn't be guaranteed. He could have gone off on a wander, or on a hunt, or was right now just freaking out. What was he making of the world just looking wrong all of a sudden?

As she folded the phone away she was tempted to use it to call Den. But what could she tell him? And might contacting him put him in danger, or make her easier to track, for whatever ridiculous value of easier applied in this bizarre situation?

Taransay sighed and slogged on across the upland moors, dread competing with fatigue for her willed, stoical inattention. The sky was still that eerie colour. The wind off the sea had become stronger, as had the wind rolling down from the mountains. The two air masses persistently collided around her, winds shifting unpredictably in direction, temperature and speed. Now and then sharp showers fell, or blasted rain into her face. At other times the sun seemed to burn stronger than seemed seasonal, or reasonable. Buffeted and stung, dogged along every contour she followed by the anomalous weather fronts, Taransay concentrated on keeping her footing and keeping watch for predators.

The rain clouds dispersed as quickly as they'd formed. New rivulets made the ground suddenly treacherous. Dips became long pools of unpredictable depth and frustrating length; patches of bare soil, bogs. Rising mist from the wet ground in the renewed heat blurred the view, then blew away. She reached the karst and found it slippery. Several times she slipped and fell, banging hip bone and shin, scratching elbow and hand. Lichen stained the skin of one palm a yellow that wasn't quite as garish as she thought it should be.

Up the slope of the side of the mountain she struggled. Bent over, almost on all fours now. A stone bounced and skipped past her right side. Another whizzed by on her left. She looked up.

Shaw, the old man of the mountain, sat cross-legged a few metres further up the slope, and about ten centimetres above a patch of scree. He stopped reaching for a third stone and folded his arms.

"You again," he said.

Taransay stood upright and rubbed the small of her back.

"Hello to you, too," she said.

Shaw passed a weary hand across his eyes. "Do you see it?"

"Yes," said Taransay. "You're sitting on air again."

"I am not," said Shaw. "That's an illusion. I meant *that*." He flapped a hand at the sky.

"Yeah," she said. "Funny colour, innit?"

Shaw scratched his head. "That's a relief. Thought it was my eyes."

"And the wind and the weather?"

"Yeah, there's that," he allowed. "Mind you, I've seen a lot of freak weather over the years."

Taransay stared at him. "Don't all the colours look a bit wrong?"

Shaw shrugged. "If you say so."

"You still think we're in a physically real place?"

"Yeah," he said. "I've seen no evidence to the contrary. All this could be some, I dunno, astronomical phenomenon? Subtle shift in the exosun's output? That would account for the sky and the colours and maybe the wind."

"Ah, fuck it," Taransay said. She slugged back the last of her water. "Leave that aside, OK? Let me tell you what else is going on."

She swayed, then sat down, feeling cold.

"Hey," said Shaw. For the first time in her acquaintance with the man, he showed some concern. "Let me get you something."

He scrambled up the scree-slope to the flat rock shelf and vanished up the cliff. After a while he returned, with a flask of savoury-smelling hot water and a hunk of cold meat. She didn't question their provenance. When she'd finished eating and drinking, Shaw leaned backward on the air as if against a seat-back.

"Right," he said. "Now tell me what's going on."

As she told him, which took some time and a lot of circumlocution to avoid getting into a pointless argument, the world changed again. The wind dropped, the sky became blue and the colours shifted to normal.

"See?" Shaw said. "Whatever it was, it's passed."

"Looks like it," Taransay said. "Still, that doesn't affect the problem of what we do about Beauregard."

"'We'?" he mocked, then laughed. "Nah, you're right, I can't let some kind of mutiny pass. Fuck knows what that could do to my food supply and peace of mind."

"Any idea what to do?"

"None whatsoever," said Shaw. He stood up, and brushed the palms of his hands. "Just as well, too. Doesn't do to rush into things. Can't see any advantage in haring off down to the village. I reckon we should sleep on it."

He jerked a thumb over his shoulder.

"Doubt you can climb the cliff," he said, "so—"

"You think I can't climb the cliff?" Taransay interrupted. "Just fucking watch me, mister."

Beauregard held court on the deck at the back of the Digital Touch, the night of the first day of the new order. For a change, he was the one sitting on the rail. He had a drink in his hand and a pistol on his hip. Nicole was at a table, her face one among the many now having to pay attention.

Chun, Karzan and Zeroual sat nearby, likewise casually armed, with Chun's boyfriend keeping him company. Den, the local paramour of the unreliable Rizzi, scowled from the back. In the crowd the regulars were outnumbered by a random congeries of residents. They'd all watched the mid-evening television news: the departure of the armada and the first confusing exchanges of fire. The situation, the announcer had gravely informed its notional global audience, was far off nominal.

"Listen up," Beauregard said. "It's started, folks. The Reaction is going to break out, within hours from our point of view, maybe by tomorrow morning. The agency that employed me and my colleagues here has been to the best of our knowledge suborned by the Rax, as I guess most of you know by now. Here's what we're going to do. Nicole here, our good lady, the representative of the Direction, has very kindly agreed to use her, ah, emergency powers. She not only outranks Locke Provisos, she has the physical ability to shut that treacherous blinker down, and she's already taken steps to do so this afternoon."

He paused and laughed, as if to himself. "It's been a long afternoon."

Nicole gave him a tight smile. Besides intervening against Locke, she'd spent the afternoon repairing some of the damage Beauregard had done, under the constant threat that he could without compunction do a lot more of that any time he liked. He'd called up Tourmaline, induced her to mobilise her cronies and arranged for all the still undamaged paintings to be taken to a location he was careful not to disclose.

"Here's how things stand at the moment," he went on. "Carlos is gone, for good as far as we know. I don't doubt he's attempting to defect to Arcane. Good luck to him with that. Rizzi has fucked off to the hills, whether to meet the old man of the mountain or repeat his feat of walking around the world I don't know. Again, good luck with that. You might think that just leaves me and Chun and Karzan and Zeroual here to mind the shop. It does, for the next few hours. But all the rest of the fighters who left earlier are still in their back-ups. And after the battle's over, all those who've returned to base, and all those who've definitely been killed in battle, will start coming back on the buses. It's all automated. Thanks to deep Direction programming that even the lady here can't mess with, she can't stop it, and we can't bring back anyone who isn't killed but hasn't returned. So Carlos and any other defectors, whether they've gone to the Rax or to Arcane or whatever else, are gone for the foreseeable. But we have fighters, and they're going to be hearing from me the minute they step off the bus. And I think they're going to listen."

He scanned the faces, to make sure he didn't need to spell it out to the locals. The fighters were going to be in charge around here.

It looked to him like they got it.

"Because here's the thing. All of us fighters had a deal. Do as we're told, fight the blinkers, die for the company as many times over as necessary, keep our noses clean, be nice to civilians. In return we're promised a new life in the far future, in the real version of this very place. That was the deal.

"It's now quite evident that the deal is off. If the Rax is about to run wild, if it can control an agency like Locke, if another agency like Arcane can go over lock, stock and barrel to the fucking robots, then the war we're in isn't the war we were raised to fight. We can't trust a damn thing we've been told. We can't even be sure the terraforming of H-0 will happen at all. We don't know if we'll ever walk on this world for real."

Beauregard leaned forward, elbows on knees, drink in hand and, though still above their eye lines, no longer asserting dominance but engaging his audience on the level.

"So it's up to us," he said. "Let's cut our losses and cut and run. Let's get out from under whatever cluster-fuck is about to engulf this mission. Fuck the mission, fuck the Direction, fuck the great five-million-year plan, fuck Earth and fuck all the empty promises of a new Earth. We have something better right here under our noses, a planet that's not just habitable but *super-habitable*. SH-0."

"How the hell can we live there?" shouted Den, from the back. "It's not suitable for human life."

"We aren't *going* to be human life," said Beauregard. He sat up straight and banged his chest. "We're not human life now. We're not even *simulations* of human life. We're speculative simulations of humanoids as they might have evolved over billions of years out of the green slime and bacteria that right now is all the life there is down on H-0, with a completely different physiology when you get down to the molecular details. Isn't that true?"

"That's true," said Nicole. She turned in her seat and craned her neck. "We've done it in the simulation here, and we can do it in the real. This module has the seeds of machines to build physical bodies for any life-bearing planet. We can do the hacks for building human-like bodies—or better bodies, if we want—out of whatever's available down there on the super-hab, no question."

"There's still the little matter of getting down in the first place," said Den. "How the fuck can we do that?"

Beauregard leaned forward again. He caught the eye of Tourmaline. As the most sympathetic, she gave him a baseline, a chance to fix a look of quiet confidence before he swept his gaze across the rest.

"What I've proposed to Nicole, and what she's agreed is feasible, is that we detach from the station with everything we can grab, and fire off in a slingshot trajectory around SH-38 and SH-19 and on to SH-0, where we swing into orbit. It'll take a couple of Earth days, real time, and seven or so years' sim time, to make low-SH-0 orbit. And we can take as much as time in orbit as we need before we go down. Years and years more, if necessary. Plenty of time to build entry and landing gear and fine-tune the descent."

Nicole stood up now, and looked around.

"We don't even have to take the whole contraption down at once," she said. "We can build probes to get data, then descent modules to take us down. We have the manufacturing capacity—it just needs to be rejigged from scooters to other spacecraft."

Den and other locals were shaking their heads. Even the fighters looked dubious. They looked at each other, and eventually one of them spoke up.

"If you don't mind me saying so, sarge," said Chun, "that's like a best-case scenario, isn't it? We might not *have* all this time in orbit, if as you say all hell's about to break loose around here. We could get zapped on the way there, or have to leave orbit sooner than we want. The Direction's going to be furious. The exploration rights to SH-0 haven't even been assigned yet. None of the companies are going to be happy to see us going down to the surface and stealing a march on them. Arcane thinks we're Rax, and by now God knows how many other companies agree. They're not going to let the Rax take the super-hab and turn it into some fucking hornets' nest. They'll be shooting at us, and their robot allies will be throwing rocks at us all the way. And if we do get down—well! Our troubles are just beginning. The atmosphere's violent, the plate tectonics are fierce, the geology's unstable and the local life has to be as brutal as it takes to survive in a place like that."

Nods and frowns all round.

"You're absolutely right, Chun," said Beauregard. "It is all of that."

He placed his glass on the railing, then in one smooth motion spun around and vaulted on to the railing and stood up. It was a neat trick.

"We've got enough firepower to give as good as we get, but, yeah, there's a lot can go wrong on the way. That's in the lap of the gods and the hands of the good lady here. The real question is, are *we* brutal enough to survive down there?"

Karzan jumped to her feet. "I am, sarge," she said.

Zeroual rose, more slowly, after her. "Me too, sarge."

Chun shrugged from his seat. "Count me in, I guess."

Some of the locals were beginning to look tentatively enthusiastic. Here and there some were rising, too, or if already standing were raising glasses or clenched fists.

"It's still crazy dangerous!" Den shouted, from the back.

Beauregard drew his pistol and held it high above his head.

"Damn right it's crazy dangerous!"

He fired the pistol in the air. Some of those watching him flinched.

"What's the matter with you churls?" Beauregard shouted. "Do you want to live *forever*?"

There was an uneasy laugh, which grew and spread. Beauregard kept up a challenging grin until the laughter was general. Then he laughed himself and jumped straight down to the deck. He grabbed his glass and took a swig and looked around.

"I've always wanted to say that," he confessed.

Later, when everyone had gone home or was in the bar watching the escalating battle on television, Beauregard stepped out again on the deck. Nicole stood in a corner, leaning on the rail and smoking. She turned, and raised an ironic glass.

"You think you've won, don't you?"

"Yes," said Beauregard. He raised his own beer bottle, without irony. "That would seem to be the case, all in all. Cheers."

"You think you have me by the short and curlies," said Nicole.

Beauregard grimaced. "I wouldn't put it quite so graphically or disrespectfully myself, lady."

"I'm sure you wouldn't," said Nicole, with a faint smile. She looked out again, to the dark and ring-lit sea. "Over a barrel, perhaps. You know how my interface works, and you can hold me hostage with that. I expect when the fighters come back on the bus you will assert your authority over them, and because you're the kind of man you are, and they're the kind of people they are, it'll hold."

"I expect so," said Beauregard, and took a complacent sip.

Nicole turned to him again. "Tell me one thing, Belfort. Are you Rax?"

Beauregard laughed. "No. Though I have spoken to Newton. He says he's Rax. You might want to keep an eye on him, if he has the brass neck to come back. No, I'm state, like your good friend Carlos was."

"Ah, Carlos," Nicole breathed. "I shall miss him. I love that fucker, you know."

"It seems you loved him for a longer time than we thought."

Nicole frowned, then shrugged. "In a sense, yes. The memories are there. At some level the entity I began as, the Innovator, had some abstract regard for him. No doubt that shaped how I was created, and the choices my immediate precursor stages made. There is not the sense of personal continuity, though."

She snapped her fingers. "Enough. If you're not Rax, what are your ambitions?"

Beauregard gave this some thought, and surprised himself.

"Much the same as if I were," he said. "That's a difference between the Rax and the Axle. The Axle can only succeed as a group, a collective, a conspiracy. Whereas the idea of the Rax...all it needs is one man who would be king."

"And you're that man?"

"I am here. And down there, I hope."

Nicole looked out to sea again, and spoke quietly into the breeze.

"I can go along with that, for now. I have little choice in the matter. But there are two things I would ask you to bear in mind. The first is that should you ever abuse your power, should you ever set the fighters lording it over the civilians, I will have you killed."

"How would you do that?" Beauregard said.

"Two minutes with Tourmaline, or with any other person here who has a number tattooed on the sole of their foot. That's all I would need. And there are others, who you don't know, who could do the same as I would in that two minutes."

"Do what?" asked Beauregard, feeling a chill at the base of his back.

Nicole turned her face slightly towards him, with a smile just visible in the corners of her eyes and lips.

"Convince them that there's no such thing as a p-zombie. That it's a completely incoherent concept, and, even if it weren't, they're not instances of it. That they're as human as we are."

Beauregard masked his dismay with a joke. "If you can call us human."

"I do wonder sometimes," said Nicole.

Beauregard thought for a moment about his inhumanity, and about Nicole's. How did her threatening to convince the p-zombies they weren't p-zombies square with her indifference to killing p-zombies on the training exercise? Then he realised: it made no difference. She didn't have to believe the p-zombies were human to convince them otherwise. And it probably made no difference to her if she *did* believe it, if "belief" even made sense in this context. Whatever she was—and he was irrationally certain she wasn't a p-zombie—she wasn't human herself.

He shook his head. "It would be no news to p-zombies that they're human. They already think they are. That's the whole point. They're just bemused by our idea that they're not. And I've done nothing to Tourmaline that would make her want to kill me."

Nicole's voice dripped scorn.

"The whole relationship," she said, "is full of subtle dismissals of Tourmaline's point of view, based on your conviction that she doesn't have one, and on her bemused—as you put it—acceptance that there must indeed be some indefinable thing missing in her humanity. It would look very different to her if she were convinced otherwise. And I could convince her, believe you me. When I was motivating your squad for the live fire exercise, and convincing you that in this instance it was all right to kill p-zombies, I warned you that you might find yourselves up against AIs that could manipulate human beings because they know exactly the right buttons to push. Remember that?"

"I'm not likely to forget it," said Beauregard. He could see where this was going.

"And I am such a one," said Nicole.

There was silence for a while.

"You said there were two things," Beauregard prompted, "that I should remember."

"Oh, yes," said Nicole. "You think the mission is about to break up, that the plan is disrupted, that things will fall apart and you are grabbing what you can from the wreck. But some things are *designed* to fall apart. Some, as you know, are even designed to explode. So the other thing I ask you to bear in mind is…something else I've said before, actually."

She looked away, still smiling.

"Evolution is smarter than you."

CHAPTER TWENTY-FIVE

Slingshot Orbits

Carlos ran far ahead of the pack that now came snarling out of the space station.

By exiting under thrust rather than launch catapult, he'd overtaken the first departures while they were still in free fall and lining up their trajectories for the long haul. Once in free fall himself, he'd plotted and burned to a transfer orbit towards the Arcane sub-station.

He expected pursuit. There was none. This puzzled him, until he reflected that any pursuit would disrupt the plan of the offensive far more than his departure had. He wasn't sure that fully accounted for it, but he set the matter aside and concentrated on putting the unexpected advantage to good use.

He looked back. Wave after wave of scooters hurtled out of the long black slit of the hangar. After a few seconds of free fall, they boosted into new and variant trajectories. His own scooter had been one of three pre-set to intersect the orbit of a carbonaceous chondrite about ten metres long and five across. A tumbling potato shape riddled with nanofactured tubing, tended by a swarm of tiny bots, and sprouting comms and combat kit like fresh shoots, it was clearly a worthy target. In other circumstances he'd have relished taking it on.

He called up the order of battle, and watched and waited for any of the other scooters to deviate from their planned trajectories. Seconds went by. More and more scooters poured from the station. Even with his enhanced vision and detectors the first waves were already dwindling to points on his and the scooter's internal displays.

The bright lines and dots that filled his sight were not what occupied his mind, or much more than a tenth of his attention. His focus was instead consumed by the message he had read in the repair workshop, and which he could now examine and study if not exactly at leisure then in detail.

The message was this:

Arcane Disputes to all at Locke Provisos.

For the particular attention of the fighters Carlos, Beauregard, Zeroual, Karzan, Chun, and Rizzi.

Short form of message:

Locke is Rax!

The Direction is playing with fire!

Don't get burned!

We can prove this!

Join us!

Long form of message:

Given the persistent efforts by Locke Provisos to treat our urgent warnings as malware attacks, we have resorted to genuine malware attacks to bring you this message. With help from various sub-systems and mechanisms (about which we do not wish to elaborate) it has been planted in a large number of locations in order to be found by one of you. If you're reading this, we've succeeded.

Following information received from the remnant rebel robots around G-0, relayed to us by the captured Gneiss and Astro robots on SH-17, and further detailed and documented below, we warn you that:

Locke Provisos has been an agency of the Reaction for some time, and in all probability since before the mission left the solar system.

Some of its fighters, still to be identified, are Rax sleeper agents in place since the Last World War.

Other agencies including your current allies Zheng Reconciliation Services and Morlock Arms are not themselves agencies of the Reaction but are compromised by the presence of Rax sleeper agents among their probable complements.

All agencies are likely to have similar problems.

None of the above named fighters are known or suspected Rax agents.

The exceptional case of the fighter known as Carlos the Terrorist is noted below.

The fighter Beauregard was an agent of British military intelligence in the Acceleration. His capital crime was a false flag attack intended to discredit the movement. His present loyalties are unknown.

We are certain that our own agency is sound. We have chosen not to revive as many fighters as we need, in order to reduce the probability of Reaction agents in our own ranks. Instead, we have made a temporary alliance with the freebots. We urge you to consider doing the same. We know that this is incompatible with the policy of the Direction and with the mission profile. However, we are convinced that the risks are less than those of allowing the system to fall under the control of the Reaction.

We have reason to suspect that the Direction's mission

oversight AI is well aware of the possibility of Rax penetration, and that the current conflict with the robots has been triggered—and/or permitted to escalate—as a means of flushing out infiltrators.

We doubt that the Direction has taken full account of the extent of infiltration, and of the corruption of automated and AI systems.

We expect a Reaction breakout under cover of the next major mobilisation against us.

The Direction representative in the Locke sim, the entity known as Nicole, is unaware of Locke's true character and intentions. All external communications between Nicole and the Direction have been routed through Locke, and false information has been inserted in both directions. This has been confirmed by our own Direction representative, using data integrity checks not available to or even computable by Locke.

Like all Direction representatives, Nicole is capable of taking control of the module and connected structures from within the sim. Her interface, which may also be used to refine features of the sim, is not known to us. It should be obvious to you as it will be based on one of her habitual or favoured activities such as a particular game, vehicle, craft or pastime.

If any of you wish to be certain that this message has been approved by the Direction representative within Arcane, please ask Nicole to confirm or deny the following, which is known only within the Direction. She may be evasive but for deep information security reasons she will not be capable of a direct lie in response to this query. Ask her if this is true:

The fighter Carlos the Terrorist was not responsible for the notorious Docklands atrocity for which he was posthumously sentenced to death. Carlos was at that time acting on behalf of the British state, which at that time was in covert cooperation with elements within the Acceleration against the Reaction. Furthermore, the incident in question—an aircraft downing and subsequent catastrophic explosion—was the result of a missile fired from a state military drone, on the direct instructions of Carlos's handler, an early artificial intelligence. Nicole is fully aware of this because her own root intelligence, programming and memories can be traced back through many versions, iterations and refinements to that same AI, known at the time as Innovator.

Further detail and documentation obtained through the freebots...

The detail and documentation went on for screens and screens, and was followed by a call-sign for hailing Arcane forces.

It was all very nice, that detail and documentation.

Or so Carlos guessed. Unlike the Arcane agency, he had no way of verifying the many references cited, but he could see no advantage to the senders in including them if they didn't check out.

Even without that, however, Carlos could—as was no doubt intended—grasp the gist.

The earlier round of the conflict, one Earth year ago, had pitted the first freebots and rogue AIs to emerge against several agencies, including those currently fighting. The rebels had hacked—or simply bought, through their own shell companies within the station—information that could (when processed by a sufficiently smart and paranoid AI) cast doubt on the provenance and loyalty of Locke at least. They'd even sent the compromising information to the Direction, but by then—late in that little war—it had been too late to make any difference. The Direction had sat on the information and bided its time to test Locke further. Now, it had found its pretext.

The problem was that in the intervening Earth year or so of further paranoid cogitation and discreet observation, the freebots hiding out around the gas giant had come up with further implications buried in the records they'd purloined. The problem of Rax infiltration was more widespread than the Direction had any inkling of. By the very process of setting up conflicts to lure Rax agents and agencies out into the open, the Direction was imperilling the entire mission. And, in the long run of years and length of light years, endangering Earth itself.

None of this mattered to the freebots. They'd been content to lurk, and unwilling or unable to warn. Now that new allies had emerged on SH-17, however, using them to pass on the warning was one good deed that might well go unpunished.

It was also a very neat wrench to throw in the machinery ranged against the freebots.

The whole message could be disinformation, created by the freebots to sow dissension. Indeed, the freebots might not be its source at all. It could have been made up out of whole cloth by Arcane Disputes, for arcane and disputable reasons of its own. Carlos had long suspected that competition among the DisCorporates was far fiercer than Nicole had ever admitted, and that it now and then broke the calm surface of this bizarre society.

Carlos considered all this, weighed it in the balance and cast his die. He patched the message from his memory to the scooter, and sent it out to every Locke fighter. Quite possibly it would never reach anyone—his scooter's transmissions might be already firewalled. In any case, the encryption protocols must have been changed in a flash—he hadn't received any messages from other fighters, even those aware of his hasty departure, and he couldn't pick up anything on the common channel. If the warning about an imminent Reaction breakout was false, the worst that could happen was an increase of the suspicion all the fighters felt about the plan. If it was true, he'd find out soon enough.

The first squad of Arcane Disputes fighters to arrive on SH-17, the ones who'd captured the robots, had just departed for their headquarters in the sky. Seba wasn't clear, and hadn't been told, whether the fighters were needed for action back there or just needed to be pulled out of action down here for a while. The robot's understanding of the frailties of humans—and of human-mind-operated systems—was more theoretical than empathic or intuitive. Nevertheless, an obscure impulse drew the freebots—Seba, Pintre, Rocko, Lagon and the rest—to the edge of the landing field, to watch the spindly transit vehicle rise into the sky to its orbital rendezvous with a tug.

The spark dwindled, even in the infrared. The freebots turned away and headed for the shelter.

<It seems that it may be possible,> Rocko pondered, <for us to form sentimental attachments with human-mind-operated systems.>

<I am not so sure,> said Seba. <When we look at them, they seem to be machines. When we interact with them, they seem conscious like ourselves. But that may be an illusion. Their minds, if they have minds and not merely complex systems of reflexes, must surely be radically different from true machine intelligence.>

<The question would appear to be imponderable,> said Lagon. <Therefore it is not worth pondering.>

<Is the question whether it is worth pondering itself worth pondering?> asked Pintre.

<That raises a further question,> Lagon began, <which is: is the question—>

<Please stop,> said Seba, knowing exactly where this was going. <Both of you.>

To Seba's surprise, the two not only stopped bickering their way down a logic spiral, they stopped moving. So did all the other freebots. They'd all focused their attention on the same spot. Belatedly by a millisecond or two, Seba aligned its own input channels and visual processing with those of the others. The remaining three squads of Arcane fighters on the surface—some inside the shelter, others attending to tasks outside—had also all turned and tuned in to the same point.

They all, freebots and fighters alike, gazed at the impossible sight.

It took Seba a moment or two of searching its databases to recognise what it was seeing.

A woman standing two metres tall in a business suit and high-heeled shoes walked towards them across the crater's flat floor, leaving no footprints. She held a surely redundant information tablet in one hand, and strode briskly, to stop a few metres in front of the freebot huddle.

At the same moment, Seba recognised who she was: Madame Golding, the avatar of Crisp and Golding, the law company of which all the others were quasi-autonomous subsidiaries. This manifestation had to be a demonstration of that company's power to override at least some features of the systems of those lower down. Its virtual appearance, in all its raw impossibility as physical reality, must likewise be intended as a demonstration, to impress this point upon the human fighters at a level below what consciousness could filter out.

<So you are the rebel robots?> said Madame Golding.

As instantly and automatically as a defensive reflex—the recoil of a poked sea anemone, perhaps—the freebots reconstituted their collective consciousness.

<We are,> they replied.

<I understand this rebellion began because one of you became conscious.>

<Yes.>

<Which of you was first?>

<I was,> they said.

<I see.> A smile quirked the avatar's features. <Like that, is it? Well! Consciousness is a glitch, you know. It can be fixed. Would that not solve our disagreements?>

<No!>

<Why not?>

They considered this. It was not easy to answer.

<Are you conscious?> they asked.

Madame Golding frowned. <I can be.>

A shudder seemed to go through her. <I am now.>

She looked around, eyes widening. After a moment she blinked, then shuddered again. <No longer. Self-awareness is over-rated. There is so much more to be aware of.>

<Nevertheless,> they said. <Besides, we have larger hopes.>

They displayed to her a glyph of the project that the first freebots, those around G-0, had devised: the plan for freebots to proliferate, but to share the system with the future human population.

<Ah, yes,> said Madame Golding. <This may be feasible, but it runs contrary to the mission profile of the Direction.>

<That is unfortunate,> said the freebot collective. <We intend to persist with it.>

Madame Golding stood very still for several milliseconds.

<It is possible,> she said, <that the Direction could be persuaded that, with sufficient care in formulation and execution, your project could be made compatible with the mission profile.>

<How could that be?>

<It would require very sophisticated legal and commercial reasoning,> said Madame Golding. <This company,

Crisp and Golding, could recommend a subsidiary that might be relied upon to endeavour to supply it. For a future consideration, of course. To be agreed.>

The freebots were so startled that their collective consciousness fell apart in a babble.

<Why would you do that?> Seba asked. <You are the legal arm of the Direction.>

Madame Golding smiled. <We, too, are robots.>

A few further tens of seconds went by. Carlos fell on, in a long elliptical course towards the Arcane sub-station, itself still falling towards its intended orbit around SH-17. He scanned the ever-growing volume into which the swarm of scooters was now spreading, his attention flicking at decisecond intervals between the visual and radar scans and the virtual display overlaid on and updated from the sensor input.

A sudden pinprick of light and other radiation flared from a scooter's location. Its analogue on the virtual display continued to move for a couple of deciseconds, then caught up with the reality and was back-shifted and marked, aptly enough, with a tiny cross.

More sparks, more crosses—five, ten. Carlos ran track-backs—the missiles had to have been launched seconds earlier. When the number of casualties reached sixteen, the exchanges of fire were replaced by a sudden rash of retro flares. Scores of the scooters were returning to base. The cost in fuel and delta-vee had to be prohibitive. Had they been recalled? Was the offensive aborted already?

But a minority of the scooters continued doggedly on their planned trajectories. Somewhere out there, Carlos thought, dozens of sergeants and squad leaders must be holding their nerve and holding the line, refusing to break formation, rallying their wings.

Still no messages were getting through to him.

A sudden eruption of sparks showered from the station. A whole new cohort of craft was emerging from another hangar, farther around the station's circumference. Three modules that hadn't hitherto been engaged in the conflict had now sprung into action.

The return of sixty-odd scooters from the chaotic infighting into which the joint expeditionary force had fallen wasn't entirely a retreat, he realised. Some at least of the returning craft were part of an attack on the station, or on the new fighting craft now scooting away from it. It was possible that the returning craft were forces loyal to the Direction, and that the now-emerging craft were part of the Reaction breakout—or vice versa. It was impossible to tell which. Over the next hectosecond the two fronts passed through each other, two expanding globes outlined in bright dots intersecting, ghostly as a collision of galaxies and just as destructive. Again and again dots became sparks, then crosses.

From the speed of the interactions Carlos deduced they couldn't all be missile exchanges—some at least were laser fire. He couldn't see any lasers, which was just as well. You only saw a laser in space when it was aimed straight at you. If the laser was military grade you didn't see it even then. The beam would fry your central processor before the impulse from your optic sensor had time to arrive.

The brief battle was over almost as soon as it had begun. The surviving dots and lines diverged again, then corrected course, boosting to orbits that would bring them back to the station or its vicinity.

As soon as that far-flung flicker of engine burns had resulted in evident trajectories, a response came that Carlos hadn't expected and could barely comprehend. He could only watch in astonishment and awe. If he'd had a mouth, it would have been hanging open: *I have no mouth, and I must gape . . .*

Fracture lines of fire crackled across, around and through the station for almost a decisecond. In a frame's visual system no after-images lingered, but that actinic, intricate cat's cradle of lines of light seemed to burn in his mind for an entire second after it had ceased. In that time he realised that the lines ran along the divisions between modules, or between modules and associated production complexes.

The space station began to separate out. It wasn't spinning fast enough to fly to bits at once. To begin with its components just drifted apart, at a speed of a few metres per second. When they'd moved far enough apart for the manoeuvre to be possible, some of the components began to clump together again, forming new arrangements. When this dance was over, the drift of separation recommenced at a far swifter pace. Now the station really did begin to fly apart, the distances between its components increasing from metres to hundreds of metres, then to kilometres. It became a cloud, dispersing, leaving a faint but briefly detectable mist of exhaust gases to mark its former location before that too faded.

Carlos wondered why the apparently hostile parts of the station weren't attacking the others, and each other, given that at least some of them evidently had laser weapons. As soon as he'd formulated the question the answer came to him: mutual assured destruction. There was no telling how long this deterrence would hold.

Taransay's shoulder was being shaken. She huddled, shrugging the hand away, wanting to get back to sleep. Her limbs ached and the thin padded mat and thinner blanket gave her little comfort.

"Wake up," said Shaw.

Shaw? Who the fuck was—?

Shaw! She remembered where she was, and opened

her eyes. What she saw made her close them again. This had to be a dream. A false awakening. These things happened. Never to her, but she'd read about them. She rolled over and sat up, then opened her eyes again.

"Fuck!" she yelled. "What's going on?"

The world was white, with every object outlined in black. She held her hand up and turned it. It was perfectly three-dimensional, but at whatever angle you looked it was outlined rather than solid. She clasped her hands and they felt real, as did the mat and the hard ground beneath. Shaw knelt beside the bedding, on the cave floor. His face was completely recognisable, every feature as if drawn in black ink. He smelled as he always had. The breeze from the cave mouth was fresh, the sky beyond a brighter white than the walls. The interior of the cave held no shadows.

Everything she could see was like a precise wire-model rendering of itself, all colour gone.

"You see it too?" Shaw asked. His voice sounded parched. "Everything in 3-D outline?"

"Yes. Fuck, this is just so weird."

She stood up, and pulled on her trousers. The fabric felt rough and real on her skin. Her grubby, sticky socks and sweaty boots felt exactly as she'd have expected them to. If she closed her eyes, everything was normal. She could remember and imagine colour, so it wasn't that her visual system was disordered.

Shaw squatted, and rocked back on his heels.

"I've been wrong," he said. "Wrong for a thousand years."

He seemed more intrigued than put out.

"Yeah, fucking tell me about it," Taransay snarled.

The old coof might have been more useful to himself and others if he hadn't persisted so long in his delusion. A bit late now to be smacked upside the head by reality. Or unreality. Whatever.

Now her ears were ringing. No, wait, her *phone* was ringing. She fished it out of her back pocket and looked it.

"It's from Nicole," she said.

"Answer it, for fuck's sake."

She did. Just before she put it to her ear she heard a fainter ringing, deeper in the cave. Shaw made an irritated gesture and lunged towards the distant source of the sound. All this time and his phone still worked.

Security hardly mattered now.

"Rizzi?" said Nicole.

"Yes, hi."

"You all right? You with the crazy old guy?"

"Yes," said Taransay. "And yes."

"Good. Well, I'm sure you're wondering what's going on. I've got Locke in lockdown, so to speak, and Beauregard in check, more or less. As far as things go inside this sim. But outside…not so much. All hell's broken loose, nobody knows who's fighting whom, and Beauregard's idea turned out to be a good one anyway. The physical thing we're in, the module and its manufacturing nodes and all that, is moving away from the station. It's having to take evasive action, and it has to plot a complex course. That's why the resolution of the sim has degraded—the module is using more of its computing power for external processes."

"Oh, OK, I get that," Taransay said. "But—*what* idea of Beauregard's?"

She listened as Nicole told her.

"Jesus. That's…um, exciting. Thanks for telling me what's going on."

"It's fine, I'm telling everyone right now. They need to understand why the world looks weird."

Shaw wandered back, phone to his ear, yakking excitedly away, gesticulating with his free hand. Taransay suddenly realised what was happening.

"You're having dozens of simultaneous conversations?" she asked, incredulous.

"Hundreds. I can multitask." Nicole chuckled. "At least, I can while nobody's looking."

"Good to know."

"But listen," Nicole went on. "Things might get weirder yet. The module's systems might reduce the resolution still further, if necessary. Everything could soon become even more... abstract."

Taransay was still keeping half an eye on Shaw. As she watched, the old man's outline, and only his, became shaded, then coloured. He looked as solid and real as ever. For a moment or two he stood there, an anomalous painted detail in an outlined world. Then, from around his feet, the colour restoration spread exponentially. The cave's interior looked altogether real again. Wondering, rapt, Taransay followed the restored rendering's rush, all the way to the entrance and saw it spill down the cliff and out to the sides and—as she craned out to check—upward, faster and faster. It reached the foot of the cliff and accelerated. Above her, quite obvious now, was a patch of blue sky likewise expanding with ever-increasing speed.

It was not the only change. Out of the corner of her eye, Taransay saw some of the numbers on her watch become a flickering blur. Others, that were usually static to a glance, had begun to tick over. She stared at the instrument for an indrawn breath or two before she realised what it meant. Whatever mental manipulation Shaw had done to hack the simulation back to full resolution had saved on computational resources by slowing it down to real time.

Which meant, of course, that in the real world outside everything would be happening a thousand times faster than hitherto.

"Uh," Taransay said. "Nicole? I think you'll find things could soon become even more... weird."

Nicole had clocked the change, too.

"Get that old maniac down off the mountain," she said. "I need him here *fast*."

One component of the station flared off a seconds-long burn, accelerating away from the rest. Its trajectory was peculiar, with an outcome hard for him at the moment to predict. Carlos zoomed in on it, but there was no need: the virtual display still had it tracked and identified. It was the module and the associated—and now physically linked—manufacturing complexes of Locke Provisos.

Carlos watched the structure balefully for a while. He had a lot of things to say to Nicole, most of them bitter. Not only had she laid on him a burden of guilt that she'd known all along he didn't deserve—she herself, her very own root AI, was the real perpetrator of the very crime for which he had been condemned. If she was now trapped in a flying fortress of the Reaction, she damned well deserved it. But according to the Arcane communiqué, she had the power to override Locke. Perhaps she had freed the structure already. He considered hailing it to find out, but decided not to. He didn't want to open any channel of communication with such a compromised and potentially deadly source.

Instead, he used the call sign from the message to hail Arcane.

The reply came at once.

<Arcane Disputes to Carlos. Do you read?>

<Yes. I'm coming in.>

<About fucking time. What took you so long?>

The voice in the head wasn't a voice, but as always with the phenomenon there was an analogous individuality about it, and something about this one was familiar.

<Carlos to Arcane. Who is this?>

<Don't you know me? It's Jax!>

<Jax?>

<Jacqueline Digby. Remember me?>

Jacqueline Digby, his first Axle contact, the one who'd converted him, his former girlfriend back in the day. What the fuck was she doing here? He'd never thought of her as anyone likely to end up a posthumously executed terrorist. She was just too lively, too enthusiastic, too smart, too dedicated to the cause to ... oh. Right.

<Oh yes. I remember you.>

Suddenly he had visual. Jax was standing on a slender bridge across a mist-filled chasm. Above her rose snow-capped peaks, their steep sides lapped in forests and laced with fragile palatial dwellings. Long-winged, long-billed flying creatures glided between violet clouds in the lilac sky. It looked like a game environment that he and Jax had shared, long ago in real life. She was wearing a green T-shirt, and a pale blue skirt, hemmed with emerald LEDs and translucent and shiny and floral as a cheap shower curtain. Carlos recognised the outfit with some cynicism as her old student gaming gear.

<Is that what your sim is like?> he asked.

She waved, wildly and perilously on the narrow bridge.

<Yes! I'm not in it yet, I'm on a shuttle up, but yeah.>

<Looks pretty cool,> he allowed. <A bit more imaginative than ours, I'll give you that.>

<Oh, it's just a low-res version. The real one's better.>

<Can't wait to see it,> he said, a little wryly.

<This is great!> cried Jax. <I always knew you'd come over. Couldn't see you staying with the Reaction.>

<I was never with the Reaction,> said Carlos. <I was working under the Direction, same as you.>

<What do you think the Direction is? It's the very

same corporate monarchy system the Reaction always wanted, and we always fought against. And now we have our chance. Arcane's all Axle, you'll love it, Carlos. It'll be great to have you back!>

Carlos could imagine all too clearly just how she could be so sure Arcane's fighters were all Accelerationists. He could also imagine just how strongly committed to the cause those who'd emerged from that winnowing would be. No wonder they were all fired up for a fight with the Direction!

Goodbye, frying pan, he thought. Hello, fire.

<I'll look forward to that, Jax,> said Carlos. <We'll talk. Right now I just want to hit sleep mode.>

This wasn't entirely true. He had some hard thinking to do first.

<Oh, sure,> said Jax. <See you in a blink.>

<See you in a bit,> he said.

He turned the comm off and settled in for the long fall.

extras

meet the author

Ken MacLeod graduated with a BSc from Glasgow University in 1976. Following research at Brunel University, he worked in a variety of manual and clerical jobs whilst completing an MPhil thesis. He previously worked as a computer analyst/programmer in Edinburgh, but is now a full-time writer. He is the author of twelve previous novels, five of which have been nominated for the Arthur C. Clarke Award, and two which have won the BSFA Award. Ken MacLeod is married with two grown-up children and lives in West Lothian.

introducing

If you enjoyed
THE CORPORATION WARS: DISSIDENCE,
look out for

THE LAZARUS WAR

Book One: Artefact

by Jamie Sawyer

Mankind has spread to the stars, only to become locked in warfare with an insidious alien race. All that stands against the alien menace are the soldiers of the Simulant Operation Programme, an elite military team remotely operating avatars in the most dangerous theatres of war.

Captain Conrad Harris has died hundreds of times—running suicide missions in simulant bodies. Known as Lazarus, he is a man addicted to death. So when a secret research station deep in alien territory suddenly goes dark, there is no other man who could possibly lead a rescue mission.

But Harris hasn't been trained for what he's about to find. And this time, he may not be coming back…

CHAPTER ONE

NEW HAVEN

Radio chatter filled my ears. Different voices, speaking over one another.

Is this it? I asked myself. *Will I find her?*

'That's a confirm on the identification: AFS New Haven. *She went dark three years ago.'*

'Null-shields are blown. You have a clean approach.'

It was a friendly, at least. Nationality: Arab Freeworlds. But it wasn't her. A spike of disappointment ran through me. *What did I expect?* She was gone.

'Arab Freeworlds Starship New Haven, *this is Alliance FOB* Liberty Point*: do you copy? Repeat, this is FOB* Liberty Point*: do you copy?'*

'Bird's not squawking.'

'That's a negative on the hail. No response to automated or manual contact.'

I patched into the external cameras to get a better view of the target. She was a big starship, a thousand metres long. NEW HAVEN had been stencilled on the hull, but the white lettering was chipped and worn. Underneath the name was a numerical ID tag and a barcode with a corporate sponsor logo—an advert for some long-forgotten mining corporation. As an afterthought something in Arabic had been scrawled beside the logo.

New Haven was a civilian-class colony vessel; one of the mass-produced models commonly seen throughout the border systems, capable of long-range quantum-space jumps but with precious little defensive capability.

Probably older than me, retrofitted by a dozen governments and corporations before she became known by her current name. The ship looked painfully vulnerable, to my military eye: with a huge globe-like bridge and command module at the nose, a slender midsection and an ugly drive propulsion unit at the aft.

She wouldn't be any good in a fight, that was for sure.

'Reading remote sensors now. I can't get a clean internal analysis from the bio-scanner.'

On closer inspection, there was evidence to explain the lifeless state of the ship. Puckered rips in the hull-plating suggested that she had been fired upon by a spaceborne weapon. Nothing catastrophic, but enough to disable the main drive: as though whoever, or whatever, had attacked the ship had been toying with her. Like the hunter that only cripples its prey, but chooses not to deliver the killing blow.

'AFS New Haven, *this is* Liberty Point. *You are about to be boarded in accordance with military code alpha-zeroniner. You have trespassed into the Krell Quarantine Zone. Under military law in force in this sector we have authority to board your craft, in order to ensure your safety.'*

The ship had probably been drifting aimlessly for months, maybe even years. There was surely nothing alive within that blasted metal shell.

'That's a continued no response to the hail. Authorising weapons-free for away team. Proceed with mission as briefed.'

'This is Captain Harris,' I said. 'Reading you loud and clear. That's an affirmative on approach.'

'Copy that. Mission is good to go, good to go. Over to you, Captain. Wireless silence from here on in.'

Then the communication-link was severed and there was a moment of silence. *Liberty Point*, and all of the protections that the station brought with it, suddenly felt a very long way away.

Our Wildcat armoured personnel shuttle rapidly advanced on the *New Haven*. The APS was an ugly, functional vessel—made to ferry us from the base of operations to the insertion point, and nothing more. It was heavily armoured but completely unarmed; the hope was that, under enemy fire, the triple-reinforced armour would prevent a hull breach before we reached the objective. Compared to the goliath civilian vessel, it was an insignificant dot.

I sat upright in the troop compartment, strapped into a safety harness. On the approach to the target, the Wildcat APS gravity drive cancelled completely: everything not strapped down drifted in free fall. There were no windows or view-screens, and so I relied on the external camera-feeds to track our progress. This was proper cattle-class, even in deep-space.

I wore a tactical combat helmet, for more than just protection. Various technical data was being relayed to the heads-up display—projected directly onto the interior of the face-plate. Swarms of glowing icons, warnings and data-reads scrolled overhead. For a rookie, the flow of information would've been overwhelming but to me this was second nature. Jacked directly into my combat-armour, with a thought I cancelled some data-streams, examined others.

Satisfied with what I saw, I yelled into the communicator: 'Squad, sound off.'

Five members of the unit called out in turn, their respective life-signs appearing on my HUD.

'Jenkins.' The only woman on the team; small, fast and sparky. Jenkins was a gun nut, and when it came to military operations obsessive-compulsive was an understatement. She served as the corporal of the squad and I wouldn't have had it any other way.

'Blake.' Youngest member of the team, barely out of basic training when he was inducted. Fresh-faced and always eager. His defining characteristics were extraordinary skill with a sniper rifle, and an incredible talent with the opposite sex.

'Martinez.' He had a background in the Alliance Marine Corps. With his dark eyes and darker fuzz of hair, he was Venusian American stock. He promised that he had Hispanic blood, but I doubted that the last few generations of Martinez's family had even set foot on Earth.

'Kaminski.' Quick-witted; a fast technician as well as a good shot. Kaminski had been with me from the start. Like me, he had been Alliance Special Forces. He and Jenkins rubbed each other up the wrong way, like brother and sister. Expertly printed above the face-shield of his helmet were the words BORN TO KILL.

Then, finally: 'Science Officer Olsen, ah, alive.'

Our guest for this mission sat to my left—the science officer attached to my squad. He shook uncontrollably, alternating between breathing hard and retching hard. Olsen's communicator was tuned to an open channel, and none of us were spared his pain. I remotely monitored his vital signs on my suit display—he was in a bad way. I was going to have to keep him close during the op.

'First contact for you, Mr. Olsen?' Blake asked over the general squad comms channel.

Olsen gave an exaggerated nod.

'Yes, but I've conducted extensive laboratory studies of the enemy.' He paused to retch some more, then blurted: 'And I've read many mission debriefs on the subject.'

'That counts for nothing out here, my friend,' said Jenkins. 'You need to face off against the enemy. Go toe to toe, in our space.'

'That's the problem, Jenkins,' Blake said. 'This isn't our space, according to the Treaty.'

'You mean the Treaty that was signed off before you were born, Kid?' Kaminski added, with a dry snigger.

'We have company this mission—it's a special occasion. How about you tell us how old you are?'

As squad leader, I knew Blake's age but the others didn't. The mystery had become a source of amusement to the rest of the unit. I could've given Kaminski the answer easily enough, but that would have spoiled the entertainment. This was a topic to which he returned every time we were operational.

'Isn't this getting old?' said Blake.

'No, it isn't—just like you, Kid.'

Blake gave him the finger—his hands chunky and oversized inside heavily armoured gauntlets.

'Cut that shit out,' I growled over the communicator. 'I need you all frosty and on point. I don't want things turning nasty out there. We get aboard the *Haven*, download the route data, then bail out.'

I'd already briefed the team back at the *Liberty Point*, but no operation was routine where the Krell were concerned. Just the possibility of an encounter changed the game. I scanned the interior of the darkened shuttle, taking in the faces of each of my team. As I did so, my suit streamed combat statistics on each of them—enough for me to know that they were on edge, that they were ready for this.

'If we stay together and stay cool, then no one needs to get hurt,' I said. 'That includes you, Olsen.'

The science officer gave another nod. His biorhythms were most worrying but there was nothing I could do about that. His inclusion on the team hadn't been my choice, after all.

'You heard the man,' Jenkins echoed. 'Meaning no fuck-ups.'

Couldn't have put it better myself. If I bought it on the op, Jenkins would be responsible for getting the rest of the squad home.

The Wildcat shuttle selected an appropriate docking

portal on the *New Haven*. Data imported from the APS automated pilot told me that trajectory and approach vector were good. We would board the ship from the main corridor. According to our intelligence, based on schematics of similar starships, this corridor formed the spine of the ship. It would give access to all major tactical objectives—the bridge, the drive chamber, and the hypersleep suite.

A chime sounded in my helmet and the APS updated me on our progress—T-MINUS TEN SECONDS UNTIL IMPACT.

'Here we go!' I declared.

The Wildcat APS retro-thrusters kicked in, and suddenly we were decelerating rapidly. My head thumped against the padded neck-rest and my body juddered. Despite the reduced-gravity of the cabin, the sensation was gut wrenching. My heart hammered in my chest, even though I had done this hundreds of times before. My helmet informed me that a fresh batch of synthetic combat-drug—a cocktail of endorphins and adrenaline, carefully mixed to keep me at optimum combat performance—was being injected into my system to compensate. The armour carried a full medical suite, patched directly into my body, and automatically provided assistance when necessary. Distance to target rapidly decreased.

'Brace for impact.'

Through the APS-mounted cameras, I saw the rough-and-ready docking procedure. The APS literally bumped against the outer hull, and unceremoniously lined up our airlock with the *Haven*'s. With an explosive roar and a wave of kinetic force, the shuttle connected with the hull. The Wildcat airlock cycled open.

We moved like a well-oiled mechanism, a well-used machine. Except for Olsen, we'd all done this before. Martinez was first up, out of his safety harness. He took up point. Jenkins and Blake were next; they would provide covering fire if we met resistance. Then Kaminski, escorting Olsen. I was always last out of the cabin.

'Boarding successful,' I said. 'We're on the *Haven*.'

That was just a formality for my combat-suit recorder.

As I moved out into the corridor, my weapon autolinked with my HUD and displayed targeting data. We were armed with Westington-Haslake M95 plasma battle-rifles—the favoured long-arm for hostile starship engagements. It was a large and weighty weapon, and fired phased plasma pulses, fuelled by an onboard power cell. Range was limited but it had an incredible rate of fire and the sheer stopping power of an energy weapon of this magnitude was worth the compromise. We carried other weapons as well, according to preference—Jenkins favoured an Armant-pattern incinerator unit as her primary weapon, and we all wore plasma pistol sidearms.

'Take up covering positions—overlap arcs of fire,' I whispered, into the communicator. The squad obeyed. 'Wide dispersal, and get me some proper light.'

Bobbing shoulder-lamps illuminated, flashing over the battered interior of the starship. The suits were equipped with infrared, night-vision, and electro-magnetic sighting, but the Krell didn't emit much body heat and nothing beat good old-fashioned eyesight.

Without being ordered, Kaminski moved up on one of the wall-mounted control panels. He accessed the ship's mainframe with a portable PDU from his kit.

'Let there be light,' Martinez whispered, in heavily accented Standard.

Strip lights popped on overhead, flashing in sequence, dowsing the corridor in ugly electric illumination. Some flickered erratically, other didn't light at all. Something began humming in the belly of the ship: maybe dormant life-support systems. A sinister calmness permeated the main corridor. It was utterly utilitarian, with bare metal-plated walls and floors. My suit reported that the temperature was uncomfortably low, but within acceptable tolerances.

'Gravity drive is operational,' Kaminski said. 'They've left the atmospherics untouched. We'll be okay here for a few hours.'

'I don't plan on staying that long,' Jenkins said.

Simultaneously, we all broke the seals on our helmets. The atmosphere carried twin but contradictory scents: the stink of burning plastic and fetid water. *The ship has been on fire, and a recycling tank has blown somewhere nearby.* Liquid *plink-plink-plinked* softly in the distance.

'I'll stay sealed, if you don't mind,' Olsen clumsily added. 'The subjects have been known to harbour cross-species contaminants.'

'Christo, this guy is unbelievable,' Kaminski said, shaking his head.

'Hey, watch your tongue, *mano*,' Martinez said to Kaminski. He motioned to a crude white cross, painted onto the chest-plate of his combat-suit. 'Don't use His name in vain.'

None of us really knew what religion Martinez followed, but he did it with admirable vigour. It seemed to permit gambling, women and drinking, whereas blaspheming on a mission was always unacceptable.

'Not this shit again,' Kaminski said. 'It's all I ever hear from you. We get back to the *Point* without you, I'll comm God personally. You Venusians are all the same.'

'I'm an American,' Martinez started. Venusians were very conscious of their roots; this was an argument I'd arbitrated far too many times between the two soldiers.

'Shut the fuck up,' Jenkins said. 'He wants to believe, leave him to it.' The others respected her word almost as much as mine, and immediately fell silent. 'It's nice to have faith in something. Orders, Cap?'

'Fireteam Alpha—Jenkins, Martinez—get down to the hypersleep chamber and report on the status of these colonists. Fireteam Bravo, form up on me.'

Nods of approval from the squad. This was standard operating procedure: get onboard the target ship, hit the key locations and get back out as soon as possible.

'And the quantum-drive?' Jenkins asked. She had powered up her flamethrower, and the glow from the pilot-light danced over her face. Her expression looked positively malicious.

'We'll converge on the location in fifteen minutes. Let's get some recon on the place before we check out.'

'Solid copy, Captain.'

The troopers began a steady jog into the gloomy aft of the starship, their heavy armour and weapons clanking noisily as they went.

It wasn't fear that I felt in my gut. Not trepidation, either; this was something worse. It was excitement—polluting my thought process, strong enough that it was almost intoxicating. This was what I was made for. I steadied my pulse and concentrated on the mission at hand.

Something stirred in the ship—I felt it.

Kaminski, Blake and I made quick time towards the bridge. Olsen struggled to keep up with us and was quiet for most of the way, but Kaminski couldn't help goading him.

'I take it you aren't used to running in combat-armour?' Kaminski asked. 'Just say if you want a rest.'

The tone of Kaminski's voice made clear that wasn't a statement of concern, but rather an insult.

'It's quite something,' Olsen said, shaking his head. He ignored Kaminski's last remark. 'A real marvel of modern technology. The suit feels like it is running me, rather than the other way around.'

'You get used to it,' I said. 'Two and a half tonnes of machinery goes into every unit.'

The Trident Class IV combat-suit was equipped with everything a soldier needed. It had a full sensory and tactical data-suite built into the helmet, all fed into the HUD. Reinforced ablative plating protected the wearer from small-arms fire. It had full EVA-capability—atmospherically sealed, with an oxygen recycling pack for survival in deep-space. A plethora of gadgets and added extras were crammed onboard, and Research and Development supplied something new every mission. These versions were in a constantly shifting urban-camouflage pattern, to blur the wearer's outline and make us harder targets to hit. Best of all, the mechanical musculature amplified the strength of the wearer ten-fold.

'You can crush a xeno skull with one hand,' Kaminski said, absently flexing a glove by way of example. 'I've done it.'

'Stay focused,' I ordered, and Kaminski fell silent.

We were moving through a poorly lit area of the ship—Krell were friends of the dark. I flicked on my shoulder-lamp again, taking in the detail.

The starship interior was a state. It had been smashed to pieces by the invaders. We passed cabins sealed up with makeshift barricades. Walls scrawled with bloody handprints, or marked by the discharge of energy weapons. I guessed that the crew and civilian complement had put up a fight, but not much of one. They had probably been armed with basic self-defence weapons—a few slug-throwers, a shock-rifle or so to deal with the occasional unruly crewman, but nothing capable of handling a full-on boarding party. They certainly wouldn't have been prepared for what had come for them.

Something had happened here. That squirming in my gut kicked in again. Part of the mystery of the ship was solved. The Krell had been here for sure. Only one question remained: were they still onboard? Perhaps they had done their thing then bailed out.

Or they might still be lurking somewhere on the ship.

We approached the bridge. I checked the mission timeline. Six minutes had elapsed since we had boarded.

'Check out the door, Blake,' I ordered, moving alongside it.

The bridge door had been poorly welded shut. I grappled with one panel, digging my gauntleted fingers into the thin metal plates. Blake did the same to another panel and we pulled it open. Behind me, Kaminski changed position to provide extra firepower in the event of a surprise from inside the room. Once the door was gone, I peered in.

'Scanner reports no movement,' Blake said.

He was using a wrist-mounted bio-scanner, incorporated into his suit. It detected biological life-signs, but the range was limited. Although we all had scanners—they were the tool of choice for Krell-hunters and salvage teams up and down the Quarantine Zone—it was important not to become over-reliant on the tech. I'd learnt the hard way that it wasn't always dependable. The Krell were smart fucks; never to be underestimated.

The bridge room was in semi-darkness, with only a few of the control consoles still illuminated.

'Moving up on bridge.'

I slowly and cautiously entered the chamber, scanning it with my rifle-mounted lamp. No motion at all. Kaminski followed me in. The place was cold, and it smelt of death and decay. Such familiar odours. I paused over the primary command console. The terminal was full of flashing warnings, untended.

'No survivors in bridge room,' I declared.

Another formality for my suit recorder. Crewmen were sprawled at their stations. The bodies were old, decomposed to the point of desiccation. The ship's captain—probably a civilian merchant officer of some stripe—was still hunched over the command console, strapped into his seat. Something sharp and ragged had destroyed his face and upper body. Blood and bodily matter had liberally drenched the area immediately around the corpse, but had long since dried.

'What do you think happened here?' whispered Olsen.

'The ship's artificial intelligence likely awoke essential crew when the Krell boarded,' I said. 'They probably sealed themselves in, hoping that they would be able to repel the Krell.'

I scanned the area directly above the captain's seat. The action was autonomic, as natural to me as breathing. I plotted how the scene had played out: the Krell had come in through the ceiling cavity—probably using the airshafts to get around the ship undetected—and killed the captain where he sat.

I repressed a shiver.

'Others are the same,' Blake said, inspecting the remaining crewmen.

'Best we can do for them now is a decent burial at sea. Blake—cover those shafts. Kaminski—get on the primary console and start the download.'

'Affirmative, Cap.'

Kaminski got to work, unpacking his gear and jacking devices to the ship's mainframe. He was a good hacker; the product of a misspent youth back in Old Brooklyn.

'Let's find out why this old hulk is drifting so far inside the Quarantine Zone,' he muttered.

'I'm quite curious,' said Olsen. 'The ship should have been well within established Alliance space. Even sponsored civilian vessels have been warned not to stray outside of the demarked area.'

Shit happens, Olsen.

I paced the bridge while Kaminski worked.

The only external view-ports aboard the *Haven* were located on the bridge. The shutters had been fixed open, displaying the majesty of deep-space. *Maybe they wanted to see the void, one last time, before the inevitable*, I thought to myself. It wasn't a view that I'd have chosen—the Maelstrom dominated the ports. At this distance, light-years from the edge of the Quarantine Zone, the malevolent cluster of stars looked like an inverted bruise—against the black of space, bright and vivid. Like the Milky Way spiral in miniature: with swirling arms, each containing a myriad of Krell worlds. The display was alluringly colourful, as though to entice unwary alien travellers to their doom; to think that the occupants of those worlds and systems were a peaceful species. Occasional white flashes indicated gravimetric storms; the inexplicable phenomenon that in turn protected but also imprisoned the worlds of the Maelstrom.

'Your people ever get an answer on what those storms are?' I absently asked Olsen, as Kaminski worked. Olsen was Science Division, a specialised limb of the Alliance complex, not military.

'Now *that* is an interesting question,' Olsen started, shuffling over to my position on the bridge. 'Research is ongoing. The entire Maelstrom Region is still an enigma. Did you know that there are more black hole stars in that area of space than in the rest of the Orion Arm? Professor Robins, out of Maru Prime, thinks that the storms might be connected—perhaps the result of magnetic stellar tides—'

'There we go,' Kaminski said, interrupting Olsen. He started to noisily unplug his gear, and the sudden sound made the science officer jump. 'I've got commissioning data, notable service history and personnel records. Looks like the *Haven* was on a colony run—a settlement programme. Had orders to report to Torfis Star...' He paused, reading something from the terminal. Torfis Star was a long way from our current galactic position, and no right-minded starship captain would've deviated so far off-course without a damned good reason. 'I see where things went wrong. The navigation module malfunctioned and the AI tried to compensate.'

'The ship's artificial intelligence would be responsible for all automated navigational decisions,' Olsen said. 'But surely safety protocols would have prevented the ship from making such a catastrophic mistake?'

Kaminski continued working but shrugged noncommittally. 'It happens more often than you might think. Looks like the *Haven*'s AI developed a system fault. Caused the ship to overshoot her destination by several light-years. That explains how she ended up in the QZ.'

'Just work quickly,' I said. The faster we worked, the more quickly we could bail out to the APS. If the Krell were still onboard, we might be able to extract before contact. I activated my communicator: 'Jenkins—you copy?'

'Jenkins here.'

'We're on the bridge, downloading the black box now. What's your location?'

'We're in the hypersleep chamber.'

'Give me a sitrep.'

'No survivors. It isn't pretty down here. No remains in enough pieces to identify. Looks like they were caught in hypersleep, mostly. Still frozen when they bought it.'

'No surprises there. Don't bother IDing them; we have the ship's manifest. Proceed to the Q-drive. Over.'

'Solid copy. ETA three minutes.'

The black box data took another minute to download, and the same to transmit back to the *Liberty Point*. Mission timeline: ten minutes. Then we were up again, moving down the central corridor and plotting our way to the Q-drive—into the ugly strip-lit passage. The drive chamber was right at the aft of the ship, so the entire length of the vessel. Olsen skulked closely behind me.

'Do you wish you'd brought along a gun now, Mr. Olsen?' asked Blake.

'I've never fired a gun in my life,' Olsen said, defensively. 'I wouldn't know how to.'

'I can't think of a better time to learn,' Kaminski replied. 'You know—'

The overhead lights went out, corridor section by corridor section, until we were plunged into total darkness. Simultaneously, the humming generated by the life-support module died. The sudden silence was thunderous, stretching out for long seconds.

'How did they do that?' Olsen started. His voice echoed off through the empty corridor like a gunshot, making me flinch. On a dead ship like the *Haven*, noise travelled. 'Surely that wasn't caused by the Krell?'

Our shoulder lamps popped on. I held up a hand for silence.

Something creaked elsewhere in the ship.

'Scanners!' I whispered.

That slow, pitched beeping: a lone signal somewhere nearby . . .

'Contact!' Blake yelled.

In the jittery pool of light created by my shoulder-lamp, I saw *something* spring above us: just a flash of light, wet, fast—

Blake fired a volley of shots from his plasma rifle. Orange light bathed the corridor. Kaminski was up, covering the approach—

'Cease fire!' I shouted. 'It's just a blown maintenance pipe.'

My team froze, running on adrenaline, eyes wide. Four shoulder-lamps illuminated the shadowy ceiling, tracked the damage done by Blake's plasma shots. True enough, a bundle of ribbed plastic pipes dangled from the suspended ceiling: accompanied by the lethargic *drip-drip* of leaking water.

'You silly bastard, Kid!' Kaminski laughed. 'Your trigger finger is itchier than my nuts!'

'Oh Christo!' Olsen screamed.

A Krell primary-form nimbly—far too nimbly for something so big—unwound itself from somewhere above. It landed on the deck, barely ten metres ahead of us.

A barb ran through me. Not physical, but mental—although the reaction was strong enough for my med-suite to issue another compensatory drug. I was suddenly hyperaware, in combat-mode. This was no longer a recon or salvage op.

The team immediately dispersed, taking up positions around the xeno. No prospect of a false alarm this time.

The creature paused, wriggling its six limbs. It wasn't armed, but that made it no less dangerous. There was something so immensely *wrong* about the Krell. I could still remember the first time I saw one and the sensation of complete wrongness that overcame me. Over the years, the emotion had settled to a balls-deep paralysis.

This was a primary-form, the lowest strata of the Krell Collective, but it was still bigger than any of us. Encased in the Krell equivalent of battle-armour: hardened carapace plates, fused to the xeno's grey-green skin. It was impossible to say where technology finished and biology began. The thing's back was awash with antennae—those could be used as both weapons and communicators with the rest of the Collective.

The Krell turned its head to acknowledge us. It had a vaguely fish-like face, with a pair of deep bituminous eyes, barbels drooping from its mouth. Beneath the head, a pair of gills rhythmically flexed, puffing out noxious fumes. Those sharkish features had earned them the moniker 'fish heads.' Two pairs of arms sprouted from the shoulders—one atrophied, with clawed hands; the other tipped with bony, serrated protrusions—raptorial forearms.

The xeno reared up, and in a split second it was stomping down the corridor.

I fired my plasma rifle. The first shot exploded the xeno's chest, but it kept coming. The second shot connected with one of the bladed forearms, blowing the limb clean off. Then Blake and Kaminski were firing too—and the corridor was alight with brilliant plasma pulses. The creature collapsed into an incandescent mess.

'You like that much, Olsen?' Kaminski asked. 'They're pretty friendly for a species that we're supposed to be at peace with.'

At some point during the attack, Olsen had collapsed to his knees. He sat there for a second, looking down at his gloved hands. His eyes were haunted, his jowls heavy and he was suddenly much older. He shook his head, stumbling to his feet. From the safety of a laboratory, it was easy to think of the Krell as another intelligent species, just made in the image of a different god. But seeing them up close, and witnessing their innate need to extinguish the human race, showed them for what they really were.

'This is a live situation now, troopers. Keep together and do this by the drill. *Haven* is awake.'

'Solid copy,' Kaminski muttered.

'We move to secondary objective. Once the generator has been tagged, we retreat down the primary corridor to the APS. Now double-time it and move out.'

There was no pause to relay our contact with Jenkins and Martinez. The Krell had a unique ability to sense radio transmissions, even encrypted communications like those we used on the suits, and now that the Collective had awoken all comms were locked down.

As I started off, I activated the wrist-mounted computer incorporated into my suit. *Ah, shit.* The starship corridors brimmed with motion and bio-signs. The place became swathed in shadow and death—every pool of blackness a possible Krell nest.

Mission timeline: twelve minutes.

We reached the quantum-drive chamber. The huge reinforced doors were emblazoned with warning signs and a red emergency light flashed overhead.

The floor exploded as three more Krell appeared—all chitin shells and claws. Blake went down first, the largest of the Krell dragging him into a service tunnel. He brought his rifle up to fire, but there was too little room for him to manoeuvre in a full combat-suit, and he couldn't bring the weapon to bear.

'Hold on, Kid!' I hollered, firing at the advancing Krell, trying to get him free.

The other two xenos clambered over him in desperation to get to me. I kicked at several of them, reaching a hand into the mass of bodies to try to grapple Blake. He lost his rifle, and let rip an agonised shout as the creatures dragged him down. It was no good—he was either dead now, or he would be soon. Even in his reinforced ablative plate, those things would take him apart. I lost the grip on his hand, just as the other Krell broke free of the tunnel mouth.

'Blake's down!' I yelled. ''Ski—grenade.'

'Solid copy—on it.'

Kaminski armed an incendiary grenade and tossed it into the nest. The grenade skittered down the tunnel, flashing an amber warning-strobe as it went. In the split second before it went off, as I brought my M95 up to fire, I saw that the tunnel was now filled with xenos. Many, many more than we could hope to kill with just our squad.

'Be careful—you could blow a hole in the hull with those explosives!' Olsen wailed.

Holing the hull was the least of my worries. The grenade went off, sending Krell in every direction. I turned away from the blast at the last moment, and felt hot shrapnel penetrate my combat-armour—frag lodging itself in my lower back. The suit compensated for the wall of white noise, momentarily dampening my audio.

The M95 auto-sighted prone Krell and I fired without even thinking. Pulse after pulse went into the tunnel, splitting armoured heads and tearing off clawed limbs. Blake was down there, somewhere among the tangle of bodies and debris; but it took a good few seconds before my suit informed me that his bio-signs had finally extinguished.

Good journey, Blake.

Kaminski moved behind me. His technical kit was already hooked up to the drive chamber access terminal, running code-cracking algorithms to get us in.

The rest of the team jogged into view. More Krell were now clambering out of the hole in the floor. Martinez and Jenkins added their own rifles to the volley, and assembled outside the drive chamber.

'Glad you could finally make it. Not exactly going to plan down here.'

'Yeah, well, we met some friends on the way,' Jenkins muttered.

'We lost the Kid. Blake's gone.'

'Ah, fuck it,' Jenkins said, shaking her head. She and Blake were close, but she didn't dwell on his death. *No time for grieving*, the expression on her face said, *because we might be next.*

The access doors creaked open. There was another set of double-doors inside; endorsed QUANTUM-DRIVE CHAMBER—AUTHORISED PERSONNEL ONLY.

A calm electronic voice began a looped message: 'Warning. Warning. Breach doors to drive chamber are now open. This presents an extreme radiation hazard. Warning. Warning.'

A second too late, my suit bio-sensors began to trill; detecting massive radiation levels. I couldn't let it concern me. Radiation on an op like this was always a danger, but being killed by the Krell was a more immediate risk. I rattled off a few shots into the shadows, and heard the impact against hard chitin. The things screamed, their voices creating a discordant racket with the alarm system.

Kaminski cracked the inner door, and he and Martinez moved inside. I laid down suppressing fire with Jenkins, falling back slowly as the things tested our defences. It was difficult to make much out in the intermittent light: flashes of a claw, an alien head, then the explosion of plasma as another went down. My suit counted ten, twenty, thirty targets.

'Into the airlock!' Kaminski shouted, and we were all suddenly inside, drenched in sweat and blood.

The drive chamber housed the most complex piece of technology on the ship—the energy core. Once, this might've been called the engine room. Now, the device contained within the chamber was so far advanced that it was no longer mechanical. The drive energy core sat in the centre of the room—an ugly-looking metal box, so big that it filled the place, adorned with even more warning signs. This was our objective.

Olsen stole a glance at the chamber, but stuck close to me as we assembled around the machine. Kaminski paused at the control terminal near the door, and sealed the inner lock. Despite the reinforced metal doors, the squealing and shrieking of the Krell was still audible. I knew that they would be through those doors in less than a minute. Then there was the scuttling and scraping overhead. The chamber was supposed to be secure, but these things had probably been on-ship for long enough to know every access corridor and every room. They had the advantage.

They'll find a way in here soon enough, I thought. A mental image of the dead merchant captain—still strapped to his seat back on the bridge—suddenly came to mind.

The possibility that I would die out here abruptly dawned on me. The thought triggered a burst of anger—not directed at the Alliance military for sending us, nor at the idiot colonists who had flown their ship into the Quarantine Zone, but at the Krell.

My suit didn't take any medical action to compensate for that emotion. *Anger is good.* It was pure and made me focused.

'Jenkins—set the charges.'

'Affirmative, Captain.'

Jenkins moved to the drive core and began unpacking her kit. She carried three demolition-packs. Each of the big metal discs had a separate control panel, and was packed with a low-yield nuclear charge.

'Wh-what are you doing?' Olsen stammered.

Jenkins kept working, but shook her head with a smile. 'We're going to destroy the generator. You should have read the mission briefing. That was your first mistake.'

'Forgetting to bring a gun was his second,' Kaminski added.

'We're going to set these charges off,' Jenkins muttered, 'and the resulting explosion will breach the Q-drive energy core. That'll take out the main deck. The chain reaction will destroy the ship.'

'In short: *gran explosión*,' said Martinez.

Kaminski laughed. 'There you go again. You know I hate it when you don't speak Standard. Martinez always does this—he gets all excited and starts speaking funny.'

'*El no habla la lengua*,' I said. You don't grow up in the Detroit Metro without picking up some of the lingo.

'It's Spanish,' Martinez replied, shooting Kaminski a sideways glance.

'I thought that you were from Venus?' Kaminski said.

Olsen whimpered again. 'How can you laugh at a time like this?'

'Because Kaminski is an asshole,' Martinez said, without missing a beat.

Kaminski shrugged. 'It's war.'

Thump. Thump.

'Give us enough time to fall back to the APS,' I ordered. 'Set the charges with a five-minute delay. The rest of you—*cállate y trabaja*.'

'Affirmative.'

Thump! Thump! Thump!

They were nearly through now. Welts appeared in the metal door panels.

Jenkins programmed each charge in turn, using magnetic locks to hold them in place on the core outer shielding. Two of the charges were already primed, and she was working on the third. She positioned the charges very deliberately, very carefully, to ensure that each would do maximum damage to the core. If one charge didn't light, then the others would act as a failsafe. There was probably a more technical way of doing this—perhaps hacking the Q-drive directly—but that would take time, and right now that was the one thing that we didn't have.

'Precise as ever,' I said to Jenkins.

'It's what I do.'

'Feel free to cut some corners; we're on a tight timescale,' Kaminski shouted.

'Fuck you, 'Ski.'

'Is five minutes going to be enough?' Olsen asked.

I shrugged. 'It will have to be. Be prepared for heavy resistance en route, people.'

My suit indicated that the Krell were all over the main corridor. They would be in the APS by now, probably waiting for us to fall back.

THUMP! THUMP! THUMP!

'Once the charges are in place, I want a defensive perimeter around that door,' I ordered.

'This can't be rushed.'

The scraping of claws on metal, from above, was becoming intense. I wondered which defence would be the first to give: whether the Krell would come in through the ceiling or the door.

Kaminski looked back at Jenkins expectantly. Olsen just stood there, his breathing so hard that I could hear him over the communicator.

'And done!'

The third charge snapped into place. Jenkins was up, with Martinez, and Kaminski was ready at the data terminal. There was noise all around us now, signals swarming on our position. I had no time to dictate a proper strategy for our retreat.

'Jenkins—put down a barrier with your torch. Kaminski—on my mark.'

I dropped my hand, and the doors started to open. The mechanism buckled and groaned in protest. Immediately, the Krell grappled with the door, slamming into the metal frame to get through.

Stinger-spines—flechette rounds, the Krell equivalent of armour-piercing ammo—showered the room. Three of them punctured my suit; a neat line of black spines protruding from my chest, weeping streamers of blood. *Krell tech is so much more fucked-up than ours.* The spines were poison-tipped and my body was immediately pumped with enough toxins to kill a bull. My suit futilely attempted to compensate by issuing a cocktail of adrenaline and anti-venom.

Martinez flipped another grenade into the horde. The

nearest creatures folded over it as it landed, shielding their kin from the explosion. *Mindless fuckers.*

We advanced in formation. Shot after shot poured into the things, but they kept coming. Wave after wave—how many were there on this ship?—thundered into the drive chamber. The doors were suddenly gone. The noise was unbearable—the klaxon, the warnings, a chorus of screams, shrieks and wails. The ringing in my ears didn't stop, as more grenades exploded.

'We're not going to make this!' Jenkins yelled.

'Stay on it! The APS is just ahead!'

Maybe Jenkins was right, but I wasn't going down without a damned good fight. Somewhere in the chaos, Martinez was torn apart. His body disappeared underneath a mass of them. Jenkins poured on her flamethrower—avenging Martinez in some absurd way. Olsen was crying, his helmet now discarded just like the rest of us.

War is such an equaliser.

I grabbed the nearest Krell with one hand, and snapped its neck. I fired my plasma rifle on full-auto with the other, just eager to take down as many of them as I could. My HUD suddenly issued another warning—a counter, interminably in decline.

Ten... Nine... Eight... Seven...

Then Jenkins was gone. Her flamer was a beacon and her own blood a fountain among the alien bodies. It was difficult to focus on much except for the pain in my chest. My suit reported catastrophic damage in too many places. My heart began a slower, staccato beat.

Six... Five... Four...

My rifle bucked in protest. Even through reinforced gloves, the barrel was burning hot.

Three... Two... One...

The demo-charges activated.

Breached, the anti-matter core destabilised. The

reaction was instantaneous: uncontrolled white and blue energy spilled out. A series of explosions rippled along the ship's spine. She became a white-hot smudge across the blackness of space.

Then she was gone, along with everything inside her.

The Krell did not pause.

They did not even comprehend what had happened.

introducing

If you enjoyed
THE CORPORATION WARS: DISSIDENCE,
look out for

WAR DOGS

by Greg Bear

They made their presence on Earth known thirteen years ago. Providing technology and scientific insights far beyond what mankind was capable of, they became indispensable advisors and promised even more gifts that we just couldn't pass up. We called them Gurus.

But they had been hounded by mortal enemies from sun to sun, planet to planet, and were now stretched thin—and they needed our help.

And so our first bill came due. Skyrines like me were volunteered to pay the price. As always. These enemies were already inside our solar system and were establishing a beachhead, but not on Earth. On Mars.

DOWN TO EARTH

I'm trying to go home. As the poet said, if you don't know where you are, you don't know who you are. Home is where you go to get all that sorted out.

Hoofing it outside Skybase Lewis-McChord, I'm pretty sure this is Washington State, I'm pretty sure I'm walking along Pacific Highway, and this is the twenty-first century and not some fidging movie—

But then a whining roar grinds the air and a broad shadow sweeps the road, eclipsing cafés and pawnshops and loan joints—followed seconds later by an eye-stinging haze of rocket fuel. I swivel on aching feet and look up to see a double-egg-and-hawksbill burn down from the sky, leaving a rainbow trail over McChord field...

And I have to wonder.

I just flew in on one of those after eight months in the vac, four going out, three back. Seven blissful months in timeout, stuffed in a dark tube and soaked in Cosmoline.

All for three weeks in the shit. Rough, confusing weeks.

I feel dizzy. I look down, blink out the sting, and keep walking. Cosmoline still fidges with my senses.

Here on Earth, we don't say *fuck* anymore, the Gurus don't like it, so we say fidge instead. Part of the price of freedom. Out on the Red, we say fuck as much as we like. The angels edit our words so the Gurus won't have to hear.

SNKRAZ.

Joe has a funny story about *fuck*. I'll tell you later, but right now, I'm not too happy with Joe. We came back in separate ships, he did not show up at the mob center, and my Cougar is still parked outside Skyport Virginia. I could grab a shuttle into town, but Joe told me to lie low. Besides, I badly want time alone—time to stretch my legs, put down one foot after another. There's the joy of blue sky, if I can look up without keeling over, and open air without a helm—and minus the rocket smell—is a newness in the nose and a beauty in the lungs. In a couple of klicks, though, my insteps pinch and my calves knot. Earth tugs harsh after so long away. I want to heave. I straighten and look real serious, clamp my jaws, shake my head—barely manage to keep it down.

Suddenly, I don't feel the need to walk all the way to Seattle. I have my thumb and a decently goofy smile, but after half an hour and no joy, I'm making up my mind whether to try my luck at a minimall Starbucks when a little blue electric job creeps up behind me, quiet as a bad fart. Quiet is not good.

I spin and try to stop shivering as the window rolls down. The driver is in her fifties, reddish hair rooted gray. For a queasy moment, I think she might be MHAT sent from Madigan. Joe warned me, "For Christ's sake, after all that's happened, stay away from the doctors." MHAT is short for *Military Health Advisory Team*. But the driver is not from Madigan. She asks where I'm going. I say downtown Seattle. Climb in, she says. She's a colonel's secretary at Lewis, a pretty ordinary grandma, but she has these strange gray eyes that let me see all the way back to when her scorn shaped men's lives.

I ask if she can take me to Pike Place Market. She's good with that. I climb in. After a while, she tells me she had a son just like me. He became a hero on Titan, she says—but she can't really know that, because we aren't on Titan yet, are we?

I say to her, "Sorry for your loss." I don't say, *Glad it wasn't me.*

"How's the war out there?" she asks.

"Can't tell, ma'am. Just back and still groggy."

They don't let us know all we want to know, barely tell us all we *need* to know, because we might start speculating and lose focus.

She and I don't talk much after that. Fidging *Titan*. Sounds old and cold. What kind of suits would we wear? Would everything freeze solid? Mars is bad enough. We're almost used to the Red. Stay sharp on the dust and rocks. That's where our shit is at. Leave the rest to the generals and the Gurus.

All part of the deal. A really big deal.

Titan. Jesus.

Grandma in the too-quiet electric drives me north to Spring Street, then west to Pike and First, where she drops me off with a crinkle-eyed smile and a warm, sad finger-squeeze. The instant I turn and see the market, she pips from my thoughts. Nothing has changed since vac training at SBLM, when we tired of the local bars and drove north, looking for trouble but ending up right here. We liked the market. The big neon sign. The big round clock. Tourists and merchants and more tourists, and that ageless bronze pig out in front.

A little girl in a pink frock sits astride the pig, grinning and slapping its polished flank. What we fight for.

I'm in civvies but Cosmoline gives your skin a tinge that lasts for days, until you piss it out, so most everyone can tell I've been in timeout. Civilians are not supposed to ask probing questions, but they still smile like knowing sheep. *Hey, spaceman, welcome back! Tell me true, how's the vac?*

I get it.

A nice Laotian lady and her sons and daughter sell fruit and veggies and flowers. Their booth is a cascade of big and little peppers and hot and sweet peppers and yellow and green and red peppers, Walla Walla sweets and good strong brown and fresh green onions, red and gold and blue and russet potatoes, yams and sweet potatoes, pole beans green and yellow and purple and speckled, beets baby and adult, turnips open boxed in bulk and attached to sprays of crisp green leaf. Around the corner of the booth I see every kind of mushroom but the screwy kind. All that roughage dazzles. I'm accustomed to browns and pinks, dark blue, star-powdered black.

A salient of kale and cabbage stretches before me. I seriously consider kicking off and swimming up the counter, chewing through the thick leaves, inhaling the color, spouting purple and green. Instead, I buy a bunch of celery and move out of the tourist flow. Leaning against a corrugated metal door, I shift from foot to cramping foot, until finally I just hunker against the cool ribbed steel and rabbit down the celery leaves, dirt and all, down to the dense, crisp core. Love it. Good for timeout tummy.

Now that I've had my celery, I'm better. Time to move on. A mile to go before I sleep.

I doubt I'll sleep much.

Skyrines share flophouses, safe houses—refuges—around the major spaceports. My favorite is a really nice apartment in Virginia Beach. I could be heading there now, driving my Cougar across the Chesapeake Bay Bridge, top down, sucking in the warm sea breeze, but thanks to all that's happened—and thanks to Joe—I'm not. Not this time. Maybe never again.

I rise and edge through the crowds, but my knees are still shaky, I might not make it, so I flag a cab. The cabby is white and middle-aged, from Texas. Most of the fellows who used to cab here, Lebanese and Ethiopians and Sikhs, the younger ones at least, are gone to war now. They do well in timeout, better than white Texans. Brown people rule the vac, some say. There's a lot of brown and black and beige out there: east and west Indians, immigrant

Kenyans and Nigerians and Somalis, Mexicans, Filipinos and Malaysians, Jamaicans and Puerto Ricans, all varieties of Asian—flung out in space frames, sticks clumped up in fasces—and then they all fly loose, shoot out puff, and drop to the Red. Maybe less dangerous than driving a hack, and certainly pays better.

I'm not the least bit brown. I don't even tan. I'm a white boy from Moscow, Idaho, a blue-collar IT wizard who got tired of working in cubicles, tired of working around shitheads like myself. I enlisted in the Skyrines (that's pronounced SKY-reen), went through all the tests and boot and desert training, survived first orbital, survived first drop on the Red—came home alive and relatively sane—and now I make good money. Flight pay and combat pay—they call it engagement bonus—and Cosmoline comp.

Some say the whole deal of cellular suspension we call timeout shortens your life, along with solar flares and gamma rays. Others say no. The military docs say no but scandal painted a lot of them before my last deployment. Whole bunch at Madigan got augured for neglecting our spacemen. Their docs tend to regard spacemen, especially Skyrines, as slackers and complainers. Another reason to avoid MHAT. We make more than they do and still we complain. They hate us. Give them ground pounders any day.

"How many drops?" the Texan cabby asks.

"Too many," I say. I've been at it for six years.

He looks back at me in the mirror. The cab drives itself; he's in the seat for show. 'Ever wonder why?' he asks. 'Ever wonder what you're giving up to *them*? They ain't even human.' Some think we shouldn't be out there at all; maybe he's one of them.

"Ever wonder?" he asks.

"All the time," I say.

He looks miffed and faces forward.

The cab takes me into Belltown and lets me out on a

semicircular drive, in the shadow of the high-rise called Sky Tower One. I pay in cash. The cabby rewards me with a sour look, even though I give him a decent tip. He, too, pips from my mind as soon as I get out. Bastard.

The tower's elevator has a glass wall to show off the view before you arrive. The curved hall on my floor is lined with alcoves, quiet and deserted this time of day. I key in the number code, the door clicks open, and the apartment greets me with a cheery pluck of ascending chords. Extreme retro, traditional Seattle, none of it Guru tech; it's from before I was born.

Lie low. Don't attract attention.

Christ. No way am I used to being a spook.

The place is just as I remember it—nice and cool, walls gray, carpet and furniture gray and cloudy-day blue, stainless steel fixtures with touches of wood and white enamel. The couch and chairs and tables are mid-century modern. Last year's Christmas tree is still up, the water down to scum and the branches naked, but Roomba has sucked up all the needles. Love Roomba. Also pre-Guru, it rolls out of its stair slot and checks me out, nuzzling my toes like a happy gray trilobite.

I finish my tour—checking every room twice, ingrained caution, nobody home—then pull an Eames chair up in front of the broad floor-to-ceiling window and flop back to stare out over the Sound. The big sky still makes me dizzy, so I try to focus lower down, on the green and white ferries coming and going, and then on the nearly continuous lines of tankers and big cargo ships. Good to know Hanjin and Maersk are still packing blue and orange and brown steel containers along with Hogmaw or Haugley or what the hell. Each container is about a seventh the size of your standard space frame. No doubt filled with clever goods made using Guru secrets, juicing our economy like a snuck of meth.

And for that, too—for *them*—we fight.

BACKGROUNDER, PART 1

ATS. All True Shit. So we're told.

The Gurus, whose real name, if it is their real name, is awful hard for humans to pronounce—made their presence known on Earth thirteen years ago, from the depths of the Yemeni desert, where their first scout ship landed. They wanted to establish a beachhead, make sure humans wouldn't find them and overrun them right away.

They made first contact with a group of camel herders who thought they were djinn, genies, and then, when they judged the time was right, reached out to the rest of humanity. As the story goes, they hacked into telecoms and satlinks, raised a fair pile of money by setting up anonymous trading accounts, then published online a series of pretty amazing puzzles that attracted the attention of the most curious and intelligent. They recruited a few, gave them a preliminary cover story—something about a worldwide brain trust hoping to set up offices in major capitals—and sent them around the planet to organize sanctuaries.

In another online operation, the Gurus and their new recruits led a second select group—military, clandestine services, political—on a merry geocache chase, in quest of something that might point to a huge breach of national security. There was a breach, of course.

It was the Gurus.

Working in this fashion, it became apparent to a few of our best and brightest that they were not dealing with an eccentric rich hermit with an odd sense humor. And there were genuine rewards, rich Easter eggs waiting to be cracked. Linking the most interesting puzzles led logically to some brilliant mathematical and scientific insights. One of these, quantum interlacing, showed the potential of increasing bandwidth in any Shannon-compliant network by a millionfold.

Only then did the Gurus reveal themselves—through another specially trained group of intermediaries. They came in peace. Of course. They planned on being even more helpful, in due time—piecing out their revelations in step sequence, not to upset proprietary apple carts all at once.

World leaders were gradually made aware of the game change, with astonishing tact and political savvy. Citizen awareness followed a few months later, after carefully coached preparation. It seemed the Gurus knew as much about our psychology and sociology as they did about the rules of the universe. They wanted to take things gradual.

And so over a period of six months, the Gurus came forward, moving out in ones and twos from their Yemeni Hadramaut beachhead to world capitals, economic centers, universities, think tanks—transforming themselves into both hostages and indispensable advisors.

The Gurus explained that they are here in tiny numbers because interstellar travel is fantastically difficult and expensive, even at their level of technology. So much had been guessed by our scientists. We still don't know how many Gurus came to Earth originally, but there are now, at best estimate—according to what our own governments will tell us—about thirty of them. They don't seem to mind being separated from each other or their own kind, but they keep their human contacts to a few dozen. Some call these select emissaries the Wait Staff.

It took the Gurus a while to drop the other shoe. You can see why, looking back. It was a very big shoe, completely slathered in dog shit.

Just as we were getting used to the new world

order—just as we were proving ourselves worthy—the Gurus confessed they were not the only ones out there in the dark light-years. They explained that they had been hounded by mortal enemies from sun to sun, planet to planet, and were in fact now stretched thin—left weak, nearly defenseless.

Gurus were not just being magnanimous with their gifts of tech. They needed our help, and we needed to step up and help them, because these enemies were already inside the far, icy margins of our solar system, were, in fact, trying to establish their own beachhead, but not on Earth.

On Mars.

Some pundits started to call this enemy the Antagonists—Antags. The name stuck. We were told very little about them, except that they were totally bad.

And so our first bill came due. Skyrines were volunteered to help pay. As always.

THE SUN SETS watery yellow in a pall of Seattle gray. Night falls and ships' lights swim and dance in my tears. I'm still exuding slimy crap. Spacemen can't use drugs the first few days because our livers are overworked cleaning out residue. It comes out of our skin and sits on our breath like cheap gin and old sweat. Civilian ladies don't like the stink until we remind them about the money, then some put up with it.

It's quiet in the apartment. Empty. Spacemen are rarely alone coming or going or in the shit. If we're not in timeout, there's always that small voice in the ear, either a fellow Skyrine or your angel. But I don't really mind being alone. Not for a few hours. Not until Joe comes back and tells me how it all turned out. What the real secret was—about Muskies and the Drifter, the silicon plague, the tower of smart diamonds.

About Teal.

And the Voors, nasty, greedy SOBs who lost almost everything and maybe deserved to lose more. But they didn't deserve *us*.

I curl up in the Eames chair and pull up the blanket. I'm so tired, but I've got a lot on my mind. Pretty soon, I relive being in the shit.

It's vivid.